Black Runs the River

Johnny Bullard
White Springs, Fla.

Black Runs the River

Copyright © 2019 by Johnny Bullard
ISBN-13: 9781695645523
All Rights Reserved

No part of this book may be reproduced or transmitted in any form or by any means, electronic or mechanical, including photocopying, recording, or by any information storage and retrieval system, without permission in writing from the copyright owner.

This is a work of fiction. Names, characters, places and incidents either are the product of the author's imagination or are used fictitiously, and any resemblance to any actual persons, living or dead, events or locales is entirely coincidental.

Edited by Joyce Marie Taylor
Cover photo courtesy of JT Bridges, Jasper, Fla.
Printed in the United States of America

"I refuse to accept the view that mankind is so tragically bound to the starless midnight of racism and war that the bright daybreak of peace and brotherhood can never become a reality... I believe that unarmed truth and unconditional love will have the final word."

       Martin Luther King Jr.
         (1929-1968)

Dedication

For Dorothy L. Bryant, White Springs, Florida, the best teacher ever. She gave me the confidence to try my hand at writing in seventh grade when she said, "You need to write, Johnny. You have a gift. Use it." Others may disagree, but she had faith in me. I will always love her and I'll never forget the inspiration she was to me. Mrs. Bryant, I love you.

I would also like to dedicate this book to my mother, Mary Lou Taylor Bullard, my brother and sister-in-law, Jerry L. and Amanda Bullard, my niece, Laura Leigh Bullard, my beloved cousins, LeAnn B. Klinger, Rhett Bullard and Paige Bullard, my dear friends, Sue and Carolyn Burkett, and Jennifer Collins.

In appreciation to my patient and wonderful editor, Joyce Marie Taylor, my beloved cousin, Michele Joyner Crummitt, Janet Moses, Cathy Jo Foster, and lastly, the book club of Madison, Florida.

❧❧❧❧❧❧❧❧❧❧

From the Eight Mile Still on the Woodpecker Route north of White Springs, wishing you a day filled with joy, peace, and above all, lots of love and laughter.

Johnny Bullard

Prelude

Extraordinarily devilish

On a moonless Saturday night in Seraph Springs on the thirteenth day of January, the atmosphere was not only dark, but damp and dreary, as well. A bitter cold had settled in like an unwanted houseguest not long after the New Year's celebrations had ended, and it showed no signs of easing up anytime soon. Most folks in this charming, old-Colonial style town in north central Florida had been fast asleep for hours, doing their best to stay warm and toasty underneath their bedcovers, in order to ride out an approaching ice storm.

Being so close to the Georgia border, Seraph Springs was not the typical Florida most people from out of state envisioned. This was *Old Florida* country with distinct seasonal changes and, oftentimes, a good ole boy mentality among its residents. It was clearly unlike south or even central Florida, with their treasured, year-round tropical climate and heavily populated and diverse cities, especially along the coast.

Tonight, in this small town in rural Campbell County, icicles dangled from the trees like Christmas ornaments, while pointy shards of ice threatened to plummet to the ground like Samurai swords from the eaves of many homes. Here, in the wee hours of the morning, the beginning of something evil was about to take place inside a remote, yet elegant riverside home that sat high up on a bluff along the historic Suwannee River. It was something so sinister that it would rival the devil's work, and it was about to be staged for just a select few to witness.

The power had gone out just before midnight, due to the weight of the ice on many of the main electrical wires throughout the town. Numerous trees had already toppled over on top of electric, cable, and telephone wires. Hardest hit was the eclectic four-block downtown area, which featured a variety of specialty shops, a couple of pubs, and about half a dozen unique restaurants, all of them closed right now, of course.

One electrical wire had snapped in two and sparked a fiery blaze that destroyed a freestanding antique shop that had been a staple in Seraph Springs for decades. Meanwhile, more trees continued toppling to the ground in and around the county, as well as neighboring counties, which were also caught up in this storm that was causing havoc for a lot of people.

The town's resources were being stretched thin, as their lone emergency crew rushed to each of the scenes as incidents were called in to 9-1-1. Since the violent ice storm was so widespread, assistance from neighboring fire stations would certainly be slow in coming, if at all.

Inside the majestic house on the hill, dozens of candles had been lit in each room to provide light. The fireplaces in the living room and kitchen were ablaze in an attempt to bring some semblance of warmth to the inside of the home, so that this dastardly deed could proceed as planned. As if it was concocted by Satan himself, tonight's icy-cold and dangerous atmosphere would be the epitome of the perfect setting to truly define what was about to take place.

Just moments after the antique grandfather clock in the downstairs parlor chimed out the two o'clock hour of the morning, there was a loud, persistent banging at the front door. It was as if death itself was pleading to come inside, away from the bone-chilling temperatures outside. In the half-darkness, after several more knocks, a man inside the home warily peeked out the window. He was clad in a pair of black wool pants and a red flannel shirt, as well as what looked to be a brand new pair of black suede hiking boots. Over top of his clothes, he was wearing a dark black, knee-length overcoat with the collar pulled up, and a red scarf twisted around his neck, making him look like Dracula reincarnated when he finally whisked open the door.

He invited the female visitor inside and then quickly glanced around the exterior of the home to be certain no one was lurking in the shadows. Feeling confident the woman had come alone and hadn't been followed, he shut and locked the door behind him.

"You'd best keep your coat and hat on," the man instructed the woman. "It's quite chilly in here tonight and I'm afraid these old fireplaces are having a tough time keeping up," he added, as he stoked the fire in the living room fireplace.

"That's quite all right," the woman said. "I'm used to the cold. Ummm… where shall I put this?" she asked, as she lifted up a large satchel she was carrying.

"Ahh, my wife will direct you," the man told her. "Please follow me."

Moments later, the man and the late night visitor exited the rear of the home and met up with the man's wife. She was standing beside a huge wooden picnic table a few yards from the backdoor of the residence.

"I see why you told me to keep my coat on," the woman jokingly said, as she pulled the collar up around her neck, but the man didn't respond. "It seems much colder back here," she nervously added, and then she slipped on the wool mittens she had previously shoved into her coat pocket.

After greeting her visitor, the wife said, "If you listen closely enough, you can hear the river waters flowing south. Do you hear it?" she asked, gleefully smiling, as she tilted her head to the side and cupped her hand behind her ear.

All she got in response from her husband, however, was a grunt, and the visitor stayed silent, except for a polite nod.

The wife looked totally out of place considering the present conditions. She was dressed in a black and gold off-the-shoulder evening gown and high-heeled gold pumps. She had only a thin, lacy shawl draped around her shoulders. The goose bumps on her arms were clearly visible even in the semi-darkness, and the tip of her nose was a dark crimson color, but she otherwise didn't seem to be bothered by the icy-cold temperature.

"I know you told me earlier you were okay, but you look like you're freezing to death, darling," the husband said. "Let me go get your coat before you catch…"

"I am quite all right!" the wife barked at him, abruptly cutting him off. "Besides, we have an extremely important task to take care of tonight and there is no time to waste. In all truthfulness, the adrenaline rushing through my veins right now is more than enough to keep me warm," she added, smiling.

"Well, then, can we get on with this, please?" her husband begged her, shivering, as he stood by the table.

"Of course, darling," she said. "Let us proceed."

Centered in the middle of the table was a large sterling silver bowl that looked as if it could have been someone's treasured antique. It was extremely heavy and very, very deep; much bigger than a standard punch bowl, in fact. The wife, it seemed, was trying to gauge whether the bowl was big enough to do the job at hand in one fell swoop, as her eyes kept darting back and forth between the satchel and the bowl.

"I think it will work just fine," she finally said. "You can place everything in there," she told the woman, as she pointed to the bowl.

"Are you certain this is what you want to do, darling?" the man meekly asked his wife. "It's not too late to change your mind."

"This is indeed what I want to do!" she snapped at him, as the woman proceeded to fill the bowl with everything that was inside the satchel. "There will be no one stopping me, not even you, my dear, sweet husband!" she growled, with her beady little eyes nearly boring a hole through his skull. "Now, hand me that lighter fluid behind you… please," she softly added, as her lips broke into a devilish smile.

"I don't know, sweetheart," he said, shaking his head. "This just doesn't seem right to me."

"You have no say in the matter!" the wife again barked at her husband. "You were not born here! Now, hand me the damned lighter fluid!" she screamed.

He sheepishly did as he was ordered, and then he watched her squirt the igniting liquid into the bowl, eagerly dousing everything in it until it was sopping wet.

"Hamp Brayerford! Damn your soul to hell!" she exclaimed, sounding as if she was the leader of a satanic cult about to crucify someone. "It was because of you that my uncle died!" she continued ranting. "It was also because of that evil, black woman… your beloved piece of chattel! That little mulatto baby she bore… dear, God! What a stupid, stupid name she gave to that child. Well, let me tell you something, Hamp Brayerford! That woman and her entire coterie are going back to their rightful places. As far as I am concerned, they can all go to hell! If you want to get rid of a colored family around here, as well as their rights to anything, you must have a friend like this," she said, putting her arm around the woman standing beside her, and then giving her a hug. "And this is what you do!" she announced, as she let go of the woman, lit a match, and tossed it into the bowl.

All three of them lurched backward as flames began to shoot out of the bowl, coming dangerously close to setting their clothes on fire. Black smoke billowed around them and then vanished into the darkness.

"Poof!" the wife exclaimed several minutes later, as the last of the smoke got swept up into the night wind.

All that was left inside the bowl were tiny, unidentifiable charred pieces of burnt paper and dark swaths of soot.

"Now, that woman will have no proof of anything!" the wife declared. "Besides, we have the best legal representation we could ask for on our side," she coyly said to her husband. "There's more than one way to deal with the likes of that woman. Who the hell does she think she is, anyway?!" she angrily shrieked, as her face turned a bright red, matching her scarlet nose now.

"Calm down, darling," the husband told her, but his wife seemed oblivious to him and his words.

"Ahhh... a match, a little lighter fluid... it works like a charm, doesn't it?" she rhetorically asked in a much calmer voice, and then she wickedly grinned from ear to ear. "Come, now," she said to the two of them. "Let's go inside and have a glass of champagne to celebrate!"

What the three of them didn't know, however, was that things were not going to turn out exactly as they expected. In fact, nothing for anyone in Seraph Springs or Campbell County, for that matter, would go back to the way it was. Something extraordinary was about to be uncovered that would forever alter the lives of many, many people.

Chapter 1

Did we do the right thing?

The late afternoon sunset was rich in intense red, orange and yellow hues, making the horizon look as if there was a blazing inferno in the western sky. All those striking colors were in stark contrast to the vibrant shades of green from the tall longleaf pines, the towering bald cypresses, and the multitude of moss-festooned Live Oak trees canopied along the river that were indigenous to this area of north central Florida. The dogwood trees were in full bloom, too, making the entire scene look like a landscape portrait from one of the masters.

"It is so beautiful here in Campbell County. It's gorgeous really," Anna Mary said with a contented sigh, as she breathed in the scene before her. "I just wish this county could thrive like the rest of the state. Then, everything would be perfect. You'd think the county administration would have gotten their act together by now. Good grief, some days it's as if we're living in Colonial times instead of 2018," she added.

It was early spring of a brand new year, and as evening began to settle in, proud matriarch Anna Mary Jarrellson Williams stood in front of the large bay window on the sun porch that overlooked the majestic Suwannee River. The old Jarrellson home where she lived with her husband, Stanley, was situated in the small community of Seraph Springs in Campbell

County.

The members of Campbell County's Jarrellson family not only knew the county of their birth inside and out, as well as their rich and varied heritage, but they were among its most prominent families, boasting among their family members a former governor of the state of Florida, and a three-term United States senator.

"Oh, my," Anna Mary said, when she spotted her reflection in the glass. "My cheeks are bright red. It seems I got too much sun today. I'll have to remember to put sunscreen on tomorrow, lest I get a freckle on this lily white skin of mine," she added with a chuckle.

She had always prided herself on having the clearest, most velvety white skin of any of the women in the county since as far back as she could remember. She never had a pimple, a blemish, and never, ever a freckle on her face.

"God forbid," she said, looking closer at her reflection, and purposely refusing to acknowledge the wrinkles that were creeping onto her countenance.

Pensively, she thought about the drive she had taken that afternoon. The drive she believed would help her recapture some of the contentment and peace she had felt in her younger days. They were days when she and her daddy, the late Dr. Richard James Jarrellson, would take off on jaunts in and around the county, heading off on adventures to no place in particular. He'd been gone now for over thirty years, but she still remembered each and every drive, and each and every story he had ever told her.

Oftentimes, he would talk about the history of the farms and specific tracts of land they passed by during their travels, as well as any and all the folks who ever lived there. She thought of the little country store out in the Flatwoods of the county; a store now long gone into oblivion, where she and her daddy often stopped to talk with the proprietor. Her father would buy them both a cold drink, usually a bottle of Coca Cola, and sometimes he'd splurge on a candy bar or a small package of crackers. The land where the little store once stood was now part of the holdings of the limestone rock company that came into town several years ago.

Anna Mary's husband, Stanley, walked into the room just then and startled her.

"A penny for your thoughts, sweetheart," he said, as he stood behind her with his hands on her shoulders, but she said nothing. "What in the world is going on in that pretty little head of yours?" he asked.

Anna Mary turned around and reached up with both hands, cradling his face as she kissed him squarely on the lips. The two of them hugged each other and then Anna Mary pulled away. A few tears began to trickle down her cheeks, but Stanley knew better than to ask her what was wrong just yet. He knew she would speak when she was damned good and ready to tell him what was bothering her. Today, it seemed, she was more than eager to talk… once she got going, that is.

"I was thinking about springtimes of long ago," she told Stanley, as she turned back toward the window. "I was reminiscing about the time I was sitting in the passenger seat of Daddy's old pickup truck. I must have been about six years old then. Daddy was driving, of course, and we had the windows down, taking in all the glorious fragrances of fresh, early spring air and all the colors of the budding flowers of Campbell County. I remember we were laughing and joking, and just having the time of our lives."

"Well, those are wonderful memories, darling," Stanley said.

"Yes, they are," she agreed. "I was thinking about Uncle Gus, too. Today, right about dawn, not long after you left to go into town, I went for a drive. When I came upon the main office of the limestone company, the outside lights around the quarry's main offices were still on. They almost blinded me for a second. They're just so bright, you know."

"Yes, they can certainly get to you if you're caught unawares," Stanley agreed with her.

"Well," she began. "Just then, something in my head turned on… you know… a light bulb, just like those lights all around the quarry, Stanley."

"Oh?" he asked.

"Yes, you see, in the beginning, my family… the Jarrellson family, that is… well, I wonder, did we do the right thing with that limestone company?"

"What do you mean?" he asked.

"Well, I know the company has helped a lot of people… a *lot* of people, including this family…." she started, but Stanley immediately interrupted her.

"Anna Mary, you can't look back," he warned her. "*We* can't look back. The Jarrellsons did the best they could with what information they had at the time, all things considered. It was the right decision. You know your family did better than most because of your Uncle Gus and his astute business acumen."

"Oh, yes, I know," she said, agreeing with him. "Especially when Uncle Gus opened up our concrete company on the other side of town," she added, smiling. "AMS Concrete," she said, as if swooning over a handsome actor at the Royal Exchange Theatre in Manchester. "Anna Mary and Stanley…" she trailed off.

"The limestone company's presence here in Campbell County, as well as your Uncle Gus's influence, helped my career with Edison Energy, too," Stanley went on. "In fact, it actually helped me advance more rapidly to the presidency of the company than I would have had I not married you and become part of the family."

"I know it helped, Stanley, but you worked hard… very hard, especially getting our concrete operation up and running. It's still doing well, I presume?" she coyly asked, and Stanley gave her a big, silent, affirmative nod.

"I often wonder if you put the right man in charge of that operation and if…"

Stanley cut her off and said, "You worry way too much, Anna Mary. Our concrete company is doing well and making lots of money. I can assure you of that."

"Thank you, dear. I'm glad to hear it," she told him. "You put a lot of your considerable knowledge into making Edison Energy a leader in the industry, as well," she said. "I am so very, very proud of you, Stanley. I've always been proud of you. I have always felt safe with you, too," she added, and she planted a soft kiss on his cheek.

"That is one of the absolute nicest compliments I've ever received, Anna Mary," Stanley said, blushing. "Thank you, sweetheart, but remember that looking back can be a painful thing sometimes. All we can do now is concentrate on what we have, not what we don't have. We need to count our blessings, too," he added. "We have been more than amply blessed."

Anna Mary sighed heavily and then she rang the bell on the wall of the sunroom. As if by magic, one of the maids appeared within seconds. Never calling the young lady by name or even looking at her, Anna Mary simply barked out an order when she heard footsteps enter the room.

"Would you please bring Mr. Stanley and me a pot of freshly brewed coffee? I know it's late in the day, but I need a restorative cup. Thank you very much," she told the maid.

That was it. Sharp, concise, and without an ounce of soul in her voice. The young Hispanic maid, responded with a, "Yes, ma'am," and off she went.

Without breaking stride, Anna Mary continued her chat with Stanley.

"There are so many stories about that land that is

being mined by the limestone company," she said. "I remember going with Mama years ago to pick wild blueberries on that one section of land the company is mining right now. It used to belong to Uncle Gus, you know. I remember the wild violets that grew there this time of year, too. When we'd go out walking, Mama would always say the same phrase over and over in some way, shape or form. She'd say the land is so green and the flowers are so pretty, but black runs the river. The river's darkness, she said, is the major storyteller of this land. I never knew what she meant until now, Stanley. At least I think I partially know the answer."

Anna Mary sat down in her favorite plush armchair just as the young maid brought in the coffee tray and placed it on an adjacent table.

"Thank you, Maria," Anna Mary said.

"You are welcome," the young girl quietly replied before adding, "I am Consuela, ma'am."

"Oh, excuse me, dear. Of course, you are."

"Shall I pour your coffee and serve it?" Consuela asked her.

"Why, yes, you may, Consuela, and thank you. Mr. Stanley takes his with a little cream and one teaspoon of sugar. I like mine black."

Consuela prepared the coffee and served it to her two employers. Anna Mary took a sip of hers and smiled wide.

"Oh, that's good. Just the way I like it," she said. "Rich and black like the river. You know, Stanley, Mama was right. Black runs the river."

Stanley had no clue what Anna Mary was talking about, but he smiled just the same and nodded to his lovely wife, as he, too, sipped on his coffee.

In the distance, the sweet, plaintive call of the Eastern Whip-poor-will began to reverberate across the huge expanse of sandy Flatwoods in this quaint, quiet town on the northern edge of Campbell County. A mildly sweet fragrance of newly budded spring flowers filled the air. Tonight, it was warm and humid, but not unbearable.

As the sun continued its descent, and as the shadows of night were about to begin their dance, those other artificial lights Anna Mary spoke of began to burn just a few miles away to the south. In fact, they were now burning more brightly than God's huge ball of light that had just disappeared into the western horizon.

From the sun room, Anna Mary had a clear shot of the lights in the distance. They illuminated a huge expanse of land, making it seem as if she was looking at a big city high up on a hill; higher than where she was at the moment. There were so many millions of bright, beaming lights that she thought, with a little imagination, could make one feel as if they were in a big limousine, pulling up to a major cinematic premiere.

It wasn't a new film, though. No, it was nothing that exciting, she thought. It was simply the same old burning lights that, every night, illuminated the corporate grounds of the county's current largest employer, G&S Lime Rock LLC.

Chapter 2

Company comes a'callin'

For many, many years, the limestone company's mammoth-sized walking draglines, powered by Edison Energy, moved with a stealthy grace across the Flatwoods of Campbell County, biting into its heart with gigantic teeth, and then methodically turning over tons of limestone-rich earth. For certain, these electrically-powered, giant earthmovers ensured there would be a wealth of smiling shareholder faces in the boardroom at the top echelons of Edison Energy.

The company, with its long tentacles reaching deep into the rich soil of Campbell County, controlled much of the altruistic and political scene in and around this area in the center of north Florida. Being the largest contributor to scores of charities in the local area also ensured the company's continued goodwill status within the community. Their quote-unquote "selfless, charitable deeds" also helped to nudge their oftentimes hand-picked political candidates into public office in the county and beyond… some of them all the way up to Washington D.C.

Meanwhile, the company's top executives fully realized that their presence and success in Campbell County was nothing short of a miracle; a miracle for them, that is. On the flipside, and even though they continued to struggle, it was also a miracle for the economically-challenged people of Campbell County who could never figure out how to keep their heads very far above water. In fact, the county had operated in the deficit for so long that its officials knew no other way to be… until "the company" came along to change things for the better, that is.

The biggest miracle, of course, was the presence of huge, seemingly unlimited deposits of a rare type of limestone rock that had lain dormant in Campbell County for hundreds of years just beneath the surface of the earth. It was the sleeping remains of long, long ago, prehistoric marine life whose skeletons and outer shells had morphed into a peculiar type of limestone rock during the time this portion of the state of Florida was mostly underwater. It was unlike any other limestone rock that had ever been discovered elsewhere in the world, which explained its exorbitant price, compared to other forms of limestone rock.

The big draglines drank from the crystal clear springs throughout the area, and they feasted relentlessly on the breast of the dark and bountiful waters of the Suwannee River. It was a river of life snaking through the county from north to south. It was a river that held many, many secrets, as well as many obstacles if one didn't stay alert to its hidden dangers. It was a river that had seen its share of abuse, too, not only from the toxic waste of the mining company, but also from contaminated sewer water that flowed downriver from the neighboring state to the north.

The major economic miracle for the company, as well as for those who came to embrace and, at times, enhance the Sunshine State's economic growth, was that paradise was indeed for sale. It was a buyer's market; not just for the limestone industry, but for numerous northern and even international interests that wanted to buy into the state of Florida. This included timber industries, railroad interests, and land developers by the dozens, and yes, even Anna Mary and Stanley's concrete plant. Yes, that big For Sale sign was out, shining like the North Star, and it was beckoning one and all to "come on down".

In the 1950s and '60s, the new Florida interstate highway system, along with the advent of air conditioning in most homes and businesses, made this tropical paradise even more enticing and desirable. Florida was also affordable with no state income tax, reasonable sales and property taxes, and a host of reasonably priced restaurants. Plus, a person could play a round of golf with his or her buddies year round… wearing shorts!

Around that same time, there was a private entity that replaced the old Florida Department of Commerce. Among other things, this new organization produced television advertising spots to entice winter-weary folks in northern states to come vacation on the white, sandy beaches of south and southwest Florida. They also heavily targeted senior citizens, who were relishing in their golden years, and who, admittedly, were tired of shoveling snow every winter. Thus, the term snowbirds took flight.

These seniors were being lured to the Sunshine

State en masse and urged to join the robins and fly south for the entire winter season. Naturally, once they got a taste of the warm, tropical Florida weather, many of them decided to make it a permanent move and reside full time in the land of beautiful sunsets, low taxes, temperate climate, and easy, comfortable living.

After a while, knowing they had a captive audience, the state's new tourism industry continued to pour tens of millions of advertising dollars into internationally renowned tourist and business interests in the more heavily populated areas of south and central Florida. The main beneficiaries of all those tourist development dollars were the dozens of cruise lines, and later, theme parks and movie studios. On any given day, each of these tourist spots welcomed nearly twenty times the amount of visitors than the entire population of little ol' Campbell County.

As one of the fifty poorest counties in the entire nation, Campbell County languished lazily and laconically on the sandy banks of the Suwannee River. In fact, the county languished for over a quarter century ever since the company came a'callin'. There was, in fact, more valuation on the tax rolls for tangible personal property than for real property because of the limestone company.

To this day, the residents of the county continue to languish with little change in population and even smaller amounts of development. After all, aside from river activities, there really is nothing to do in the county and nothing to look at other than the raped land

and the thinned forests, due to activity from companies such as G&S Lime Rock.

The public schools in Campbell County had been declining in enrollment for many, many years because there was little industry other than the limestone rock company. Not everyone was keen on working there, either, although, many residents felt they had no other choice if they wanted to survive and take care of their families.

The folks in the county were under anesthesia, drowsed, if you will, as if in a drug-induced dream. A dream from which they felt they would never awaken. If nothing else, most county officials were content with the low property taxes and the cooperation of its largest employer and largest taxpayer, the limestone company.

They were also thankful for the generosity of the company toward their schools and the scholarships they offered, as well as club donations and library funding, and for providing employment for their residents, whether those residents liked working there or not. They employed many out-of-towners, too, who temporarily relocated inside the county or commuted back and forth to take advantage of the higher wages the company afforded them. All in all, the company, most anyone would tell you, had been and was still good for the area.

No one in management at the company would dare say it out loud, but the county had been good to them, as well. Despite what had been accepted on the surface as a warm and fuzzy feeling about the company, as well as the sense of security it provided for its workers, it was not that old familiar grandmotherly or maternal feeling.

The company, at one time, employed thousands of people. Now they were down to just a few hundred employees. According to state authorities, limestone is categorized as a non-renewable resource because of the amount of time it takes to regenerate. Needless to say, with all the mining that had already been done, limestone just wasn't as plentiful in Campbell County as it was twenty-five years ago.

In truth, according to critics and non-critics alike, the company existed and only moved its mammoth-sized industrial equipment across the limestone-rich land of Campbell County for the sole purpose of making money... lots of money... period.

Throughout the years, since its inception, the company's ownership had changed hands a few times, from one powerful entity to the other with some name changes along the way, all the while riding the highs and lows of the world's rich limestone market. They were always mindful, however, of keeping their costs at a minimum and their profit margins as high as possible, even with all their generous contributions to the community, which tells you just how lucrative the limestone business really is, especially in a limestone-rich area such as Campbell County that boasted the rarest type of that rock.

Prior to the time the company set up shop in

Campbell County, folks used to comment on the prolific growth of longleaf and slash pine trees in the area. Many said that it was as if the pine trees had fertilizer "put to them". In truth, they had been richly fertilized; fertilized by the mineral-rich soil of the county; fertilized by minerals that were unashamedly considered collateral damage as the draglines massively mined the land to sell its limestone product around the world. Limestone has an enormous diversity of uses, including construction material, road base, and railroad ballast, and, of course, Portland cement.

In the early days of the company, and after very little investigation, by the way, their top executives discovered that the price to be paid for goodwill in Campbell County was not exorbitant in cost at all.

They had at their disposal a master of public and human relations; a guy by the name of Dale Mills Fitzgerald. He had been raised in Savannah, Georgia, educated at the University of the South in Sewanee, Tennessee, and later went to the Wharton School of Business up in Philadelphia where he received his MBA.

Dale's father, a well-known corporate attorney in Atlanta, Georgia, developed friendships with many of the nation's industrial executives, including those who were heads of Florida's limestone industry. In fact, the limestone industry was such a major client that it required a great deal of the firm's time. So, Dale's father opened a branch of his firm in Lakeland, Florida, in order to cater more easily to those clients. He put his son in charge of the venture. Within three months, Dale and his family moved to Lakeland, although, it turned out to be only a short stay.

Through their association with Dale and with all the invitations from him and his wife, these Florida clients and company executives soon discovered the delights of the golf links at Augusta and Sea Island where the law firm's home office owned numerous luxurious cottages. Each cottage was equipped with all the modern conveniences one could hope for, plus fully stocked bars, and private pools and hot tubs. The so-called cottages each had about five-thousand square feet of living space and would comfortably accommodate twelve to fifteen guests quite nicely. Most importantly, each cottage was fully staffed with cooks, maids, laundresses, and pool maintenance staff. They were all conveniently located on well-tended and beautifully maintained golf courses, and they were utilized for the firm's most select clients.

Into this lavish and privileged world, Dale was born and groomed, and he turned out to be the ideal scion of a family who smoothly, graciously, and professionally made their fortune from the good fortune of their clients. In other words, he was a master at using other people's money to make a profit.

Dale was a good-looking man with a self-effacing manner about him that he could turn on and off at will. It was clear that he felt just as at home shootin' the bull with a farmer, while leaning against a farm tractor out in the middle of a plowed field, as he was in a tuxedo in a luxurious private club or seaside resort. People, it seemed, never had a problem opening up to him. They'd invite him into their home for a meal with their family, they'd ask him to join in on a dove shoot, a deer hunt, a day on the river, or a deep sea fishing expedition. He just fit in anywhere and everywhere.

Dale and his stunningly beautiful wife, Molly, had twin daughters with long, blonde, curly locks, named Melissa and Priscilla, Missy and Prissy respectively. The family eventually relocated to Campbell County and soon became regular fixtures at Seraph Springs United Methodist Church. Molly, as it turned out, was an expert pianist and it didn't take long before she won the hearts of all, playing for special occasions and events in the community, as well as in church during Sunday services.

Through many friendly visits around the county, Dale discovered things about individuals that one can only discover while actively seeking the story of a stranger, which was something he was very good at doing without raising any suspicions. Campbell County's citizens, including all its elected officials, did not remain strangers to him for long. Dale found out a great deal about all of them and he was always looking for ways that the company might enhance their lives. It was sneaky and perhaps a bit sinister, but that was the way the game was played.

For those Campbell County folks who enjoyed playing cards, betting on horses, or other games of chance, they might find themselves the winners in a drawing for an all-expenses-paid weekend trip to Las Vegas for a company celebration event.

For the avid hunters, they might find themselves invited to join company executives for a Montana elk hunting excursion, or to go bird hunting at a Central American destination, complete with deluxe lodging and five-star gourmet meals.

Then, for those lovers of just plain leisure, there were numerous invitations from the company to attend decision-making workshops, or a long weekend at a beach resort. These workshops would either be held on the southeast coast of Georgia or the southwest coast of Florida. Evenings would be spent in palatial dining rooms, eating exotic meals, and listening to orchestral music, while participating in company meetings, if they cared to, that is. It was not a requirement.

In truth, the company employed business practices that were as old as the sea with those they were courting. In a poor and struggling north Florida county, this type of courting was new and exciting, and it was all dressed up in newly purchased resort and cocktail wear, and travels to all-expenses-paid destinations for conferences in venues that were far beyond their economic means or imagination had the company not been providing these wonderful learning opportunities.

No expense was spared for Campbell County's residents who were making these seasonal pilgrimages. The bulk of them, of course, were the elected officials, but there were quite a few citizens who were considered to be extremely influential in the community, so they were given special treatment and invitations, as well.

The company retreats and conferences brought about a feeling of friendship, whether it was a phony friendship or not, between the local community and the company, which translated into an easy working relationship, at least on the surface. It made the oftentimes controversial decision-making of the company easier to swallow, thereby maximizing profits for the company in the long run. All the while, the humble yet illustrious Dale, the ever-loving public relations man, continued to schmooze with the community to keep human relations at a satisfactory and acceptable level.

The company was booming on a wave fueled by the sounds of laughter and camaraderie, the tinkling of ice cubes inside highball glasses, and the sweet scent of cigar smoke rising above the intoxicating aroma of barbecued chicken and ribs piled atop half a dozen large, gas barbecue grills. It was a huge revelry of well-dressed, well-groomed company executives, along with numerous county officials and a smattering of local, privileged residents.

Over the years, school-aged children had frequently been bused in from outside the county to dig for and uncover ancient shark's teeth, small fossils and other treasures in Campbell County that hearkened back to a time when most of the state of Florida had been underwater… under the ocean, if you will. The squeals of delight when a child or even a grown adult would uncover one of these relics could be heard for miles, it seemed.

Meanwhile, just a few hundred yards away, the company draglines were busy at work, digging through the sandy soil and scraping up every last ounce of precious limestone from the land. The endless supply of this lime rock in Campbell County was beyond the imagination of anyone at the company. Many residents often wondered what other unique treasures the draglines had dug up over the years, and they also wondered what the company did with those treasures.

Just a few days ago, something odd happened on a strip of property once owned by Anna Mary Jarrellson Williams' late uncle, the internationally renowned artist, Spencer Augustus Jarrellson.

Gus's family, at one time, owned over one-hundred-thousand acres of land in Campbell County. Needless to say, because of the family's stature in the county, no one ever dreamed that the giant shovel of the dragline would dare appear on any Jarrellson property. Yet, there it was. The shovel was so large that two regular-sized pickup trucks could have easily driven onto it and had plenty of room to spare.

This super-sized shovel that for years had been scooping up tons of north Florida sand, soil, and limestone, would, with one big scoop, miraculously and purely by accident, unearth one of the county's most gruesome, most often-discussed, and still unsolved mysteries.

It was just before dawn on a warm, spring day,

deep in the heart of Campbell County. On precious land that used to belong to one of the founders of the county, one of G&S Lime Rock's mammoth, electrically-powered walking draglines, the Number Three, as it was known among the crew, had just been stopped dead in its tracks by order of Hoyle Malphus, who was commandeering the behemoth machine. Stopping a moving dragline was not something one could or would do easily. At least, not without approval from on high, unless you wanted to get fired or severely reprimanded.

From the cab above, Hoyle had been watching the beast move across land that was once covered with second growth longleaf pines, and before that, covered with the Jarrellson family's Sea Island cotton. Even though his eyesight wasn't what it used to be, with early stage cataracts in both eyes now, Hoyle could still spot a deer fifty yards away through the scope of his rifle. He could also see there was something in the ground ahead of him that shouldn't have been there. Whatever it was, it was brightly sparkling in the dirt from the glare of the headlights of the dragline, just as he was about to make a deeper scoop into the earth.

He immediately radioed the main power station and told them to kill the juice to the dragline. Once the machine stopped, Hoyle, who was a rugged old man in his sixties, took his sweet time climbing down the gigantic machine. Once on the ground, he lumbered toward where he thought he had seen the bright glittering object. With his bare hands he began to scratch at the dirt. Seconds later, he turned toward his buddy, who was still watching from inside the cab of the dragline.

"Foye!" he yelled. "Foye! Bring me a small shovel!"

Hoyle's coworker, seventy-one-year-old Foye Dicks, arrived minutes later, huffing and puffing after climbing off the dragline, and looking as if he was about to have a coronary.

"This better be good, Hoyle," Foye warned him, as he struggled to catch his breath.

Hoyle didn't say a word. He just grabbed the shovel from Foye's outstretched hand and proceeded to turn over shovelfuls of dirt. After the third shovelful fell to the ground, the two men's jaws simultaneously dropped and they turned to look at one another. Foye yanked his handkerchief from his back pocket and wiped his sweaty brow, as he shook his head from side to side.

"Boss, you better phone the superintendent and tell him to get his ass out here now," Foye told him.

"You think I don't know that?!" Hoyle barked at him.

The two men were both old enough to have heard all the rumors, some crazier than others, that had floated around the county throughout the years, so this was a big deal… a very big deal if this was what they thought it might be.

After a long, deep breath to clear his head, Hoyle grabbed the radio from his belt loop and punched in the numbers 9-1-1-9-9-9-9, which was the secret emergency code that would take him directly to the Day Supervisor at G&S, who was an ingratiating young man by the name of Wilfred Simms. When Hoyle told him he had cut the power to the dragline, Simms started yelling like a banshee. However, once Hoyle told him what he had discovered, Simms changed his tune and said he would immediately contact the public relations office of the company.

"Well, I guess we just sit and wait now," Hoyle told Foye after he ended the call.

"Yes, sir," Foye said, still shaking his head, as he stared at the sight before him. "Just sit and wait."

Chapter 3

Oh, dem bones

It took about twenty minutes for the limestone company's public relations manager, Dale Fitzgerald, and Campbell County Sheriff Bartow Lewis to arrive at what could potentially be a murder scene on Jarrellson property in Seraph Springs. The two of them came in separate vehicles, both of them kicking up dust, dirt and pebbles before coming to a screeching halt directly behind the dragline. By now, the morning sun was just breaking through the rain clouds to the east, making it easier to see the lay of the land.

After the perfunctory professional greetings between all four men, Dale and the sheriff casually walked over to the area in question. For several minutes, all four men simply stood motionless staring at the incredible sight before them. Nobody said a word.

Buried in the ground in front of them, about two feet apart in the dug up soil, were two human skulls, both appearing to have been buried face up, as their eye sockets were aimed toward the sky. The skull on the left had five, shiny gold teeth still intact in its upper jaw, as if the skeletal head was grinning from behind a black curtain at a Halloween party. Or, perhaps, it was more of a haunting grimace. Whatever it was, the gold teeth were what Hoyle had seen sparkling in the dirt under the glow of the dragline's lights as it dug into the earth just before dawn.

Right beyond the two skulls there were other bones protruding from the sandy soil that looked to be arms, legs and feet... remnants of human bodies that had been buried in the earth for God only knew how long.

The sheriff immediately noticed something curious about the two skeletons.

Once he had them both completely unearthed, he mumbled, "Well, would you look at that? The sternums are missing from both these bodies."

"Yeah, it almost looks as if they were removed by design," Dale said, taking a closer look at the two skeletons.

"Well, ain't that jes' somethin'?" the sheriff mumbled again, shaking his head, clearly dumbfounded.

"It sure is," Dale agreed. "It's rather macabre that the breast bones on both bodies are missing, don't you think?" he asked the sheriff.

"Yeah, the main bone that protects the body's most vital organ, the human heart, is just plum gone," the sheriff said, scratching his head.

Sheriff Lewis, not a man to ever make a hurried decision, snatched his cell phone from his pocket and immediately phoned Florida State Attorney Stephen Marcus, who answered the phone after four rings with a yawning and lazy, "Hello."

The first thing out of Sheriff Lewis's mouth was, "Mr. Marcus, I think there's somethin' here you need to see for yerself... and the sooner the better," he added, in his unmistakable southern drawl.

"Say what?!" Stephen shouted. "Bartow, you been dippin' into that moonshine again?" he asked, obviously recognizing the sheriff's voice, but then he managed a soft chuckle.

"Now, you know I ain't touched the stuff in years, Mr. Marcus," the sheriff rebutted. "In all seriousness, I need you here immediately and I think the Florida Department of Law Enforcement should be notified, too."

"The FDLE?!" Stephen gasped. "What the hell, Bartow? It's seven o'clock in the damn morning!"

"Yes, sir, I know it is," the sheriff calmly answered. "Well, actually, I think it's closer to eight now. Anyway, I can assure you it will be well worth yer while to climb outta that bed, get yer'self dressed, and then get yer sorry ass over here to look at what we jes' found. This is somethin', I'm thinkin', if we ain't here to oversee things, the nosy press will get a holda' this story and have a dang heyday," he told him. "I like you, Mr. Marcus. Always have. I'd like to see you stay in office, too," he added. "I'm sure you're likin' that hundred-and-fifty grand you're pullin' in every year."

"Bartow, first of all, if you're gonna call me at the break of dawn, you can at least call me by my first name."

"Oh... yeah, sure thing, Stephen," the sheriff said.

"Secondly, what the hell can be so important that you had to wake me at such an ungodly hour?"

"Well, now, I'm gettin' to that," the sheriff said. "It's actually somethin' we've talked about in this town long before you ever ran for office. It's somethin' that's been a mystery here for over twenty-five years, in fact. By the way, this ain't the break o' dawn, Stephen. Hell, us country folk been up for hours."

There was a short lull in the conversation and then Stephen spoke again, almost in a whisper this time.

"Are you talking about what I think you're talking about? Is it about those boys who went missing and were never found?" he asked. "Those vagrant boys? Are you talking about that, Bartow?"

"Well, now, for a sleepy man, you're suddenly wide awake now, ain't ye?" Sheriff Lewis teased him. "Yes, sir-ree. I think we done found 'em," he said. "Some of 'em, anyway. There were four of 'em that went missin'. I think I got two of 'em here in front of me. It looks like they been here awhile."

"Wow… let's hope we find the other two," Stephen said.

"Yeah, let's hope," the sheriff said. "There's a couple folks I want you and me to talk to as quickly as possible. One of 'em is Mrs. Dee Dee Wilson Fernandez, and the other one is old Judge Wesson."

"Oh? And why is that, sheriff?"

"Well, Dee Dee's late uncle, old man Hamp Brayerford, had a keen interest in that "missing boys" investigation. I believe you may have met the man once or twice."

The sheriff knew Hamp had kept a detailed

notebook, or diary, if you will, where he had jotted down all his thoughts, observations and suspicions about that particular case. He figured now was as good a time as any to pass along that interesting little tidbit to Stephen while he had him on the phone, and so he did.

"Yeah, Hamp tried numerous times to force the state of Florida to continue the crime investigation until it was solved," the sheriff continued. "Even with all of Hamp's influence, and it was a substantial amount, he kept gettin' stonewalled in his efforts. It's hard to believe all that happened so long ago, nearly twenty-five years now."

"That doesn't surprise me," Stephen said. "Sometimes cases are just hard nuts to crack, especially murder cases with no bodies."

"You're right on that, son. Anyway, Hamp often brought up the investigation about those missing boys in conversations with other folks over the years, which is how I found out about his extensive notes, even though he never showed 'em to me. He always swore there was a lot more to it than people thought. He may have been right," the sheriff told Stephen. "I liked the old man and I never knew him to dwell on much of anything, unless it was a huntin' trip or maybe when he was concentratin' on a loved one who was in trouble. He dwelled on that investigation, though. He damn sure did. That's the truth, Stephen. I hunted and fished with him a lot, and that case seemed to have haunted the old man."

"Well, if this Dee Dee lady still has all that

documentation done by her uncle, we'll certainly want to see it," Stephen said.

"I can almost guarantee she still has it," the sheriff assured Stephen. "Somethin' else…" he added, as he scratched the whiskers on his chin. "Judge Wesson was on the bench when all them boys went missin'. He's retired now, but that old man's memory is phenomenal, or at least it was the last time I spoke with him, which was just a few weeks ago. So, like I said, we need to talk to both of 'em."

"And we will," Stephen said, sounding much more awake now. "Maybe I'll bring in my forensics specialist, too," he added.

"Your predecessor in the State Attorney's office, Mr. Alton Culpepper, had the case closed," Sheriff Lewis explained. "He told the press and the community that every possible stone had been turned over, and that every person who could be questioned was indeed questioned. However, there was no compelling evidence to bring anyone to trial, nor enough evidence to continue the investigation. He said there was an absence of proof. No bodies were found. There was a lotta diggin' and a lottta huntin', but not one body did they find. Ain't that somethin'?" he rhetorically asked. "Said it was costin' the taxpayers too much money. Funny thing is, he didn't take a political lickin' for it, either. In fact, he was praised for it. Can ya believe that?" the sheriff asked.

"Sounds about right," Stephen said, with a tinge of sarcasm in his voice.

"A lot of folks felt... well... them boys was wanderers... not from around here, you know?" the sheriff went on. "No need in spendin' tons of taxpayer money on somethin' such as that... you know... for them kinda vagrant folk. As I recall, as soon as one of the detectives knocked on the door of one of the members of the Jarrellson family, who is now deceased, the investigation came to an abrupt halt. I mean like instantly! It wasn't long after that, maybe a year or two, that Mr. Culpepper purchased that beautiful home he always wanted up in the mountains of North Carolina. Sure did. Right smack dab in the middle of a world-class golf course. Beautiful place. He showed me pictures one day."

Stephen didn't say much about that, other than a tired, "Hmmm..."

"Well, I been here in this county a long time," Sheriff Lewis said. "I'm sure there's folks here who don't much care what I think. What I do know is, since I been sheriff there ain't been no dead bodies dug up in this county. It sure as hell looks like we got some now, though. We'll see what the medical examiner has to say."

"Yeah, I'll call him as soon as we hang up," Stephen said. "We definitely need to talk to Dee Dee and the judge, but first we have to stop the limestone company from doing any more digging in that area. Then, we need to thank them and the dragline operators for discovering something I'm sure they never intended to uncover."

"I wonder if I should phone Mr. Stanley and Mrs. Anna Mary Jarrellson Williams," the sheriff suggested. "You realize these bodies are on some of her Uncle Gus's property, right?"

"Let's wait on that until we know more, Bartow."

"Yeah, I guess you're right. One thing's for certain. We need to keep this out of the newspaper until we have a lot more answers."

"Stupid question, but why is that so important?" Stephen asked.

"Because we don't want things gettin' messed up on this case by someone who might still be alive, you know? Someone who may have killed these boys... or someone who knows who did."

"I suppose you're right, Bartow," Stephen said. "Aww, hell, of course, you're right. I'm still not fully awake yet."

"Okay, then," the sheriff said with a heavy sigh. "For now, I'm gonna talk to Mr. Fitzgerald here and these two men on the dragline to see if they can offer any more information."

"That's good," Stephen said. "Tell them to keep their mouths shut, though. Scare the hell out of them if you have to. Just do what you need to do. We don't want anyone talking about this right now," he added, as if it was his bright idea to keep things quiet and not the sheriff's.

"I'll take care of it," Bartow assured him. "Wait... hang on a sec, Stephen."

While the two men had been talking on the phone,

Hoyle was busy shoveling and he uncovered yet another skeleton.

"Sheriff, it looks like there's three bodies altogether!" Hoyle yelled to him, as he wiped the sweat from his forehead.

"Bartow!" Stephen barked into the phone, obviously overhearing what Hoyle had just said. "Bartow! What the hell is that man doing disturbing the crime scene? You need to get him the hell away from there!"

"Aww, don't be gettin' all excited there, Stephen. We got things under control. I am the sheriff of this county, you know."

"Yeah, well, just the same! Make him stop!"

"Hey, Hoyle!" the sheriff yelled. "Mr. high-and-mighty-state-attorney here says to put down that damn shovel, you hear?"

"Yes, sir," Hoyle sheepishly replied, but then he grinned when the sheriff winked at him.

"One of these days, you old coot," Stephen snarled into the phone. "One of these days."

"Hey, you know you love me," the sheriff quipped with him.

After a brief, uncomfortable silence, Stephen asked the sheriff a question to move things along.

"So, Bartow, do you have any sort of description of these missing boys? To your recollection, that is?"

"Yes, I sure do. You can look it up for yourself, I'm sure, but I'll tell ya what I know. First off, there was four of 'em altogether that went missin', like I tol' ya. Each one of 'em was Caucasian, of course, and they was all about five feet eight or nine inches tall. They was slightly built, but wiry, and they was all hired by Mrs. Anna Mary's uncle, Gus Jarrellson. They was doin' some work on a piece of land he had that went all the way down to the Suwannee River. The limestone company now has the rights to dig on that property. In fact, we're standing on part of it right now."

"Don't ask me how I know, but that crazy professor, Dr. Curtis Osborne, lives on part of that property old man Gus owned," Stephen said. "Gus, it seems, left a small strip of his land to Miss Agatha Campbell, and you're right…"

"Ahh, yes, Miss Aggie," the sheriff interrupted him. "Did you know she delivered 'ol man Hamp Brayerford?"

"No, I didn't know that. Anyway, that land goes all the way down to the river like you said. Before she died, she deeded it to the professor for a dollar."

"Eh, I know all about that," the sheriff lazily replied, as he chewed on a cigar that he just popped into his mouth. "You ain't tellin' me nuttin' new," he added, totally preoccupied with getting his cigar lit.

Meanwhile, he kept staring at the three skeletons out of his beady little eyes that always looked like they weren't fully opened. High Sheriff Snake Eyes is how the African Americans in Campbell County referred to the sheriff, but only behind his back. Of course, the sheriff wasn't an idiot, and he knew darned good and well exactly what the people in his county thought of him, as well as all the nicknames they had given him. He didn't care, though. His favorite saying was, "I'm just doin' my job."

"Looks like nothing gets past you, eh, sheriff?" Stephen asked.

"Nope. Not a whole lot," he replied, as a smile spread across his face. "That's the reason I done tol' you... we need to find out who is responsible for this... the living or the dead. We could have a killer runnin' loose, you know."

"I realize that," Stephen said.

"Remember, no press," the sheriff went on. "We're gonna take our time on this one. It could blow the lid right off this county. Like I said, I been here a long, long time. Right now, everyone needs to stay just as quiet and calm as these bones have stayed for all these years. Trust me, son. When the bones get ready, they'll talk to us. They always do."

"I'm sure they will," Stephen agreed.

"There's more than one skeleton in most closets here in Campbell County," Sheriff Lewis went on. "Sometimes, folks move their skeletons from one closet to another closet, but sooner or later, those skeletons get found out," he added with a chuckle, as cigar smoke circled around the big silver star above the brim of his white-straw cowboy hat. "Yes, sir, they get found out."

Chapter 4

An unpleasant task

Judge John Wesson was sitting behind his desk staring out the window of his plush office, which wasn't far from Campbell County's historic courthouse in the quiet little town of Turpricone. In fact, the office was within walking distance, as it was just two short blocks to the west. The judge had made the trek back and forth many, many times over the years.

As soon as he arrived at his office this morning, he immediately opened one of the north-facing windows, which was something he rarely did. Most times, he, like so many others nowadays, preferred the even-comfort temperatures of air conditioning, which he'd become accustomed to, ever since he had the central air unit installed back in the late 60s.

Today, however, he felt as if he needed something to invigorate his body and his mind. He wanted to breathe in some fresh, brisk, spring air and enjoy all the varied fragrances of the flowering blooms out on the lawn. As the curtains rustled ever so slightly, the cool breeze seemed to be helping to clear his thoughts. He needed to shake off some of those darned old cobwebs that kept getting trapped in his brain of late. Plus, he hadn't enjoyed a good night's sleep since Sheriff Bartow Lewis phoned him the other day regarding the discovery of skeletal remains on some old Jarrellson property by the dragline crew of G&S Lime Rock. As if he didn't already have enough on his plate, he now had to deal with an age-old mystery that had just been dug up.

After retiring from the bench, the judge returned to practicing law on a part time basis, just to stay active in his waning years. He was still referred to by the townsfolk as Judge Wesson, though, and would probably be called that until the day he died.

He kept his old judicial office as a place to study, hold private conferences, and counsel a select few private clients on occasion. Right now, he was waiting for two extremely special clients to arrive, Dee Dee Wilson Fernandez and her cousin, Carl Alvin Campbell. It had been quite a few months since he had seen either one of them. Their history went back many, many years, and he considered them as part of his family.

The aroma of freshly brewed coffee and the light fragrance of homemade lemon pound cake filled the air inside his spacious office; an office that was dripping in excesses of all sorts, down to the solid gold drawer pulls on his massive, antique oak desk. His long-time legal assistant, Mrs. Sara Nell Townsend, still came in on an as needed basis and today was one of those days. As always, she arrived early.

"Sara Nell, I'm feeling my age today, all eighty-two of them, especially since the task that lies ahead of me is not a pleasant one," Judge Wesson blurted out when she walked into his office.

"Well, good morning, Judge," she said. "I'm sorry to hear you aren't feeling well."

"Oh, I imagine I'll get over it soon enough," he mumbled.

For the last forty-seven years, among the many other legal and administrative tasks Sara Nell performed for the judge, she had also dutifully supplied refreshments for client visits. Today was no different. Most of the refreshments she brought in were baked goods homemade by Sara Nell herself, who was an excellent cook. The judge had commented on several occasions that he wondered how she found time to do all that she did on a daily basis. Her answer was always a simple one. "I just love doing it," she'd say.

Judge Wesson motioned for her to have a seat in front of his desk, which was something he often did when he needed a friendly ear to get things off his chest. Sara Nell was a good listener and she had been the most loyal confidante anyone could have ever asked for over the years. She could keep a secret like nobody's business, which is why Judge Wesson trusted her with his life.

"I know my clients will be upset today, to say the least, but my duty is to uphold the law," he started, and Sara Nell nodded. "As unpopular and politically incorrect as it might come across to Dee Dee and Carl Alvin, I have to tell the truth about this nasty business with Anna Mary and Stanley, and all that it involves. I feel especially bad for Destini, though."

"I know you do, Judge," Sara Nell said, nodding

again and obviously knowing full well what her boss had to do today, since she had helped him review all the paperwork. "You always tell the truth," she added.

The judge was referring to Destini Wilson Abamu, a close, close friend of both Dee Dee and Carl Alvin. She was also the former black mistress of the late Hamp Brayerford, who was Dee Dee and Carl Alvin's uncle. Destini bore Hamp a child out of wedlock, the late Easter Bunnye Wilson. Bunnye died at the age of twelve in a house fire trying to save her beloved great-grandmother, Mama Tee, who also died in the fire.

"You, me, Dee Dee, and Carl Alvin… well, we're like family, you know?" the judge rhetorically asked. "We've all known each other for years, so this isn't going to be easy."

Judge Wesson stood up from his big, black leather chair, went over to the table where Sara Nell had placed the cake and coffee, and proceeded to pour two cups of the steaming hot brew, one for him and one for Sara Nell. Then, he carefully laid two slices of cake and placed them on his favorite antique china dessert plates, again, one for him and one for Sara Nell. It was a ritual that she knew not to interfere with or interrupt. After all, the judge was a true gentleman when it came to the treatment of women, and he wanted to make sure everyone knew it.

As he sauntered back to his desk, he silently thanked God for the gift of the day and asked the good Lord for strength and wisdom, as he often did. Then, he started aimlessly chattering, as if he was in a trance and reliving days gone by.

"This county, while remaining so much the same, changes all the time," he wistfully said. "Sometimes those changes are pleasant and welcome, but oftentimes they're extremely unpleasant. Today is one of those unpleasant changes, Sara Nell."

"Yes, it is," she agreed, as she took the cake and coffee from his outstretched hands. "Look at it this way, though," she told him. "At least you are being well paid to be unpleasant," she added, to which he grinned ever so slightly.

Once he was seated again, he took a small bite of his pound cake.

"Ummm... moist and delicious as always, Sara Nell," he complimented her.

"Thank you, Judge," she said, smiling from ear to ear.

After a few more bites, the old man washed it all down with a generous gulp of coffee. Then, he seemed to drift off again for a few minutes, as Sara Nell slyly watched him.

"Do you remember all the young children flyin' past this office on their bicycles after school let out, and all the sweet, little girls who would roller skate up and down, and up and down the sidewalk?" he asked her, smiling, as if he was still living in those moments.

"I sure do," she said.

"I remember one time a tearful Carl Alvin come in here with his legs all skinned up from the knee down to his ankles, and with a pretty good chunk of flesh gouged from his shin. Ohh… and there was pretty little Dee Dee sittin' beside him, sayin', don't cry, Carl Alvin, don't cry. The judge is gonna make it all better. Do you remember that day, Sara Nell?"

"Yes, I do, and I recall you didn't know what to do with him, so you reached into your pocket and pulled out two peppermint candies."

"That's right, and I told him, son, suck on these as hard as you can and all that pain will drain away. Remember that?"

"Yes, I sure do, and you had the easy part," Sara Nell teased him. "I was the one who had to clean up his scrapes, find the Bandaids, and then give him a cold soft drink to calm him down."

"Heh, heh, heh… that you did, sweetheart," he said, all smiles. "All I know is that by the time they left, both he and Dee Dee were laughing again." He paused a moment, and then continued. "I remember all those days they played with my granddaughter, Amy Elizabeth, and how much love and attention they lavished on her," the judge went on, and then he fell silent.

For just a few moments, Judge Wesson became extremely emotionally distraught… something he'd been doing a lot lately. He immediately snatched a crumpled up handkerchief from his coat pocket and wiped his teary eyes, turning his back on Sara Nell as he did so. He wasn't a man who normally gave in to his emotions, especially in front of other people, so it was a little embarrassing for him. Today, it was clear that his heart ached with the burden of news he was carrying, which he soon had to deliver to both Dee Dee and Carl Alvin, two people he dearly loved as if they were part of his own flesh and blood.

"Let me warm up your coffee," Sara Nell said, and she grabbed his cup and went over to the refreshment table, in order to give him time to collect himself.

A lot of the folks in Campbell County were related to one another in some way, shape or form, whether legitimately or illegitimately, and whether they were black or white. Sometimes it was hard to keep track of who was who, even for some of the elders of the community. The Judge knew them all, though, and all their history dating back decades, and so did Sara Nell.

The Jarrellson Williams family had kept the judge – in his capacity as an attorney – on retainer for a number of years. The Jarrellson Trust had been his first major client in the county when he was a young attorney just starting out. That one account alone kept food on his table during all those lean years when clients were few and far between.

Throughout the ensuing decades, he had watched the Jarrellsons make numerous family and business decisions... some that truly burdened him. They were decisions he would not have made, but he was their legal representative. As long as he stayed within the bounds of the law, he had no right to question their wishes or their motives, and they never asked for his opinion when they had their minds set on something.

It saddened him some, but he knew the Jarrellson

family never viewed him as a real friend nor a social equal. For the most part, he was fine with that. In the end, he was paid handsomely by them for the services he provided, so it was worth the hurts and the slights.

The Jarrellsons, in their minds, had no social equals in Campbell County, or even the entire northern portion of the state of Florida, except perhaps the Lord himself. The family was known to utilize and tolerate others, but they were, unto themselves, a closed society, if you will. Meanwhile, everyone in the county simply accepted the way they were and dealt with the situation without prejudice.

Judge Wesson had already decided, in this case, that if he had to drop the Jarrellson Williams clan as clients, he would do so willingly. He would protect Dee Dee, Carl Alvin and even Destini with all of his might. Since part of what was involved in this current legal situation could possibly be the well-being of his beloved granddaughter, Amy Elizabeth, there was no way in hell he was going to have that happiness threatened.

He figured he'd begin the meeting by asking Dee Dee about the late Hamp Brayerford's research involving the missing boys case without telling her anything about the recent discovery of the skeletal remains that were just dug up on Jarrellson property. He hadn't even mentioned it to Sara Nell yet, since the sheriff had just told him two days ago and swore him to secrecy. He and the sheriff both agreed that it would be best if the judge asked Dee Dee for Hamp Brayerford's notebooks, rather than the sheriff.

The judge knew he had to be careful how he approached her, though, since Dee Dee was not only brilliant, but extremely intuitive. If he wasn't careful, she might figure things out on her own. Carl Alvin was no slouch, either, but he lacked a lot of common sense, something Dee Dee prided herself on. Then, he would slowly ease into the information he truly dreaded sharing with them. That was the plan, anyway.

"We'll see how it plays out," he softly said, as he heaved a heavy sigh.

"Are you okay, Judge?" Sara Nell asked, after she sat back down.

"Oh, yeah... I'm fine," he told her. "I'm just dreading this meeting."

Chapter 5

Bad news, worse news

When Carl Alvin and Dee Dee arrived at Judge Wesson's office that morning, the old grandfather clock in the lobby was still chiming out the nine o'clock hour. The judge, who had just emerged from the restroom, greeted them both with hugs and kisses, and then directed them to his office and toward the table with the cake and coffee. Sara Nell was right behind them and she helped them with their refreshments, but not until after receiving her share of kisses and hugs from the duo.

Once everyone was seated, the old man glanced grim-faced back and forth between Carl Alvin and Dee Dee, who were seated side by side in front of him. Dee Dee was turned sideways chattering away with Sara Nell, who was sitting to her left, and she was quite animatedly telling her about Destini and the soon to be new addition to the Abamu family.

After a few seconds, the judge straightened up in his chair and cleared his throat. The look of gravity in his eyes was something Carl Alvin immediately picked up on.

"I don't like that look on your face, Judge," Carl Alvin told him. "You're scaring me. In fact, this whole impromptu meeting has me concerned."

The judge sat stone-faced, as he ever so slightly nodded his head in agreement.

"Destini and Matt are so excited about the new baby," Dee Dee rambled on to Sara Nell, totally unaware of the tension going on between the judge and Carl Alvin. "You know, when she had that miscarriage last April, nobody thought she'd ever get pregnant again. I guess that young hottie she's married to is quite the fertile dude, huh? We were all shocked when she announced she was pregnant again last July. I'm just so happy for her."

Finally, Dee Dee turned around, glanced toward the judge, and immediately picked up on the same sense of dread that Carl Alvin had already noticed on the judge's face and in his eyes.

"Uh-oh, what's up, Judge?" she asked.

Judge Wesson meekly smiled at her and then he nervously adjusted his glasses.

"So much for well thought out plans," he muttered under his breath, but no one heard him.

It was time, he knew, to delve into the unpleasant business right off the bat, since Dee Dee had already brought up Destini's name.

"Dee Dee, Carl Alvin..." he began. "I want you to listen closely. This is probably one of the hardest things I have ever had to relate to you. It's about the Jarrellson Trust."

Both Dee Dee and Carl Alvin sat up a little straighter in their seats and now focused their full attention on the judge.

"Your Uncle Hamp's great-grandmother was a Jarrellson, as you both know, and she owned some timber properties jointly with Hamp's estate," he said. "The one in particular that we'll be discussing today is the parcel of land down near Mama Tee's farm that borders up to Camp EZ. You two remember all of that business, right?"

"Yes, sir, we do," Dee Dee said, looking over at Carl Alvin for an affirmative nod, which he gave her.

"It's such a large tract of land that it's kind of hard to ignore it," Carl Alvin told the judge.

"Well, it seems that after repeated offers from Anna Mary and Stanley for that forty acres of land, Destini has shown no inclination in the least that she is willing to sell it," the judge informed them. "That land abuts the area where Anna Mary and Stanley are planning to build a boat landing and park in memory of their son Watson and his wife. I'm not sure if either of you knew that or not."

"Well, it's not news to me," Carl Alvin piped up.

"Me, either," Dee Dee said.

"We've heard all about it already, Judge," Carl Alvin said. "The way we figure, it's Destini's land and it's her decision whether or not she wants to sell it. It should be none of our business."

"Yes, son, I tend to agree with you, but… oh, Lord, I wish I didn't have to relate this to y'all, but I do," the judge said, shaking his head.

"Goodness, Judge, what could possibly be so bad?" Dee Dee asked, as her eyes grew wide. "You look just awful. What is it? Tell us… please," she urged him.

The judge inhaled a deep breath and said, "Well,

you see… Anna Mary and Stanley have Elwood Ellison Carter's law firm out of Jacksonville on retainer. They're an excellent firm, as I'm sure you are both aware. They are good at what they do and the Jarrellsons are longtime, valued clients of theirs."

Dee Dee and Carl Alvin both nodded, so the judge continued.

"You realize that by blood, Anna Mary is related to your late Uncle Hamp through his mother, Mrs. Lillian, right?" the judge rhetorically asked, and Dee Dee and Carl Alvin nodded again. "Well, since Destini never married your Uncle Hamp, for obvious reasons, and since their child who was born out of wedlock… little Bunnye, God rest her soul, is dead now… well, Anna Mary and Stanley have decided to contest your uncle's will," he explained. "They are bringing suit against the estate as plaintiffs Jarrellson Trust/Anna Mary Jarrellson Williams, President, versus Destini Wilson Abamu."

There was a collective gasp from both Dee Dee and Carl Alvin, but they said nothing just yet. Meanwhile, the judge continued.

"They are contending that, in essence, Destini was no more than a concubine and that she has no legal rights any longer to any of the Brayerford properties, since Bunnye is now deceased," the judge explained. "Furthermore, they are contending that the money Destini received at the time of Hamp's death is excessive, given the fact Bunnye is dead, and that those funds should be put back into the Brayerford Trust for investment. You know that Anna Mary receives money from that trust each year, don't you? Actually, she receives a lot of money... a little over a hundred-thousand dollars a year, in fact."

"She also gets two-hundred-thousand a year from her late Uncle Gus, doesn't she?" Dee Dee asked.

"I believe you are correct, honey," the judge said.

"You've got to be kidding, Judge!" Carl Alvin shouted, as his face turned an awful shade of crimson. "Surely, all of this is a joke of some sort, right?" he asked, obviously in shock that Anna Mary and Stanley would initiate such a legal proceeding against Destini. He looked over at Dee Dee, who seemed just as stunned as he was. "Surely, they can't be that damned greedy!" he went on, and then he rose from his seat and began pacing the floor.

"No, son, I'm afraid it's not a joke," the judge told him. "You'd best sit back down, though, and fasten your seatbelt because there's more. Lots more."

Reluctantly, Carl Alvin sat back down, but he was still fuming. You could almost see smoke coming out of his ears.

"I have to tell both of you... Destini stands a huge chance of losing the property left to her by your Uncle Hamp," the judge solemnly said.

For once in her life, the usually spunky and spirited Dee Dee was truly speechless, as she looked over at Carl Alvin's beet red face.

"Anna Mary and Stanley are willing to concede that Destini can receive an income of fifty-thousand a year, and that she can keep her job at Camp EZ," the judge continued. "They also said she can keep the health insurance she has now, which has been paid for by the Trust since Hamp's death. They have directed me to advise the two of you to remove Destini and Matthew Abamu from Hamp's old house at Camp EZ within 90 days."

Dee Dee reached into her pocketbook and pulled out a silver flask. With her lips pursed, her nostrils flared, and her eyes looking almost as beady as the sheriff's, she stood up from her chair.

"Any of y'all want a hit?" she asked, looking around at everyone. "I damn sure need one," she added, as she poured some liquor into her nearly empty coffee cup.

"Dee Dee, it's not even ten o' clock in the morning yet!" Carl Alvin protested.

"I can tell time, Carl Alvin!" she barked at him. "In this case, time doesn't mean a damn thing," she said a little softer. "I need a drink."

"I will certainly join you, honey," the judge chimed in. "I'm sure Sara Nell will join us, too."

"My goodness, y'all haven't changed one iota," Carl Alvin said, shaking his head, but at the same time he offered his cup to Dee Dee, so she poured him a shot.

"This is all very hard to take in, I know," the judge went on, as Dee Dee poured him a hefty shot of bourbon. "I hate it for Destini and I hate it for this county. I talked to Anna Mary and Stanley until I was blue in the face, but they refuse to budge. Oh, and here's another thing. Those original deeds to Mama Tee made out by your Uncle Hamp, as well as the original Photostat copies of the Wilson farm properties... well, they have all vanished. Vanished without a trace," the judge explained.

"Oh, my God!" Dee Dee gasped. "Are you kidding, Judge?"

"No, honey, I'm afraid I'm not kidding. In fact, most of the deeds that were transferred over to Destini, and any and all court recordings of them have gone missing, too. There's nothing in the filing cabinets, and nothing on any of the computers at the courthouse or elsewhere. There's just nothing to be found anywhere. I really hate to say this, but I have some serious misgivings about this entire matter. I truly do."

"This is outrageous!" Dee Dee shouted, as she poured herself another shot. "How can all that stuff just disappear?!"

"Calm down now," the judge told her. "We all know the clerk of the court, Sterling Randolph, is Anna Mary's closest friend. That bug-eyed fool spent more time at the Jarrellson house than she did at her own, if you ask me. Years ago when Anna Mary was getting ready to go off to college in Virginia, everyone wondered how Sterling was able to afford to go there as well," he added. "It was a very prestigious college and the Randolphs were poor as dirt at the time."

"Uncle Gus, no doubt," Carl Alvin piped up. "Sterling was related to the Jarrellsons by blood through Anna Mary's great-grandmother Adamson, in case you didn't know."

"Those bastards... really," Dee Dee mumbled, shaking her head. "To stand up at Mama Tee's funeral and take on and do all they did, and now this?!" she shrieked. "Lord, I would just love to beat them both with a gall berry whip until I couldn't swing my arms anymore! I'm serious! I would! Stanley, hell, you could expect this from him, that Yankee, carpetbaggin' nobody, but Anna Mary? Dear God! And as good as Destini always was to the two of them. If you ask me, I think this is Stanley's doing."

"With respect, Dee Dee, I think you're wrong," the judge interjected. "I think Anna Mary Jarrellson Williams is the culprit. She should have pursued a career on the stage if she hadn't have been so wealthy. I've watched her through the years. She is truly adept at acting. I've seen her at funerals crying out of one eye and winking out of the other one. I've seen her when sugar wouldn't melt in her mouth, cozying up to them poor, illiterate white people and under-privileged African Americans... taking them fruit and whatnot, and when they'd get themselves into a tight situation, she'd loan them money. I've seen her smile, as she put her signature on foreclosure papers with no more emotion in her eyes than a cold-blooded killer. Anna Mary, you have to remember, learned at the feet of a master... her Uncle Gus."

"You could be right," Dee Dee said.

"Well, I have to tell you children, the Jarrellsons, unlike your Uncle Hamp, didn't care who they had to walk on, whether black or white, to get what they wanted. They always saw it as their due," the judge said.

"That's true," Sara Nell chimed in. "I've seen it many times over myself."

"When Anna Mary and Stanley invited me over to their house with old man Elwood Ellison Carter, Esquire himself present, I was immediately suspicious," the judge said. "I can't believe the man is still alive, let alone still practicing law. Anyway, Anna Mary had the maid pour coffee and then she told me what they intended to do. I mentioned to her about Destini and the baby, and what Hamp had specified in his will, and do you know what she did? She took her compact out of her purse and looked at herself in the mirror."

"That sounds like Anna Mary," Carl Alvin muttered.

"She said, excuse me, Judge, I want to make sure I look my best. Then she said we all grew up here and that Destini wasn't the first African American woman to have a light-skinned baby. She said Destini was a maid, a cook, a nanny... nothing more."

"Of all the nerve!" Carl Alvin shouted.

"That ain't all," the judge continued. "She said that Destini will still have more than she ever had in her life with this new legal agreement, and that she never was, except with those silly pulpwood girls and misguided Dee Dee and dear little effeminate Carl Alvin, any more than that... a maid, a cook and a nanny."

"Say what?!" Dee Dee shrieked.

"Yes, ma'am, she said y'all was just so needy," the

judge went on. "Then, she says, 'We are just putting her and her African missionary husband... is it her husband? Is he a citizen now, or should he be deported? We will cross that bridge later. Destini must be put back in her place, but we'll do it with generosity,'" the judge ended, looking exhausted after trying to remember all of Anna Mary's nasty and cruel comments, and mimicking her voice as best he could.

"Lord, have mercy!" Carl Alvin yelled, as his face got redder.

"There's more," the judge said. "Anna Mary said that Destini and her husband, and all her collective family can stay in church day and night with fifty grand a year they didn't deserve, but not one acre of family land would go to *that crowd,* and there would be no interest accruing in the bank."

"Of all the nerve!" Dee Dee shouted, with a face as red as Carl Alvin's now.

"Anna Mary told me that if you two want to keep Destini on at the Camp, that's your concern, but the rest by law, she said, is mostly hers," the judge explained. "She also said Destini's connection to Hamp Brayerford is over with."

"Well, I'll be," Dee Dee said, shaking her head in disbelief at all she had just heard. "We'll just see about that, now, won't we?"

"Oh... something else Anna Mary said," the judge added as a footnote. "She said it nearly killed her great-grandmother Adamson and caused her to go to an early grave when she learned about her precious daughter's serious interest in Hamp Brayerford, Sr. She said that on her dying bed, Cousin Mamie Lila told her daughter, Lillian, that if she married into that trash, no matter how much money the Brayerfords made or had, that trash always reverts, always does."

Chapter 6

Revelations

It took quite a while for Judge Wesson to get Dee Dee and Carl Alvin calmed down after all he had just told them. Dee Dee even left the office for about twenty minutes to run down to the liquor store for more bourbon, since between them all they had emptied the little flask already.

Around eleven o'clock, when Dee Dee returned, she suggested they go out for lunch at the new diner downtown, but the judge said he had a few more things to discuss with them first.

"Why don't we wait until noon?" he suggested. "That way, most of this delicious pound cake Sara Nell made will have dissolved in my stomach to make room for some more good eatin'."

"Okay, sounds good," Dee Dee said, and she sat back down in front of the judge's desk.

Just then, Sara Nell came in and quietly took her seat.

"Come on, Carl Alvin, you're gonna wear a hole in that dang rug if you don't stop that damned pacing," Dee Dee told him. "Come sit down… please."

"Yes, Carl Alvin, do sit down," the judge urged him.

"More hooch, anyone?" Dee Dee asked, as she poured some of the bourbon she had just bought into her coffee cup.

Everyone shook their head in the negative this time, though.

"Suit yourselves," she said. "It just leaves more for me."

"All right, back to business," the judge announced. "You realize that Anna Mary and Stanley know all about your past life down in Jacksonville, Carl Alvin," he said, looking directly at him. "They also know all about your uhh… well, your uhh… your close friendship with that national football star, Grant Martin, who's now a well-respected member of the business community."

"And who's also married to your granddaughter, Amy Elizabeth," Dee Dee interjected. "Ain't that right, Judge?" she asked, really beginning to slur her words now.

Before the judge could respond, Carl Alvin shouted, "Oh, for godsakes! This is outrageous!"

"Outrageous or not, I'm afraid they have threatened to go public with all that nonsense if they don't get what they want," the judge told him.

"That's a bunch of bull!" Carl Alvin shouted again. "You tell them if they want to play dirty and do that, then I'll have some pretty interesting things to say publicly about their Uncle Gus, as well as their dear departed son, Watson. You tell them that, Judge!" he yelled, and then he got up to pace the floor again.

"Well, son, I'm not surprised that you might have something to say about Watson, but Gus… well, now, that does pique my interest," the judge said, lifting an eyebrow, and not seeming the least bit bothered by Carl Alvin's temper tantrum.

"Let's just say Uncle Gus took a keen interest in young people... young male people with no place to stay, except in his little cottage," Carl Alvin began. "He was such a good Samaritan," he sarcastically added, rolling his eyes. "It was even commented on in the Turpricone News how he exemplified such a kind heart to provide vocational training and other types of employment training for some of those juvenile delinquents who were picked up by the sheriff and placed in our county hospitality center."

"You mean the jail, don't you?" Dee Dee asked, laughing.

"Yeah, whatever," Carl Alvin said. "Hush up, Dee Dee. Anyway, the newspaper even carried an article once about his... how shall I put this? His benevolence to the young men."

"I forgot all about that," the judge said, scratching his chin. "Sara Nell, your memory is a lot better than mine. Do you have anything you'd like to add?"

"Well, first of all, Dee Dee, I want you to know I thought the world of your daddy and your uncle Hamp. They were gentlemen of the old school, if you will," Sara Nell began.

"Why, thank you, Sara Nell," Dee Dee said, and then she hiccuped. "I appreciate that."

Sara Nell smiled, shook her head, and continued. "They were just wonderful, wonderful people. Judge Wesson often allowed me to write letters for the two of them, as well as type up other correspondence for them, always with their permission, of course. I also helped your Uncle Hamp keep those volumes of notes up to date about those poor young boys who went missing years ago. He never got over those boys not being found and that case being dropped so quickly. Frankly, neither have I and..."

"Miss Sara Nell, do you have any of that Knock-Out headache powder?" Carl Alvin asked, stopping her mid-sentence, while the judge heaved a sigh of relief at the interruption.

"As a matter of fact, I do," Sara Nell said. "You hang tight and I'll bring you some, along with half a glass of sweet milk. I keep some on hand in the fridge in the kitchenette. Just bought some this morning, as a matter of fact. It works wonders with that headache powder."

"Thank you, Miss Sara Nell," Carl Alvin said. "I love you."

"I love you, too, honey. Be back in a jiff," she said and off she went.

Judge Wesson took this opportunity to speak to Carl Alvin and Dee Dee in private.

In a whispered voice, after motioning them forward, he said, "When you go home, Carl Alvin, I want you to think… really think about what you said to me about Gus Jarrellson helping those boys from the jail. I want you to think about what you *knew*, not what you *think* you knew. Remember, all of this happened a lot of years ago, so I need you to think really hard and be accurate."

Carl Alvin nodded, but it was clear he didn't know what the judge was getting at.

"Now, Dee Dee, I want you to find those notebooks or tablets where Hamp kept all that information about the case of those missing boys," the judge went on. "I want you to bring them to me at my home."

"Sure, I'll do that, but why?" she asked.

"I don't want to get into that right now," he said. "Just do it, okay?" he asked, and she nodded. "Don't say a word to anybody, not even Sara Nell for now. Both of you. Not a word. You got it?" he sternly asked.

Again, both Dee Dee and Carl Alvin nodded.

"I'll take those notebooks you give me over to Tallahassee and put them in a safety deposit box that I keep over there," the judge explained. "We don't want them kept here at the local bank. That could be too risky. Now, both of you, until I tell you, don't you breathe a word of this to anyone, you hear? Not to Sara Nell, not to Destini, not to the other girls, not to anyone. Please, please, please, I beg of you, keep this quiet. There could be a lot riding on this. More than you can possibly imagine."

The judge was so intense with his statements that Dee Dee and Carl Alvin looked shaken, not to mention confused and intrigued.

"We understand, Judge, and we will do exactly as you asked," Dee Dee said, and then she looked over at Carl Alvin, who nodded in agreement.

About that time, Miss Sara Nell, ever the gracious lady and efficient employee, came back into the room with the milk and headache powder for Carl Alvin. She had both on a small silver tray and set it on the front of the judge's desk. A small linen napkin had been placed on the tray, as well.

"Judge Wesson, may I say something in regards to what you all were discussing earlier?" Sara Nell asked.

The judge looked at her, rather surprised, but he said, "Uhh, sure, go ahead, Sara Nell."

"Well, you know what I remember most about that time was you and your wife, Mrs. Iris, taking me over to that fancy dinner held on the St. Johns River at that beautiful art gallery. They were having a showing of Mr. Gus Jarrellson's landscape artworks. I believe it was mainly his oil paintings they were showing. I still have the pamphlet from that show, by the way."

"Yes, I remember that day," the judge said.

"Well, I distinctly remember this one particular mural out of the five pieces of his work that were on display in the back of the room," Sara Nell continued. "It was a haunting piece... really mysterious, quite frankly. It was as if I was looking though a veil of Spanish moss that was hanging from the tree branches over the water... it was dark, dark water, but you could tell the water was moving, rather like a river, you know," she explained. "Behind it was a sunset, and ohh... the color of that sunset... it was quite unsettling. It gave me the shivers, actually. I believe the color is referred to as sienna, almost a blood red color.

Behind the sunset, bright, white lights were burning, and circling overhead in that ominously red sky were two or three vultures, or maybe they were buzzards. I can never tell the difference."

"I do believe buzzards and vultures are synonymous," Dee Dee piped up, still slurring her words a bit and obviously getting tipsier by the minute. "Aren't they, Carl Alvin?"

"How the hell should I know? Go on, Miss Sara Nell," Carl Alvin said, and then Dee Dee shot him a dagger that could have killed an elephant.

"Well, like I said, the river in the painting really looked like it was flowing. It even had foam on top. It was so realistic," she went on. "There seemed to be more than just paint on that mural, though, and that foam..." she said, as if still in awe. "I reached up and touched it and it felt like pieces of bone or rocks were mixed into the paint. It was strange. Anyway, I remember the work was entitled, *Black Runs the River*."

"Wow, it sounds really creepy, doesn't it?" Carl Alvin asked.

"Yes, I remember thinking so at the time," Sara Nell agreed. "The largest of the other four paintings was one that made me smile and even brought tears to my eyes. I recall how Mr. Gus loved Gloriosa Lilies. They bloomed in profusion on his property during the spring and early summer. They were so beautiful and lush. The most I have ever seen all in one place. That was the largest painting... the one of the Gloriosa Lily. The other three, let me see... one was a Trumpet Lily, one was of a Nightshade plant, and the last one was a hot pink Oleander. The collection was titled *Flowers of Home*. I'll declare I had not thought of that in years," Sara Nell said, as if she had just emerged from a fog. "That series is going to be shown here before too long in the gallery built in Mr. Gus's memory."

"Very interesting recollections, Sara Nell," the judge told her, and she smiled.

"Yes, very interesting," Carl Alvin said. "Aren't all those flowers that he painted poisonous?" he asked.

"I do believe they are," the judge said.

"Anyway, I sure remember that wonderful dinner you and Mrs. Iris took me to after the show," Sara Nell continued. "It was down near the river… a nice place with steaks and seafood, and the most wonderful cheesecake for dessert. I don't know, though. I came away from that art show feeling really uncomfortable for some reason."

"It sure sounds like it," the judge said.

"Well, forgive an old lady for talking so much," Sara Nell said. "Oh, Judge Wesson, I almost forgot. Mrs. Iris phoned while I was in the kitchenette and she wanted me to remind you that Amy Elizabeth and Grant are coming for dinner tonight. She said she wanted you home before five this afternoon."

"Thank you, Sara Nell," the judge said. "I plum forgot about dinner tonight with all this other mess goin' on."

"Oh, one last thing, Judge, if I might," Sara Nell said. "I don't mean to get into anybody's business here, but…"

"Sara Nell, anything you say will be appreciated," the judge interrupted her.

"Well, I remember, because my niece works at the Greyhound bus station here in town… has for years, actually. You know her, Judge. Sweet Ella Ruth?"

"Yes, ma'am, I do," he said.

"Well, you know when strangers come into town, a person takes notice and remembers certain things," Sara Nell continued. "We talked about a week ago, Ella Ruth and I, about a summer afternoon many years ago when some young men came into town. There were about four of them, I think, all young and all Caucasian. They had been working for one of those federal programs down in south Florida. When their time was up, they started their journey north again to their hometowns, but their money ran out and Turpricone was as far as they could ride the bus. Ella Ruth said she remembers they got off the bus and started going around town trying to find work. I saw them, too, later that day. They were clean-cut boys, not unkempt. One of them evidently had some really odd dental work done, as several of the crowns on his front teeth were gold. I do remember that about him."

"That is odd," the judge said.

"One of them had hair that was a little long in the back. I remember Sheriff Lewis picked them up because there were several complaints from some folks around town that they were vagrants. I don't know that the boys were vagrants," Sara Nell said. "I think they might have just been down on their luck. Anyhow, as you might know, from time to time the late Mr. Gus Jarrellson, God rest his soul, would go down to the jail, and he and the sheriff would play checkers, sometimes late into the night."

"Yeah, I remember hearing about that," the judge said.

"Well, nobody would think the two of them would enjoy each other's company, but they did," Sara Nell went on. "I know the sheriff took it mighty hard when Mr. Gus... well, no need to mention that. We know what happened."

"Yeah, the bastard off'ed himself in the bathtub... on a ship out in the middle of the ocean, no less," Carl Alvin interjected, seeming ecstatic that Uncle Gus had met his maker.

Sara Nell seemed overcome with emotion all of a sudden, so Dee Dee handed her Carl Alvin's linen napkin to dab the tears from her eyes.

"You big dope," Dee Dee muttered to Carl Alvin, and then she turned toward Sara Nell. "It was a terrible time, dear," she said, trying to comfort her. "Would you like a glass of water?"

"No, thank you, honey, but I appreciate you asking," Sara Nell said. "Anyway, as I was saying, Mr. Gus told the sheriff he had some work he needed done outside his studio and also out on some property close to the river. He said he'd be responsible for those young men, pay them, and get them on their feet, so they could go on to wherever it was they were headed."

"Gee, how nice of him," Carl Alvin snidely remarked, but Sara Nell ignored him, while Dee Dee jabbed him in the ribs.

"The sheriff talked to the boys, and they agreed to the deal, from what I understand," she went on. "During the next few weeks, they did a lot of work out there for Mr. Gus. They helped him clean up around his studio, clean fence rows, and they got his yard and that landing down near the river in really good shape again. I remember not long after they started working for Mr. Gus, they came to town and bought a few clothes, got haircuts, and I thought they were really nice. After about a month, month and a half, Mr. Gus told the sheriff and several others, that those boys would be leaving. All but one, that is. The one with the gold teeth. He said the boy was going to stay a bit longer and do some more work. Mr. Gus himself went down to the Greyhound station and bought the other boys' tickets. One of them was going to Baltimore, Maryland, another to New York City, and the other one would be heading back to somewhere up in Michigan. Not Detroit. Oh, where was it? A college town up there."

"Ann Arbor?" Carl Alvin suggested.

"Yes, that's it," she said. "Thank you, Carl Alvin. So, Mr. Gus paid for those tickets, and the boys were supposed to get on the bus, but they weren't leaving from here in Turpricone for some reason. Mr. Gus said he was driving them over to Pittstown to take the bus from there. Maybe he wanted to show them the music park. I don't know."

"Yeah, maybe," the judge said.

"Well, I know they left, because no one ever saw them again," Sara Nell said. "I do know the one boy stayed a little longer, maybe a few days or weeks. He even did a little work for us, Judge, taking care of the yard here at the office."

"Well, now, he sure did, Sara Nell," the judge said "I remember now. He was that nice, young, New England boy… the one with the gold teeth."

"That boy, gosh, I wish I could remember his name," Sara Nell said, scratching her head.

"Was it Thomas?" the judge asked.

"Yes! Yes, it was Thomas! His last name… wait… it will come to me. Caldecott? No, Endicott? Yes, that was it! Thomas Endicott. It sounded refined and upper crust, don't you think? He spoke eloquently, too, for such a young boy. Anyway, he told me something that I never knew. He said Mr. Gus trained in Cincinnati, Ohio to be a mortician, and that he was a licensed funeral director. I never knew that."

"Me, either," the judge said.

"Thomas said Mr. Gus worked for several years at various funeral homes, until he got enough money saved up to go overseas and study art. Then, the Jarrellsons sold a big tract of land they owned over near Pittstown to some developers. It was a sizeable sum for the early 1950's, as I recall. It was enough that Gus took his share, went to see some friends who had connections to Wall Street, and the rest is, as they say, history."

"Yes, he hit it lucky," the judge said. "He got rich, especially from all that money he put into utilities."

"Well, eventually Ella Ruth sold Mr. Gus a ticket for that young boy to go back up north, somewhere close to Boston, Massachusetts, I believe," Sara Nell explained. "Well, like I said, they were, I thought, nice young men."

"Well, thank you for your detailed input, Sara Nell," the judge said.

"Oh, not a problem," she said, and then she glanced at her watch. "Well, since I am a dinner guest at your house this evening, I need to head home and get ready. I have two pecan pies I need to make this afternoon. Oh, your wife told me to invite Carl Alvin, Dee Dee, and Mr. Ricardo, too. She said to tell y'all this is family, so she wasn't apologizing for it being last minute."

Everyone had a good laugh and Dee Dee said, "You tell Mrs. Iris we will be there. How should we dress?"

"Strictly casual, dear," the judge piped up. "I'm grilling steaks, so no sports coats, no evening gowns, just casual and comfortable. We will expect you at five, okay?"

"Sounds good to me," Carl Alvin said, and Dee Dee nodded in the affirmative.

"One more thing before you go, Sara Nell," the judge said. "That memory of the art show you shared with me earlier... do you have any idea where that mural is now?"

"It's about to be shown at the gallery named for Mr. Gus next week, as a matter of fact," she said. "Isn't that exciting?"

"Hey, I'm helping with the opening of that show," Dee Dee chimed in. "I hope we have a good turnout."

"Oh, I think we will have a record attendance," the judge said, grinning like a Cheshire cat and looking squarely at Dee Dee and Carl Alvin. "I do believe Anna Mary and Stanley will be overwhelmed with the response she'll have for that show. Overwhelmed," he said again, slyly winking at Dee Dee and Carl Alvin, as Sara Nell left the room.

"Am I missing something?" Dee Dee asked.

"You're not missing a thing, young lady," the judge told her. "Just remember, Black Runs the River," he added, quite solemnly. "Buzzards overhead... my goodness... and bright lights in the background... white lights like looking through moss," he kept rambling. "Boy, that Sara Nell sure has a good memory, doesn't she?" the judge asked, although, it was clear he was merely talking to himself. "Sunset the color of blood... now, ain't that something?"

"Uhhh, Judge? You okay?" Dee Dee asked him.

"Oh, now, don't you mind me," he said, blushing. "I'm just a ramblin' old man. Remember now, you two. Not a word about any of this to anyone. Not a word."

"Well, I don't know what you're up to, Judge, but I think it's time me and Carl Alvin got the heck out of here. We've got a dinner party to get ready for. So much for lunch today, eh?" she added.

She went around behind the judge's desk, kissed him on the cheek and hugged his shoulders.

"Okay, go on, now," he told her. "Go use some of that charm on your husband, drink yourself some good, strong coffee, and get the two of you to the house by five o'clock this afternoon."

"Yeah, try to sober up before then," Carl Alvin teased her.

"You, too, Carl Alvin," the judge said. "Go on home and do what I asked you to do. You, too, Dee Dee. I need those notebooks. And don't you worry, son. Don't you worry one little bit. Just know that the Lord works in mysterious ways... he surely does."

❦❦❦❦❦❦❦❦❦❦

FIVE O'CLOCK came and went at the judge's home that afternoon with no sign of either Dee Dee or Carl Alvin. At about six-thirty, Dee Dee called and apologized up and down for not showing up, claiming she had fallen asleep when she got home and had just awakened. In truth, she had passed out from all the bourbon she had consumed earlier in the day, but she wasn't about to tell the judge that.

"That's okay, Dee Dee," the judge told her. "I'm just glad you're okay. Is Carl Alvin with you? He hasn't shown up yet, either. The rest of us have already eaten, but there is still plenty left to go around."

Dee Dee said she had no idea where Carl Alvin

was, but that she would try to track him down, and then the two hung up.

Dee Dee fell back asleep just seconds after speaking with the judge. Carl Alvin, on the other hand, had evidently decided he wasn't in the mood to face Grant or Amy, especially after what Judge Wesson had told him about Anna Mary's plan to make public their little tryst. He did call the judge the following morning, at Dee Dee's insistence, and he apologized for not showing up and not even bothering to call.

"I completely understand," the judge told him. "Don't worry, son. We'll catch up later."

Chapter 7

Neighbors helping neighbors

The majority of the folks in Campbell County knew absolutely nothing about what had been uncovered at the old Jarrellson property. It had been about a week now since the discovery. There were a few rumors going around, though, which pissed off the sheriff big time, since no one was supposed to talk about it yet. However, at this point, no one actually believed any of the rumors, and no one rushed out to the site to check things out firsthand, as it was in a bit of a remote area.

Over the last twenty-five years, it seemed, the folks in the county became more and more complacent about ever learning what had happened to the four missing boys. Memories of all the newspaper headlines, and all the local gossip about the investigation that went on at the barber shops and beauty salons in town had faded into oblivion.

Even fewer people knew what Anna Mary and Stanley Williams were in the process of litigating to force Destini and her husband, Matt, out of their home and more or less out of the picture completely in Seraph Springs, if they had their way. One individual in the community was about to learn some things about certain people in Seraph Springs that would eventually shake up the town, maybe even more so than Destini's planned ouster by Anna Mary and Stanley Williams.

Her name was Nadine Lloyd, one of Destini and Dee Dee's closest friends.

Nadine was in her kitchen enjoying a morning cup of coffee when the telephone rang. After she picked up the receiver, she heard the familiar voice of Miss Bessie Robinson, the longtime postmistress of Seraph Springs.

"Nadine, I'm so glad I caught you. I need your help," Bessie said, sounding like a desperate woman.

"Oh, hi, Miss Bessie. I'll do what I can to help. What's up?" Nadine asked.

"Well, Mr. Claude Clements had a stroke yesterday on his way home from work and he ran into a ditch out near Watson Estates."

"Oh, dear!" Nadine gasped. "Is he okay?"

"He's in the hospital in Gainesville," Bessie said. "Fortunately, it's not as bad as we originally thought, but he's going to be out of commission for a few months. Anyway, we really need your help."

"Uh, yeah, sure, but I don't know what I can do," Nadine said.

"Well… Claude only worked part time here at the post office," Bessie explained. "There are about sixty boxes on his route, most of them out near the big produce farm, Feed the World Organics, and a few just north of there at Watson Estates. You know… that development the Jarrellson Trust built after Mr. Gus… well, you know… took his own life."

"Yes, I know that area," Nadine said.

"Well, Claude's maiden sister, Inez, has always depended on him for everything, you know. My nephew, Dewitt, is going to drive her down to see Claude tomorrow and the hospital has arranged for her to stay there until he's able to come home."

"Oh, how nice of your nephew… and the hospital."

"Yes, it is," Bessie said. "Inez, however, is worried about all those cats of hers. She has over twenty of them, I believe, and she takes care of them like they were human babies."

"I can understand that," Nadine said. "Cats are cool creatures."

"So, my question is, do you think you could help me with Claude's mail route until he gets better and comes home?" Bessie asked. "I really hate to ask, but right now I don't have any other choice, and you already know the area," she added. "It would take much too long to advertise the position and even longer to train a new person, assuming anyone would even apply for such a short-term job."

"Wow, I wasn't expecting that," Nadine said, clearly taken aback. "What time would I have to be there?"

"Well, just come in to the post office by nine o'clock tomorrow morning, if you would, please. We have some uniform shirts here that I'm sure will fit you, so just wear a pair of jeans and a t-shirt or whatever, and when you get here you can change. I'll have Betty Sue bundle the mail for you before you get here. I'd say you should probably be finished with the route by noon or maybe just a little after. It's a short route with some interesting folks, particularly out in Watson Estates."

"Well, since I don't have any real commitments at the moment, other than taking the kids to school and picking them up in the afternoon, I think I can handle Claude's mail route... for a short time, that is," Nadine said. "I'll also tend to all those cats, if that's okay. The children will love that, Miss Bessie. I know Miss Inez has always been a faithful member of the church and has helped Mama's Bible Drill group on numerous occasions. Mama will be happy to help me out with the cats, as well. Tell Miss Inez not to worry about a thing here at home. It's all under control until she and Mr. Claude get back. Oh, by the way, how badly damaged is Claude's old Buick? My husband, Louie, I'm sure wouldn't mind fixing it if it isn't too beat up, that is."

"Actually, the car fared quite well," Bessie said. "No real damage, from what I've been told, but thank you for offering Louie's services."

After the two women chatted for a few more minutes, Bessie said she had to go, so she wouldn't be late for work.

"I can't thank you enough for helping me out, Nadine," Bessie told her. "I'll see you tomorrow then," she added, and they hung up.

The next morning, Louie got the children off to school, but not before Nadine kissed them all goodbye and warned them, "Y'all be good at school. I better hear only good things. If I have to come to that school for y'all acting ugly, there'll be the devil to pay."

On her drive over to the Seraph Springs Post Office, Nadine felt a little apprehensive, as she had never done anything like deliver the United States mail before. It seemed like such a privilege and honor to work for Uncle Sam. Not to mention, she had to be careful and precise with such precious and personal cargo as a person's mail.

When she knocked on the backdoor of the post office, she was immediately greeted by Betty Sue Matheson, one of her old classmates from high school and the current postal clerk. Between Betty Sue and Miss Bessie, the post office ran like a well-oiled machine with no complaints from customers for the last ten years, at least.

Betty Sue had spent most of her working life at the post office in Seraph Springs, as had her mother before her. She flashed her ever-ready smile to Nadine and said, "Come on in, hon. I am so glad you're here."

"I'm glad I could help," Nadine replied with a nervous smile. "I hope I don't screw things up, though."

"Oh, you'll do just fine, honey," Betty Sue told her. "Poor Mr. Claude, huh?" she asked, shaking her head. "He would be so happy to know that you are taking over his route. He's always thought a lot of you, as well as your sister, Wanda Faye, and your mama, Sister Jewell."

"I know he has," Nadine said. "He's one of Mama's best customers. He's always buying her cakes from the Bible Drill group. In fact, I heard from Miss

Bessie that the sheriff found half of one of Mama's marble swirl cakes wrapped in tin foil on his car seat when he had that stroke."

Betty Sue's bottom lip began to quiver and she pointed to a small metal table by the door. "Look," she said, and so Nadine did.

There, wrapped in tin foil, were the remnants of her mother's cake, which still looked edible and not squashed except on one end. Out of the corner of her eye, Nadine spotted a fresh pot of coffee on the counter that had just finished brewing. So, she snatched the cake, set it on one of the mail sorting tables, took Betty Sue by the hand, and told her to have a seat. She sliced some cake for both of them, poured two cups of coffee, and grabbed another chair so she could sit down beside Betty Sue.

"Aww, thank you, Nadine," Betty Sue said, as she wiped tears from her eyes. "I think this is just what I need right now. I just feel so bad for Mr. Claude, you know. I mean, it could happen to anyone… even me."

"Nah… you're healthy as a horse, Betty Sue. You worry too much," Nadine told her, trying to comfort her and make her feel better. "So, tell me, is there anything specific I need to know about this mail route?"

"No, not a whole lot," she said, after gulping down a big swallow of the hot coffee. "There's about fifty folks on your route, plus a few new folks over the last several months, actually. Of course, you know about Feed the World Organics, who gets the bulk of the mail. Oh, and you know about the Jarrellson family selling about eighty acres up that way two or three years ago, right?"

"Yeah, I heard that," Nadine said.

"It's just north of Feed the World Organics. I'm sure you remember when young Dr. Watson passed away," she said, and Nadine nodded. "Well, Mrs. Williams... Anna Mary, that is, well, she said that land had been a special place for him when he was younger, but she just couldn't bear to keep it."

Upon hearing this, Nadine's face didn't betray what she was thinking. She, among a few select others, knew Anna Mary's decision had nothing to do with sentimental value. It did, however, have everything to do with the fact it was the site where old man Gus's cabin used to be before it was torn down. It was where young Watson Williams was systematically and horrendously molested by his great-uncle, Gus Jarrellson.

"Anyhow, there's a development out there called Watson Estates," Betty Sue continued. "It's broken up into about sixteen five-acre lots. Oh, and the trees and the landscaping out there is spectacular... it's just beautiful."

"It sounds like it," Nadine said.

"Newly-paved little roads wind down into and around the entire development, and the homes they built there! My goodness! They each have to be worth at least three-hundred-thousand dollars or more! Nobody thought they'd be able to sell any of those lots, but they tell me Stanley Williams has a friend in Orlando who's a real pro at real estate marketing. Believe it or not, all the lots sold within about three months of each other. So far, about a dozen houses have already been built. All but one of those houses is now occupied."

"I've seen the place from the main road, you know… River Road, but I haven't been up in there in years. That development goes all the way down to the river, if I'm not mistaken," Nadine said.

"It does, and Anna Mary and Stanley want to create a nice little park there on about five acres. They plan to build a monument in the middle of the park that will be named in honor of Dr. and Mrs. Watson Jarrellson Williams, their son and daughter-in-law," Betty Sue explained. "It should be a nice place with a family picnic area and barbecue grills, and some playground equipment, as well as a boat ramp and canoe launch area. All I know is they want to spend a good wad of money on it."

"Yeah, I'll bet they do," Nadine said, trying her best to hide her cynicism.

"Oh, and I saw the rendering of the monument. It's a beautiful dark marble and it will stand about six feet tall. The wording will be something on the order of: *In loving memory of Watson Jarrellson Williams MD, and Selena Dubois Jarrellson Williams, his devoted and beautiful wife. They loved life and this river, and our prayer is that their love of the Suwannee River will live on through others. Given with love by Mr. and Mrs. Stanley Williams and Mary Selena*

Williams."

"Wow, you sure memorized that, didn't you?" Nadine teased her.

"I just thought it was so touching," Betty Sue told her.

"Yes, it is, Betty Sue. I know the grief they suffered when Watson and his wife were killed in that automobile accident over in England. By the way, that daughter of theirs is one of the most beautiful girls I think I have ever seen."

"She is a beautiful child," Betty Sue agreed. "Anyway, I want you to be careful on this mail route, Nadine. There are a few shady characters living up there in Watson Estates, and they do some really strange things sometimes. I don't believe any of them would harm you, but just be careful. Most of them aren't from here. I believe they moved here from south and central Florida."

"Betty Sue, you should know by now that I can take care of myself and that I am pretty much shock proof," Nadine assured her. "I've been through too much already and seen way too much in my life. Nothing shocks me anymore."

"Don't' be so sure of that," Betty Sue said, as she gently laid her hand on top of Nadine's. "There's always something new to experience, and you may just get an education on this little mail route."

"Well, don't worry, Betty Sue," Nadine assured her. "I'm looking forward to it."

Chapter 8

Here comes the mail

Claude, the hospitalized postal delivery guy, was a big, husky man, not to mention at least a foot taller than Nadine. Consequently, it took her a few minutes to get the seat of the mail truck in a comfortable position, so that she could at least reach the pedals. Soon, she was off, though, waving goodbye to Betty Sue, who was watching her from the backdoor of the post office, as she zipped out onto the highway. With the steering wheel on the right side of the vehicle, driving was a bit of a challenge at first, but after a few blocks she felt mostly at ease, even enjoying the novelty of it a little bit.

"Since I'll never travel over to Europe or Asia, this will be my *driving on the wrong side of the road* adventure… kinda, sorta," she said, and she laughed. "Stay on the right side of the road, Nadine. Don't be stupid now," she reminded herself, and then she broke out into laughter, as she cruised along the highway on the way to her first stop, Feed the World Organics.

As Betty Sue had told her, Feed the World Organics received the bulk of the mail, two entire bins worth, in fact. They were quite heavy, too, so she had to make two trips back and forth from the truck to the main office, since she had forgotten to bring along the hand truck that Betty Sue had suggested earlier.

"Everything else on this route should be a breeze

now," Nadine said, as she got back into the truck to continue on her way.

A few minutes later, she entered through the impressive gates of Watson Estates.

"Wow, this is much nicer than Betty Sue let on," she said in awe. "It looks like its own little city in here," she added, as she glanced around. "Cool!" she added, and then she pulled off onto the shoulder of the road to make sure she had the right bin of mail at the ready.

Inside all the remaining mail bins, aside from the usual utility bills and marketing materials, she noticed a gross of glossy, colorful pamphlets in a rubber-banded bundle. She snuck a peek at one of them, since they weren't in sealed envelopes, and she saw they were invitations going out to all the folks on her mail route.

"Hmmm… this is interesting," she said. "It looks like there's an art exhibit coming up in two weeks at the new Spencer Augustus Jarrellson Art Gallery here in Seraph Springs."

The pamphlet, which was printed on high quality paper with vivid, colorful photographs, explained that it was to be an evening affair with a reception and brief remarks by Anna Mary Jarrellson Williams. She was to speak about her uncle, Spencer Augustus Jarrellson. A showing of several of his works was to include a series of watercolors entitled, *The Flowers of Home*, as well as a mural entitled, *Black Runs the River*.

"Well, Nadine, stop stalling," she chastised herself. "You've got mail to deliver."

The first residence she approached was located

down a long, winding drive. The home was magnificent, just like Betty Sue had described. It was rather like a storybook cottage, she thought, but it was an expensive storybook cottage.

There was a large fieldstone terrace out in front of the house and it was surrounded by dozens of rose bushes. They were all in bloom, too, in various colors of the rainbow. There were also multiple flower beds throughout the yard that were filled with an assortment of daylilies and amaryllises. The most beautiful scene, she thought, was a small valley-like area behind the house through which Wilson Creek flowed. It was completely covered with wild coreopsis and phlox.

"Wow!" Nadine mouthed, as she prepared to pull up to the mailbox.

Standing by the mailbox ready to greet her was a frail looking woman, rather emaciated actually. She politely waved at Nadine and motioned for her to stop. Beside her, on a diamond-studded leash, was a beautiful Pomeranian, who began jumping up and down like a Slinky, and barking like a rabid dog the closer Nadine got.

The woman's hair was dyed a platinum blonde and it was styled into a chin-length Cleopatra pageboy cut. She was wearing a snap-front house-dress and on her feet were a pair of espadrille canvas shoes. When Nadine got close enough, she noticed a huge pair of emerald shaped diamond solitaire earrings, at least two carats in each ear, and they were set in a platinum gold. Her eyes were covered with a pair of oversized, round sunglasses that had a thick, white frame. Aside from the frumpy dress, she reminded Nadine of actress and entertainer, Carol Channing.

"Hush, now, baby, and be sweet to the nice mail lady," the woman said, as she moved her sunglasses up above her brow to check out Nadine's face. "Hello," she said, and she extended her hand to Nadine. "I am Neva Wesley, and I have lived here about six months. This is my sweet little Princess," she added, as she scooped the dog up into her arms.

"Well, nice to meet you, Mrs. Wesley," Nadine said. "You, too, Princess. My name is Nadine Lloyd. I'm taking Mr. Claude's place on this route for a short time. He suffered a health setback and will be out for a while."

"Oh, my!" the woman gasped. "I am so sorry."

"Well, he's going to be fine, Mrs. Wesley, and he should be back before we know it."

Nadine noted that Mrs. Wesley's voice sounded like she had smoked too many cigarettes in her lifetime and may have drunk a few too many vodka tonics, as well. Her skin was freckled and sun damaged, especially on her face, and she had lots and lots of wrinkles, but she had the most brilliant blue eyes and a kind smile. She guessed her to be about seventy years old.

"Please, call me Neva," the woman said. "Or *Miss* Neva, if you prefer. I know how you southerners are in this town," she added, smiling.

"Miss Neva it is, then," Nadine told her. "Wesley… hmmm…" she said, scratching her chin. "By any chance is your son the new OB/GYN doctor over in Turpricone?"

"The very same," Neva said, smiling wide. "That's my son, Dr. Warren Wesley, M.D. He's been in practice there for about two years. I moved here from Old Lyme, Connecticut and had this home built several months ago after my husband passed away."

"Oh, I'm so sorry," Nadine said. "So, how are you liking our part of the world?" she asked her.

"To tell you the truth, I love it," Neva said. "You see, I love to garden, and I don't mean to brag, but just look at my yard and my gardens," she added, as she gestured behind and around where she was standing. "Someday, when you have a little bit of spare time, I'd like to show you what I've done out in the backyard. It's absolutely stunning, if I do say so myself."

"You do have some pretty gardens here and a beautiful home," Nadine told her.

"Sometimes, I get a little lonely, though. I don't have a lot of friends here. I imagine part of the reason is because I haven't joined the Woman's Club and I'm not a churchgoer."

"Well, Miss Neva, you know what? I'm going to invite you to a baby shower on May the first," Nadine told her. "That's a week from now. You don't know her, I'm sure, but her name is Destini Abamu. I'm the hostess for the baby shower given in her honor and I want you to come as my guest. That way, you'll get to meet some of the ladies from around this area. It will be held at Camp EZ. Have you heard of the place?"

"Are you talking about the famous Camp EZ? The one once owned by the late Mr. Hamp Brayerford?" Neva asked.

"Yes, ma'am, that's the place. May I ask how you know Mr. Hamp?"

"Well, I didn't know him, but my husband did and he spoke well of him," Neva explained. "You see, my husband was a physician up in New York City at Cedars Sinai Hospital. We had an apartment in the city and we would go to our other home in Connecticut on weekends and holidays. His specialty was cardiology. Mr. Hamp's sister, Mrs. Bessie Campbell, was a patient of his for many years. Such a nice lady, and oftentimes she was accompanied on her trips up to the city with Mrs.... oh, now, who was it?" she asked, scrunching up her face as she thought. "I'm trying to remember the woman's last name. Oh, I know. It was Wilson."

"Mrs. Hattie?!" Nadine gasped. "Mrs. Hattie Wilson?"

"Yes, that's it," Neva said. "Wonderful, wonderful woman. Always dressed so ladylike and she had the most charming Southern accent. It was like water gently flowing down a stream."

"Yes, Mrs. Hattie is something else," Nadine agreed.

"Another of my husband's patients was a Mr. Stanley Williams, who, I understand, still lives in this area."

"Yes, ma'am, he does. Mr. Stanley sort of married into the area, if you will," Nadine tried to explain without being too cynical. "He married Anna Mary Jarrellson, whose family, at one time, owned this property on which your home is sitting, as well as about half the rest of the county before the War Between the States, or as Anna Mary likes to say, the war of nawthun aggression," she added, trying her best to sound like the snooty Anna Mary.

Both of them shared a good laugh and even the dog seemed amused, as she started barking again.

"Princess, that will be quite enough," Neva scolded the little mutt, and she immediately quieted down again.

"I hope this county is getting beyond all of that old history," Nadine said. "I believe we are, but some folks do try their best to keep it alive and talk about Uncle Jim and Cousin Justice at Cold Harbor, as if it happened just yesterday. There are some great stories to be told about this area, though, I have to admit."

"I knew Mrs. Williams' uncle quite well, the famous artist, Spencer Augustus Jarrellson," Neva said. "You see, my dear, Old Lyme, Connecticut is still somewhat of a retreat for a lot of artists. Mr. Jarrellson leased a home and studio there for many years. He worked there during the late spring and summer months. My husband and I knew him quite well."

"Well, now, Miss Neva, what a coincidence. It really is a small world," Nadine said with a smile. "Here, let me hand you your mail, along with an invitation to a showing of Mr. Gus's work at the gallery here, named in his honor, by the way," she added, as she grabbed all of it from one of the mail bins.

"I'm sorry. What did you call him, dear?" Neva asked.

"Mr. Gus," Nadine repeated. "We called him Gus… short for Augustus, you know."

"Oh, I see," Neva said, nodding her head. "I do believe I will plan on attending this event." She paused a moment and then said, "Earlier you mentioned stories about this area. Do you know any of them?" she asked, as if she had all the time in the world to listen.

"Well, I will share one with you, but after that, I need to be on my way and get the rest of this mail delivered," Nadine told her.

"Okay," Neva said. "That's fine."

"Well, let's see. Anna Mary Jarrellson's great-great grandfather, Amos Augustus Jarrellson was the captain for the county's Home Guard and he marched off at the beginning of the war. Unfortunately, he was captured quickly and placed at a prisoner of war camp in Elmira, New York in the dead of winter. Consequently, he lost nearly all the fingers on his right hand and a couple on his left hand due to frostbite."

"Oh, my," Neva said, cupping her hand over her mouth and seeming completely enthralled with the story so far.

"He eventually came home to a huge tract of land with very few folks to help him tend it, but he went to work," Nadine said. "Even with his hands in the shape they were in, he created a big garden and hired whoever he could to farm small parcels of the land. He never cheated the workers and always treated them with respect. Even though the Jarrellson family had to sell off a lot of acreage to help ends meet, they managed to hold onto about half of what they had before the war started. They believed wholeheartedly in education and sold some of their land to pay for legal and business educations for their family members. Their descendants used that education to help the family as a whole, and they were able to persevere and prosper over the ensuing years. They weren't like a lot of folks who lived in the past and were knocked flat by it."

"They sound like an interesting family," Neva said.

"That's one way of putting it," Nadine replied with a crooked grin. "Another surname you might hear a lot in this town is the Brayerford name. You already know about Mr. Hamp. Anyway, they didn't have much at all before the war, but their marriages into the Adamson and Jarrellson families, and with them being decent, down to earth farmers with a mind for business, it put them forward on the right path. The late Mr. Hamp was such a good friend," she added, as her eyes welled with tears. "He was a great man, a truly great man, who had a heart for people of all walks of life. I loved him dearly."

"Ohh, I do understand," Neva said, and she reached out to pat Nadine on the arm. "Losing someone we truly love is not easy. I have heard such good things about him. I wish I had gotten to know him. It's very much the same in New England… different church, same pew," she added with a genuine smile. "I have so enjoyed talking with you, Nadine. If I invited you for lunch one day, would you join me?" she asked.

"If it's on a Saturday or a Sunday afternoon, Miss Neva, it's a date," Nadine told her. "Now, I really must go. I enjoyed our little chat."

"Me, too," Neva said, and the two women waved goodbye to each other.

Nadine had a good feeling down deep in her soul after visiting with Miss Neva, as she continued on her mail route. She didn't much care what others might say. She knew Yankees were a different breed, but she had met some Southerners who were more than curious, too. She knew in her own mind that there were pleasant folks everywhere from all walks of life.

"Miss Neva is certainly one of those pleasant folks," Nadine said, smiling wide as she turned the corner onto the next block. "I wonder why she wears those great big sunglasses, though. They look a little ridiculous."

Chapter 9

The glow of the river

The Smoking Pig Grill had been a fixture in Campbell County for decades. It was situated on the main drag through the town of Seraph Springs and you couldn't miss it if you tried. Aside from the colorful red, black and white flags surrounding the parking lot, the top of the chimney had been designed to look like a black and white hog. It boasted a huge, oversized snout, making the smoky aroma of pork ribs, and barbecued chicken and beef look as if it was emanating directly from the pig's nose.

The restaurant was also the unofficial gathering place in Campbell County for the local men's breakfast and coffee group that was held on weekdays, Monday through Friday. A group of about fifteen to twenty men, a few of them happily retired already, would meet at the restaurant beginning at about seven o'clock in the morning. After eating, some of them would hang around until well after ten o'clock, while others went off to their respective jobs.

As Nadine approached the restaurant on her second day on the job as a fill-in mail carrier, she couldn't help but laugh out loud.

"Everyone thinks women are the ones who sit around and gossip all the time," she said, shaking her head and giggling, as she watched three elderly gentlemen enter the restaurant chit-chatting like old mother hens. "Gossip sure ain't gender specific. Never has been," she muttered. "Especially in *this* town!"

She knew from personal experience that men could swap tales of gossip just as quickly and eagerly as women could, and they did it with such finesse.

"They have a way of repeating gossip that makes it seem like it isn't gossip at all, but valued talk that's useful," she mumbled, as if she was jealous of their technique. "Yeah, right," she added, and she laughed.

This morning, there were a lot of pickup trucks and SUV's in the restaurant parking lot, more than usual, actually. Every one of them looked to be in need of a good washing, too, as they had several layers of greenish-yellow, spring-induced pollen stuck to the windows, as well as white sand road dirt on the rear ends of most of the vehicles. Campbell County was one of many counties in the region that had as many, if not more, dirt roads than paved roads, so the dirty cars were a familiar sight, especially during the drier months.

"Well, lookie there," Nadine said.

She had just spotted a familiar, shiny black 1969 Cadillac Fleetwood parked along the curb. The car used to belong to Anna Mary's late mother, but since Anna Mary refused to drive the big monstrosity, as she called it, she gave it to Stanley, who, oddly enough, kept it in tip-top condition, considering the fact he wasn't really a connoisseur of vintage cars. Unlike the other dirty cars in the parking lot, the Cadillac looked as if it had just come off the showroom floor.

Since the death of his son, Watson, Stanley only

drove the car to Seraph Springs Methodist Church on Sundays and to the Smoking Pig Grill during the week, where he had become a fairly regular member of the morning breakfast group. It was, in fact, a men's only group with the rare exception of one woman by the name of Dee Dee Wilson Fernandez, whenever she happened to pop in unexpectedly, that is.

"Oh, look! Here comes Dee Dee!" Nadine exclaimed when she spotted her coming from the opposite direction.

She slowed down the mail truck and waved to Dee Dee, motioning for her to turn in front of her and on into the parking lot of the Smoking Pig. Dee Dee waved back and then blew Nadine a kiss.

How Dee Dee had wormed her way into that circle of gossipy men was a mystery to many folks, but Nadine knew the reason why. Just like herself, Dee Dee was also one of those shock-proof type people. Nothing much ever fazed her, at least on the surface. She was an expert at talking down-to-earth common sense with the best of them. She had spent most of her formative, growing-up years in a man's world, mostly hanging out with her father, the late Carter Wilson, and his best friend, the late Hamp Brayerford, who was Dee Dee's uncle. She could ride a horse, shoot a Remington 700 hunting rifle or a Smith & Wesson 9 mm handgun, and she could hunt and fish as expertly as any man in the county. All the men knew it, too, which is why they offered her so much respect.

Dee Dee's aunt, Hattie Wilson Campbell, would

oftentimes cringe at her niece's antics. That was the reason at the age of fifteen, Dee Dee was sent off to Ashley Hall in Charleston, South Carolina for finishing school. It was a long, long summer with Anna Mary Jarrellson as her mentor and chaperone. Their totally opposite personalities often clashed, but they somehow managed to get through the summer without killing each other. Some folks in town said that even with Anna Mary's extra tutelage, Dee Dee's finishing didn't altogether take.

While Dee Dee could hold her own against anyone at any type of elegant sit-down dinner or society luncheon, and while she could make small talk like nobody's business, she could also lapse into the local, colorful expressions with the best of the good ole boys. She could pepper her conversations with enough well-placed cuss words to make the men's club crowd gasp every now and then, but they always laughed along with her and never at her.

Dee Dee also had the good sense not to show up at the men's club breakfast every weekday, lest they think she was becoming a nuisance, or that she was infringing on their manly rights. As it was, they never knew when she would pop in. When she did, however, it never failed that a chair was slid out for her by any one of the men around the table, who seemed to compete for her attention. Without question, she would sit down and be able to enjoy her time with "the guys", and vice versa. She was the only female in Campbell County ever to gain that notoriety, and no one ever questioned it, nor did they think it was odd in any way, shape or form. It was just the way Dee Dee was, like her or not.

All the joking and all the conversations she had with the men were always paired with respectful comments, such as, "Miss Dee Dee, you just won't do," or "Miss Dee Dee, you've got some kind of memory," or "Sure enough, Miss Dee Dee." They never patronized her and they never called her anything but Miss Dee Dee.

"I wish I could join you now, Dee Dee," Nadine said, as she continued past the Smoking Pig Grill and onto her first stop at Feed the World Organics. "I'll just bet you're gonna have a big old time with those good ole boys," she added, and she laughed.

&&&&&&&&&&&

THIS MORNING, the talk in the breakfast group was all about the Suwannee River, specifically, a section of the river from the mouth of Wilson Creek on down for about a mile southward.

"I'll tell you what, boys. I have never seen anythin' like it," said Theodore "Junior" Thomas, who was the chief deputy for Sheriff Bartow Lewis. "I remember one day, me and Duke Wilson put out some set hooks and we were just about finished checkin' 'em," he began. "When darkness fell, we looked through the woods up by Wilson Creek and it seemed like the water, which y'all know is fed by three springs… well, it seemed to turn a greenish-yellow color and it was glowing in the dark. As dark as the river is, the water skimming the top seemed to be shimmering… it almost looked like an oil sheen."

"Oh, come on now, Junior," Judge Wesson said. "Are you sure you and Duke didn't get into a good bit of that whiskey old man Hamp Brayerford had stored away near that camp?"

Everyone sitting around the table laughed. Everyone except Dee Dee, that is.

"You know, Junior, I find what you said very interesting," she interjected. "About three weeks ago, my husband and I were out for a walk on some of our property through which part of that creek runs. It was about the same time of day, too, about twilight. I don't mind telling you, we had enjoyed a few drinks that day," she added, which drew quiet laughter from the boys. "I thought for a minute I was seeing things, but Ricardo said he saw it, too. Anyway, we continued walking, and as we got closer to the creek, it was like there was a light shining on some of the lowest hanging moss on the trees over top of the creek. We walked a little further and we both saw what you just described."

At this, the table went silent. None of the men would dare dispute Dee Dee's word. They knew enough to know that you may not like what she says, but she was known for her honesty and for telling the truth. She'd been called upon more than once by folks in the area to vouch for various things, and if she verified it, you could pretty much bank on it.

"I wonder what it could be," Stanley piped up, discreetly inserting himself into the conversation.

On the surface, Dee Dee thought Stanley appeared to be as puzzled as everyone else, but she had a feeling he knew exactly what was behind the glow in the river water, especially after what Judge Wesson had told her. She had asked the judge if he would come by Camp EZ to pick up her Uncle Hamp's notebooks, since she never got around to dropping them off at his house, and he did so right after dinner night before last.

It seemed to Dee Dee that everyone around the table this morning, except maybe for Stanley, assumed that the glowing water in Wilson Creek was caused by either the limestone company or Feed the World Organics, one of which might be illegally dumping chemicals into the river.

One person present at the table this morning was Phil Brainard Jr., who definitely had some idea of what would make water glow, but he was not about to say out loud what he thought. He and Dee Dee had been discussing it off and on for quite a while. Phil also knew enough about the limestone business to have suspicions about their possible involvement, and he voiced those concerns to her several times.

Phil had retired early in life, due to the fact he got tired of the corporate rat race and longed for a simple life back in his hometown of Seraph Springs. Plus, he could afford it. Prior to his retirement, he gained notoriety as one of the nation's most respected environmental attorneys at the Federal Department of

Environmental Protection and his exorbitant salary proved it. Then, he went on to serve on the staff of a prominent Washington, D.C. law firm and consulting company that specialized in environmental issues, again, with a more than generous salary.

He'd had enough of that lifestyle, though, so he and his wife agreed that living in Campbell County was what they both preferred. So, they built a nice three-bedroom brick home on a piece of property that the late Mama Tee Wilson had deeded to them. It was clear to everyone who knew Phil and his wife, Elyse, that they both truly enjoyed rural living. Elyse soon fell in love with the art of quilting and needlework, and she joined a group of women who restored vintage quilts. They met once a week over in Pittstown.

In the fall of last year, Elyse encouraged the group to take a trip to Asheville, North Carolina to view a traveling exhibit from the Whitney Museum of Art in New York City that featured heirloom quilts. Dee Dee graciously hosted the entire group at her mountain retreat log cabin, which was just a few miles from the museum.

This morning, Phil's ears perked up when the subject of Wilson Creek's spooky green illumination by night came up, but he said nothing. Instead, he pretended to be engrossed in the latest edition of the Turpricone News, while he sipped on his coffee.

In truth, Dee Dee knew that the thought of something or someone purposely emitting radioactivity into the river frightened him. He told her recently that, in his mind, the thoughts and suspicions that many folks in the county held about Feed the World Organics could very well be true. He actually had the right thought process going, but he had no idea that the actual culprit might very well be sitting beside him at the table right now.

Meanwhile, Stanley didn't change his serene facial expression one iota upon hearing about the glowing water. He simply sat quietly and sipped his coffee, stirring it every now and then. Dee Dee could tell just by looking at him, though, that on the inside he was anything but serene.

The back and forth chatter of the shining, glowing water in Wilson Creek went on for another fifteen minutes. Mr. Elton Lewis, who owned one of the area's electrical supply companies, offered his opinion from the other end of the table.

"You know, my granddaddy told me the original Jarrellson homestead was situated someplace on the banks of that creek," Elton began. "The reason the Jarrellsons chose the site was because that creek is one, if not the only creek in this county that's fed by several springs. When the weather is dry, there's places along that creek where the water runs crystal clear for quite a few yards downstream. Do you think that's what y'all were seeing?" he asked.

"No, sir, Mr. Elton," Dee Dee disagreed. "I know that place you're talking about. I've seen it. Daddy told me that some of the old chimney bricks that were in the main part of that old house are still there. He said it was the county's first two-storied house with chimneys at both ends. The house was built there, he said, because of the springs, and because there's a special type of clay that forms on the east bank of the creek."

"I know what you're talking about," Junior interrupted. "It's one of the only places in the county where that clay is located. The brick in the chimneys of that original old house were made from the clay out of the bank of that creek and fired in a kiln that was right there on that property," he explained. "There was a long walkway leading up to the house made out of those bricks, too."

"You're right about that, Junior," Dee Dee said. "That house burned down in the late 1880's. Daddy said there had been a big house party out there in the fall of the year and several men had been invited to hunt. Supposedly, one of them was careless with a lit cigarette, and since the house was made of heart pine lightard, it didn't take long for it to burn to the ground."

"Oh, yeah, I remember that," Junior said. "The Jarrellsons then moved into town and built that big house on the river where Mr. Stanley and his wife, and that pretty grandbaby of theirs live now," he added.

At that, Stanley said, "Thank you, Junior. That baby, our beautiful Mary Selena, means the world to us, although, she's not a baby anymore."

Dee Dee reached over, patted Stanley's hand, and then she winked at him. In her mind, though, she was thinking, "You smug little bastard. You think you can act? I'll show you what real theater is!" She never let her face betray what she was feeling, though.

Everyone talked a while longer about a variety of goings-on within the community, including some juicy gossip about a big bar fight a couple nights ago, the result of a domestic dispute gone haywire, that sent three people to the hospital.

There was some discussion, too, though not a lot with this crowd, about the upcoming exhibit of some of Gus Jarrellson's paintings at the new gallery. The gallery, it turns out, was once one of the Jarrellson family's brick cotton warehouses that was restored with a lot of money and effort into a beautiful art gallery. It was named in memory of the late Spencer Augustus Jarrellson.

Most of the group sitting around the table were not that interested in the fine arts. However, being well-mannered Southern boys, they nodded in approval when Stanley mentioned the opening, and a couple of them said, "That's nice."

Phil rose from his chair and picked up his check, as well as the checks of everyone at the table.

"Well, now," Dee Dee said, smiling wide. "Thank you, Phil."

"My treat," Phil said, as the others at the table echoed the same thanks.

Right before Phil walked away toward the cashier, he slyly slipped a napkin into Dee Dee's hand. On it was written:

Meet me at Camp EZ tonight at 8 p.m. We need to talk!

Chapter 10

The truth comes out

Once Nadine finished delivering the mail to the folks living in Watson Estates that afternoon, she left the development and continued to her next stop, which was to a man named Mr. Chadwick Clement Clark. She had no mail for him the previous day, so this was her first time seeing his place.

His residence was located about half a mile outside of Watson Estates, down a winding, woodsy road that was barely wide enough for her little mail truck to fit on the pavement without sliding off onto the sandy shoulder. The road, though, was well-maintained with not a single pothole. It was obvious to her that the owner took great pride in his property, assuming he was the one who had the paved road installed, she thought.

"Well, of course, he did," she muttered. "The county sure didn't do this out of the goodness of their heart."

When his huge, double-wide manufactured home came into view, she was in awe, as she'd never seen a mobile home look so elegant before. The place was surrounded by a high chain link fence, and inside the yard was a uniquely manicured lawn with all sorts of exotic shrubs and bushes.

"Wow," she thought. "This looks like something out of an architectural design book."

Aside from the home, there was also a large outbuilding constructed to resemble a garage. It also must have served as a storage shed, she figured, since the doors were wide open at the moment and she could see inside.

"Goodness, that's a lot of stuff," she thought.

Then, she spotted, who she assumed to be Mr. Clark, sitting atop a brand new John Deere mowing the grass on the side of his house. She noted that for a man she guessed to be in his mid-fifties, he was in good physical shape. She also took note of the expensive running shoes he was wearing.

"I wonder if he's one of those 5K runners," she thought. "Or maybe he just likes nice shoes," she thought again, and she chuckled.

Inside the garage, she saw both a canoe and a kayak, so she figured because of his close proximity to the river, he probably often engaged in those leisurely pursuits.

When he saw her drive up to the mailbox, he waved at her and she honked the horn back at him. Seconds later, he was over by the fence. When he hopped down from the big mower and unlatched the gate, out of nowhere came one of the biggest blue-grey pit bulls she had ever seen. The dog barked at first, but when Nadine spoke to Mr. Clark, the big fellow rolled over onto his back just like a puppy during playtime. Nadine couldn't help but laugh at the dog's antics. She then introduced herself to Mr. Clark and he, in turn, introduced himself to her.

When she handed him the invitation to the art exhibit, she watched him raise his eyebrows, but he said nothing, other than, "May I offer you a cold soft drink or a bottle of water?"

"No, sir," she told him, smiling. "Thank you for asking, though. I have to finish up with this mail route and it looks to be a long afternoon. Have a good day, Mr. Clark."

Although she only had about sixty stops on her route, they covered a wide swath of geography and it took time getting to each one. A few hours later, she pulled into the post office parking lot, drove around to the rear entrance, and heaved a sigh of relief that her work day was nearly finished. It was just about to strike three o'clock.

"Finished by noon, my butt," she mumbled. "Maybe it gets better with time."

As soon as she walked in the door, she got a whiff of freshly percolated coffee.

"Oh, that smells heavenly," she said to Betty Sue.

"Come on in and take a load off," Betty Sue told her. "Let's talk a few minutes before we bundle up some of this mail for tomorrow."

"Don't mind if I do," Nadine said with a pasted-on smile, as she poured herself a cup of steaming hot coffee. "Oh, geez, I forgot about this part of the job... bundling mail... ugh," she quietly mumbled, but thankfully, Betty Sue didn't hear her.

"So, tell me about some of the folks you met on your mail route," Betty Sue urged her, evidently more than eager to hear some juicy gossip.

"Well, let's see," Nadine began. "I met Miss Neva yesterday and what a sweet, old woman she is. I invited her to Destini's baby shower luncheon at Camp EZ. Oh, and I met Mr. Clark, today."

Betty Sue raised an eyebrow. "Now, honey, that one has a story, you hear me? Since we have some time, I'll tell you part of it."

"Okay, I'm always up for a good story," Nadine said, as she continued to sip on her coffee.

"You would think with him living in that double-wide mobile home, even though it's well maintained, and he has that equally well-maintained Range Rover that's several years old, that maybe there's not much of a story there."

"Do tell," Nadine encouraged her. "Oh, can we sort some of this mail while we chat?" she added, as she really wanted to go home.

"Yes, certainly," Betty Sue said, and then she continued her story. "Well, Mr. Clark... I'll call him Chad, so you don't get confused. Well, he was more or less turned out to pasture by his daddy because he refused to go to work in the company business. His daddy was a huge industrialist and land developer in the northeast," she began with relish. "It was somewhere up in Connecticut, and he also had holdings in New York, Delaware... everywhere, or so I have been told. Chad's mother died under rather mysterious circumstances, while she and Chad's father were down in the Bahamas on his company's yacht."

"Oh, my," Nadine said.

"Oh, my, is right," Betty Sue agreed. "Here's the really strange part, though. The sea, supposedly, was as calm as it could be that day and Chad's mother used to be an Olympic swimmer. She won an Olympic gold medal, actually, and she was still in terrific shape. On that fateful morning of her death, it was reported that she ate her breakfast onboard the yacht, drank a glass of orange juice and a cup of coffee, read the morning paper, and then she went into the water for a short swim."

"Hmmm, not a good idea to go swimming after eating, or so Mama always told me," Nadine interjected.

"I guess not because she drowned, and there was no sign of foul play of any kind, according to the authorities," Betty Sue continued. "No autopsy was done and it wasn't long after that, maybe six months or so, that Chad's father remarried his third cousin, Abigail Claire Clark," she added.

"Okay, now this is getting even more interesting," Nadine said with a chuckle.

"Well, the woman didn't even have to change her last name," Betty Sue said, rolling her eyes. "The two of them never had a child together, thank goodness. According to Miss Neva, she knew a little bit about the story since her late husband and the elder Mr. Clark were both members of the Yale Club in New York City. They also saw each other socially from time to time. She said young Chad was sent to a very prestigious boarding school in Massachusetts and he only came home on holidays. During summer breaks he was sent to exclusive summer camps in the Adirondacks."

"Nothing like shipping your kid off, huh?" Nadine mumbled.

"Mr. Clark's father was very busy adding to his already tremendous fortune," Betty Sue went on. "Honey, he could have bought and sold Campbell County a thousand times. Of course, Clark wasn't their real name, you know. They changed it when they came to this country from Russia around the turn of the twentieth century. Their surname, according to Miss Neva was a Hebrew surname, although they changed it to Clark and then became Episcopalian. I am told that Abigail Claire Clark's folks often frequented the synagogue in Newport, Rhode Island. It's one of the oldest… in fact, I think it *is* the oldest synagogue in the nation."

Without even taking a breath, Betty Sue continued to ramble on, as Nadine sat quietly sorting the mail, mesmerized by how much Betty Sue knew about people.

"Chad, at one time, was a national champion at dressage and he won championships here in the United States, as well as in Europe. I've heard there is one big room in his home that's filled with ribbons and trophies and photos, even a couple pictures taken of him and members of the British Royal Family."

"Wow, that's cool," Nadine said.

"Supposedly, Chad's father supported all of this, but here is the proverbial twist in the story," Betty Sue continued. "Chad was a clinical counselor for a short time, and he wound up working at that place... what was it? Ocean Breeze Rehabilitation Clinic? Yes, that's it," she said, and then she went on. "It was where the late Dr. Watson Jarrellson Williams was a patient. You know... after that unfortunate business in China, and then when he was hooked on alcohol and pain medication."

"Yes, I remember all that," Nadine said. "Go on, honey, this is good stuff."

"Well, it seems that the one they paid off to "cut and run" as it were, that Monty Wu guy... well, it turns out that he wasn't the one with whom Watson was close to. No, no, they say it was Mr. Chadwick Clark."

"Really?!" Nadine gasped.

"Yes, really, but the story gets a little better, honey," Betty Sue went on. "Monty Wu was fixated on Watson, and when he discovered that Chad was more of an interest to Watson than he was, well, that's when things got ugly... real fast. The story goes that while Chad was asleep one evening, Monty Wu took a carving knife and he nearly cut Chad's face to pieces."

"Oh, my goodness!" Nadine gasped. "I noticed a few scars on his face, but they looked like maybe acne scars or something. I mean it was hardly noticeable."

"Well, he rarely goes out in public," Betty Sue explained. "He's got a Hispanic housekeeper, a little Guatemalan lady named Pilar Gonzalez, who does most of his grocery shopping for him, as well as going out after anything else he may need. There is one thing that is really interesting about him, aside from his love of gardening, which he does rival Miss Neva on that."

"He does have a pretty yard," Nadine agreed, interrupting her.

"In addition to his advanced degree in clinical counseling, he first trained and still is a chemical engineer," Betty Sue said. "He received his degree from Cornell University in New York. He supposedly lives off a trust fund left to him by his mother."

"Must be nice," Nadine said.

"Well, her family owned vast amounts of property in the Connecticut Valley, and when that property developed… to use an old expression… they got well off of it. The grandmother's name was Victoria Eugenia Firestar Holt and the family owned a huge national company that made tires for automobiles across the United States. As I stated earlier, his father cut him completely out of his will when he refused to come into the family business. From what Miss Neva said, though, that decision Chad made could have been forgiven. However, when Chad's father found out about the situation that took place at Ocean Breeze Rehabilitation Clinic… well, that was it. He was done with Chad forever… period."

Nadine was about to get up, thinking Betty Sue was done, but she wasn't.

"Supposedly, it was a physician friend of Watson's who resided in London who did most of the corrective surgery on Chad's face," Betty Sue continued. "When you think about it, it really is quite a small world."

"Yes, it is," Nadine said. "Why in the world do you think Chad wants to be here in Seraph Springs when he could be living anywhere in the world?"

"That, honey, is the sixty-four-thousand-dollar question many people have asked," Betty Sue replied. "Thus far, no one has come up with an answer. He is such a recluse and minds his own business, you know what I mean?" she rhetorically asked. "As I told you, he rarely leaves that property, except for doctor visits and dermatologists down in Gainesville from time to time. Some folks have said they've seen him out jogging or canoeing on the river. Despite the fact that he's very understated and tasteful in choosing clothes and shoes for himself, he does wear a gold link bracelet that I'll bet you is one-hundred grams of gold. It's absolutely beautiful."

"Yes, I noticed that when I was there," Nadine said. "You know, he's not a bad looking man, even with those scars on his face. If he grew a beard, he'd be a knockout."

"While sorting the mail every day, I noticed a lot of huge manila envelopes that came from the Federal Environmental Protection Agency up in Washington, D.C.," Betty Sue said. "Evidently, he reads a lot because he gets a lot of boxes of literature from scientific companies that deal with groundwater quality. He also receives quarterly reports from his mother's trust, the Firestar-Holt Trust, and he makes regular contributions to the science departments at the schools in Seraph Springs and Turpricone," she explained.

"Boy, I guess when you work at the post office you learn a whole lot about people," Nadine said with a yawn that she didn't try to cover up.

Betty Sue nodded, and then she continued, again, without even breaking stride.

"Monty Wu never knew, nor did anyone, I suppose, that Chad's interest in Watson had been only that of a devoted clinical counselor to his patient," she said. "Watson's story of abuse and neglect, growing up the way he did with parents who were more or less indifferent, and his search for what he thought was love with his uncle Gus, and later, what happened in China, was a story that traced much of Chad's own past, quite frankly. Watson was well on his way to recovery when he left Ocean Breeze Rehabilitation Center. It seemed to Chad, as he recovered in a New York City Hospital after the facial cutting, that Watson had found happiness in the final couple years of his life. For this, he was grateful. No one, except Chad, his maternal grandmother, and the chief of staff at Ocean Breeze, Dr. Samuel Geiger, knew the reason why Chad's attack was not made public, and Monty Wu was never charged. All the evidence went up in smoke in a small fire before Monty Wu left Panama City under the watchful eye of Dr. Geiger and the sheriff of the county, as well as a private investigator from New Orleans, Etienne Deauville, a former agent for a major federal agency in Washington D.C."

"My goodness, Betty Sue. How did you find out about all of this, and how do you keep all of it straight in your head?" Nadine asked.

"Ohh, it's just a natural talent, I guess, and I will never reveal my sources," Betty Sue replied, red-faced, but it didn't stop her from continuing. "Monty Wu put all his letters, all his copious notes, as well as photos and films of him and Watson into that huge fire at Ocean Breeze. He had stored all of it in two safety deposit boxes that he emptied, as well as a secure hiding place under the floorboards of a storage shed on the grounds of the rehab center, which was also destroyed."

A stunned, "Wow!" was all Nadine could come up with, as she listened to this tale of intrigue.

"It was the appearance of the box from the storage shed that sent Monty Wu into the rage that propelled the attack on Chad," Betty Sue went on. "You see, Chad knew that Watson's chances for recovery would be shattered forever if any of this became public. So, he told law enforcement officials there would be no charges brought against Monty Wu, and he made sure the cashier's check he wrote for fifty-thousand dollars went straight to Monty Wu, so that he could disappear. Then, he traveled to New York City on a chartered plane to undergo numerous surgeries to try to correct all the facial cuts. He had a lengthy recovery, as you can well imagine. His scars, many of which have since disappeared, were nothing compared to the permanent damage to Watson's life. It was a wound from which

Chad knew his patient would never recover."

"Ain't that the truth?" Nadine piped up.

"No one in this area knows about the volume of research done by Chad on the ongoing operations involving groundwater quality at various spots around here where the creeks and branches discharge into the Suwannee, Withlacoochee and Alapaha Rivers," Betty Sue continued. "All of this was being done because of conversations he had with Watson before his death about the changes to the water quality in Campbell County. No one knew the reason for Chad's many trips out of the country to places in Central and South America, supposedly to collect tropical and subtropical plants for the fabulous gardens on his property. No one knew of the hours upon hours he spent on meticulously labeling each plant species he tended for the benefit of very few who visited his private haven. No one knew of the meticulous care he tended to two big ornamental ponds on his property that were filled with several varieties of exotic koi fish. Most importantly, no one knew, not even Chad, of the secrets that lay on a piece of land just beyond his well-tended acres. Acres of land now owned by Destini Wilson Abamu… acres of land now desperately wanted by Anna Mary and Stanley Williams."

Nadine was aghast and asked, "What secrets?"

"Well, I know quite a bit, but that is one secret that was never divulged to me," Betty Sue told her, and then she continued. "No one, other than Chad, knew that Dr. Spencer Augustus Jarrellson had been a guest on his father's company yacht when his mother drowned. No one knew, except Chad, that in his father's private art collection were three original oils done by Mr. Gus. They were paintings depicting brightly clothed individuals on a Caribbean island that was deeply involved in voodoo practices."

"Holy cow!" Nadine muttered, still in shock at all she was hearing coming out of Betty Sue's mouth.

"What people did know was that Chad was very clean and neat, he kept himself in good physical condition, he respected his neighbors, and since his appearance in Campbell County, several charitable organizations and foundations have received hefty contributions… heftier than had been received in the past, that is."

"Gee, now that you mention it…" Nadine said, scratching her chin.

"These contributions were made anonymously, too," Betty Sue explained. "Folks thought they knew, but they didn't know, not entirely, anyway. Chad kept a large part of his life very private. It was the way he chose to live. His comings and goings in his Range Rover and his Ford utility truck are very rare, but you know, it's kind of an odd thing. Some of our regular river fishermen like the Thomas twins, John and Ron, claim they've seen someone who they believe strongly resembles Chad at the mouths of some of the creeks and branches of the river and he has these little glass containers with him. It's always late in the afternoon or even after dark, and he's out there scooping up river water."

"I wonder what he's looking for," Nadine said.

"I wonder myself," Betty Sue replied. "Folks like him are a real puzzlement to me. That's for sure," she added.

"Well, I need to get going," Nadine said. "I've got kids and a husband to feed soon."

"Okay, honey," Betty Sue said. "Thanks for letting me bend your ear."

"Not a problem," Nadine told her. "See you tomorrow," she added, and out the door she went. "Good grief," she muttered, as she slipped behind the wheel of her car. "That woman can talk! Sheesh!"

Chapter 11

Down by the riverside

One person who wasn't wondering what Chad Clark was up to was Phil. Always somewhat of a loner himself, Phil would walk the trails along the Suwannee River at odd hours of the day and night when no one else was around. Many times, when the weather was just right, he would launch his canoe and silently paddle up and down the river. He told his wife, who wasn't much into canoeing, that he truly enjoyed the quiet solitude of the river, and she never complained about his special alone time.

"We all need our space every now and then," she had told him. "Goodness knows I need mine, too."

It was on one such canoe trip that Phil decided to take a break after two hours of steady paddling, so that he could re-nourish his body. He tied his canoe off onto a protruding cypress tree branch near the mouth of Wilson Creek and then he spread a small blanket on the bank, so he could sit without getting his pants too wet or sandy. On his canoe outings, he'd usually bring along something simple to munch on like crackers and sardines, which is what he brought with him today. His drink of choice was always bottled spring water, which he kept in a small cooler.

After he finished his snack, he was just about to doze off for a little nap when he heard a light rustling in the bushes behind him. At first, he thought it might be a raccoon or even a deer looking for scraps of food or a drink of water from the river.

"I just hope it's not a snake or, God forbid, an alligator or a rattlesnake," he mumbled, as his eyes scanned the area where he thought he heard the noise.

He breathed a sigh of relief when he spotted Chadwick Clark, the other infamous recluse of Seraph Springs, just a few yards down the river bank to the south of him.

Since Seraph Springs was the gossip capital of Campbell County, Phil was well aware of Chad's reputation for being a loner like himself. Today, however, Chad seemed to be in a congenial mood. He waved, shouted a hearty, "Good morning!", and then he surprised Phil when he came over and sat down beside him.

The two men began chatting like they were old college buddies, talking about the crisp weather, the flow of the river and how high the water level was today. Phil recognized at once that Chad wasn't the common, garden variety Campbell County local. The man's insight into environmental issues, and the discussion the two engaged in about groundwater toxicity in various places around the country was a refreshing change for Phil. At the end of their visit along the beautiful sandy bank of the majestic Suwannee River, Phil asked Chad if he might call on him at some time in the future.

Chad nodded his head, and said, "Absolutely."

That, in and of itself, was the beginning of a

friendship that was based solely on common interests and scientific backgrounds.

Consequently, the two of them talked on the phone quite often after that first conversation on the river. About once a month, they would head off to explore a new part of the river, usually in Phil's canoe, which was a little larger than Chad's. They were almost always early morning day trips where they would take samples of water at various creeks and branches that were offshoots of the Suwannee. Once collected, all the water samples were later tested in Chad's private laboratory behind his home.

Phil was probably the only person in Campbell County who figured out the reason Chad chose to live in Seraph Springs, although, it took him many months to discover why. The two of them had become such close friends that Chad soon bared his soul about much of his life, and he even told Phil the story behind the scars on his face.

Even after he figured out why Chad was in Seraph Springs, Phil's opinion of the man never altered. He knew that for someone like Chad to have emotions so intense, he had to have greatly suffered the pain of rejection and its resultant heartache, as well as the pain of extreme disappointment. The two separate careers Chad had chosen, clinical counseling and chemical engineering, required extreme focus and Phil knew both jobs required a complex mind. Yet, at the core of that complex mind was a yearning for something else, which was clearly evident to Phil. Chad, he knew, was holding back, but Phil didn't want to press him on it, lest he lose a best friend in the process.

He knew there had to be more to the story because Monty Wu was never charged with the crime of cutting Chad's face. To Phil's knowledge, neither Stanley nor Anna·Mary had ever been made aware of anything other than the original story of Monty Wu and his relationship with their son, Watson, that had been created by their attorney, Elwood Ellison Carter.

Chapter 12

Baby on the way

Every single chair around the huge oak dining room table at Camp EZ would be occupied very shortly for an evening of joy, camaraderie, scrumptious food, and lots and lots of baby shower gifts for the expectant mother, a hugely pregnant Destini Wilson Abamu.

Camp EZ, a magnificent hunting retreat on a massive swath of acreage located in Seraph Springs, was the perfect location for Destini's baby shower. The Camp included a quietly elegant hunting lodge that was built by its founder, the late Hamp Brayerford, who spent over a million dollars constructing just the lodge alone. That was a lot of money several decades ago. Upon his death at the reading of the will, it was disclosed that Mr. Hamp had deeded the camp to Dee Dee and Carl Alvin, his niece and nephew, who have successfully been running and managing the property ever since.

This evening, seated at the head of the table where Mr. Hamp used to sit, was Phil. He was given the seat of honor and respect by his lifetime friend, confidante, and former nanny, Destini, who was seated to his right. To his left sat Dee Dee in all her nouveau riche elegance. Aside from Phil, the only other man in attendance was Carl Alvin, who was sitting at the opposite end of the table enjoying a glass of wine.

As she had promised days ago, Nadine brought along Miss Neva, whom she had met on her mail route. Even though it was a cloudy day, the old woman was still wearing those huge, strange looking sunglasses. It was bugging Nadine so much that she had to ask her why she always wore them.

"Oh, honey, I just had cataract surgery not too long ago and my doctor told me to always wear sunglasses when I go outdoors," Neva told her.

"Oh, okay," Nadine said, nodding her head and pretending to understand, even though they were indoors now and she still had the sunglasses on.

Aside from that little quirk of hers, everyone at the party seemed to warm up to her immediately and made her feel more than welcome to join their tight-knit group for an evening of fun. Meanwhile, everyone was waiting for the remainder of the guests to arrive.

Destini's due date was two weeks away and it was clear to everyone that her huge belly was becoming very uncomfortable for her, to say the least. Destini was a trooper, though, and she kept a big smile on her face for most of the evening.

Destini had Phil's hand clasped in hers as he began to relate stories about Chadwick Clark's interest in the environment, and how much he enjoyed their burgeoning friendship. Both Destini and Dee Dee shared eye contact as he spoke, but Phil was so engrossed in what he was saying that he didn't notice the sly winks back and forth between the two women.

"Now, let me see, Phil, baby," Destini interrupted

him, still referring to him as one of her babies since she practically raised him. "It seems to me that the name Chadwick Clark is a name I remember. Let me think a minute." She closed her eyes tight and moved her lips, mouthing the man's name, "Clark... Clark... Chadwick Clark. Oh!" she exclaimed. "I know who he is! Oh, yes, he was a young man who knew my baby, Watson. Yes, I remember now. He used to phone the house all the time after Watson came home. Yes, they talked quite often, but when Watson married Miss Selena, I noticed Chad wasn't on the guest list. I always thought that was a bit odd. I recall he had a voice similar to Mr. Stanley's. It was very, very New England-ish. I do remember that. Was he born and raised in New England, Phil, or am I remembering wrong?" she asked.

Phil just shook his head and smiled, and then he leaned over and kissed Destini on the cheek. He didn't even bother answering her question.

"Now, what was that for?" she asked, raising her eyebrows, as her cheeks turned red. "If you think that kiss is gonna influence what I put in your Easter basket this year, you're dead wrong. I already got your basket done," she added.

"Does there have to be a reason for me to kiss you on the cheek?" Phil asked her, and then he winked at Dee Dee, who was watching the charming exchange between them.

"Not at all, baby. I do appreciate you, honey, but like I said about the basket..." Destini started, but she got interrupted.

"My Lord, that cheek kiss wasn't about the basket, Destini," Phil chided her. "Even though, you are the only person in the whole wide world that I know of who puts together and sends out Easter baskets to grownups. Every Easter, no matter where I was living, here'd come that Easter basket," he said to the others around the table, and he laughed.

"And wasn't you always glad to get it?" Destini defiantly asked him. "Tell the truth, now, and shame the devil if you don't," she added.

"Yes, I am always happy to get your Easter baskets," he assured her. "To tell you the truth, I would have been deeply hurt if you had ever forgotten to send me one. My wife always laughs when those baskets arrive. She says I act like a little kid."

"Well, that's all right then," Destini said. "What I wanted you to know with those Easter baskets was that you are my baby and always will be," she added.

Dee Dee chimed in, "As if there could be any mistaking that, with or without the baskets. My God, Destini, nearly every conversation of any length with you over the past twenty some odd years has included something about your baby, Phil."

"And what's wrong with that?" Destini defiantly asked.

"I didn't say there was anything wrong with it," Dee Dee said, defending herself. "I just remember you bringing out all those photographs you carried around with you in your purse. "This is Dr. Watson Jarrellson

Williams Jr., medical doctor," you would tell people. "He's all grown up and doing well." Dee Dee then held up her hand as if she was showing people a photo. "This is my baby, Phil," you'd tell folks. "He's a big shot attorney up in Washington, D.C. Yes, ma'am, he goes everywhere in the world as a lawyer for the United States government. He's even met several of the presidents and was presented before the Queen of England. My baby is smart. I mean real smart. I am so proud of my baby,'" Dee Dee said, mimicking Destini's voice like a professional impressionist.

Meanwhile, Phil's face kept getting redder and redder, while Destini never let go of his hand, but it didn't stop him from talking.

"What I was going to say, Destini, is that I always knew you were one of the smartest individuals ever," he told her. "No one could challenge me to think more differently nor any more diversely than you during my childhood. I can recall you listening to me jabber away and then you'd ask me if I had considered this or that," he added. "Then, when I would complain about how Daddy and Mama were treating me... and you know what I'm talking about, Destini... you'd say, "Well, honey, there's always a rainbow after a storm. If you just give the Lord a chance, he'll show it to you.""

"And wasn't there always that rainbow?" Destini asked him.

"Well, if there wasn't, just you saying it to me made me think there was," Phil answered. "Anyhow, I figured if I mentioned Chad's name to you, something might register."

"It more than registered, honey," Destini said. "Old man Elwood Ellison Carter, who is still Mr. Stanley and Mrs. Anna Mary's lawyer... well, he got into his cups one afternoon when he came to their house here in Seraph Springs for the weekend. I was workin' for 'em at the time. It wasn't long after Watson and Selena's deaths, and they were goin' through all that stuff with the baby, Mary Selena. Well, Mr. Stanley and Mrs. Anna Mary were late comin' back from a doctor's appointment down in Gainesville. She finally called and asked if I could stay a little later. She wanted me to put out some cheese and crackers, mixed nuts, olives, and a little cocktail tray. She also asked that I be available to get Mr. Carter settled in, and then stay through the cocktail hour. She said they'd be home by six, so I agreed."

"Of course, you agreed," Dee Dee piped up. "You were a good employee."

"Whatever," Destini said, rolling her eyes. "Anyway, after a couple of those big bourbon and water drinks, the old man began to talk some. After the third drink, with me just sittin' there bein' friendly, he began to talk even more. You know, a lot of white folks of his generation always looked upon the help as a fixture... like furniture. We were supposed to be there, do our jobs, and not hear nothin', but I heard a lot. A whole lot. Up until today, though, I never thought too much about what he said that day. He talked about my dead baby, Watson, and all that unfortunate business with Monty Wu. Then, he talked about how addicted Watson was to alcohol and opiates after he came back from China. It was bad, according to Mr. Carter. He told me this young man, Chad, was a clinical counselor who was working with Watson even before he went into that fancy hospital over in the Panhandle. He said the guy even put his practice on hold up in Philadelphia, somewhere near Malvern, I believe, so that he could help with Watson's condition."

Dee Dee's eyes were eager with anticipation, and so were Phil's, as they listened intently to Destini's recollection. Destini needed a break, though, so she took a sip of milk, and then immediately scrunched up her face.

"This sure ain't as good as a cup of coffee, but I'm trying not to drink so much of it until the baby comes," Destini said. "I don't want my baby to be all jittery, you know."

Everyone laughed, and then Dee Dee encouraged her to continue with her story.

"Where was I?" Destini asked. "Oh, yeah, well, just outside of Malvern, Pennsylvania was where Chad and that private detective that the Williams' had hired found Watson. It was someplace way out in the country and there was a caretaker who lived on the property, along with Watson. Mr. Carter said Watson would phone in grocery orders to some man and his wife, and they'd go pick them up for him from the local grocery store and deliver them to Watson."

"Wow, that's odd," Dee Dee said, and Destini nodded before continuing.

"The pharmacy delivered to him, too, or rather, the man who acted as the pharmacy employee delivered his drugs to him. The liquor store delivered to him, as well, on quite a regular basis, from what I was told by Mr. Carter. By the time Chad and that detective man, what was his name? Let me see… Mr. Bascom Phillips, yeah, that was his name. Anyway, by the time they found Watson, he was in real bad shape, both physically and mentally."

"Gee, who knew he was so screwed up?" Dee Dee asked, shaking her head in disbelief.

"Yes, he was bad off," Destini said. "Anyhow, the plot thickens," she added, and she paused a moment to have another sip of milk. "That man who was serving as Watson's drive-in pharmacist overheard enough when he made his last drop-off that he knew where Watson was going for rehab, and get this! He was Monty Wu's cousin, so he stayed in contact with him, prodding him on, knowing Watson's weaknesses. As you can see, he was the only person with whom Watson had any interchange with for about six months, as far as talking face to face."

"Let me stop you for a second," Dee Dee said. "Malvern, Pennsylvania… I've been there. One of Aunt Hattie's roommates from her boarding school days was from Charleston, South Carolina. She had a son who went to some posh boy's boarding school up there, and I remember it was one where the boys could bring their own horses to school. They got to board them in really nice stables right there at the school. Isn't it funny, all I can remember about that trip are those stables, and the fact that handsome young man, Mark... ahhh, Mark Cooper St. Croix was his name. I have never forgotten him," Dee Dee said, smiling, and evidently still smitten with the guy.

"I'll bet!" Destini exclaimed, rolling her eyes at her. "You better not be bringing up his name around your man, Señor Fernandez!"

"Oh, don't be silly. He'd understand," Dee Dee said. "I was young and I was innocent back then."

"You were young, all right," Destini said. "Let's just leave it at that, Dee Dee. You were young."

"Hey!" Dee Dee protested, but then she laughed. "Well, you do have a point," she agreed. "I batted my eyes around that boy until he didn't know what hit him. He loved horses and I swore to him that I had such an interest in them, when, as you know, I really never had that much interest in horses at all. Ohh, those big, blue eyes and that gorgeous blonde hair... Ohh, he was such a handsome thing. By the time he finally kissed me in that smelly old stable, I felt as if I was standing in front of the Tivoli Fountain in Rome."

"Now, now," Destini said. "Let me move on, Miss Romance Novel."

"Oh, you're no fun anymore, Destini," Dee Dee said with a heavy sigh.

"All right, now, where was I?" Destini asked.

"Mr. Clark and Mr. Phillips found Watson," Dee

Dee reminded her.

"Yes, old man Carter told me how the Williams' had chartered a private jet with an attendant physician to fly Watson down to Pensacola. Then, a medical transport company drove him to the rehabilitation center in Panama City. When he arrived, Chad was there. As I said earlier, he left his job up north and was now part of the staff at the rehab center."

"Don't you find that a bit odd that he would do that?" Dee Dee asked, looking at Phil.

"I thought so, until the old man said that Chad had been educated at a boardin' school before he went off to college," Destini explained. "Since he was rarely visited by his parents, he embraced Roman Catholicism with an intense fervor."

"Omigod, fervor? Did you just use a five-dollar word, Destini?" Carl Alvin joked with her.

"I'm just repeatin' what the old man told me," Destini said, and she shot him a dagger. "Anyway, he even considered becomin' a Catholic priest, but because of his maternal grandmother, whom he loved dearly, he decided against it. His maternal grandfather was dead at the time, and the old lady, it seems, told Chad she simply couldn't go on in life without him being close at hand to offer her comfort, support, and guidance, as Chad's mother was her only child. Chad took a course in clinical counseling, according to Mr. Carter and, as he knew of Watson's great neediness, as well as a lot of what happened here with Mr. Gus…" Destini trailed off, closing her eyes for a moment.

Dee Dee, for one, was remembering all those monsters from Destini's past when she saw firsthand what Mr. Gus was doing to young Watson. All those painful feelings sprang to the surface as she was speaking, and they affected her facial expressions. Fresh tears were now streaming down Destini's cheeks, but she pressed on.

"Mr. Carter said there was always talk of Chad havin' more to do with Watson than purely professional consultation, but there was no proof of that," Destini said. "Chad simply realized how fragile Watson was, so he attended to his patient with care and compassion, until that unfortunate business with Monty Wu. Goodness, he said Monty Wu was so jealous thinkin' Chad was involved with Watson that his plans to use Watson for his own selfish purposes had been foiled. That's when he lashed out with a knife and cut Chad's face somethin' awful. According to Mr. Carter, it took some of the best plastic surgeons in the country a long time, and it took many surgeries to get Chad's face to where it was presentable without him lookin' completely deformed."

"That's about the same story I heard directly from Chad," Phil said, shaking his head.

"Old man Carter said it was the decision of his clients, the Williams', to put all the business of Chad, Monty Wu, and others completely behind them," Destini continued. "He said given Chad's dedication to Watson, he wondered if the Williams' were just being churlish, but that was his personal opinion, not a professional one. So, for months after Watson's return to Seraph Springs, Chad had no contact with him."

"Such a shame," Dee Dee said.

"I still remember that old man slurrin' his words that afternoon," Destini said, speaking about the attorney, Mr. Carter. "It was right before Mrs. Anna Mary and Mr. Stanley walked in the door that evenin'. The old man looked at one of Mr. Gus's paintings that was hangin' on the wall in the livin' room... it was the one of the old Adamson house. I remember he mumbled somethin' about voodoo paintings and Chad's father."

Destini was full on crying now, so Dee Dee reached into her purse and grabbed some tissues for her to dry her eyes and blow her nose. In the mean time, most of the other guests had arrived and had taken their seats at the table, while casually chatting with one another.

"Maybe the reason the old man was in such agony that night, as he drank himself into oblivion, is because of somethin' I have never spoken to another soul about... until now," Destini said, ignoring the other guests. "I have kept it in my heart all these years. For some reason, Chad was drivin' the car with Watson and Selena as passengers the night they were killed in that automobile accident in London," she confessed. "He had gone there for another surgery on his face. On one of his first public outings, he was invited by Watson and Selena to go with them to her aunt's country estate just outside London. So, it was Chad who was drivin' the car that foggy night. Watson was in the front seat and Selena was in the back. Chad was seriously injured and spent many more months in the hospital recovering. Several weeks later, when the doctors and his grandmother thought he might be able to handle it, he was told about Watson and Selena's deaths. According to Mr. Carter, Chad was so distraught that he had to be sedated for several days afterward. Once he was released from the hospital, he became a virtual recluse."

There was silence and astonished facial expressions from Dee Dee and Phil. Their mouths were agape and neither one of them seemed to be able to speak.

Just then, Nadine announced that the buffet table was ready and that everyone should go fill their plates. From one end of the table to the other was everything from roast beef sandwiches to fried chicken, and sides of all different kinds. Of course, there were also several of Miss Jewell's dessert cakes to choose from, along with homemade ice cream.

Later, after everyone finished eating, it was time to open presents, and there were a lot of them. Destini received everything imaginable that a new baby would require, including a brand new crib with matching changing table, and an antique baby carriage that Dee Dee had found for her during her travels around the state with her husband.

"My Lord!" Destini said, with a look of astonishment on her face.

"My Lord, indeed," Dee Dee echoed her. "I think

you're all set here, Destini. There's enough stuff here for two babies."

"My Lord!" Destini said again, still with the same strange look on her face, although, a little more intense now.

"What?" Dee Dee finally asked her. "What's wrong, Destini? Did we forget something?"

"It looks like we're gonna have to conclude this baby shower," Destini said. "My water just broke. Dee Dee, you or Phil, or somebody, please get in touch with Matt. He's at the school board office over in Turpricone. You have his cell number, don't you, Dee Dee?"

"Calling right now, honey," Dee Dee said, suddenly calm and cool as a cucumber, taking control of the situation. "Phil, you get Destini out to the car," she added. "We have a baby on the way. Nadine, you need to find someone to take Miss Neva home."

"Done!" Nadine shouted.

A few minutes later, Phil helped Destini up from her chair and they slowly started for the door. After Dee Dee got off the phone with Matt, she grabbed the overnight bag that Destini had been toting around with her for the past month. On the way out to the car, Dee Dee phoned Duke and Essie, Destini's brother and sister-in-law, who weren't able to come to the baby shower. On her heels were Carl Alvin, Wanda Faye and Nadine, all ready to accompany Destini to the hospital.

"Gee, isn't today Good Friday?" Dee Dee asked Nadine out of the blue.

Before Nadine could answer, Destini suddenly stopped in her tracks, nearly causing a pileup of people.

"Did y'all hear that?" Destini asked.

"Hear what?" Dee Dee asked her.

"It was Mama Tee!" she squealed with delight. "I heard her plain as day! She said Queenie, with God nothing is impossible!"

"Oh, my God!" Dee Dee shrieked, about to burst into tears. "Mama Tee spoke to me! Did you hear that, everyone? Mama Tee talked to me!"

Chapter 13

The tip of the iceberg

The small maternity ward waiting room at Campbell Community Hospital was packed wall to wall with Destini's friends and family. Even though her amniotic sac had broken, Destini's baby girl was being very stubborn about wanting to leave the comfort of her mother's womb.

"Do you know it's been close to twenty-seven hours since we got here?" Carl Alvin asked, followed by a big, mouthy yawn. "What the heck is that woman doing in there? Is she waiting for Christmas to have this baby, or what?"

"I think she's waiting for Easter," Dee Dee chimed in, laughing, not really knowing how right she might be. "I'm with you, though, Carl Alvin. I wish she'd hurry up. I would love to go home and take a shower."

"Me, too," Nadine said. "I'm starting to stink."

Just then, Duke and Essie arrived with Pastor Jackson and his wife from Mt. Nebo A.M.E., Destini's home church.

"Sorry, no baby yet," Carl Alvin nonchalantly mumbled, as they sat down.

Wanda Faye, Nadine and Dee Dee were all sitting in a row on one side of the room, while Matt, of course, was wearing out the carpet as he paced the floor. He had told Destini from the very beginning that he didn't want to be in the delivery room with her when she had the baby and she never fought him on it.

Just then, a very young Dr. Celia Campbell emerged in the doorway. She was the great-granddaughter of Campbell County's medical pioneer, the late Dr. Sidney J. Campbell, who was one of the most revered citizens of the area.

"Wanda Faye, Nadine, and you, too, Dee Dee!" Celia called out from the doorway. "Destini is asking for you girls now. Will you come with me, please?"

"Oh, wow! Is this it?" Dee Dee asked her. "Is she having the baby now?"

"Any minute," Celia said, smiling. "Matt, Destini said you could come, too, if you'd like."

"If you don't mind, I think I'll just stay here," he said, looking as if he was about to faint.

"You don't know what you're missing, Matt," Dee Dee teased him, and then she winked at him right before she slipped out the door.

The girls followed Celia down the corridor to where Destini was and they were immediately met at the door by a nurse.

"Please put these on before you go inside," she told the girls, pointing to a stack of green medical gowns and white surgical masks that were laid out on a table just outside the door to the labor room.

"I'll be back in a few minutes," Celia told the nurse, and she hurried down the corridor to the nurse's station.

Wanda Faye stepped into the room first and walked over to where Destini lay atop one of the four beds that were in the room. For the moment, there were no other women in labor, so they had the entire room to themselves.

"How's it going, honey?" Wanda Faye asked her, and then she grasped Destini's hand in hers. "You look a little tired."

"I've had better days, old friend," Destini said. "Business is about to pick up, though, or so the doctor says. I have waited, you see."

"Waited for what?" Dee Dee asked. "Honey, we've all been waiting for this baby for well over twenty-four hours now."

"What time is it, Dee Dee?" Destini asked her.

"It's almost midnight. In six more minutes it will be Easter Day," Dee Dee said, and then she caught her breath.

All three girls stared at each other with a look of shock on their faces, and then all eyes were trained on Destini.

"Could one of y'all call for Dr. Campbell, please?" Destini asked much too calmly.

As if she heard Destini's request, Celia entered the room, all decked out in her own gown and mask. She took one look at Destini's face, lifted the bed sheet to check her dilation, and said, "It's time, Destini. Are you ready?"

Destini answered with a loud shriek and she squeezed Wanda Faye's hand so hard that her fingernails broke through the skin of Wanda Faye's palm. It was all Wanda Faye could do not to let loose with a shriek of her own, judging by her facial expression. There was barely enough time to wheel Destini into the delivery room, but minutes later, after some grueling pushes on Destini's part, the joyous first cries from the baby's healthy lungs filled the room.

At eleven minutes after midnight on Easter morning, with her three best friends surrounding her, Destini gave birth to a beautiful, bouncing baby girl, weighing in at eight pounds, seven-and-a-half ounces.

A short time later, once mother and daughter were cleaned up, Matt came in to be introduced to his daughter. Destini proudly handed the little bundle of joy to her husband, who seemed reluctant and extremely nervous at first. As he gently held her, though, his face lit up, and then he kissed his daughter's forehead.

"My beautiful Easter Lily," he said, smiling.

"That's what she'll be called," Destini announced.

"How's that, honey?" Dee Dee asked her, raising her eyebrows. "I thought you had already decided to call her Destiny with a "Y".

"I changed my mind," Destini said. "It woulda been too confusin'. Besides, that baby died, remember? So, she will be called Lillian Delphine Abamu… Lily for short."

"Ohhh… how sweet of you, Destini," Dee Dee said, as her eyes filled with tears.

"Lillian, in honor of Mama Tee, and Delphine for your middle name, Miss Dee Dee," Destini explained.

Essie and Duke had just entered the room and

Essie exclaimed, "Lord have mercy! This poor chil' won't ever be called just plain ol' Lily. You know that now, don't you, Miss Destini? From now on, she's gonna be Lily Dee," she added, and then she took the baby from Matt's arms.

Tears were streaming down Dee Dee's cheeks now, as she repeated the name Lily Dee over and over.

"Thank you, honey," she said to Destini. "Thank you so very much," she added, before kissing Destini's cheek. "I think I shall go outside now and wait for Ricardo on one of the benches out there. He's supposed to be here in just a few minutes. I will see you in a little bit." To Nadine and Wanda Faye, she said, "You know, y'all have called me Queenie since I can remember because you claimed I was always directing you. Well, I'm about to do it again. It's time for us to give the rest of this family some time together. I see through the glass over there that Phil and Carl Alvin are champing at the bit to get in here, so they can oooh and aaah over this baby, too. Miss Essie, you let us know when we should come back, okay?"

"Essie ain't got a say!" Destini protested. "I will have the say as to who comes in here!"

"Begging your pardon, Destini, but I do got a say," Essie corrected her. "Dee Dee, you go on and meet up with your husband. Take Wanda Faye and Nadine with you, and tell Carl Alvin and Phil to come on in. Bye, now, y'all, and we'll see you later. Boys, y'all come on in now!" she yelled. "Queenie on her way out!"

A woman of few words, Essie was definitely heard

and understood when she spoke. Dee Dee, though, had to have the last word, verbalized or not, and she mouthed to Destini and Matt, "See you later."

"Bye, Queenie… bye, Queenie…" Essie trailed off.

When Carl Alvin and Phil walked into the room, Destini motioned them over to look at her new baby.

"A gift from God," Phil said. "A gift from God, and no one deserves it more than you and Matt."

"Carl Alvin, you're the owner of Camp EZ, you and Dee Dee, that is, but this new mama has a request," Destini piped up.

"You name it, honey," Carl Alvin told her.

"I want you to ease on back to the Camp, take you a good, long rest, take a shower, and then come back to me with some fried catfish, some grits and coleslaw… oh, and some hushpuppies. Oh, and I want some of Miss Jewell's cake, too."

"Sure, when do you want it? Today or tomorrow?"

"I want it tonight for supper," she ordered him, and everyone had a good laugh. "Bring a cake or two for the doctor, the nurses and all the staff up here, too. They all been so good to me. I know Miss Jewell's been busy bakin' lots of cakes, and I want these folks to enjoy some of it."

About that time, the telephone rang in Destini's room and she whispered to everyone, "Guess who?" and they all laughed, knowing it had to be Dee Dee.

Destini put the phone on speaker, but soon had to turn the volume down, as Dee Dee put forth as only Dee Dee could.

"Now, I'm gonna tell you something, Destini!" she started quite loudly. "Any of your friends can bring you pretty clothes for your baby's trip home, and even first day and second day outfits, but remember one thing! I am providing the christening gown for Lily Dee! Actually, I guess I should say Carl Alvin and I are providing it, since the gown was ours and it hasn't been used since!"

Dee Dee stopped ranting and everyone in the room could hear her huge intake of breath. She seemed to have calmed down, as her voice then returned to normal.

"By the way, Destini, me and the girls have decided to take your baby shower stuff to your home and get it all set up for you, since you so rudely interrupted our little shindig," Dee Dee teased her.

"I can't wait," Destini said. "I should be home tomorrow, I think."

"Sounds good," Dee Dee said. "I can't believe you put me on speaker phone, Destini. Anyway, I'm out in the parking lot waiting for Ricardo. Nadine and Wanda Faye went home to shower and change, which is what I would like to do. First, though, I would like to see Carl Alvin and Phil, if you could send them out here for a minute, please. Let me say again…"

"We understand, Dee Dee!" Destini shouted, and then she and the others in the room had a good laugh. "Besides, I haven't even thought that far ahead to the christening. I love you and I'll talk to you soon," she added, as she tried to subdue her laughter. "Carl Alvin and Phil, I think you boys better get on out there. She's waitin' on ya."

"Oh! One more thing!" Dee Dee shouted. "You still there, Destini?"

"I'm still here," Destini said, shaking her head.

"Since you and Matt will be at the Camp with your new baby and you'll be busy for a while, guess who's going to host Lily Dee's christening luncheon for you?" Dee Dee asked her.

"I can't imagine," Destini said. "Let me guess… Miss Jewell? Sister Velma? Essie, over at the House of Prayer fellowship hall?"

"Good guesses, honey, but no cigar," Dee Dee told her. "No, ma'am, it will be Anna Mary Jarrellson Williams. It will be held at the Jarrellson ancestral home on the Suwannee in her solarium dining room that looks out across the river."

"Get the hell out of town!" Destini guffawed.

"I'm dead serious!" Dee Dee told her. "I damn near fell out of my chair when she phoned and insisted on doing this. You know darned well it will be perfection carried out to the "nth" degree, too."

"Well, that's mighty kind of her," Destini said, although her voice sounded skeptical. "It will probably be the first time ever that her fine china and sterling silverware that she keeps holed up at Continental Planters Bank will ever have African lips touch any of it. Plenty of African hands have washed those dishes and that silverware, including mine, but in the nearly two-hundred years of them having that fancy stuff, I'll be the first black woman to actually eat off of it. Kinda makes me feel like a Rosa Parks or something," she added, with a crooked grin.

"Well, you are correct there, but, honey, don't get too high up on your moral high horse just yet," Dee Dee warned her. "I would say that you, Matt, and Lily Dee being the guests of honor for the christening luncheon will have more to do with that forty acres of land you own that borders Watson Estates. It's right there on the river and out of any flood zones, and I'm sure they'd like to see it brought in under their development umbrella."

"Dee Dee, you're not the only one who's thought about that," Destini said. "I thought about it long ago when they originally put that development where it is. Mr. Stanley and Mrs. Anna Mary started gettin' extra nicey-nice with me, but here's the thing, Dee Dee. There's a sliver of land, about seven acres I'd guess, between their land and mine that belongs to that man… I think he's from south Florida. You know… that guy who lives in that old camper. He works at the library and also teaches two courses in botany at the university over in Tallahassee. I believe his name is Dr. Curtis Osborne."

"Oh, that's right. I forgot about him," Dee Dee said, lying through her teeth, as she knew darned well who the man was.

"When he's not cleaned up, he is some boogery looking man with that unruly, red, curly hair and them wild lookin' eyes," Destini said. "He's owned that piece of property for about twenty years or so. If you can believe this, he bought it from Miss Aggie Campbell. Actually, some folks say she done flat out give it to him."

"Okay, enough chit-chat," Dee Dee abruptly stopped her. "You need some rest, honey, so tell the boys to come out to my car. I decided to wait here for Ricardo instead of on that hard bench by the hospital entrance."

"Okay, Dee Dee, they're on their way," Destini said, and the two women hung up.

When Carl Alvin and Phil made it out to Dee Dee's SUV, they noticed her head was resting against the steering wheel, as if she'd fallen asleep or something. When she heard them talking, she lifted her head

"Good Lord, Dee Dee," Carl Alvin gasped when he saw her face.

Dee Dee wasn't just crying, she was weeping, which was something she rarely did, at least not in public. Carl Alvin immediately hopped in the front passenger seat and put his arm around her to comfort her.

"Why was I so stupid to say that about the christening gown, knowing Bunnye was also christened in it?" Dee Dee asked through her sobs.

"For once in your life, Dee Dee, I want you to listen to me," Carl Alvin told her. "I know it's usually the other way around, but this time you need to listen to me. You are so happy for Destini and Matt and they both know it. We all know it. Hell, you were so happy that you bought out the damned florist and had it sent to her room. You were over the top, girl!"

"I guess I was, huh?" Dee Dee replied, as her face broke into a smirk.

"All you did with this christening gown business was to share something that was precious to you," Carl Alvin went on. "Trust me, Destini knows that, and I'm certain she doesn't fault you for anything."

"Are you sure?" she asked, still sobbing.

"Yes, I am absolutely sure," Carl Alvin told her, as he held her tight. "Now, here," he said, and he whipped out his handkerchief. "You're getting all that gooey snot all over my brand new shirt."

During this exchange, Phil had hopped into the backseat.

"Guess what I have in this tote bag," he prodded the two of them, and then he pulled out three Styrofoam cups and a big bottle of Kentucky bourbon. "Let's drink a toast to Lily Dee and to happy times for Destini and her family."

"Damn you're good, Phil," Dee Dee said, and she reached around and pulled him toward her, so she could plant a kiss on his cheek, which left a well defined lipstick print.

After their first toast ended, Ricardo arrived. He had pulled into the lot and was parking his car right beside them. Carl Alvin hopped out and got into the back seat with Phil. By the time Ricardo got into the front seat, Dee Dee had already fixed her face and spritzed on a little perfume. Then, she gave her husband a big, juicy kiss on the lips. Phil was Johnny-on-the-spot and had already poured Ricardo a drink, after which everyone toasted the new baby again.

"We need to talk," Dee Dee then blurted out. "We *all* need to talk. Tomorrow afternoon, Judge Wesson is coming out to the Camp to see me and Carl Alvin. I need you there with me, too, Ricardo," she added. "Phil, I want you there, as well. It's going to be an emotional day. The judge is bringing his nephew, St. John Culpepper."

"St. John Culpepper?" Ricardo asked, clearly amused. "Now, that is some kind of name," he added, and he laughed a little too hard.

"Ricardo, honey, I love your name, but with a name like Ricardo most folks around here have decided to simply call you Rick, so I'd leave that one alone," Dee Dee reminded him.

"Understood, sweetheart," he said, scrunching up his face, and then he turned to Phil with his arm outstretched, adding, "Hey, hit me again, willya?"

"Comin' right up," Phil said, and he poured him another shot of booze.

"Just so you know, Ricardo, St. John's mama was sanctified, religious, and she loved the Gospel according to Saint John," Dee Dee explained. "She died giving birth to that baby, and so his daddy, Mr. Elbert Culpepper, decided to name him St. John."

"In this part of the world, there's a story behind everything," Carl Alvin told Ricardo.

"I can see that," Ricardo said, chuckling.

"Anyway, I need you guys there with me for moral support," Dee Dee told the three men.

"You need support, Dee Dee?" Carl Alvin asked, laughing.

"Yes, by God, I do need support," she sternly replied. "As per Judge Wesson's request, I fished out all of Uncle Hamp's old notebooks that he kept about a particular murder case in this county. I was supposed to drop them off at his house the other day, but I needed time to make copies of everything first, so I suggested he come by Camp EZ tomorrow," she explained.

"That reminds me... I never got back to him either," Carl Alvin interrupted her.

"Well, you can talk to him tomorrow, Carl Alvin," Dee Dee said. "Anyway, all of this murder stuff happened about twenty five years ago and the case was never solved. Uncle Hamp kept every single newspaper clipping, and every letter written to him by some guy from the state of Washington, who came here to do some investigative journalism on the matter," she continued. "To make a long story short, over a period of about a year-and-a-half, four young, male hitchhikers is what they called them, but they weren't... anyway, whatever they were, these guys were between the ages of seventeen and twenty-five, and they went missing and were never found."

"Oh, yeah, I remember hearing about that," Phil said, nodding his head.

"One of those boys did occasional odd jobs for a few folks around town, including the judge," Dee Dee went on. "It was said that some of those young boys worked for Gus for a while over where that crazy Dr. Curtis Osborne lives now. You know... on that little piece of land he got from Miss Aggie. She, by the way, was once engaged to the late Spencer Augustus Jarrellson, in case you didn't know, but the Jarrellson family didn't approve of her."

"Imagine that," Carl Alvin jokingly interjected.

"Well, Miss Aggie kept that piece of land that abuts up to Gus's old property," Dee Dee continued. "It seems Gus never had the nerve or the inclination to ask her to sell it, but the Jarrellson Trust did through their attorney, Ellwood Ellison Carter over in Jacksonville. Oh, the money they offered," Dee Dee said, shaking her head. "It was fifty... a hundred times what the land was worth, but she would never sell it. For some godforsaken reason, Miss Aggie had an interest in a subterranean cave on the property, the only one anyone knows of on this part of the Suwannee. So, she asked around and heard about this Dr. Curtis Osborne from that little man... you know, that nice, handsome looking guy. Gosh, if he hadn't been married... oh, well..."

"Who are you talking about, Dee Dee?" Carl Alvin asked.

"I'm talking about Mr. Tate "Sonny Boy" Esmerian," she said. "My God, that boy could dance. His father, Mr. Tate Sr., was the CEO of Florida-Georgia Timber and Pulp Company. He wasn't bad looking, either, but Sonny Boy was some kind of handsome. If he had been taller, he would have been male model material, and that is the truth."

"Geez, Dee Dee, quit drooling," Carl Alvin teased her. "For godsakes, your husband's sitting right there."

"That's okay," Ricardo said. "It's just Dee Dee being Dee Dee."

"Anyhow, as handsome as he was, Sonny Boy was somewhat of a nerd," Dee Dee continued. "He was smart when it came to technology, though. It seems he and his daddy never got along. I believe the family came here from up north, someplace close to Philadelphia where his mother's father was a major banker. They lived out on the Main Line, Villanova, and she was a sophomore at Bryn Mawr College. Meanwhile, his father's family owned a chain of pharmacies. They literally came to this country with nothing but the clothes on their backs, but they were both brilliant and they worked hard. Both families, I am told, had summer homes near Cape May on the Jersey Shore and so they more or less grew up together. They didn't socialize there or in the city, however… two different worlds, you know… but someplace on the beach or in town or somewhere, Sonny Boy's parents became friendly with one another."

"How do you know all of this stuff?" Ricardo asked her.

"I just do," Dee Dee said, with a wicked little grin. "So… Sonny Boy's father was pursuing a degree in forestry and forest management, and later he got a graduate degree from the University of Georgia. That was when Sonny Boy's mama discovered she was going to have a baby... little Sonny Boy. The Main Line family, though, with a pedigree longer than the River Nile, completely turned their backs on her. So, she and Sonny Boy's dad wound up having a rough time of it. Consequently, the father wound up having a rough time with Sonny Boy. He resented the boy, actually, and he wasn't kind to him at all. Sonny Boy, I guess, internalized all of that hatred by blaming his father for not providing a more promising future for him. The Main Line family, I am told, eventually gave Sonny Boy's mother an annuity. It was a hefty one with an agreement that she would never show her face anywhere near Villanova or Cape May ever again. They said they never wanted to lay eyes on her, her husband, nor any of her children, who, other than the annuity she would receive, would be considered per stirpes by the family."

"What in the hell are per stirpes?" Carl Alvin asked. "It sounds like a damn disease or something."

"Oh, for goodness' sake, Carl Alvin. You need to learn some ten dollar words every once in a while," Dee Dee chastised him. "A per stirpe is a term used in wills to describe how property should be distributed when a beneficiary who has children dies before the will maker."

"Oh... well, you could have just said that in the first place," he told her.

"Whatever," she said. "So, one day, Sonny Boy decides to go see his grandparents. Don't ask me why, but he did. He'd been drafted into the military and was in the area at a naval station in Cape May. Sonny Boy, being who he was, never made it past the foyer. He later told some of his friends that the butler came to the door and said the family did not wish to receive him. Of course, he was hurt, but he never let on to anyone."

"I guess his mother never told him that she was banished, eh?" Ricardo asked.

"Evidently," Dee Dee said. "Anyway, Sonny Boy was never much of a people person, but he was great with the ladies. He never stuck with one, though, until he found this little Melanie Wilkes type girl that he later married. She was a real mousy type and gave birth to three children in four years time! Can you believe that?"

"Hey, Ricardo, pass me that bottle," Carl Alvin said. "It looks like your wife is going to be talking for a while," he added, laughing.

"Sure thing," Ricardo said, and he handed him the bottle of bourbon, but not before refilling his own cup.

Dee Dee shot them both daggers, but she continued anyway.

"Sonny Boy and his wife were rarely seen together in public," she went on. "He did the grocery shopping, and his mother's trust fund helped send the children to boarding school. I am told he could verbally browbeat her into submission, and that during the time he was director of a technology company, he had a number of female acquaintances. He viewed any opportunity as a step up the ladder, and his main mantra was "next". He never looked back on anything, only forward. He really was quite brilliant. You have to give him that, and he got a lot accomplished. He just wasn't the type you wanted to bring to a cocktail party, unless you just wanted to look at him."

"There's nothing wrong with that," Carl Alvin piped up.

"Of course, you'd say that, Carl Alvin," Dee Dee said, laughing. "Anyway, Sonny Boy always had a strange kind of communication with people who were different, if you will. I don't know this for certain, but I heard that his conversations with Chad, and later Curtis, were difficult to understand. You see, there was a rumor that Sonny Boy was destined to become a naval officer, but he was suddenly stricken with liver cancer and the medical prognosis wasn't good. At that point in time, he was asked to leave the armed services, and so he finished his undergraduate and graduate degrees in record time. Then, he went to work for an international technological company. His people skills hadn't improved, though, so the company sent him to professional development sessions on how to get along well with others. It was through his acquaintance with Miss Aggie, who evidently found Sonny Boy charming, that the two of them developed a friendship of sorts. In fact, Miss Aggie even found a liver donor for him, as the disease was really beginning to wear him down. I hear he's doing fine now."

"This is getting harder and harder to follow," Ricardo said. "Are you almost done?"

"Yes, I'm almost done," Dee Dee said, giving him the evil eye. "Where was I? Oh... Miss Aggie introduced Sonny Boy to Curtis, who was presenting one of those "Eating Healthy" programs at a nutrition dinner that was hosted by the local drug store. Sonny Boy was co-chair of that group, along with Valerie Rose Teeter, who shared her story about being bullied and being called the Blue Whale in high school. Now, she's a fitness guru, although, to see her in a pair of tights... well, I digress."

"Why, Dee Dee Fernandez, you have no room to talk," Carl Alvin teased her. "Have you looked at your behind..."

"Carl Alvin, I'm gonna smack you," she said. "I'm in great shape still. More than I can say about you."

"Hrmpph," Carl Alvin grunted.

"Anyway, this Valerie woman married a man who had this diet frozen pizza thing for weight loss and he sold millions of them to folks all over the Southeast. The two of them lobbed off about two-hundred pounds altogether. They're not any prettier, but they're thinner. Valerie is a sweet thing, though. I always liked her, but I'm getting way off track."

"Ya think?" Carl Alvin asked, and Dee Dee again gave him a look to kill.

"It seems that Sonny Boy and Curtis shared a passion for raising goldfish and rare Japanese koi," Dee Dee continued. "They had a number of ponds dug on Curtis's property and they spent a lot of time devoted to their hobby. The ponds are fed by springs, you know, and they're all over the property."

"I thought you were almost done," Ricardo said, as he glanced at his watch.

"I am, I am," Dee Dee said. "Just stay with me here. Anyway, I heard some of those fish sold for premium prices all over the country. With Sonny Boy's stellar computer skills, he created a website to sell the fish. It seems their little side enterprise had become quite lucrative. They never had too many ponds, nor did they raise a huge number of fish, but their clientele was select."

"That's all well and good, but what does any of this have to do with the missing boys?" Carl Alvin asked.

"Well, it seems that one day, while taking a break, they went into an old storage shed that was built by Miss Aggie," Dee Dee went on. "There, in an unlocked safe, they found numerous newspaper articles going back years about those four hitchhikers and even further back, there were diaries… diaries written when Miss Aggie would visit with Gus at his studio. The diaries seemed to reveal a good bit about what could have occurred. It was rumored that Curtis and Sonny Boy decided to turn them over to the State Archives who, after reading them, turned the diaries over to the proper state and federal authorities. No one knows what's going on with the case right now, but what we do know is that there is an interest in Uncle Hamp's notebooks."

"Gee, honey, I can't wait until tomorrow," Ricardo said. "Sounds like we've got a real mystery on our hands."

"Ya think?" she asked, rolling her eyes.

"I just hope I can keep up," Ricardo said with a chuckle.

"Yeah, me, too, Dee Dee," Carl Alvin said. "That was a lotta stuff you just threw at us."

"I think this is just the beginning," Dee Dee said. "I don't like using clichés, but I do believe this is just the tip of the iceberg, if you know what I mean."

Chapter 14

The invitation

Chad pulled into the parking lot of a quaint, unassuming barbecue restaurant outside of Elsberry, a small, mainly rural town about seventy miles south of Seraph Springs. He rarely traveled too far from the comfort of his home, but Phil had been adamant that he needed to meet with him and that it needed to be someplace away from Campbell County.

Reluctantly, Chad had endured the hour-and-a-half trip down the interstate in his Range Rover. He was dressed in blue jeans, a dark red polo shirt, and a Tractor Supply ball cap pulled down low on his forehead. Upon entering the restaurant, he immediately spotted Phil at a corner table near the back of the establishment, since there were just a handful of patrons eating lunch at the moment.

Phil motioned him over to where he was sitting with Curtis, whom Chad had met only briefly just a few weeks ago. It had been late in the afternoon when the two of them converged on each other as they traveled in opposite directions in their kayaks on the Suwannee River. They exchanged the usual introductions and pleasantries, and then paddled on their separate ways.

Both men stood up as Chad approached and then they all shook hands, as Phil re-introduced Chad to Curtis.

"Yes, Dr. Osborne, I recall we met on the river not too terribly long ago," Chad said, and they all sat down.

"Yes, we did, and please, call me Curtis. Just don't call me that crazy professor like some folks do," he added with a chuckle. "I really do enjoy getting out on the river, especially this time of year. It's so beautiful and serene that it relaxes my mind," he added.

"It certainly is beautiful," Chad agreed. "I can identify with that relaxation part myself. I love the river, mostly for that reason. It's one of the best mental therapies in the world. I can spend a couple of hours along the Suwannee and I come back feeling refreshed and renewed. It gives me very positive vibes about myself and the world at large."

"I can identify with that, too," Phil said. "I never dreamed when I left my job in Washington D.C. that I would make the decision to come back to Campbell County to live."

"What made you decide?" Chad asked.

"Well, my childhood nanny and best friend in the whole world, who loved me then and still loves me now, by the way, would never forgive me if I hadn't come back."

"Who would that be?" Chad asked.

"Destini Wilson Abamu," Phil said. "She owns part of the Brayerford properties now."

"I haven't met her, but I've seen photos of her in the local newspaper," Chad said. "She's very active with the Margot Smith Center for Women, isn't she?"

"Oh, yes, Chad, that she is," Phil said, and then he

turned to Curtis. "I don't know if you know it or not, but she owns the property just down the river from you where Wilson Creek runs down into the river."

"*Does* she now?" Curtis asked, raising his eyebrows. "That's quite interesting. In the past, I've tried walking up on that property, just to have a look around, you know, but I could never get past all those barbed wire fences and all the posted trespassing signs."

Phil chuckled, and said, "Yes, well, that's Destini for you. I believe she had those fences put up about a month or so after the reading of Hamp Brayerford's will where he left her all that land, so that she would know exactly where her property ended and yours began. Right behind her, though, the land lines do a funny zigzag that's a little hard to figure out. The rest of that land is owned by the Jarrellson Trust."

"As in Anna Mary Jarrellson?" Curtis asked.

"The very same," Phil said. "Only it's Anna Mary Jarrellson Williams now."

"Oh, okay. I knew her uncle quite well," Curtis said.

"Wow, you knew her uncle, Gus?" Phil asked, seeming surprised.

"I'm sorry, who?" Curtis asked.

"Her uncle, Gus Jarrellson," Phil repeated. "I'm sorry... perhaps you knew him as Spencer Augustus Jarrellson."

"Ahh, that's funny," Curtis said. "I only knew him as Mr. Jarrellson. I never knew his full name until I got to know Miss Aggie Campbell. I didn't know folks referred to him as Gus, though, until now. I met Miss Aggie at a water management meeting once and we talked for a bit. She invited me to her little piece of heaven, as she called it, and we became good friends. She told me she and Mr. Jarrellson had been life-long friends. She said he even deeded her the seven acres of land where I now live. She was quite a lady, that Miss Aggie."

"She was that… a great beauty in her time, according to Destini's grandmother, Mama Tee," Phil said. "Excuse me, the late Lillian Tecola Wilson."

"How in the world did they come up with Mama Tee out of Lillian Tecola Wilson?" Curtis asked.

"You know what? I never asked," Phil said, chuckling. "One of these days I'll be sure to ask Destini," he added, and he smiled. "Anyway, Miss Aggie and Gus had evidently been an item when they were younger. It was serious there for a while… a bit too serious for the Jarrellson family, evidently, according to Mama Tee. The county might be named after the Campbells, but the Jarrellsons considered themselves kind of… how shall I put this? Kind of the royal family of this area."

"Oh, I can see that," Curtis said, nodding his head.

"How do you mean?" Chad piped up. "I knew Anna Mary and Stanley's son, Watson, quite well. He spoke about them all the time, but I didn't notice any of that uppity attitude in Watson… never, in fact."

"You wouldn't have, Chad," Phil said. "He was as down to earth and genuine as they come, but he was flawed…"

Before Phil could say anything further, Chad held up his hand.

"Say no more," Chad told him. "You know, his parents never once told Watson that I tried calling him several times after he came back home here. They never once mentioned that I was in the car when Watson and his wife were killed, either. They never once…"

"Acknowledged you were living at all?" Phil asked, filling in the blanks for him.

"No, they never acknowledged me in the least," Chad said, clearly still holding a grudge against Anna Mary and Stanley.

"Don't feel you are in exclusive company," Curtis said. "They have never once acknowledged me, either. I've never been invited into that big home of theirs… not one time. They never acknowledged my parents, either, other than when my father had to sign papers with them for the sale of a large portion of their mineral rights. Stanley and Anna Mary are a closed corporation, as far as I can see. Nobody gets inside."

"You got that right," Phil said. "Ohh, they visit occasionally with their attorney, Mr. Carter and his wife over in Jacksonville. Then, every other year, they visit with an old maid aunt that Stanley has up in the New England area for about three days, but that's about it. Rumor has it that the only reason they go up to his aunt's place is because she has some antique furniture that they want. You know… museum quality things, but the Williams' are mostly low key and they try not to draw attention to themselves."

"Except for the water that flows through their property that looks like a damned glow stick sometimes," Chad interjected. "I know kids hang out around that area and do ecstasy, you know… that hallucinatory drug. I wonder… do you think pills like that could cause the water to glow in the dark in Wilson Creek?"

"No, I don't think so," Phil said, shaking his head.

"Do you think the water is full of radioactivity?" Chad asked. "Do you think possibly there's something in those woods that could be poisoning the water?"

"Yes, I think there could be, but I have no proof," Phil told him.

"If you ask me, I think someone in that royal Jarrellson family is up to no good, and whatever it is, they have become addicted to doing it," Chad suggested. "I think it's time somebody did a little investigating. They're probably doing much greater damage to the environment here in this town than the limestone company, Feed the World Organics, or anyone else could possibly do, if my hypothesis about what's there is true," he added. "In fact, I think they could potentially be doing more damage than all that human waste South Georgia flushes down the Withlacoochee River, to which the government is turning a blind eye, mind you. I think the Jarrellsons would gladly let anyone believe it was any one of those other entities causing major problems with the water, and not them and whatever it is they're up to."

"My goodness, it certainly sounds like something's going on," Curtis said, shaking his head. "My property is a bit farther up the river from Wilson Creek, so I hope I'm in the clear. When I first came here, I remember I would see all kinds of wildlife hanging around my place, but it's a totally different story now. All I've seen lately back in the woodsy area are a few white-tailed deer with tumors all over their skin. They're dying from a sickness or something... rabbits, too. It's really kind of eerie."

"Yes, isn't it?" Chad rhetorically asked. "You have to wonder, don't you, why folks would go to so much trouble to protect such a small piece of property. Also, why aren't the Jarrellsons using their own property to put their proposed memorial park for Watson and his wife? Goodness knows they have enough vacant land. Why do they need to buy Destini's property? I find that very odd."

"Yes, I do, too," Phil said. "Before we talk ourselves to death, though, we should probably order. The waitress has been by here three times already," he added with a chuckle, and then he motioned the young lady over to the table.

All three men ordered the rib special and sweet iced tea, since the waitress suggested it was the best iced tea in town. After she poured the tea, she told them it would be a few minutes before the ribs were brought out.

Chad, who was born and raised in the New

England part of the country, took one sip of his tea and said, "Oh, wow, that will run your glucose right on up there, now, won't it? Oh, my! Sweet!" he added, scrunching up his face.

"It's the regional favorite," Curtis said, laughing, as he sipped on his.

"Nice, big slices of fresh lemon, too," Phil added.

Just minutes later, the waitress set down an appetizer sampler tray on their table, which surprised everyone.

"I'm sorry, but we didn't order this," Phil told her.

"I know," the waitress said, smiling. "I don't know her name, sir, but she is without a doubt one of the most charming and funny ladies I have ever met, and boy, is she beautiful… glamorous, actually," she added. "She said to tell Little Phil that this appetizer was from the one and only."

"Really?" Phil asked, clearly stunned.

Phil couldn't see behind him, but soon there were two soft arms reaching around his neck, and then a pair of lips placed a big, juicy kiss on his cheek. An unmistakable voice then whispered loud enough that everyone at the table could hear.

"My God, what a handsome man you are," the sultry voice said. "You didn't tell me this was a foursome. All that "My God'ing" you were doing last night, and now this. Well, it looks like a good time to me, and you know my motto, honey. I am not here for a long time. I am here for a good time."

Curtis and Chad were dumbfounded and both their

faces turned a bright shade of pink at the woman's brazenness, but not Phil's.

He merely said, "Dr. Curtis Osborne, Mr. Chadwick Clark, may I introduce to you Miss North Central Florida. The only girl to wear the crown forever. Seriously! She was really crowned that! She was also Miss Florida, and first runner-up in the Miss America pageant," he explained.

Dee Dee smiled wide and said, "All true, my darling, and if the judges that year had not been going for talent like that little pudding-faced thing from Kansas who beat me... oh, she was so sweet and she had that cute little lisp. I juth love America and I want world peath, she told the crowd."

Phil was laughing now, and he said, "Yes, I recall that girl. We were all watching the show on TV. I always meant to ask you, Dee Dee. Did that girl really trip after she was crowned, or did you push her?"

"Why, Phil Brainard, I do declare. You know I am a lady. Nevuh would I *evuh* do such a thing," she replied, feigning hurt feelings in her best and most exaggerated Southern accent.

"Gentlemen, this is Mrs. Dee Dee Wilson Fernandez," Phil proudly said. "Mrs. Ricardo Luis Fernandez, femme fatale of the Suwannee Shore."

Dee Dee extended her hand to both Chad and Curtis, and said, "Very nice to meet you gentlemen. As you can see, I am taken, but if I weren't... my, oh, my, such handsome gentlemen. Phil, aren't you going to offer me a chair? Ask me to join you?"

"Would it matter if I didn't?" he jokingly shot back at her. "I guess you eavesdropped when I was on the phone with Chad the other day, huh? Those lynx ears of yours perked right up, I'm sure."

"Well, it was really more the professor here that interested me, Phil," Dee Dee said. "So intelligent and eccentric," she added, as Curtis's face turned a bright red. "But you're right, Mr. Chadwick Clark," she swooned. "Honey, you know you make the blood pressure of many matrons in Campbell County rise to dizzying heights when you're out jogging along River Road in the mornings with no shirt on and that gold bracelet glistening in the early morning sun. As for me, it's not the bracelet I've been observing. It's the way you run, Mr. Clark. You are so gifted. Truly. Did you ever do any exotic dancing? You could have, you know."

Dee Dee was on a roll, batting her eyelashes at him, until Phil cleared his throat and gave her that look of his that meant she was about to cross the line of decency.

"Okay, let's move along," Dee Dee said. "Professor, I've been hoping to meet you for a long while. Indeed, I have. Ever since I heard cousin Aggie speak about you."

Curtis nearly spit out his iced tea. "She spoke about me?" he asked, as he wiped his mouth with his napkin.

"Well, of course, Professuh," Dee Dee said, with all the southern charm she could muster. "Actually, she didn't have to tell me about you. No, sir. You have more facial hair now and you have aged very well, I must say. You were always the most handsome thing with those beautiful blue eyes of yours. You may not recall the incident, but I do. It was at the Blue Hole years ago near the Suwannee River during the Florida Folk Festival. Suddenly, there you were like the statue of a patrician Greek god coming down that sandy bank with those sparkling blue eyes."

"Oh, my God," Curtis mumbled, as his face turned even redder. "And you were in a hot pink bikini. You were, without a doubt, the most beautiful thing I had ever laid eyes on. I was afraid to even approach you, but you..." he trailed off, shaking his head.

"Let's not share all our memories, shall we?" Dee Dee coyly urged him.

"Well, I, for one, would like to hear the rest of the story," Phil said.

"People in hell want ice water, too, Little Phil, but they don't get it, and you are not going to get the rest of this story, except to say the professor here was a major turn-on for a small town girl who was young and innocent... well, young. I was young," she said, rolling her eyes. "He was the first young man I ever seriously kissed. Right out in public, too! I threw caution to the wind. I do recall, Professor, you were with a couple of those boys who were working at Gus Jarrellson's place at the time. Do you remember that?"

All ears at the table came to attention waiting to hear Curtis's answer.

"Yes, I do" he said.

"Well, that's what I would like to speak with you about," Dee Dee said. "It's also the reason I have come over to this table, other than to share my considerable charm with such handsome gentlemen."

With that she reached into her purse, pulled out three printed invitations, and handed them to the men. As the three of them read the invitations, Dee Dee voiced what was written on them.

"Cocktails next Saturday at five in the afternoon honoring my mother and father-in-law's visit here," she said. "It'll be a small gathering. Just the family. The adult family, that is. Plus you gentlemen and maybe a few others. Phil, I have already spoken to your wife, Elyse, and invited her. She's helping me with the table decorations and the flowers."

"*Is* she now? Well, that's news to me," Phil said.

"Nothing much for you to do, Phil, except put on some khakis, a nice dress shirt, maybe a blue blazer, and a pair of brown loafers, and come along with your wife. By the way, no neckties allowed. Professor, after the guests depart that night, I would like to discuss a couple of other matters with you."

"Matters such as...?" he asked.

"Such as glow in the dark water in Wilson Creek, and your association with those boys who worked with Gus Jarrellson," she explained, and Curtis's face turned an ashen white.

Dee Dee opened her compact, inspected her makeup, and put on a bit more lipstick, all the while saying, "Excuse me for doing this, gentlemen, but I left a good bit of my lipstick on Little Phil's cheek and I don't want Ricardo asking any questions."

Dee Dee then stood up and all three of the men stood up, as well, out of gentlemanly respect.

"Oh, now, no need to rise from your chairs," she said, and then she extended her well-manicured hand to each of them. "It has been a delight, gentlemen, and most interesting. Yes, indeed. I shall look forward to seeing all of you at Camp EZ next Saturday."

"I don't get out all that much, Mrs. Fernandez," Chad said, evidently in an attempt to get out of attending the party.

"I can't imagine why," she responded. "For someone as handsome to look at as you are, you're being rather selfish. You've already broken the hearts of so many girls, just by jogging along the river pathway. Don't you think you should afford some of our local citizens a closer look at you from in front rather than from behind? Please, do come, Mr. Clark. There are many people I would like for you to meet."

"Well, then," he said, blushing. "How can I refuse you?" he asked, as his face turned red again.

"See you all soon, and thank you, Little Phil," she said.

"For what?" he asked.

"For your voice, darling," she said. "It always did carry. If you didn't have such a strong speaking voice, I wouldn't have overheard you on the phone when you mentioned to Mr. Clark about coming here. I managed to piece it all together, though."

"I can see that," Phil said, smiling.

"Say you love me, Phil."

"Damn it, you know I do. I always have and always will."

"And why is that, Little Phil?"

"Because I know you love me, too," Phil told her. "You've always had my back and you've always looked after me."

"I still am," she said. "I needed a facial this morning in Gainesville, but I wouldn't have come had I not still been watching your back, honey. You're a smart man, but you're swimming in shark-infested waters now, sweetheart. I was spawned in them. The water can look so peaceful at times, but it can also be treacherous."

"I know what you mean," Phil said.

"Do you, darling? Do you, indeed? Bless your heart," Dee Dee said.

She turned and waltzed toward the door, about to make a Dee Dee exit as only she could do. All eyes were on her and she knew it, as she wiggled her fanny, slid on her sunglasses, and daintily put on her little white gloves.

Before walking out the door, she turned and said, "Oh, by the way, I may have a major announcement to make at the party. See you soon," she added, and she was out the door.

Chapter 15

If words could kill

Unbeknown to Phil, Chad, Curtis and Dee Dee, sitting two tables behind them at the barbecue restaurant was a group of young people in their early twenties having lunch. They had been snorkeling in the crystal clear waters of the Ichetucknee River that morning. One of them was young Anna Elizabeth Randolph.

The girl was a bit of a snob and she didn't know a whole lot about anything in particular, but she heard enough of the conversation at the nearby table to realize something was up and that she should probably text her mother, Sterling Randolph, with the details. Sterling was the clerk of the court for Campbell County in the town of Turpricone. It was a bit of a lengthy text by Anna Elizabeth, but it explained all it needed to, as far as Sterling was concerned when she received it.

Mama, Phil Brainard is here with that crazy Professor Osborne and that man who lives out near Watson Estates and jogs along the river. They were talking about the water in Wilson Creek and something about glowing water coming from Anna Mary and Stanley's property. I couldn't hear the rest. You should maybe let Anna Mary know. Sounds like some big secret thing. I did hear the word radioactive, though. Oh, and Dee Dee Fernandez was there, too. Love you, Anna."

Within two seconds after reading her daughter's text message, Sterling was punching in the numbers to

Anna Mary's home phone.

"Hello, Anna Mary. Are you alone, honey?" she asked when Anna Mary picked up on the fourth ring.

"Why, yes, I am, Sterling. Good afternoon, by the way," she stiffly said. "Stanley has gone to Jacksonville on business today. He won't be back until much later this evening."

"I need to talk to you now and it needs to be face-to-face. I think it's important," Sterling told her. "I'm leaving the office in about thirty minutes and I can come straight over to your place, if that's okay."

"Well, Sterling, I know you are sometimes given to the dramatic, but I hear something in your voice that tells me you are deeply concerned about something. Come on over, then. I have plenty of shrimp salad left over from yesterday's lunch and it's such a beautiful day. Perhaps, we could have a light meal out on the terrace."

"Yes, that sounds good," Sterling said. "Thank you. I'll see you in about forty-five minutes," she added, and the two women hung up.

The late luncheon with Sterling had been most unsettling for Anna Mary. Sterling didn't stay long and she barely ate any of the shrimp salad, stating she really needed to get back to the office. As soon as she left, Anna Mary started pacing the floor in the sun room. Her mind was racing with all kinds of thoughts.

"I must think clearly now," she kept telling herself. "I must think clearly and I have to be absolutely certain of my words."

When the antique grandfather clock in the living room struck four in the afternoon, she went upstairs. For several minutes, she rifled through the clothes in her huge walk-in closet and finally decided on a light blue, linen sheath, and a pair of silver evening sandals. She hung the dress on the back of the closet door and then she rang for the maid. Consuela arrived within seconds.

"Consuela, please draw my bath," she told her. "Then, come back in about a half hour and help me dress. If you would, please see to it that cocktail fixings are ready downstairs by six-thirty. Mr. Stanley will be home by then. We shall have cocktails at seven, dinner at eight, and there will be no need to use the big dining room. We will dine instead at the smaller table in the sunroom."

"Very good, ma'am," Consuela said. "May I help you off with your dress?"

"Thank you, yes," Anna Mary said. "If you would unzip me, please, and take off these pearls. Tonight, I wish to wear my diamond and sapphire pendant, and the sapphire ring... the one my Uncle Gus gave me when I turned sixteen. Will you see to it?"

"Oh, yes, ma'am," Consuela responded.

While Consuela was busy filling the tub, Anna Mary was looking at her reflection in the mirror, while trying to gather her thoughts. As soon as Consuela left the room, Anna Mary got into the tub and picked up the phone that was sitting on a nearby table. She called the boarding school in New Orleans to inquire about her granddaughter, Mary Selena, who would soon be turning fifteen years old.

She found it hard to believe that time had flown by so quickly. Mary Selena had turned out to be just as beautiful as her mother, who was absolutely stunning. Consequently, she was very popular at school.

A while back, Anna Mary had set up a conference between herself, the Mother Superior at the school, and Mary Selena. During that meeting, Anna Mary decided to allow Mary Selena to be a full-time boarding student at the school until graduation.

Today, simply talking with Mary Selena brightened Anna Mary's outlook on things. She told her granddaughter that she was looking forward to seeing her again in Seraph Springs in a few days. When Mary Selena asked about Destini, Anna Mary winced.

"She is doing just wonderful, darling," Anna Mary told her, in her most convincing, syrupy sweet voice. "I haven't seen her new little one yet, but they are calling her Lily Dee. Her Christian name is Lillian Delphine Abamu."

"Ohh, that's a beautiful name," Mary Selena said.

"They will both be here for the christening luncheon I'm throwing here at the house," Anna Mary told her. "Oh, but darling, you will already be here during your school break, you know, so you may indeed see her before I do. I have so much to do leading up to that event. It's been good talking to you, my darling. I love you. Oh, and do buy yourself something pretty for the christening luncheon, sweetheart. Better yet, phone Mrs. Hortense and pick out the fabric and have it made," she added. "I would suggest something in a pale pink or white."

"Gee, if you want me to do that, I shall," Mary Selena gleefully said, which made Anna Mary smile.

Mary Selena was not aware, but her grandmother had already chosen the dress, the shoes, and the hat from Mrs. Hortense, who promised to have the entire ensemble ready and waiting for her when she called.

After emerging from her bath and drying off, Anna Mary again rang for Consuela, who helped her dress for the evening. Tonight, she used more eyeliner than usual, as well as a darker shade of mascara, as she wanted her total effect to be more dramatic than usual.

Admiring her finished efforts in the full length mirror in her bedroom, Anna Mary seemed quite satisfied. Everything about her oozed power and control, but yet showed femininity at the same time.

"You look perfect, Anna Mary" she told herself, as she continued to admire her reflection.

That evening, she waited for Stanley in her usual chair out in the sun room. When her husband arrived at seven o'clock on the nose, Anna Mary had already prepared his favorite cocktail for him, as well as one for herself. They sat and chatted about his trip to Jacksonville for about an hour, and then Anna Mary rang the bell for dinner.

After they finished eating, and when the dinner dishes were cleared from the table, Consuela served the coffee and a light fruit cup dessert.

"Consuela, when you finish in the kitchen, you and the entire staff can go home," Anna Mary told her. "Consider it my Easter present to all of you," she added, with a pasted-on smile.

"Thank you, ma'am," Consuela said, smiling from ear to ear, and she left the room.

"That was mighty generous of you, sweetheart," Stanley said.

"Yes, it was, wasn't it?" she replied.

Draped on the back of Anna Mary's chair was a beautiful evening shawl that Uncle Gus had bought in Italy for her years ago. It was one of her favorites. She handed it to Stanley, who gently wrapped it around her shoulders.

As soon as Consuela poked her head in and said she and the staff were leaving, Anna Mary looked over at Stanley and smiled.

"Let's walk down to the bluff, Stanley, and sit for a bit in the summerhouse," she suggested. "I had the staff put out some candles there."

"Are you trying to seduce me, Anna Mary?" Stanley asked, blushing, and having no idea what was about to be thrust upon him.

"In a manner of speaking, Stanley, I suppose I am, but what I want is not your body, honey," she said. "I want a confession of words. An intercourse, if you will, of words, and in particular tonight, the truth. We have always believed in truth, haven't we, Stanley? You've always told me you prided yourself on the truth."

"Why, yes… yes, Anna Mary, tha… that's true," he

stuttered, clearly caught off guard by her sudden change in attitude.

"Answer me this, Stanley. Have I ever, at any time in our marriage, ever said anything even remotely resembling criticism about any member of your family?"

"No, you haven't, dear," he answered, seeming even more confused and flustered the more she spoke.

"Well, you will soon hear it, my dear," she said. "All in good time."

She reached into her evening bag and retrieved one of her rare handmade cigars. They were small cigars, about the size of a cigarette, but they smelled similar to a big old stogie. She didn't smoke them often, but tonight she felt as if she needed one to calm her nerves. After she lit it, she inhaled deeply, and then she blew the smoke out through her nose in true redneck fashion.

"You know I don't like for you to smoke, Anna Mary. We have discussed this," Stanley chastised her.

"You have stated your objection, Stanley, but have I ever answered you or told you I would give up a couple of small cigars a month?" she asked him. "I'll answer that for you. No, I have not, and no, there has been no discussion."

"Just the same..." he began, but she cut him off.

"Small communities and family connections in small communities are so... how did you put it one time, Stanley? Provincial? And yet, so useful and helpful?" she asked, but she obviously didn't want an answer from him. "You see, Stanley, your part of the world up north never knew what it was like to be humbled, to be a conquered people. We knew about it down here, and if we didn't know, we had people from your part of the world coming here to remind us quite often, just as you have throughout the years in your own subtle way."

"Now, wait a minute, darling," he said, but she cut him off again.

"You had a superior educational system, more culture, better opportunities, more of everything, Stanley. In your case, and I have never brought this up before, but here it goes... except money and connections. You didn't have that, Stanley. You had no problem utilizing both those things from my family, though, and they have served you well, haven't they?" she asked, as she took another drag off the cigar.

"They have served us both well, Anna Mary, and I don't particularly like your tone!" he adamantly told her.

"I don't particularly give a damn what you like, Stanley," she said. "I have given a damn in the past, but I don't tonight. A lot is going to hinge on what I am about to ask you, Stanley," she added, and then she straightened her shoulders and inhaled some more from her cigar. "Have you been up to some foolishness out on that Wilson Creek tract up in the woods near where the head waters come out of the river swamp?" When he stalled, she asked him again. "Have you, Stanley?"

She carefully watched him from behind her heavily made-up eyes, while fondling her sapphire pendant with her free hand. She kept watching him like a hawk that was about to swoop in on an unsuspecting squirrel.

"What do you mean, foolishness, Anna Mary?" he asked her.

"I mean... what I am asking you, Stanley, is have you been up to some foolishness?" she repeated. "Some foolishness you have kept from me? Some foolishness that was done on my family's property? Some foolishness that is now being bantered around in restaurants by certain people here in this county?" she berated him. "Look out at the river, Stanley. You can hear it flowing, but you can't see the water, can you?" she rhetorically asked. "No, it's a dark night," she went on. "There's no moonlight shining on it, is there, Stanley? And yet, I hear near the mouth of Wilson Creek, the water shimmers at certain times. It glows in the dark, Stanley. So, I did a little research and what I found led me back to you, Mr. Stanley Williams, summa cum laude graduate of Georgia Tech, first in your class in electrical engineering. What I have found is most disturbing. So answer me now, Stanley, what have you been up to on my family's property?" she sternly asked, although, never raising her voice.

"*Your* family property?! *Your* house?! *Your* Uncle Gus?! *You, you, you*!?" he shouted at her. "I never had anything over which I had any real control, Anna Mary, since the day I said *I do* to you! Never!"

"Stop shouting, Stanley," she ordered him. "It's

unbecoming."

Stanley took a deep breath and continued in a softer tone.

"About twenty years ago, when Watson went off to school up north, the company I work for began thinking about building a nuclear power plant here in Campbell County and they asked if I knew of a small area in which to conduct some experiments. Someplace secluded, someplace out of the way of curious eyes. I told them I did, and so, I agreed to their proposal."

"Let me finish this for you, Stanley," she said. "You agreed to allow them to place this little experiment far up in the swamp on my family's property, and *you*, Stanley, have taken joy, if you will, from time to time, in being in control of that experiment... your little creation. You couldn't let it go even after you knew, Stanley, that it could cause us all a world of trouble. You kept at it, didn't you? Well, I am here to tell you, Stanley. That little experiment is coming to a close. I am telling you, Stanley, and I have never been so blunt before in my life. It better be destroyed and all evidence of it gone within a month, or Mr. Gentleman Stanley Williams, you can leave this place with nothing but a sandwich and a damned road map!" she added, screaming quite loudly now. "Do you understand me, Stanley?!" she shouted.

"I understand you are overwrought," he calmly told her, and then he stood up from his chair and looked down his nose at her.

It was the look that did it. It sent her over the edge.

She mashed out the cigar in the ashtray, stood up from the table, and slapped Stanley so hard across the face that he stumbled backward and fell to the floor. The impact of her punch was hard enough that his front teeth bit into his lower lip and it began to bleed.

"Damn you, Anna Mary! Damn you!" he shouted.

Then, he hurried to his feet and snatched a napkin from the table to sop up the blood.

"Damn me, Stanley?! Damn me?!" she yelled at him. "How dare you?! How about damn you and your whole damned carpetbagging family?! They sent you south to find a good Protestant heiress, didn't they?! Your mama told me all about it one day," Anna Mary said, as her voice dropped a few octaves. "Well, you succeeded, Stanley, beyond their wildest dreams. What did it cost me? What did it cost? I'll tell you what it cost me, Stanley. It cost me my only child, my daughter-in-law, and my Uncle Gus. Oh, yes, Stanley, you bear the blame for that one, too!"

"Anna Mary, you've lost your mind," Stanley said, and he sat back down at the table.

"I warned you years ago about hiring that damned girl, Destini, too," Anna Mary continued. "I told you about her voodoo grandma, the one who had visions," she added, making a funny face and rolling her eyes around. "I told you how Destini wanted to work in this house, but my daddy would never let her. What I didn't tell you when you hired Destini was that my Uncle Gus thought it was a mistake. My mama thought so, too, and so did I, but you insisted. You said she was a nice, compliant girl with plenty of gumption and common sense. Look what it got us, Stanley!" she shouted. "Death! Heartache!" she screamed.

"I have no idea what you're talking about!" he shouted back at her.

"I have said what I was going to say to you, Stanley," Anna Mary said, calming down to a mild roar now. "I am tired. I am sick, and I am tired. I am sick that you have lied to me all these years, and I am tired of lies and liars, and being put down. You listen to me before I go upstairs, Stanley. Don't you dare follow me up to our bedroom. Our son's old room is all made up for you. I want you to stay in there, Stanley. That's where you will sleep. I want you to feel Watson's spirit all around you. I want you to feel the grief each time you look at those walls, Stanley."

"You moved Watson's things after I expressly asked that nothing be touched?" he asked her, wide-eyed.

"You have asked for enough, Stanley. You asked that nothing be touched, and yet you never opened the door and went inside. You're going in there tonight, though, Stanley. All your things have been moved in there," she told him.

"How did you explain that to the help?" he asked. "The move… the change? What did you tell them?"

"They were happy to do it and I offered no explanation," she said. "You always offer the help too much and you give them too much attention, Stanley. Too many explanations. They are the help, don't you understand? The help. Like furniture is furniture, help is help. They are paid to do a job and they do it. Then, they cash their checks and go home. If I choose to tell them anything more, I do, but since you asked, I told them you've been having trouble with your sinuses lately, as you often complain, and that your sleep patterns made me so restless that *we* decided this would be best. It puts you way down the hall away from me. Don't you dare speak to me, say anything to me, or acknowledge me in any way, other than daily pleasantries, until you come up with a plan that destroys that experiment of yours. Do you hear me?"

Stanley didn't say a word. He just stared at her in total disbelief.

"This could bring down the entire Jarrellson legacy in this county, and I won't have it," she went on. "I will not have it. You are disposable, Stanley. I hate to convey it to you, but you always were. The thing is, Stanley, I loved you, and I was in love with you. I fought for you, knowing what you were coming into, knowing what it could cost us both, but I always counted on the truth from you, Stanley. No deception. So, tonight, since lying and deception seems to be the game you've been playing, look into the eyes of a person who made up that game," she said, staring directly into his bloodshot eyes. "I invented the game and I mastered it. How the hell do you think this family lost and then regained so much of its power without a little chicanery and masterful deception, Stanley? The damned book you learned from, my dear, well, I wrote it. I authored it... volumes of it. So, tonight, you sleep in our dead son's room. A son you helped damage and kill, and you think about what your plan will be to clean up your experiment, Stanley. Then, you let me know what you're going to do."

If anyone was looking for the definition of shell-shocked, they'd have to look no further than Stanley's face right now. It was a mess, with blood still oozing from his lip, and his eyes red and glassy, and filled with tears.

"Your lip should stop bleeding soon," Anna Mary told him. "Oh, don't cry, Stanley. I can't bear that. It doesn't impress me. The more you cry, the less you'll urinate," she said, laughing, as she recalled a clever phrase she had heard in the past from her mother. "When you're ready to talk, Stanley, I will be waiting... but don't take too long," she added, and she turned away from him and prepared to leave the sunroom.

Stanley was beside himself, as the only word to come out of his mouth was, "Bitch." Thankfully, for him, Anna Mary was too far away from him to hear, otherwise, who knows what she would have done.

Before walking out the door and going up to her bedroom, Anna Mary had one more thing to say.

"Unless you want our summer house to burn to the ground, Stanley, I suggest you go snuff out those candles Consuela lit earlier," she ordered him.

With that, Anna Mary stormed out of the room, leaving Stanley behind in a state of utter frustration, which pleased her to no end.

Chapter 16

At the river I stand

The sweet mixture of aromas from a variety of specially-prepared ethnic foods, along with the lively sound of an accomplished pianist playing old jazz standards was intoxicating this evening at Camp EZ. Add to that the fragrance of beautiful blooming flowers, as well as the laughter of dozens of guests, and the great room of the lodge seemed magically transformed into a spectacular Hollywood gala. Everyone present appeared to be having the time of their lives at this somewhat impromptu cocktail party hosted by Dee Dee and her husband Ricardo.

This magnificent million dollar camp built along the banks of the Suwannee River by Dee Dee's late uncle, Hamp Brayerford, was now the property of Dee Dee and her first cousin, Carl Alvin Campbell. This party was to entertain Dee Dee's in-laws, who had come up from Miami for an unexpected springtime visit.

Knowing how much they loved parties and laughter, Dee Dee always planned something for them each time they visited. She outdid herself this time. Even though she had encouraged her guests to dress in business casual attire, most of them dressed up for the occasion. Dee Dee herself was decked out in an apricot-colored chiffon cocktail dress that was accessorized with large turquoise and coral earrings, as well as gold evening sandals.

As she gleefully worked the room, she made certain everyone was being attended to properly. She so wanted the entire evening of revelry to be enjoyed by everyone, especially Ricardo's family, which was now her family, too.

Among those friends to whom she was close, only Wanda Faye and her husband Dink had been able to attend. Nadine and Louie had promised their children they'd take them to a movie in Pittstown, and Nadine said there was no backing out, as they had already prepaid the tickets. Miss Jewell, Wanda Faye said, was at home in bed nursing a springtime allergy.

Destini and Matt, for the time being, were staying in Mr. Hamp's old cabin. It had been lavishly refurbished recently, yet it didn't lose any of its rustic charm. The two of them were busy taking care of their new baby, Lily Dee, and as much as she wanted to come to the party, Destini told Dee Dee that she wasn't quite up to socializing at the moment.

Meanwhile, most everyone who had shown up was buzzing about the upcoming art show of the late Gus Jarrellson's works. One small group of women were chatting it up about the news of Stanley's aunt giving Stanley and Anna Mary her prized sterling silver service. It was supposedly made by a master silversmith in New England before the Revolutionary War.

Dee Dee and Carl Alvin had decided it would be best to invite Anna Mary and Stanley to the cocktail party, for one reason, and one reason alone. They wanted to see if they would actually attend. As was usual protocol for them, they arrived fashionably late. Many people believed Anna Mary always did this just to make a grand appearance, which was probably true. She never failed to impress and tonight was no exception.

When she entered the room, Dee Dee muttered to herself, "Whoa, someone has been to the safe deposit box and pulled out some of the *real* Jarrellson jewelry."

Anna Mary was wearing a simply cut, navy blue, linen cocktail dress with a neckline that was a bit lower than usual for her, exposing a tad too much of her cleavage, Dee Dee thought. Ever the lady, though, she had the most beautiful ecru colored, lace evening shawl draped around her shoulders to cover up much of her over-abundance. She carried with her an antique, ornate, hand-painted fan, which she unfolded when she sat down, languidly waving it back and forth, as if she lived in a different century. The most attention, however, was drawn to her jewelry.

She wore the famous Jarrellson diamond and Ceylon sapphire jewelry suite that her ancestors had purchased long before the War Between the States. Ceylon sapphires are the rarest in the world and the most sought after, as they need no artificial enhancements to achieve their vivid, light blue color. The entire jewelry suite had been hidden away deep in the river swamp to avoid being taken by the Yankees during the war, and later the carpetbaggers, or so the story went.

Tonight, the ornate necklace, with a magnificent

center stone surrounded by diamonds and seed pearls, looked to be ablaze under the bright lights above, and it accented Anna Mary's stunning blue eyes. The bracelet that clung to her wrist and the ring that sparkled on her finger boasted matching diamonds and sapphires.

From her ears hung huge, four carat diamond tear drop earrings that were also surrounded by sapphires. They sparkled like tiny bursts of lightning as she moved her head.

Anna Mary's regal carriage and her nearly six foot frame added to the dignity of the jewelry. People always said Anna Mary "wore" her jewelry; it didn't wear her. She carried it off with a quiet dignity, as if she were wearing only a simple gold chain around her neck or even nothing at all, as nonchalant as she was about it all. She was born and bred to pull off any event with great elegance, including wearing this king's ransom of heirloom jewels.

Before getting ready to come to Dee Dee's cocktail party, Anna Mary talked at length with her good friend from New Orleans, Sally Robichaux, whose husband did a great deal of business in Latin America. They discussed the manner in which the upper crust of Latin society, especially Cuban-American society, attired themselves, as Anna Mary wanted to fit in.

As if taking a page from Sally's playbook, as well as her own sense of creativity for her role as doyenne of the town, Anna Mary slowly scanned the room. Oh, yes, the people at the party were impressed, talking in circles and admiring her jewelry. She immediately began to make the rounds with Dee Dee leading the way, so she could greet everyone, leaving Stanley behind to talk with Carl Alvin and the male members of the Fernandez family.

The party was definitely enjoyed by everyone, and as the evening was coming to a close, Dee Dee interrupted the pianist and asked if it was okay if she could play something. The pianist complied and Dee Dee sat down, immediately launching into a medley of show tunes. She suggested the guests listen carefully to the last song of her piano medley.

As she was about to end her charming display of piano magic, she broke into the traditional "Brahms Lullaby", known to some folks as "Rock a Bye Baby". She played it softly and sweetly, tickling the keys with her dainty fingers. As she played, she kept her eyes on her husband, who soon became very emotional. His eyes filled with tears, but they were tears of happiness.

It was probably the best kept secret of the century on Dee Dee's part, but when Ricardo rushed to his wife's side, arms outstretched, she could hold it in no longer.

"We're having a baby!" she shouted.

Standing behind her at the piano was Anna Mary, who had been turning the pages for Dee Dee as she played. She seemed as stunned as everyone else was at the pronouncement, but she whispered to her, "My best wishes to you, Dee Dee. The greatest journey of your life is about to begin."

Anna Mary, known for her stoicism, then began to

cry. She cried hard enough that she had to motion for Stanley to come to her from across the room. He rushed over and handed her his handkerchief. Then, in a startling gesture that caused everyone in the room to gasp, Anna Mary slipped the famous Jarrellson sapphire ring from her finger and she placed it on Dee Dee's right ring finger. The center stone was oval, probably about four-and-a-half carats, and it was set in platinum, but it was the considerably sized diamonds that caught everyone's eyes.

"Oh, no, Anna Mary," Dee Dee said, shaking her head, and remembering full well what the judge had shared about Anna Mary being the consummate actress. "You will want to save this beautiful ring for Mary Selena, darling."

"No, no, I want you to have it," Anna Mary told her. "You need to have something wonderful to remember this day for as long as you live. It is truly one of the great events of life, Dee Dee."

Dee Dee looked at the ring on her finger and she thought about Anna Mary and Stanley and what they were trying to do to Destini; what they were trying to do to all of them. She thought about the comments the judge shared, but she didn't allow those thoughts to show on her face to betray the expression of gratitude and humility she was properly displaying now.

Taking Anna Mary to her bosom, Dee Dee whispered, "Thank you. Thank you so much."

For a few moments, she thought about forgiving Anna Mary. She thought how Anna Mary, in some ways, had been a victim just as much as her son, Watson, and just as much as so many members of the Jarrellson family, who fell helplessly to the charms and direction of the late Gus Jarrellson. She knew that forgiveness was a process, but she wasn't ready to forgive Anna Mary just yet. Not until she saw how everything played out regarding all the legal mumbo-jumbo with Destini.

In her heart, Dee Dee still felt Anna Mary had been urged by Stanley to do much of this land-grabbing nonsense. She despised him, but then, she always had. He wasn't one of them. He never would be. He didn't even try to be.

Her darling husband, Ricardo, was his own man, but in Ricardo she had found a love that was simply unconditional. He accepted her, her friends, and pretty much everyone he met unconditionally, as she did his family. She wondered if all the love she felt in her heart at this moment, and what she might find out tonight from Curtis, might possibly help to bridge so much of the needless disdain and pain between her and the Williams'. She prayed it would.

Dee Dee held up her hand with the ring and took Anna Mary by her other hand, and said, "This sapphire and diamond ring, beautiful though it is, represents so much more to me than the jewel itself. It represents joy, despair, struggle, triumph, and tragedy. The ladies who proudly wore this ring for the past one-hundred-and-seventy-some-odd years, since it was purchased in England, were very familiar with everything I have mentioned, and everything in between. Life frequently is what happens in between great events, and is as precious as the great events themselves," she explained, as her eyes filled with tears. "The first Jarrellson lady to wear this ring lived in a log house with no heat and no air conditioning. She struggled through miscarriages and she had a very hard life. She helped her husband by sacrificing and sacrificing, again and again, to become a great mother and a great lady, just like the lady who gave me this ring tonight. I ask Judge Wesson, if he would, to lead us all in a prayer of thanksgiving. Ricardo, come hold my hand, darling. Everyone... please join us in a circle. I want to be able to see you and feel your love, as my husband and I begin our family here in this land we call home... this great state of Florida. Carl Alvin, honey, come hold my hand on this side. You hold Anna Mary's and she'll hold Stanley's and right on around."

Anna Mary was weeping aloud now. Meanwhile, Wanda Faye was smiling. She told Dink she could hear Mama Tee's voice whispering in spirit, "You tell em, Queenie!"

"I can actually hear her cackling like she always did when Dee Dee was doling out marching orders," she told Dink.

The judge, who asked for silence from everyone, began to pray. Dee Dee sank to her knees, as did Ricardo, and then all the family followed suit. The flickering light from the candles behind her caught the huge sapphire and diamonds, and cast a play of prismatic light on the ceiling. Dee Dee looked up and saw that light, and in it she found the hope she needed to step forward and be a woman of strength and peace... and a good mother.

She cried some, but when the prayer was over, in true Dee Dee fashion, she shouted, "Ricardo, you better lift me up from this floor, baby! You know this may be one of the last times you see me, even with your help, be able to get up and down like this. If I do this much longer, I'll have to audition for the circus as an acrobat or something."

Dee Dee's aunts, Hattie and Nanny, were standing across from her, and both of them were shaking their heads back and forth.

"My God, when I think of all the money we spent on that girl for finishing school in Charleston," Hattie said to Nanny.

Nanny didn't respond. She simply nodded in agreement, while everyone else laughed.

"Carl Alvin, did you mention something about homemade ice cream or did I dream that?" Dee Dee asked, once she got up to a standing position.

Carl Alvin winked at Wanda Faye and they both laughed so hard it made their eyes water.

"Yes, ma'am, we have some made," Carl Alvin told her. "We've got some of Miss Jewell's cake, too," he added.

"Do you want chocolate swirl or coconut cake with your ice cream?" Wanda Faye asked her.

"Hell, give me some of each," Dee Dee said. "Pile

it on, honey. I'm eating for three now."

"Do you know whether you're having a boy or a girl?" Wanda Faye asked, obviously not catching the word "three".

"I don't know as of yet," Dee Dee said. "Did you not hear me, though? I said I'm eating for three."

"What?!" Wanda Faye shrieked when she caught on. "Twins! Dee Dee, you're having twins?!"

"Well, I will tell you, at this point the doctor says there is a good possibility we may be welcoming two babies rather than one."

"Well, now!" Carl Alvin shouted. "This calls for a toast!"

Everyone in the room toasted the parents to be, and there were hugs and kisses all around.

"When is this blessed event going to happen?" Carl Alvin asked.

"Well, unless nature changes her calendar, and I don't think she will, I should have something over which we can truly give thanks for before Thanksgiving," Dee Dee said.

"I am so happy for you, darling," Carl Alvin said, and he hugged her. "I'm so happy for both of you," he added, and he hugged Ricardo, too. "I'm just so happy for our family."

Aunt Hattie and Aunt Nanny came forward for hugs, both of them chattering away about the layette for the babies and the christening gowns. This, in turn, set off Ricardo's mother, who began speaking Spanglish so fast that no one could understand anything she was saying, other than to know she was truly excited about becoming a grandmother.

Dee Dee, ever the gracious hostess, kept her wits about her and remembered the main reason for the calling of this little party. It was to chat with Curtis. She motioned for him and Chad to stay put, while most of the other guests were preparing to leave. Dee Dee then asked Ricardo, Carl Alvin and Judge Wesson if they could hang back as well, while the others left the lodge.

She loved the other guests and was related by blood to many of them, but these were the people who were the core of her existence, and she wanted them to be present when she asked Curtis questions, so that they could hear his answers, too.

Darkness had fallen across the vast acreage of slash pines, scrub palmettos, and white sand roads where the Suwannee flows through it. As Dee Dee stood at the door bidding her guests goodbye, she glanced out at the river below, which was flowing as it always did. She was trying to collect all her thoughts, while the remaining guests gathered around the dining room table.

Her thoughts had been churning around like whirling currents in the river for days, but tonight her thoughts needed to be clear and concise, moving slowly and with a deliberate cause, just like the waters in the river that ceaselessly flowed out to the Gulf of Mexico.

In a low whisper, she recited to herself the first line lyrics of an old African American gospel song:

At the river I stand, guide my feet, hold my hand.

Chapter 17

The inquisition

Once the bulk of the guests had departed Dee Dee's cocktail party, the catering service quickly cleared the last remaining remnants from the affair and departed, as well. Dee Dee's in-laws had gone up to their room for some much needed rest after their exhaustive trip from Miami to Seraph Springs, plus all the excitement of the party.

Dee Dee then invited her remaining special guests to join her in the study, formerly the study of her uncle, the late Hamp Brayerford. Earlier that day, a large conference table and chairs had been brought into the room to accommodate everyone who was going to attend this somewhat impromptu meeting.

Aside from Dee Dee, there was Ricardo, Carl Alvin, Phil, Judge Wesson, and Chad and Curtis. Dee Dee directed Judge Wesson to sit at the head of the table. Just then, Sheriff Bartow Lewis, State Attorney Stephen Marcus, a young, female court recorder, and the judge's nephew, St. John Culpepper, entered through a side door. Dee Dee asked them to have a seat near the judge.

On the table, in front of each chair, Dee Dee had provided bottled water and crystal drinking glasses, as well as small dessert dishes and silverware. In the middle of the table there was a variety of snack type foods, as well as slices of Miss Jewell's chocolate marble cake.

Meanwhile, Chad and Curtis, neither of whom had sat down yet, were nervously looking around the room, as well as back and forth at each other, obviously caught off guard and wondering why so many officials had just joined the meeting. To say they looked uneasy was an understatement.

"Excuse me, but what is the purpose of all this?" Curtis asked Dee Dee, with a facial expression that seemed to beg the question, "Have I been betrayed?"

"The purpose of all this is to ascertain the truth, Dr. Osborne," the state attorney interjected, as he took his seat beside the sheriff. "The purpose is to lay some things to rest," he added, looking Curtis square in the eyes. "I think we can do this easily enough, and then we can move on to some interesting findings."

"I don't understand," Curtis said, looking as if he was about to bolt from the room.

"Curtis, I'm so sorry," Dee Dee said, and she went over to place her arm around his shoulders. "It wasn't my intention at all to make you feel uncomfortable or railroaded. The same goes for you, Chad. I'm sorry," she told him, and then she returned her attention to Curtis. "It's just that something has happened here in Seraph Springs and we think you and Chad can help us understand it better. It has to do with the strange river glow at Wilson Creek," she explained, which seemed to ease both their minds for the moment.

"Before we go on, though, Dr. Osborne and Mr. Clark…" the judge began.

"Please... call us Chad and Curtis," Chad interrupted him, sounding a bit more relaxed now. "I think we can dispense with all the formalities. It makes me feel as if we're on trial here or something," he added with a smile, and Curtis nodded in agreement.

"Of course," the judge said. "Please, everyone, have a seat and we shall begin."

Once everyone was seated, the judge continued.

"Some of the things we're going to ask at this meeting will be very compelling, if you will, and we will not go on if either of you would like to have legal representation present with you," he said, as he glanced back and forth from Chad to Curtis. "Let me just say that either myself or my nephew here would be happy to serve as your legal counsel and advise you about anything you may not want to answer or discuss, as this meeting is being recorded," he said, nodding toward the court recorder, who was sitting on the other side of him.

"Well, I have nothing to hide," Curtis said. "So I'm fine."

"Same goes for me," Chad said.

"All right, then, let's get on with it," Stephen, the state attorney curtly began, since he was evidently tasked with taking the lead in this somewhat odd meeting of the minds. "I'm going to ask you a series of questions," he said. "Dr. Osborne... I'm sorry... Curtis... did you work for the late Spencer Augustus Jarrellson of this county during the time from the spring of 1993 until the beginning of fall, 1993?" he asked.

"Yes, sir, I did," Curtis said with a nod.

"Would you say you became well acquainted with Mr. Gus Jarrellson?"

"Yes, sir, I did become well acquainted with him," Curtis flatly answered. "He was a talented and fascinating man."

"Did you ever know Thomas Endicott?" Stephen asked.

Curtis thought for a moment, and then said, "Yes, I did know him."

"Now, Curtis, I am going to show you some photographs," Stephen continued. "They might be quite disturbing to you, but I think you should see them."

Stephen then pulled out a folder from his briefcase. Inside was a color display of photographs of the three recently unearthed skeletons. The gold teeth in the skull of the skeleton in the middle of the photo display were clearly visible and obvious.

"These skeletal remains were discovered here in Seraph Springs a few days ago," Stephen explained. "On some old Jarrellson property, to be more specific," he added.

The sheriff, a naturally astute observer, was watching Curtis's face, which had morphed into a look of pure horror as he stared at the photos. Soon, his eyes began to water and then he clammed them shut, as if he was trying to ward off old demons from coming back to haunt him. Seconds later, he inhaled a deep breath, opened his eyes again, and then quietly spoke.

"That looks like it could possibly be Thomas Endicott," Curtis said, pointing to the skeleton in the middle. "I remember that gold dental work he had. It was unmistakable, for sure. I know he came from a prominent family up in the New England area of this country. Otherwise, he wouldn't have been able to afford gold crowns like that. Personally, I thought it was a bit of an extravagance and even overkill, but he seemed to be proud of that golden smile."

"Do you know who the other two skeletons could be?" the sheriff asked, pointing to the photographs.

"It was a long time ago, but I believe the one on the left might be Joseph Raymond Sutton. He was from Ann Arbor, Michigan, if my memory serves me correctly. This last one, with what looks to be a hairline fracture on his skull, is most likely Patrick Sean O'Reilly. I recall he was from Philadelphia or somewhere thereabouts. I remember him telling us about falling during an ice hockey game when he was a young teenager in junior high. He said some big brute on the other team hit him from behind, and when he fell, his head hit the ice really hard. I think he said he needed about ten stitches."

"Do you have any idea how these boys might have died?" the sheriff bluntly asked.

For a few moments, Curtis sat stone-faced, as if he had drifted off into a dark, dark place. Dee Dee looked over at him and saw that his right leg had developed a nervous tic, making his whole body shake. She reached over and put her hand on top of his.

"It's all right, Curtis," she said. "No one here is going to hurt you or judge you. We're just trying to get at the truth."

In a show of support, Chad put his arm around Curtis's shoulder, and said, "I'm right here with you, Curtis. There's no need to be afraid. Everyone here is your friend."

"Thank you, Chad, and you, too, Dee Dee," Curtis said, and he straightened up in his chair. "Well, Sheriff Lewis, I think I might have an idea how they died. It's a dark and horrific story," he added, and then he cleared his throat. "I'm ashamed I haven't told anyone in all these years, but for a long time I was frightened for my own life had I said anything about what happened. For the longest time after that, I totally blocked those memories from my mind to keep from going mad. I finally realized that I had to come back here and face head-on the place from where I ran away."

"So, that must mean you were the fourth missing boy, right?" the sheriff asked him.

"It certainly seems that way," Curtis said.

"Please continue, Curtis. We'd like to hear more about your time with Gus Jarrellson," Stephen urged him.

"Well, Mr. Jarrellson had us all working for him. There were four of us who had ridden the bus up here from Miami and we were looking for work, so that we could earn enough money to get back to our homes up north. Mr. Jarrellson had us clearing land, working on his landscaping, and doing miscellaneous repairs on several of his outbuildings," Curtis explained. "One of those buildings was air conditioned with a large central air unit and it was kept locked at all times. No one was ever allowed to go inside, though. The place had no windows, either, which I found to be quite odd."

"Could that building have been his art studio?" Stephen asked.

"No, sir, I don't think so," Curtis said, shaking his head. "His studio was in another building and we all went inside it quite frequently. In fact... and I am not proud of it... but since I needed the money, I posed in the nude for several of his paintings. He paid me generously. One of his most famous artworks, "Narcissus in Paradise", is actually a painting of a much younger me," he explained, as his cheeks turned red.

"Did you ever have any sexual relations with Mr. Jarrellson?" Stephen asked.

"Oh, no, sir, I did not!" Curtis adamantly replied. His eyes turned wild and he stiffened up in his chair. "He never propositioned me, either!" he added, again very adamantly.

"Let's move along," Stephen said, taking a breath. "You inherited the piece of land you currently live on from Mr. Jarrellson's good friend, the late Miss Agatha Campbell. Is that correct?"

"Yes, sir, it is."

"What was the nature of your relationship with her?" Stephen asked.

"I was her friend, her confidante, and I did odd

jobs for her," Curtis explained.

"Did she ever give you anything of a personal nature, like property... except for the land, that is?" Stephen asked.

"Uhh... well, yes, sir, she did," Curtis said with some reluctance.

"What did she give you?" Stephen pressed him.

"It was a detailed journal... a very detailed journal," Curtis said.

"Do you still have that journal?" the sheriff interrupted.

"Yes, sir, I do," Curtis said. "Actually, she gave me several journals. In truth, the bulk of them were more like the diaries of a lovelorn woman. I was originally going to turn them over to the authorities, but I was really messed up at the time... mentally, you know."

"Where are they now?" the sheriff gruffly asked.

"I normally keep them in my safety deposit box at the bank in Turpricone, but Chad asked me to bring a few of them with me tonight," Curtis said. "I was under the impression he and I were going to have a private discussion about it later after this meeting," he added, and he shot Chad a disapproving look.

"I'm sorry, Curtis," Chad meekly said.

"That's okay, Chad," Curtis said with a heavy sigh. "I imagine it had to come out into the open at some point... and it may as well be now. I actually just made copies of the more relevant stuff, since I want to keep the original journals in safekeeping. It would have been a little awkward carrying it all around with me all evening here at the party."

"That's fine," the sheriff told him.

Curtis then reached into his coat pocket, retrieved a small stack of papers and straightened them out on the table in front of him.

"May I?" Curtis asked the sheriff.

"Yes, please," the sheriff told him. "We're ready to listen when you're ready to start reading."

Chapter 18

The journal

All eyes inside the spacious study at Camp EZ were trained on Dr. Curtis Osborne, the eccentric professor who lived in a tiny camper on a small parcel of land in Seraph Springs that was given to him by the late Agatha, "Miss Aggie" Campbell. He was about to read from a detailed journal she had given to him many years ago. It was filled with shocking statements about the late Gus Jarrellson and the evil deeds he, along with Miss Aggie, had inflicted upon three innocent young men. After nervously clearing his throat, Curtis began to read some of Miss Aggie's journal entries.

"Good Friday, 1993," Curtis started. "Today, Gus is going to begin work on a large mural. Last night was not easy, but while semi-gods require sacrifices of flowers or food, real gods require blood. Gus already sent the other boys back to the jail. The four boys who were living with him stayed behind, which included the Endicott boy, Thomas. They all worked hard today digging a large hole in the ground where Gus told them he would be moving some brush."

"I'm sorry, you said brush?" the sheriff asked.

"Yes, sir," Curtis said. "You know, like tree limbs and such."

"Oh, okay, go on," the sheriff urged him, and Curtis continued reading.

"Gus told Thomas to pack his suitcase, while he quickly fed the other three and sent them off to bed. When Thomas came back, Gus said he wanted him to have a good, healthy dinner before he put him on a bus to Boston over in Pittstown. He prepared a salad, grilled salmon, and a unique dessert. In it were small paper-thin slices of Gloriosa lily bulbs that he had ground up and mixed into a pudding, and he served it to Thomas for dessert."

"Aren't those poisonous?" the sheriff asked.

"Yes, they are," Chad piped up. "I actually read up on them several years ago. It's a beautiful plant, but the entire thing is poisonous, from the stalks to the leaves to the flowers. They're mostly indigenous to Southeast Asia and India, so I imagine Gus must have had them imported."

"Interesting," the sheriff said. "Please continue, Curtis."

"There was also a huge amount of Secobarbital Sodium in the pudding, as well," Curtis resumed reading. "I stole this drug from the prescription cabinet at the hospital to aid my beloved Gus with his artwork. Thomas died a fairly peaceful death and with a full stomach. We then carted him out to Gus's special room where he laid him on the slab. Then, he made the incision and drained all the blood from his body. The blood was then placed in the big cooler. A mallet was used and with a saw, he severed the breast bone and saved it to dry."

As Curtis was reading, Dee Dee noticed it was dead

quiet in the study. It was as if no one was breathing, much like the contents of Miss Aggie's journal.

"This is incredible," Dee Dee muttered to Phil, shaking her head. "I guess that explains the air conditioned shed with no windows."

Curtis took a sip from his water glass and then resumed reading.

"We did this, in turn, on two of the other boys in subsequent days. The fourth boy simply disappeared one day and he didn't return until after Gus had died."

"Looks like you dodged a bullet, Curtis," the sheriff said.

"Yes, sir, I guess I did," Curtis said. "In hindsight, I think I must have figured out what was going on and so I ran off and never looked back," he added. "These next entries are a few years later."

"Please continue," the sheriff told him.

"I knew the boy the minute I saw him," Curtis read. "At this time in my life, I feel the boy is owed something since Gus never paid him, except for money to go to the movies or into town for a haircut. He was a good artist's model, too. I am becoming very fond of him, so I shall leave him my property, as I want nothing further to do with this place."

"Well, that explains a few things," the sheriff said, as Curtis took another sip of water. "Is there more?" he asked.

"Yes, there is," Curtis said. "A lot more."

"If you need to take a break, you let us know," Dee Dee told him, and he nodded before proceeding.

"There is one thing I want to add in this journal that is very important," Curtis continued reading. "In that subterranean cave on my property, I once gave refuge to a young man for a couple of days. He came down here to see the wedding of Dr. Watson Jarrellson Williams. He was a young man by the name of Chadwick Clark."

"Oh, wow," Chad mumbled, as if he had just been found out.

"He later wrote to me and then phoned me, telling me all about being in that terrible accident when Watson and Selena were killed outside London," Curtis went on. "He was driving them, you know, and there was a reason he was driving them. Watson had hurt his arm playing cricket and his arm was in a sling. Chadwick was visiting there at the time to have surgeries done on his face. That boy was a godsend to Watson. Anna Mary and Stanley never acknowledged that boy or his goodness in any way. They should have."

"Well, I guess secrets can only stay secret for so long," Chad interjected, and then Curtis continued reading after taking another sip of water.

"I decided I wouldn't make the same mistake Anna Mary and Stanley did in life, which is why I am willing my land to Curtis Osborne. It is the least I can do to make amends. I know I shall be judged for the death and burial of those three boys and rightly so. Their blood was used in many of my longtime paramour's paintings, especially in his mural, *Black Runs the River*.

Their breast bones were dried and ground up with a mortar and pestle, just as we ground up the poisons that went into their food. It was a nice touch to his paintings, giving them much more depth."

"Holy Mother of God!" the sheriff gasped, as everyone else sucked in their breaths in horror.

After another sip of water, Curtis continued, as if unfazed by what he had just revealed to the people sitting around the table.

"In the end, everyone will assume I had a stroke and fell into the river," he read. "I have planned it that way. So, now, I am on my way to the bridge downtown to jump into the dark waters of the benevolent and oh so majestic Suwannee River. Before I jump, I shall swallow enough of the same poison that Gus and I gave to those poor boys. I want to feel what they felt. I want to experience their pain and agony. I won't last long, I'm certain, as my heart is weak and my body is frail. I do hope Dr. Osborne will forgive me. More importantly, I hope Almighty God forgives me for what I have done. Those poor boys, so young, but in a way, through Gus's art, they shall live forever."

"Oh, my God!" Dee Dee shrieked. "This woman was insane!"

"I tend to agree with you, Dee Dee," the sheriff said.

"One last thing before I go," Curtis continued reading. "I believe Chadwick Clark may have had a slight fixation on Watson. I know human nature quite well and if he ever hears about any of this, there is one thing I want to say to him from the grave. Find happiness, my boy, and at this time, happiness may be in the room with you. Reach out to it."

Chad looked as if he wanted to slide down in his chair and hide under the table, but the others in the room didn't seem to grasp what Miss Aggie had written, except for maybe Carl Alvin.

"That's all I brought with me tonight," Curtis said, barely above a whisper. "The rest of the journal entries are kind of mundane, except for the love letter type stuff she wrote about Gus. Some of that was literally pornographic."

Everyone in the room was in a shocked stupor, it seemed. Even the young court recorder, who had to stop several times during the reading to wipe her eyes, looked stunned out of her mind. Curtis then laid his head on the table and he wept, while Chad consoled him by rubbing his back. Dee Dee finally asked St. John to take him to his car and also to drive him home. She asked Phil to follow them, so he could bring St. John back to Camp EZ.

Once they left, the sheriff asked, "What do we do now? What do we do? Everyone who is guilty is dead."

"Yes, they are, and thank God for that," Dee Dee said. "Some of the living, though, have an opportunity now to right some wrongs, don't they, Judge?" she asked, turning to look him in the eyes.

"I don't think I'm following you, Dee Dee," the judge said.

"Well, I'll tell you what, Judge," she began. "I think

you should take the sheriff and the state attorney with you right now, and you should call on Mr. and Mrs. Stanley Williams. You should make them very aware that all of this... I mean *all* of it will be made public."

"It will hurt them mighty bad, Dee Dee," the sheriff said, shaking his head. "They've already endured so much, especially Anna Mary," he added.

"Yes, they have, Sheriff, yes, they have," Dee Dee agreed. "And yet, I heard through a friend of mine in Jacksonville that Anna Mary was having a baby gift wrapped for Destini. She's going to tell her not to open it at the christening luncheon she is throwing for her tomorrow afternoon, but to take it home with her and open it then," she added. "Do you know what's in that present? That beautifully wrapped gift?"

"I'm not following you, Dee Dee," the sheriff said.

"Tell him what's in the present, Judge," Dee Dee said, and the judge wasted no time in complying with her wish.

"What's in it is notice of a lawsuit brought by Anna Mary and Stanley against Destini... in essence, stripping her of all that Hamp Brayerford left her in his will, except for a small income and health insurance," the judge said.

"Oh, my," the sheriff said, stunned, since he was well aware of what Hamp Brayerford had left Destini in his will. "Do you think they'll win the suit?" he asked the judge.

"I think they probably will, but when this mess becomes public... *if* it becomes public, it would be a hollow victory for them," the judge told him.

"Did those boys, aside from the Endicott boy, come from well-to-do families?" the sheriff asked.

"No, not that I'm aware of at the moment," the judge said. "Oh, by the way, the bodies have all been positively identified through DNA as the boys Curtis named to us a little while ago. There will be an article in the newspaper about this any day now, I'm sure."

"Will the article mention who killed them?" Dee Dee asked.

Judge Wesson stood up from his chair and cleared his throat.

"I think the deal might work out this way, if you will indulge me a moment," he started. "Gus's mural will most likely sell at the art gallery auction that's coming up, and it will probably fetch several million dollars from what I am hearing. As for the Turpricone News, the crime of who killed the three boys will remain unsolved. However, their bodies will be identified by name. As compensation for the pain and suffering of the families, the Jarrellson Trust, since the bodies were found on Jarrellson property, will give all proceeds from the sale of the mural to the families of those boys. It will be an altruistic way of saying Campbell County is very apologetic for your long-term grief, and the case will be closed."

"With the addition of one very important stipulation," Dee Dee interjected. "Anna Mary is to leave Destini alone. She will not serve her those papers. Carl Alvin and I have talked it over. We have enough land between us that we are willing to deed a section each to Anna Mary and Stanley, and give Stanley a position on the board of the Bank of Pittstown, but Destini's inheritance remains intact. If Anna Mary or Stanley renege on any part of the agreement, we will make that journal public, which we are going to keep in a safe place, by the way. I'm certain Curtis will have no objections to any of this."

"My God! What a monster that Gus Jarrellson was!" Chad suddenly shrieked, shaking his head, as if it just now sunk in what Gus had done. "All that money and all that talent, but such a sick and twisted mind! Dear God, help us all!"

"Amen to that," Dee Dee agreed.

֎֎֎֎֎֎֎֎֎֎

IT WAS CLOSE to nine-thirty that evening when everyone dispersed from Camp EZ. The sheriff, the judge, and the state attorney had all piled into the sheriff's brand new, big, black SUV and they called on Anna Mary and Stanley at about quarter to ten. The lights were still on inside the home, which meant they most likely hadn't turned in for the night yet. Solemnly, yet diligently, the three men marched up to the front door and the sheriff rang the doorbell.

The scene at the Williams' home that night was not a pretty one, to say the least, but an agreement was reached, albeit begrudgingly on the Williams' part.

After the trio of news-bearers left the Jarrellson

home and were well down the road, Anna Mary let loose a tirade of obscenities aimed directly at Stanley.

After she calmed down some, she told Stanley, "You'd better get that damned boat down at the landing ready right now. I want you to check on how far along Sonny Boy Esmerian has come with blowing up that damned experiment of yours out at Wilson Creek."

"How do you know about me and Sonny Boy?" he asked her, clearly stunned that she knew about their relationship.

"Stanley, I know everything," she told him, rolling her eyes. "Now, go check on Sonny Boy, you hear?"

"I'm going, Anna Mary, I'm going," Stanley muttered. "You can count on me to take care of things," he added, and he started for the backdoor.

Anna Mary thought for a moment and then sternly said, "I think not! No, sir, I've changed my mind. I will be going with you, Stanley. I want to witness this thing with my very own eyes."

"What?!" he gasped. "You can't be serious!"

"I am dead serious!" she told him. "I am going with you, Stanley. You don't actually think for a minute that the good name of this family is going to be left to your capriciousness, do you?" she asked him.

"Well, Anna Mary, I think we can pretty well assume that the family name, if this goes public, will become a dirty... a *very* dirty name thanks to your beloved Uncle Gus. Let's see... molesting our son? Killing young boys? Using the love of an old woman to cover it up? Now, trying to get more property and money from Destini? Did I miss anything, dear?"

"Only one thing, Stanley, only one," she told him. "Right now, I won't tell you what that is. I'll save it until after your little experiment is totally destroyed. I want us... that means you and me, Stanley... I want us to be on the river or at least near it when this goes down, and I want to look you straight in the eyes when I reveal it to you. Yes, sir, I surely do."

"Fine," Stanley said, and then he straightened his shoulders. "While you're pondering that, whatever it may be, I want you to also think about this. Your Uncle Gus, that sweet old man that you always adored, is the one who authorized Edison Energy to build that nuclear plant on your precious Jarrellson property," he added, and then he turned his back to her and stormed out the door, almost running, as he headed down toward the river.

"Stanley Williams, you're a damned liar! Do you hear me?! You wait up for me!" Anna Mary screamed, as she hurried to catch up to him. "You no good...!" she trailed off, spouting off more obscenities than he had heard come out of her mouth in the entire time he had known her.

As Anna Mary's voice drifted off into the darkness of the woods and the thick night air, Stanley's thoughts were all over the place, but there was one thing he wanted right now more than anything.

"I wish there was a magic wand that could make this evil woman disappear!" he yelled.

At that very moment, a bright bolt of lightning lit up the sky, immediately followed by the loudest clap of thunder Stanley had ever heard. Two seconds later, the skies let loose with buckets of heavy raindrops.

Not far behind him there was a big thud that shook the ground. Then, Anna Mary's voice began screaming, "Stanley! Stanley! Come back here! I'm hurt, Stanley! I'm hurt!"

Against his better judgment, Stanley turned around and rushed toward her relentless yelling. When he found her, she was lying on the ground face up, all muddy and soaked from head to toe. A thirty-foot pine tree was lying on the ground about a foot in front of her. It was all he could do not to laugh.

"We'll have to take care of this experiment of yours tomorrow, Stanley," she told him, as the rain continued to pelt them. "I seem to have twisted my ankle, or maybe even broken it. Help me up, Stanley. Let's go back to the house."

Dutiful husband that he had been for so many years, Stanley did as she directed, but he had to get in the last word, as he carried her back to the house.

"This was a stupid idea, Anna Mary," he told her. "A stupid, stupid idea."

Anna Mary was so beside herself that for once in her life she could think of nothing to say.

Chapter 19

No more lies

That same night, Chad was sitting in his living room trying to read a magazine and get his mind off what had just been revealed at Camp EZ, but he couldn't get past the first paragraph of the first article. He just kept reading it over and over again, and losing track of what he had just read. Nothing, it seemed, was sticking in his brain. Nothing except the vile, grisly way those three boys had been murdered.

He went out to the kitchen and poured himself a glass of Pinot Grigio, hoping it might relax him a little.

"Oh, this is awful," he said, scrunching up his face after he took a sip. "It's as flat as roadkill," he added, and then he dumped it down the sink.

He thought about going out for a jog, but he gave up that idea. It was much too late already. Plus, he was exhausted. As he stood in the kitchen, staring out at the night sky, he recalled what Miss Aggie had written in her journal about him.

"I pray you find happiness. It may be very close to you. Closer than you can imagine."

At that very moment, there was a knocking at the front door.

"Oh, crap," he muttered.

He hurriedly yanked on his pants and slipped into a t-shirt before putting on his toupee. When he opened the door, there stood Carl Alvin.

"Chad, I am tired of pretending," Carl Alvin blurted out. "I am tired of the charade I have lived for so, so long. I would like for us to become better friends. I would also like for you and me to fly down to Barbados for a few days. Just to get away, you know? Would you like that, Chad? Would you do that with me? I have some business to attend to first, but my schedule will be all cleared up by Friday after next, if that works for you."

Chad seemed taken aback at first and it showed on his face. The more he stared at Carl Alvin, though, the more he realized what was actually going on and it seemed to please him.

"I would love to go to Barbados with you, Carl Alvin, but I'll have to phone the vet's office in the morning and make sure they can send someone over to pick up my pets and attend to them while I'm gone," he said.

"No need for that," Carl Alvin told him with a mischievous grin on his face. "It's all been taken care of."

"Really? How?" Chad gasped, but then he caught himself and he smiled. "Your cousin, Dee Dee, right?" he asked.

"Yes, the vet is a dear friend of hers," Carl Alvin told him, smiling wide. "So, you handsome Yankee boy… you'll come with me for maybe a week or two?"

"You bet I will," Chad said, smiling back at him.

"Excellent!" Carl Alvin gleefully shouted. "I'll make all the travel arrangements, so don't worry about any of that. Just make sure your passport is in order and up to date," he added, and then he reached out and took Chad by the hand. "I can't wait," he said, smiling like a kid on Christmas morning. "We're going to have such a marvelous time together. We'll just go and forget about all this craziness for a while. I am so ready. Aren't you?" he asked Chad.

"Oh, yes, I've been ready," Chad told him. "In fact, I have been ready for a long, long time."

"Well, then, I shall talk to you tomorrow," Carl Alvin said, and he turned to leave. Before exiting the front door, he swung around and said, "I'll bet you look much more handsome with a bald head. Bald is in, you know," he added, and he walked out the door.

Chad was clearly embarrassed. When he looked in the mirror by the front door, he saw how crooked the darned toupee was on his head. A few seconds later, he burst out laughing, thankful that his long-held secret of being bald was finally out in the open.

Later, as he was lying in bed, minus the toupee, he realized that for the first time in a long, long time, a sense of peace had settled over him.

"This feels good," he said, rubbing his baldness and thinking about the trip to Barbados with Carl Alvin. "It feels really, really good."

Chapter 20

Memories of Walter Drake

Dee Dee was up at the crack of dawn the morning after the big powwow with Curtis and Chad, anxious to see how the entire day would play out. To start things off, little Lily Dee would be christened at around ten-thirty at Mt. Nebo A.M.E. Church, and then a large crowd would descend upon the magnificent Jarrellson house up on the hill for her christening luncheon.

"First things first, though," Dee Dee said, as she prepared to take a shower. "I need to talk to Destini and let her know what's been going on, so that she doesn't think we've purposely been keeping her out of the loop."

When Dee Dee arrived on Destini's doorstep at around eight-thirty, the first thing out of Destini's mouth was, "Okay, who died?"

"Oh, you silly woman," Dee Dee said, laughing. "No one has died... well, maybe I should take that back. Some people died, but it was a long time ago. About twenty-five years to be exact."

Just then, Phil pulled up in the yard. A few minutes later, the three of them were sitting around the kitchen table enjoying a cup of coffee, while Matt and Lily Dee were asleep in the bedroom.

"So, what were you about to tell me about some people dying?" Destini asked Dee Dee.

After Dee Dee and Phil caught her up on the discovery of the skeletal remains, as well as all that had happened yesterday with the reading of Miss Aggie's journal by the crazy professor, Destini said she had her own stories to tell.

"I remember when all that stuff happened," she said, and then she stood up from her chair. "You know what? I'd better go get Matt up, so he can take a shower while Lily Dee is sleeping. I don't want us to be late to the christening."

"That's a good idea," Dee Dee told her.

As soon as she was out of earshot, Dee Dee asked Phil not to say anything to Destini about what Anna Mary and Stanley had planned to do to her and he agreed it was best to keep that private for now. When Destini came back into the kitchen, she was rarin' to talk, starting just where she left off.

"Those poor, young boys who went missing," she said, shaking her head. "I recall something else that happened about that same time, and oh, how I wish Mama Tee was still alive. She used to have all kinds of nightmares and visions, as I'm sure I've told y'all before."

"Yes, we know all about them," Dee Dee said, looking over at Phil.

"Well, she often told me it was like those boys were being moved into something dark and cold," Destini said. "She said the one who was moving them was not the one the law was even questioning."

"She was definitely onto something, that sweet, old

Mama Tee," Dee Dee fondly said, and then she heaved a heavy sigh, as a lone tear trickled down her cheek. "I sure do miss her."

"Now, don't get me started," Destini warned her. "Today is supposed to be a happy day. My baby, Lily Dee, is getting baptized."

"You are absolutely right, my dear," Dee Dee agreed. "So... you were saying?"

"Well, I remember Mama Tee screaming in her sleep... screaming over and over, "That ain't it! The water's on fire, but that ain't it!" She had that dream more than once, too. So, I asked her, Duke asked her, Essie, we all asked her what she was dreaming about, but she never would say much. All she ever told us was there's some things best left unsaid, and there's some things, if you don't know for sure, you don't need to go huntin' to find an answer."

"That's Mama Tee for you," Dee Dee said. "Ever the wise woman."

"She said most folks thought about huntin' from the perspective of being the hunter and not the hunted," Destini continued. "Yeah, that's what she said. I asked her what she meant by it, but she wouldn't say no more than that. I can still hear her screams, and I can still hear her yellin' those words in her sleep. The water's on fire, but that ain't it. I wish I knew what she was talking about."

"Yeah, me, too," Dee Dee said.

"I remember there was a man who would come by from time to time and bring Mama Tee a sack of them

Satsuma oranges and then visit with her for a while," Destini went on. "I don't know how they knew each other, but he was an unusual sort, to say the least. When I asked why he didn't come around no more, Mama Tee said he moved away to south Florida. I think his name was Walter Drake, or something like that.

"Well, that's a new one on me," Dee Dee said. "Never heard that name before."

"Well, he was a pleasant enough guy, but one time he brought a little red and white Chihuahua with him. Duke and Essie's big ol' bulldogs aggravated the heck out of the poor little thing the whole time he was there," she added, laughing.

"I can only imagine," Phil said, laughing with her.

"Mama Tee always said there were some folks who just needed to talk, and that this guy, Walter, was one of 'em. I remember during their few visits, Mama Tee hardly ever got a word in edgewise. He was either talking about his dogs, his exotic birds, his mother, his ex-partner, who died at the age of forty-two…"

"I'm sorry," Dee Dee interrupted her. "His ex-partner? You mean like a gay partner or a business partner?"

"A gay partner," Destini replied. "All's I know is he left Walter everything and Walter said he blew it all. On what, I don't remember. Mainly he talked about his father, who he said was an industrialist in the cosmetic and fragrance business. He said he provided quite well for him, until he found out about his sexuality and lifestyle, that is. Seems his father had hired a private detective who discovered his little secret. So, when his father made out his will, he left nothing for Walter, who said it came as no surprise to him. He said his father left everything to Walter's older sister and brother by his dad's first marriage. Since Walter hardly ever had a thing to do with either one of them, what little he did get, he had to go to court for it. To make a long story short, the sister and brother, both much older than him, were left yachts, ski resorts, island retreats, luxurious condominiums, one in Fisher Island and the other in Palm Beach, as well as trust funds that were quite substantial."

"Boy, Destini, that is one good memory you have," Dee Dee said.

"What can I say? I was a bored little kid there for a while with nothing to do but eavesdrop on my Mama Tee," Destini said, laughing. "I do have a good memory, though. Yes, I got the memory of an elephant," she added, still laughing.

"Well, have you left anything out?" Phil asked.

"Well, let's see. Hmmm… Oh, yeah, Walter was left enough money to live on comfortably, or so he said. It was a pittance compared to his siblings, though. He said he lived in a really nice double-wide home with a few of his mother's furniture items. He said his parents divorced when he was young, so there were only a few pieces of nice jewelry, but a lot of memories. Those two siblings of his got the lion's share and they never wanted to have anything to do with Walter."

"Wow, what a sad story," Dee Dee said.

"It sure was," Destini agreed. "When his settlement came, he said there was a clause in it that stated as long as he didn't rock the boat, then his income would keep rolling in. Mama Tee said the one thing Walter did have was a top rate mind, although, it had never been put to good use, since he never worked outside the home."

"Again… so sad," Dee Dee said.

"His life revolved around his pets, his well-tended yard, and his hair, which looked real, but it wasn't. He said he went bald before his twenty-first birthday."

"Omigod! Really?" Dee Dee gasped.

"Really," Destini said. "Walter said he always had a steady stream of men who visited at odd hours and left as hurriedly as they arrived. The rumor around town, he said, was that he liked big barrel-chested men, who were younger in age and preferably married. He said he wasn't into sharing any of what he had with anyone, which didn't make much sense to me, since these men had wives, but what do I know? Maybe he was talkin' about somethin' else.

"Yeah, maybe," Dee Dee said.

"On occasion, it was rumored he would even offer a guy gas money to drive over and meet him if he liked his looks and lived in the area."

"Oh, my word," Phil said, cupping his hand over his mouth.

"Yeah, he kept very much to himself and socialized little, if any," Destini said. "He had few friends, mainly because he was incapable of cultivating any, I suppose.

He, more or less, loved only three folks; me, myself, and I," she added, ending her long ago recollections of a man named Walter Drake, for whatever it was worth.

Destini, it seemed, was blessed with inheriting many of Mama Tee's uncanny, insightful abilities, but it would be a while longer before she would make the connection between Walter Drake and Chad.

Chapter 21

A celebration of life

Precious newborn, Lily Dee Abamu, was fast asleep in the arms of her mother, wearing the same christening gown that was worn by her half-sister, the late Easter Bunnye Wilson-Brayerford. It was also the same gown that Dee Dee and Carl Alvin had worn at their christenings. It was a vintage, white cotton gown with a floral border eyelet across the bodice and hem, and came with a matching bonnet, appropriate for either a boy or a girl.

Lily Dee made a pretty picture before an altar decorated with pale pink roses and, of course, huge vases full of white Casablanca lilies and Easter lilies. Destini had asked Dee Dee if she would do the honor of playing soft, background gospel music on the piano during the ceremony and she gladly accepted.

Anna Mary had called Dee Dee on her cell phone that morning. First, she advised her that Mary Selena wouldn't be able to attend as planned, due to a last minute exam her English professor had sprung on the class. Then, she begged out on attending the christening service herself, claiming she had hurt her ankle, and that Stanley was over in Jacksonville for the morning. When Dee Dee asked if the christening party was still on, Anna Mary assured her it was and that her ankle was healing, but she needed to stay off it as much as possible. Of course, she didn't offer any explanation as to how she hurt her ankle and Dee Dee didn't ask.

The aging Reverend Aloysius Jackson was now standing in front of the pulpit wearing his long black robe with a white stole around his neck. Even as old as he was, his signature boisterous sermon was still intact, as Destini and Matt stood before him with their newborn child. Throughout his sermon, as usual, there were lots of hearty "Amen's" from the entire congregation.

When it came time for the actual christening, the reverend dipped a single Easter lily into the silver bowl containing water from the River Jordan. It had cost Dee Dee a small fortune to have the holy water shipped to the church via overnight courier, but she told Destini she was happy to do it.

Soon, the reverend ended his sermon and the music died down to a point where it was barely audible. Everyone in the congregation was now on their feet, as Reverend Jackson asked Destini what the baby should be named.

"Lillian Delphine Abamu," Destini proudly said, and then she looked over at Dee Dee, who was smiling from ear to ear, as her eyes filled with tears of joy.

Reverend Jackson took the baby from Destini's outstretched arms. "In the name of the Father, the Son, and the Holy Ghost, I announce that ye shall be named Lillian Delphine Abamu!" he shouted, as he sprinkled the holy water onto the baby's forehead. "Glory to God!" he shouted again.

The entire congregation, including every member

of Destini's family, her extended family, and all of her closest friends who had come to celebrate with her, joined in and shouted, "Glory to God! Amen!"

When the service was over, there was quite a long photo session with everyone wanting a picture of themselves with Lily Dee and her proud parents. Then, the entire group from the church departed for the Jarrellson home at the top of the hill, some of them with a slight trepidation in their heart, specifically, Dee Dee, Lily Dee's godmother, and Carl Alvin, the child's godfather.

On the way to the luncheon, Dee Dee, who had insisted on driving and leading the procession of vehicles, chatted away with Carl Alvin, who was sitting in the front passenger seat. Ricardo and Chad were sitting in the back seat.

Finally, Dee Dee turned onto the half-mile long gravel drive of the Jarrellson home. It was bordered by wild azaleas in full bloom and in every color; formosa, light pink, white, and the ever popular salmon colored hue. It was as if Anna Mary had set the azaleas on a timer to bloom at just the right moment.

"Well, everything looks pretty and serene outside," Carl Alvin said. "I just hope the same atmosphere prevails inside."

"You and me both," Dee Dee agreed.

Anna Mary was inside putting the finishing touches on the tables in her sunroom when she heard cars pulling up outside. She had gone all out for this christening brunch event, or as all out as she could bear to go, under the circumstances. She was still slightly limping, due to her sprained ankle, but other than that, she looked none the worse for wear after her little spill in the woods last night. She had decided to attire herself in something simple today, which was really out of character for her, but she felt she needed to play down her holier than thou attitude in order to blend in better with her guests. One last look around the room and she seemed quite satisfied with everything.

Even though Anna Mary was playing down her appearance, the table she had set was quite the opposite, thanks in part to Dee Dee's insistence. At each place setting were the most beautiful Porthault linens that had been hand embroidered with violets and pink roses. All of the napkins were also embroidered, but with the Jarrellson family crest.

About half a dozen or more heavy silver chafing dishes lined a massively large mahogany side board. Off to one corner of the sunroom, a bar had been set up and one of Anna Mary's hired servants was already in place, ready to serve mimosas, Bloody Mary's and screwdrivers to the guests.

Moments later, after Destini stepped into the sunroom, she handed Lily Dee to Matt, who was right behind her, and then she proceeded to the bar where she was asked which of the three drinks she preferred.

"I'll have a screwdriver," she told the young man. "It's one of my favorite mixed drinks. I gotta do somethin' to try and relax while in the company of…" she started to say, but then she thought better of it and simply said, "Never mind."

Within seconds, the young male server handed her the drink in a crystal glass and she thanked him.

"I still don't know why Anna Mary offered to do this for me," she said to Dee Dee, who had come up behind her and ordered a mimosa.

"Well, you know Anna Mary," Dee Dee said. "Anything to make herself look good," she added, rolling her eyes, as she accepted the mimosa from the server.

There were four round tables in the middle of the sunroom that sat eight guests each. The centerpieces were an elegant arrangement of pale pink roses, violets, fishnet fern, and Lily of the Valley, which Dee Dee had specially flown in for the event, since Anna Mary had told her days ago that she wasn't going to bother with centerpieces.

The famous Jarrellson antique silver flatware adorned each place setting. The flatware had been specially designed for the Jarrellson family during the turn of the century by a famous silversmith flatware company in London. Each piece was engraved with a beautiful cursive "$\mathcal{J}$".

Evidently anxious to get things rolling, Anna Mary asked Reverend Jackson to bless the food and the occasion, which he did in fine style, followed by many more raucous "Amen's" from the entire group.

Again, although Anna Mary was simply dressed, she spared no expense in hiring a harpist from the Jacksonville Symphony, who played throughout the entire event, just so she could flaunt her upper echelon heritage, no doubt, Dee Dee figured.

As the brunch came to a close, all who had assembled in the Jarrellson family's sunroom to celebrate the birth of Destini and Matt's new baby thanked Anna Mary for her hospitality and for all the delicious food. Anna Mary pulled Destini aside and quietly slipped her a boxed gift, saying it was a present for the baby. She also asked her to wait to open it until she got home.

"Well, sure," Destini said. "I'll open it when I get home… and thank you, Anna Mary. Thank you for everything," she added, and she gave her a warm hug.

Once the last of the group had exited the front door and piled into their vehicles to head back from whence they came, Anna Mary shouted for all the maids and other hired help to join her in the sunroom.

"Make it snappy, now!" she yelled to them. "I've got work for you to do!" she added, as she hobbled back into the sunroom. "Damn you, Stanley," she muttered. "You did this to me, you slimy little bastard."

Chapter 22

Radioactive thoughts

Few people in the state of Florida were still alive who knew about the experimental nuclear plant. In Campbell County, only Stanley and Sheriff Bartow Lewis had knowledge of it, and the sheriff's knowledge was limited at best. According to sealed court records, when Edison Energy first approached the idea of experimenting with nuclear power for their many power plants across the state of Florida, they decided to test it in what was then a fairly remote area in Campbell County. It happened many, many years ago and quite frankly, it was a miracle that the press never got wind of it.

Right after breakfast the morning of the christening party, Stanley had retreated upstairs to Watson's old bedroom where his wife had banished him to. He told Anna Mary the previous day there was no way he was going to participate in the christening event and watch the charade of feigned happiness on her face concerning the arrival of Destini's new baby.

"I hope Anna Mary is happy now," Stanley muttered to himself later that day after all the guests finally left.

As for him, he was definitely not happy about anything. He decided to take a short nap, so he'd be well rested for the long night that lay ahead of him.

After turning down the bedcovers, he lied down and stretched out his body, desperately trying to get comfortable on the old twin size bed, but not having much luck.

"I didn't want to burst your bubble about your beloved uncle, Anna Mary, but you asked for it, and you'll find out soon enough," he mumbled to himself, as he thought back to the day this entire nightmare had begun.

The Jarrellson family, specifically just their spokesman at the time, Anna Mary's Uncle Gus, allowed Edison Energy to construct a small plant on Jarrellson property to experiment with the feasibility of nuclear power. It was not without remuneration from Edison, either, and as a side benefit and added bonus, it also furthered Stanley's climb up the corporate ladder. No one else in the Jarrellson family had the slightest clue what was going on.

The test plant was built deep in the heart of Jarrellson land and it was well-camouflaged from discovery by anyone. At the time of its construction, there were no permits issued and the knowledge of what was being done was extremely limited to just a handful of people in the state.

The property where the plant was located was in a prime spot, high up on the bank of the river and far out of any flood zone. It was where Anna Mary wanted to begin construction of the memorial to their son, Watson and his wife, but first, he and Anna Mary had to get the land back from Destini, which was already in the works and soon to be finalized, since Anna Mary had served Destini with the papers from the attorney today at the christening party.

Even though Destini owned the property, she had only checked on it one time in a quick drive-by just weeks after the reading of Hamp's will. She had made it clear to everyone that she didn't want the land to be disturbed. She wanted it kept in its natural state, which is why she had it immediately fenced in.

The plant had officially been shut down for years already, but Stanley, who had decided to make the test plant a secret scientific retreat for himself, went there every now and again to keep tabs on the place and assure nothing had been disturbed by any outsiders. On occasion, he would even activate the plant, which gave him a thrill and an unimaginable high, as if he had just snorted the finest Colombian cocaine.

The original fuel rods for the plant were deeply immersed into the headwaters of Wilson Creek and, as far as Stanley knew, they had been operating long enough to have become slightly radioactive, which, for some unknown reason, never concerned him much.

What he had discovered in his research over the years was that when uranium nuclei fission into smaller nuclei, the fission products all become radioactive. They emit beta radiation, which consists of fast moving electrons. Nothing can go faster than the speed of light in a vacuum, but in water, light travels a bit slower. It's called Cherenkov radiation.

Stanley had learned this and much more during his

research, which is why he had been so adamant about getting back the land that Hamp Brayerford had willed to Destini. After all, that's where the nuclear plant was located, unbeknown to Destini, of course.

As the years progressed, Stanley had convinced himself that he needed that property on the river to keep the experiment going that he had engineered all those years ago with Edison Energy, who, by the way, had used Campbell County as a guinea pig. Stanley often wondered if Hamp had any knowledge of the plant, but since he was dead now, that question would never be answered.

Stanley was now being forced by Anna Mary to destroy all evidence of the nuclear plant, which was something he didn't want to do. After the recent late night visit from the judge, the sheriff, and the state attorney, however, things sped up tremendously, as it had now become an urgent matter. There was no time to wait for the final deed to the property to make it through the courts. Things had changed drastically, especially since Anna Mary had stuck her nose into things that were none of her business, as far as Stanley was concerned.

"I wish I could spare you the pain of knowing your supposedly beloved Uncle Gus had a part in this, Anna Mary," Stanley said, as he stared at the ceiling. "Quite frankly, though, now that you've shown your true colors, I don't give a damn if I hurt you or not."

Stanley, it seemed, had finally reached a breaking point with his wife and he vowed not to take any more of her humiliating and degrading behavior toward him.

"It's time to assert my manhood," he declared.

All in all, Stanley had no trouble allowing folks to believe what they wished about what was causing the creek water to glow. In fact, it was much better for him if they thought it was caused by the limestone company or even Feed the World Organics.

All he knew now was that Anna Mary wouldn't stop her relentless badgering until the place was destroyed. Soon, though, all evidence of the test reactor and its potential long-term harm to the environment would be obliterated and buried forever, even though it would require trespassing onto Destini's land.

That was the plan, anyway, and it would be carried out around midnight tonight. Stanley sat up and fluffed his pillow, and then laid his head back down, as his eyes filled with tears.

"That monument would have been so beautiful," he mumbled, as he dozed off into a deep sleep.

Chapter 23

Vengeance is mine, sayeth the Lord

"Oh, thank goodness all those people are gone," Anna Mary mumbled, when the last of the baby christening guests had left her home. "I thought they would never leave."

Seconds later, she called her entire staff into the sunroom. Once everyone quieted down, she spoke.

"I realize all of this beautiful bone white china that was used here this afternoon is new, but I want it all thrown away immediately," she told them. "I never want any of it to be eaten from again. Do you understand?" she asked the staff, and everyone nodded. "I want all of the silverware to be placed into boiling water with heavy duty bleach, and then it is to be sent back to the vault at the bank in the same boxes it arrived in. I want each box marked, as well, with today's date and the name Destini Abamu. This silverware will never, ever be used again in this home." She thought a moment and then added, "Although, if Mary Selena wants it, that's fine with me. My lips, however, shall never touch it ever again. Understood?"

Again, all the staff nodded in the affirmative.

"All these crystal goblets," Anna Mary went on, pointing to them on the tables. "I want you to throw them away, as well. I don't want my mouth touching any of it. It's bad enough that I had to acquiesce and have that trash come into my home, but this was a one shot deal. I can assure you of that!" she exclaimed, going off on a rant that never should have been said out loud, especially to her help, some of whom were African American.

No one flinched, though, as Anna Mary continued to spew her deep-seated hatred.

"Can you imagine they were all hinting earlier at wanting to borrow the Jarrellson christening gown for Lily Dee? Fat chance on that one!" she shouted. "I pretended I couldn't find it. Ha! If you think for a minute I would allow that *thing* to use my family christening gown for her *issue*, you can think again," she declared. "I am surprised they didn't wrap that baby in some African cloth with bird bones around her head and neck," she said, laughing. "They probably would have if that silly Dee Dee hadn't given them her christening gown. Oh, well, I hope I never get that needy. I do hope Destini opens her gift from me on the way home. I would pay anything to see the expression on Mrs. Destini Abamu's face when she does."

Little did Anna Mary know, but Stanley had entered the room. His attempts at taking a nap had failed miserably, due to the uncomfortable bed and the sunlight streaming in through the lace curtains. He witnessed her entire tirade about Destini and her friends. In fact, she was still ranting on and on to the help, as if she thought they actually cared what she thought about anything.

"To think Dee Dee thought she could scare me into surrendering to her will regarding Destini and that baby of hers..." Anna Mary trailed off, and then she spotted Stanley by the doorway staring at her. "Oh, Stanley, there you are, dear. I want you to call our attorney, Mr. Carter, and check on the status of Matthew Abamu. I want to know under what circumstances he has been allowed into this country. Use every contact we have, right on up to the White House, if you have to. I want that Bible-beating piece of baggage deported back to Africa as soon as possible. I want his bitch, Destini, to grieve, grieve, and grieve some more. She must grieve the way I have grieved. She deserves every bit of grief I can send her way," she added, and then she started toward the window to look out onto the Suwannee River.

"Don't you think you're being a bit too dramatic and just a tad too vindictive, Anna Mary?" Stanley asked her, as he motioned for the help to get busy clearing the tables.

Anna Mary whipped around as if an electric shock had struck her, bad sprained ankle and all. She marched quickly across the room to where Stanley was standing tall and erect, at first not even noticing the darts of pain shooting up her leg.

"The only thing keeping me from screaming at you and slapping the hell out of you right now is the fact that this foot is throbbing," she admitted. "Besides, your lip hasn't healed yet," she added with disdain. "So, do what you do best, Stanley. Shut up and leave. Go somewhere for a while. Get out of my sight, because I am going to limp out onto the terrace, smoke a cigar, and savor the moment of Destini Wilson Abamu's expression when she opens my present. Leave me now, Stanley," she added, and she dismissed him, as she would a servant.

❧❧❧❧❧❧❧❧❧❧

MEANWHILE, Destini had asked Matt to take the baby home and put her to bed because she and Dee Dee had some things to talk over, and also that Dee Dee had a few more baby things to give her, which was sort of half true. Duke and Essie eagerly offered to drive Matt and the baby home, stating that they wanted some time with their favorite new niece, and that it would not be out of their way. Truth be known, Destini just wanted a break from mothering for a bit.

"I love that little baby, but goodness gracious, she can sure wear me down," Destini confessed to Dee Dee after Matt, Duke, Essie and Lily Dee left.

"I'll bet," Dee Dee said. "Gee, I can't wait until mine are born," she added with a chuckle.

"Oh, your time is comin'," Destini promised her. "Yes, ma'am."

On the way to Camp EZ, Destini, who was in the passenger seat of Dee Dee's SUV, decided to defy Anna Mary's request. She unwrapped the gift that was given to her and inside was a gold bracelet for Lily Dee.

"Well, lookie here," Destini said. "Isn't this just beautiful?"

"It sure is," Dee Dee said. "What's that other stuff in the box?" she asked.

"I don't know," Destini said, and then she pulled out a sheath of legal-sized papers that had been folded in half.

"Oh, no," Dee Dee grunted. "I don't believe this."

After Destini quickly scanned the first couple pages of the documents, she looked over at Dee Dee in shock, and then she wailed, "Lord have mercy! Leopards don't never change their spots, do they?!"

"I am so sorry, Destini," Dee Dee said, shaking her head and having a hard time keeping her eyes on the road.

"You knew about this?!" Destini asked her, raising her eyebrows. "Why didn't you tell me?!"

"I thought it was a moot point," Dee Dee told her. "I thought it was all over with when the sheriff, Judge Wesson, and the state attorney met with Anna Mary and Stanley the other night. I was certain they had come to an understanding with Anna Mary and Stanley. I guess we were all mistaken. We tried, honey. We all tried as hard as we could to change their minds. I actually thought Anna Mary would use better judgment."

"Well, I guess there's no accounting for what grief and anger can do to a person," Destini said. "I know she blames me for a lot. She always has. She hated Mama Tee. Never made any bones about it, either, but to stand up at her funeral and Bunnye's funeral and…"

"Act?" Dee Dee rhetorically asked, filling in the blank for her. "Anna Mary; the consummate actress. That whole Jarrellson clan are, and always have been experts at acting, especially if it meant they'd get what they wanted. She has to want your land and your money terribly much to risk damaging her uncle's quote-unquote stellar reputation. Boy, oh, boy, when word gets out about what he did..." she trailed off. "You know, she has placed it all on the altar fire now, though. It looks like we'll just have to let the chips fall where they may."

After a brief lull in the conversation, Destini said, "No, Dee Dee, I don't want you to do that, and you tell everybody else who knows about this the same thing. If Gus's secret gets out, it will affect that sweet baby, Mary Selena. I won't have that. I just won't," she adamantly said.

"I don't agree, but if that's really what you want, then I'll let everyone else know," Dee Dee assured her.

"Thank you," Destini said. "According to this paperwork, I'll have more than enough to live on, even with all of Anna Mary's manipulation, so, no. Let Anna Mary and Stanley run with it. Let them think they've won the battle. Things have a way of working out, you know. They always do. As for me, I am putting my faith in God. He has never failed me yet and he never will," she added, and she shoved the paperwork and the bracelet back into the box.

Chapter 24

They all fall down

Stanley Williams, at age fifty-four, was in great physical shape and he prided himself on it. Tonight, he was paddling his prized, extremely expensive, handmade wooden canoe down the Suwannee River. Anna Mary, oddly or not, had purchased it for him on their first wedding anniversary. At that time, the canoe cost well over fifteen-hundred dollars. Since it was in pristine shape, it was probably worth ten times that now.

Stanley loved his canoe, and he loved nothing better than paddling up and down the Suwannee River, especially in the early morning hours or right before dusk when there was a full moon. For him, it was always a peaceful getaway where he could just be Stanley Williams and not Anna Mary Jarrellson's husband, a label he had grown to despise.

Tonight, however, she had robbed him of that bit of peace when she insisted on coming along. He had a terrible stress headache right now, mainly because of Anna Mary and her constant carping, which she hadn't stopped for the last several days. Even now, she just kept bitching about one thing after the next, like a vinyl record that had gotten stuck on the turntable.

He finally had all he could take and he turned to her and said, "Please, please close your mouth. Damn!

You sound like Dee Dee, for godsakes. Shall I call you Dee Dee Dumb Ass, now? I have brought you with me, Anna Mary, just as you asked, but for the love of God, shut the hell up! Do you want to alert someone who might be out along the river that we're out here this time of night?"

For once in his life, Stanley had actually put Anna Mary in her place. For the moment, anyway, because she did indeed shut up.

It was just after midnight when Stanley tied off the canoe a short distance up the river away from Wilson Creek. In the distance was the sound of a purring engine that turned out to be a souped-up golf cart/ATV sort of vehicle that evidently had a powerful muffler on it because the engine was super quiet. Behind the wheel was Tate "Sonny Boy" Esmerian, who had come to rendezvous with Stanley.

"Well, I see we have some company tonight," Sonny Boy said to Stanley, clearly taken aback, yet looking somehow amused.

"Yes, I'm afraid so," Stanley muttered. "She insisted on coming... oh, and she knows all about this place, so let's get on with our mission."

Sonny Boy seemed a bit unnerved for a second or two, but he finally said, "Well, Stanley, if you say it's okay, then who am I to argue with you? What are you waiting for? Hop in," he told the two of them.

Stanley helped Anna Mary up onto the back of the vehicle, whether she wanted to sit there or not, and then he hopped up into the passenger seat next to

Sonny Boy. A second later, Sonny Boy hit the gas pedal and sped off through the scrub bushes and woods, aiming toward the secret site of Stanley's beloved nuclear experiment.

Not only was Sonny Boy an expert in the art of lovemaking, dancing, and technology, but he was also an expert on how to detonate sensitive sites, such as those involving structures of a nuclear nature. He was one of only a few individuals trained in this very specific field. He had even gone on to teach classes on the subject at Edison Energy, as well as do consulting work for them.

On the other hand, Stanley was one of the most brilliant men Sonny Boy had ever known, and he had told him so on numerous occasions. What Stanley didn't know, however, was that Sonny Boy had made love to his wife, Anna Mary, many afternoons while Stanley was in Jacksonville or elsewhere for business. Then, later, on those same days, he would meet up with Stanley for dinner in the evening to discuss scientific and technology topics, as if nothing unseemly or illicit had just gone on behind the scenes.

Sonny Boy had evidently discovered that many times, the seemingly untouchable Southern belle lady-to-the-core types, who wore white gloves and spoke in soft, sultry voices, saying words like "nevuh" and "forevuh", never enunciating the letter "r", were oftentimes absolute sex freaks in the bedroom. Anna Mary happened to be one of those women, which might explain why Stanley put up with so much out of her, aside from her money, that is. Even with Sonny Boy's vast experience, though, he caught himself blushing at many of their intimate times together.

Tonight, Sonny Boy's task was specific. Rather like playing a game of Contract Bridge, when you held a three, no-trump hand and knew it. He had already spent many grueling hours undoing wiring, removing equipment, and testing and re-testing every minute detail, so that the little nuclear power plant at Wilson Creek – Stanley's beloved pet project – could be destroyed with very little sound and without a trace of evidence left behind.

When the trio arrived at the site, Sonny Boy didn't say, "We will *try* to detonate the plant now." Instead, he confidently declared, "Are you both ready to say goodbye to all that is here?"

"I'm damn sure ready," Anna Mary said, as Stanley helped her down from the ATV. "In fact, I'm always ready, Mr. Esmerian," she coyly added, and then she winked at him, making sure, of course, that Stanley wasn't watching her.

There was something in her tone, though; something in the way she enunciated that last statement that made Stanley finally realize that something had been going on between his wife and Sonny Boy. He didn't quite know what, but he knew Anna Mary well enough, and he knew her discipline well enough as a consummate actress who always played a part. In fact, he had learned early on that most of the families in the South played to a theater every day of their lives, whether there was an audience or not. The upper class folks of the South played the most impressive roles, and his wife was among the most adept of actresses.

There was one role, however, that Anna Mary had never been able to fake and it wasn't honesty. She had that one down pat and could fake it with the best of them. She once told Stanley, "Dahlin', once you learn to fake honesty, the rest is a piece of cake."

The one thing she couldn't fake was passion, especially in her voice. He knew that because, as a woman, she had desired him for a long time throughout their relationship. It was the one thing that kept him tied to her with such blind devotion for so long. That desire had waned considerably over the past couple of years, though. It had waned enough that he was ashamed to admit it, even to himself.

Like other men who weren't getting what they wanted from home, Stanley had employed the services of a friend in Miami and he was able to enjoy several passionate encounters with a few extremely beautiful escorts. They were young ladies of considerable charm.

The first time he cheated, he felt ashamed of his infidelity, because he truly did love Anna Mary. He had from the beginning of their courtship. He knew for a fact, or at least he thought he knew, that he was the first and only man she had ever been with, but lately, he wasn't so sure of that.

He soon got over the guilt of his infidelities, as he was still quite a virile man. He felt that since his wife wasn't being a wife, even after he had given up most everything for her, that he deserved some comfort in the arms of a woman. A woman who could at least pretend he was the best lover she ever had. He was a disciplined man, though, and so he never carried on the affairs close to home. He also made sure his Miami contact knew that he never wanted the same young lady twice, as he wanted no emotional attachment. That was reserved for his wife, insane as it sounded, even to Stanley.

What concerned Stanley the most at the present time, was that in Anna Mary's voice, when she spoke to Sonny Boy, there was definitely a connection between them. It was like a jolt of electricity... like some sort of emotional attachment between her and Sonny Boy. He was sure of it. In fact, he could almost smell it on both of them. Even with that sick feeling stuck in his gut, and with more than a little resentment, he and Anna Mary stood side by side and watched from afar as Sonny Boy pressed the magic button. Within seconds, Stanley's beloved nuclear experiment became a thing of the past. Everything had simply vanished. It truly was a magical moment... or it should have been.

Stanley reached into his vest and felt the handle of his Smith and Wesson M&P .22 caliber pistol. It was an excellent pistol with a solid aim, and the best part was that it had a silencer. He intended to use it tonight, but he wasn't sure on whom at the moment.

Meanwhile, Anna Mary was laughing loud and hearty, like the Wicked Witch of the West in the ever popular film, *The Wizard of Oz*.

She looked at her husband and said, "Well, Stanley, now that your little playtime toy is over and done with, I have two things for Mr. Esmerian."

She walked over to where Sonny Boy was standing and she and handed him a sealed white envelope.

"Inside is notice of a wire transfer to your bank account in the Grand Cayman Islands," she told Sonny Boy.

Sonny Boy tore open the envelope, inspected the document, and then gave Anna Mary an approving smile, after which she clasped her hands around his face and kissed him passionately on the lips. It was a knowing kiss, for sure, and a long one, as if they had kissed this way numerous times in the past. The shocking part was that neither of them seemed the least bit apprehensive or embarrassed about their public display of betrayal, while Stanley was standing right there watching them.

"Now, Stanley, do you remember that I told you there was one last thing I needed to tell you once this sick experiment of yours had been blown up into oblivion?" Anna Mary asked, although, she didn't wait for him to react or respond. "I'm leaving you, Stanley," she flatly blurted out. "I'm divorcing you, and then Sonny Boy and I plan to marry once he leaves that mousy little wife of his," she added, and then she again kissed Sonny Boy full on the mouth.

"Are you kidding?!" Stanley shouted. "You're almost old enough to be his mother, for godsakes!"

Neither Anna Mary nor Sonny Boy paid any

attention to what Stanley was yelling, and neither of them heard the click of Stanley's pistol when he disengaged the safety catch, as they were so engrossed in yet another kiss. When their lips parted, things took a drastic turn for the worse.

Sonny Boy dropped to the ground first with a shot to the forehead. It hit him squarely between the eyes and killed him instantly. Then, another shot rang out and Anna Mary went down with a bullet to the chest. As she fell to the ground gasping for air, Stanley calmly went over to her. He knelt down beside her and then gently cradled her in his arms, looking at her through his glazed over eyes.

"I had every intention of letting you go to your grave without knowing this important tidbit of information about your heritage, Anna Mary," he told her, as she lied there looking up at him with incredulity in her eyes. "My heart just won't let me, though. You see, Anna Mary, your Uncle Gus wasn't really your uncle at all. He was your father, which makes you an illegitimate bitch."

Anna Mary's eyes grew wide with disbelief, as she stared into Stanley's stone-cold face. Words escaped her. Moments later, her body went limp and her heaving chest became motionless.

Stanley gently closed her eyes, laid her on the ground, stood up, and took one last look at the two dead bodies. He found himself totally devoid of emotion of any kind. Then, he abruptly turned around and looked toward the river, as if he was going to go back to his cherished canoe and back to his home, and pretend none of this had ever happened.

Unfortunately for Stanley, he was a true coward. Always had been. In one swift movement, he put the barrel of the gun into his mouth and pulled the trigger.

As he breathed his last few breaths, he thought about Anna Mary's secret paternity and how it pleased him to get in one last dig before she died.

"No one will ever know who your father really was," he whispered, and then it was lights out forever for Stanley Williams.

It seemed that Stanley was the last of the known survivors who knew about the big, scandalous Jarrellson family secret. The only other people who knew were Uncle Gus and Anna Mary's mother, as far as Stanley was aware, but they were both dead, and now, so was Stanley. Time would tell if there were others who knew.

Chapter 25

A bloody mess

Curtis was in his kayak paddling down the Suwannee River the following morning. It was just after dawn and all the leaves on the trees were still wet with dew. The air was crisp and clean, and the sun was just peeking above the horizon. An entire chorus of birds was chattering back and forth up in the trees, as if having a philosophical conversation among themselves. Others were circling the sky above him, taking short respites on the tree limbs, and then calling out to their brothers and sisters before taking flight again.

As Curtis neared Wilson Creek, he spotted a wooden canoe tied up to a tree just a few feet from the river. It was gently bobbing from side to side, as the river current flowed south on its eventual way toward the Gulf. From the looks of it, he figured whoever owned it must have spent a large sum of money on the vessel. For a few minutes, he glanced all around him, but saw nobody in the area. He even called out to see if anyone would answer him, but no one did.

"That's odd," he said. "Who would leave such an expensive canoe tied up here and then take off? More importantly, who in this town would even own such a canoe? It's gotta belong to a tourist, for sure."

As far as he could tell, this was the area of land just beyond the river bank that Destini owned. As the sun rose higher in the sky, he noted that the fencing wire that enclosed the property had been sliced open in one spot. It looked large enough that a small car could probably squeeze through it without scratching the paint, so he decided to explore. As many times as he'd passed by the area, he had never noticed the fence being cut like it was.

"Heck, what else have I got to do this morning?" Curtis asked himself, and he laughed.

After tying off his kayak, he slipped through the fence and began walking. Since he had nothing pressing to do today, other than catch up on some reading, he decided to walk until he got tired. About two miles in to the property, which was mostly scrub bushes, oak trees and lots and lots of weeds, he saw about half a dozen vultures circling overhead.

"Must be a dead animal... maybe a deer or a wild pig," he thought, and he continued walking.

He came upon a thick growth of jasmine and then some high huckleberry bushes. When he squeezed through all the bushes, he looked ahead of him.

"Oh, my God!" he gasped. "Oh, my God!" he gasped again.

Three people were lying on the ground within close proximity of one another. It was a gruesome scene with pools of dark, red blood soaking the ground all around them. Half of one man's skull had been blown off and a woman looked to have been shot in the chest. He couldn't get a good look at the other body from where he was standing, other than to see that it was a man whose face was a bloody mess. He sure as hell didn't want to get any closer. In fact, the scene was so grisly that he had to turn away and vomit. Not knowing if the killer was still lurking nearby, he took off like a bat out of hell and ran back to the river where his kayak was tied up.

"Oh, my God!" he kept muttering as he ran. When he got closer to the river, it struck him like a bolt of lightning. "Oh, no! I wonder if that canoe belongs to the killer! Oh, crap!"

He made it back to his kayak in one piece, although, he was so out of breath he thought he was going to have a heart attack. The canoe was still there, and as far as he could tell, there was no one else around. He wasted no time in getting out of there as quickly as he could.

ೞೞೞೞೞೞೞೞೞೞ

CURTIS DIDN'T know why he pulled his truck into Neva Wesley's driveway, but he did. He was in a total state of panic when he knocked on her door and begged her to call 9-1-1.

When the operator answered, he shouted, "This is Dr. Curtis Osborne! Three dead at Wilson Creek! Gunshot wounds, all three! Tell the sheriff quickly!"

Then, in what seemed like a split second, Sheriff Bartow Lewis was patched through on the call.

"Who is it, professor?" the sheriff asked him. "Who's dead up there?"

"I can't be certain, but I think it might be Mr. and Mrs. Williams, and Mr. Sonny Boy Esmerian," Curtis replied, still panicked out of his mind, as Neva stood beside him rubbing his back.

Bartow shouted, "Say again, Dr. Osborne?! I don't think I heard you correctly!"

Still shaking like a leaf and in a state of complete shock, Curtis repeated, "Mrs. Anna Mary Jarrellson Williams and her husband Stanley, and Mr. Sonny Boy Esmerian. They're all dead up there on Destini's property by the river!"

"Oh, God," the sheriff muttered. "Oh, dear God. I'm on my way," he added, and he hung up.

Then Neva mumbled, "Oh, Lord," and Curtis fell to the floor. He had fainted and was out like a light. Neva couldn't get him to wake up, so she phoned her son, Dr. Warren Wesley.

"Mom, I'm busy," Warren said, after noting the Caller I.D.

"You're always busy," she hurriedly said. "I think you better come here now, Warren, and come quickly."

After she briefly explained what had happened, her son said, "I'm on my way, Mom."

Warren told his receptionist to cancel his appointments for the rest of the day and he rushed out to his car. On his cell phone, he dialed Judge Wesson's number, and then he sped out of the parking lot. The judge happened to be the legal representative for the hospital board.

After explaining to the judge what had just gone

down, the judge dropped his head to his desk and began to sob. After he collected himself, he said, "Warren, call this number," and he rattled it off to him.

"Whose number is it?" Warren asked.

"Just call the number," the judge told him. "You'll know when she picks up."

A sweet Southern voice answered the call and said, "This is Dee Dee Fernandez."

"Ahh... Mrs. Fernandez, this is Dr. Warren Wesley. Could you please come to my mother's home at Watson Estates right away? You met her recently, I believe. I really need your help. Judge Wesson asked that I phone you. Something terrible has happened. Is your husband there with you?"

"As a matter of fact, he is," she said. "Dr. Wesley, what's going on? You're frightening me."

"I am truly sorry, Mrs. Fernandez. Please allow me to speak to your husband."

Reluctantly, Dee Dee handed the phone to Ricardo, who gave her a puzzled look.

"Yes?" he asked, with the phone to his ear.

Moments later, Ricardo started shaking his head and then he tightly closed his eyes. All the while, Dee Dee was watching his facial expressions. He hung up the phone and then took his wife's hands in his.

"My darling, I have some distressing news to tell you, but I don't want it to affect you and our little ones," he said, looking down at her baby bump.

"What is it, Ricardo? Please! Is it Aunt Hattie? Aunt Nanny? Is it Destini? What?!" Dee Dee shrieked.

"No, my darling, it is Anna Mary and Stanley, and Sonny Boy Esmerian," he solemnly told her. "They are all dead. It seems it might either be a triple murder or a murder suicide. The authorities are on their way now."

"Did the judge say where this happened?" she asked.

"Somewhere on that property that Destini owns down by the river."

Dee Dee said nothing for a long, long time. Tears just oozed from her eyes and kept on oozing until streams of them were rolling down her cheeks and onto the floor.

Finally, she boldly stated, "I never liked Stanley, and he never liked me. Daddy and Uncle Hamp always told me, do business with Yankees, but never trust them or bring them into your inner circle."

"And yet, Dee Dee, you love and trust me, right?" Ricardo asked her.

"Correction," Dee Dee said. "I adore you, Ricardo, and, of course, I trust you implicitly. You are no Yankee, though. If you had been, I might have been tempted to desert the teachings of childhood for you. My goodness, that day in the bathroom… that towel draped around you when I walked in… You know, I always wanted to ask you, but never did. Did you do that on purpose?" she asked, trying to distract her mind away from the tragedy of what she had just been told.

"I will never tell," Ricardo said, with a sly grin. "I will never, ever tell."

"Omigod, Destini!" Dee Dee suddenly gasped. "I

have to tell her about this, Ricardo! Oh, my gosh, Mary Selena... Destini has to know what's going on. She's that child's guardian now!"

"I'll phone Destini, my darling," Ricardo told her. "Let's get going now and check on the professor."

"Ohhh, Ricardo, you go check on him, please, honey. I have to go see Destini. I have to be the one to tell her in person."

"Whatever you wish, darling," Ricardo said. "Just be careful driving."

"I'll be fine," she said, and she grabbed her purse and darted out the front door.

Destini and Matt were sitting in matching rocking chairs on the screened porch of Uncle Hamp's old cabin, which was where they were currently living. Destini was quietly humming an old gospel tune and rocking Lily Dee, who was sound asleep, while Matt was reading yesterday's Turpricone News.

"Well, now," Destini said, smiling when Dee Dee pulled up in the driveway. "Look what the cat drug in."

Dee Dee walked up to the porch, and the expression on her face was what Destini immediately picked up on. That, and her bloodshot eyes.

"Dee Dee, honey, could I get you something?" Destini asked her. "A glass of ice water? Something a little stronger?"

"No, Destini," Dee Dee said. "I have some news for you. Some terrible, tragic news. Anna Mary and Stanley are both dead."

Destini was so stunned that all she could do was

close her eyes and take a few deep breaths.

"Isn't it just awful?" Dee Dee asked her. "I think I'm still in shock."

"My God," Destini mumbled. "What happened?"

"I'm not sure yet," Dee Dee said. "I just found out from Dr. Warren Wesley. The only thing I know for sure is that they are both dead, as well as Sonny Boy Esmerian. The authorities are on their way right now out to that strip of land of yours down by the river."

"Oh, no! My land? Who found them?" Destini asked.

"I believe it was Curtis. You know... the crazy professor."

A few seconds passed while Destini absorbed the news. Meanwhile, Matt retrieved Lily Dee from her, saying he would put her down in her crib for a while.

"You know... all day, day before yesterday, a screech owl kept screaming down in the swamp," Destini said. "I heard him plain as day, and I told Matt that owl is screaming, "Death, Death, Death!" Oh, my Lord... Matt!" she yelled, and her husband came back out on the porch.

"I need you to call Essie," Destini ordered him, and then she stood up and began pacing back and forth on the porch. "Dee Dee, can you get your husband to charter us one of them planes? We need to go to New Orleans right now. I need to give this news to Mary Selena in person. She'll be devastated."

"Isn't she flying in here tomorrow, anyway?" Dee Dee asked.

"Tomorrow is too late," Destini told her. "Before you call Ricardo, get on that cell phone of yours and call the judge. Tell him to call old man Elwood Ellison Carter over in Jacksonville and let him know he better not be calling Mary Selena. Not until after I speak with her, anyway. Tell him Mary Selena will be home here first thing tomorrow morning. Matt, you get Duke to help you move the baby's things and our clothes and stuff up to the Jarrellson house," Destini said, barking out orders like a drill sergeant.

"Say what, Destini?" Matt asked. "We don't need to be moving up there, honey."

"We may not need to, but we're going to," Destini told him. "That is Mary Selena's home. That chil' has already lost her daddy and her mama, and now her grandparents, too. Thank God them evil things that was Stanley's parents are dead. Pit vipers, they was. I hate to say it, but so was Mr. Stanley... and Anna Mary! I don't mean to speak ill of the dead, but I know them two was after me. I know they hated me for no other reason than that their son Watson loved me. I also know they would hate even worse me going into that big house of theirs, but I'm goin'. I don't really wanna go, but I have to be there for that chil', at least until we see what arrangements are going to be made for her."

In the mean time, it had been about an hour since Curtis's 9-1-1 call to the local authorities. Every law enforcement agency in the tri-county area was now at the scene of the crime or on their way, including Sheriff Bartow Lewis, who had arrived first.

Chapter 26

Thy will be done

As Destini had requested, Dee Dee was able to convince Ricardo to let them have use of his company jet to transport her and Destini to New Orleans. They boarded the plane at a small private airport in Pittstown later that afternoon, and within a couple of hours they were standing at the curb outside New Orleans Lakefront Airport hailing a taxi.

Now, it was off to Anna Mary and Stanley's cottage home in the Garden District where Mary Selena was living. There, out on the front porch to greet them were Lady Arabella Simpson Keyes, Mary Selena's maternal great-aunt, who was visiting from London, and the ever-gracious hairdresser extraordinaire, Eileen Paquette, otherwise known to her friends as Miss Sissy. Her still handsome-as-ever assistant, Justin Boudreaux, was standing beside her.

As is the custom in the Deep South, food had been prepared for those "coming in", as the late novelist Harper Lee of *To Kill a Mockingbird* fame had written. "Neighbors bring food with death," she had written.

Young Mary Selena, who was now fifteen years old, appeared in the doorway, dressed in a beautiful white sundress, as she watched Destini and Dee Dee come up the walkway.

"Oh, it is so good to see you both!" she squealed with delight, and she and the two women shared a group hug. "I'm so sorry I missed the christening party, Destini. I had such a beautiful dress to wear, thanks to my generous grandmother, Anna Mary. You know, I was going to take a commercial flight in the morning. I had my ticket and everything. Thankfully, it's refundable," she said, laughing. "You really didn't have to come get me on a private plane, Dee Dee, but I'm glad you did. Maybe you two just wanted to do some shopping here in New Orleans?" she teased them.

Dee Dee motioned for everyone to go inside, so that Destini could speak with Mary Selena alone, and so they all vanished into the kitchen.

"Is everything okay?" Mary Selena asked.

"I need to sit down, baby," Destini said, as she pointed to the swing on the east end of the porch. "Come sit with me, Mary Selena, and let's talk for a few minutes, okay? I know it's a surprise for you seeing us here today. I wish I could be the bearer of happy news, but I'm not. There's no other way to put this, honey…" she trailed off.

Destini then cradled Mary Selena's head against her breast, as she had cradled the girl's father so many years before.

"Baby, Mrs. Anna Mary and Mr. Stanley are dead," Destini blurted out. "We don't know too many of the details yet, but we do know they are both dead."

Mary Selena abruptly pulled away and looked up at her with terror-filled eyes.

"What did you say?" she asked.

Destini tightly closed her eyes and whispered,

"Help me, Lord Jesus." Then, she repeated, "Baby, your grandparents are dead."

Mary Selena just kept staring at her, and then she began to cry. A few seconds later, she stood up and screamed at the top of her lungs. It was just a lot of nonsensical words, but it was enough to bring Dee Dee out onto the porch, as well as everyone else who was in the kitchen.

"Destini, tell me this isn't true!" Mary Selena screamed, as she beat her fists against Destini's chest. "Say it isn't true, Destini!" She turned toward Dee Dee and shouted the same thing. "Say it isn't true!"

Dee Dee was beside herself, but she was able to keep her composure.

"Honey, I can't tell you that," Dee Dee told her. "What I can tell you is that Destini, myself, your aunt, Miss Sissy, Justin… baby, we all love you. We do with all our hearts," she added, and she hugged the weeping child.

"What will happen to me?" Mary Selena asked through her sobs. "I'm an orphan now."

Destini turned Mary Selena around to face her.

"Honey, you are far from being an orphan, as long as I have breath in my body," she told her. "For years, your daddy and Phil were like my very own children. You, young lady, you're my child, too. Always have been," she said. "We have to go home right away to tend to the arrangements for Mrs. Anna Mary and Mr. Stanley. You'll be coming with us, but I don't want you worryin' about nothin', you hear me? I'll be there, your aunt will be there, Dee Dee will be there... all of us, includin' Wanda Faye, Nadine, Carl Alvin, Duke and Essie... honey, you got more people that loves you than you could ever know. Now let's get inside and get your bag packed, okay?"

"Just one thing, Destini," Mary Selena said, reverting back to her stoic, ladylike self, and with pure bravery in her voice. "I want the service for my grandparents to be a celebration of life, not a testament to death. I don't want anyone wearing black. I want pretty pastel colors, and I want the flowers and everything to reflect a happy springtime. I insist on that. I will not wear black."

"Honey, I wouldn't have had it any other way," Destini told her. "You think I would have a black garment touch my baby's shoulders even at a time like this? No, ma'am, we will do just as you wish. Now, let's have a little somethin' to eat and let's let Dee Dee rest a bit. She's havin' twins, you know," she added with a huge grin. "Then, we'll all head back home."

Late that night, about eleven-thirty, everyone disembarked from Ricardo's private jet at the same airport in Pittstown where they had started their journey. Matt, who was holding Lily Dee, was there to greet them, along with Ricardo and Carl Alvin.

The next day, a meeting was set up at the Jarrellson home for two in the afternoon with Anna Mary and Stanley's attorney, Ellwood Ellison Carter. Only those mentioned in the will were invited to attend, along with Judge Wesson and Lady Arabella. Destini asked that

Mary Selena be spared any more grief for the moment, and Mr. Carter agreed she should not be in the room when he read the will. Duke and Essie offered to look after Mary Selena while the legal part of this terrible tragedy was taken care of.

Meanwhile, Dee Dee and Carl Alvin arrived in separate cars. Chad had accompanied Carl Alvin to the meeting, but he stayed in the sunroom with Mary Selena and Duke and Essie.

Mr. Carter's countenance was not a happy one, as he sat at the head of the table inside the study. It was there that he read the Last Will and Testament of Anna Mary and Stanley Williams. It involved millions of dollars in Jarrellson Trust money, thousands of acres of land, and some minor bequests to servants, as well as to Sterling Randolph. At the mention of Sterling's name, Dee Dee rolled her eyes.

"No surprise there," she whispered to Carl Alvin.

None of the servants had responded to Mr. Carter's invitation to attend, but then, it wasn't surprising, since it was a known fact they all despised Anna Mary. Sterling Randolph told Mr. Carter on the phone that she was much too distraught to even think about attending and she pretty much hung up on him.

What was surprising was how much Anna Mary and Stanley had left Sterling. It was nearly half a million dollars.

"I'll bet you she wishes she would have come," Dee Dee said to Carl Alvin.

Another surprise was when Mr. Carter read that the

Jarrellson Ceylon Sapphire Suite would be left to Dee Dee. Everything else was left in trust for Mary Selena, until she reached the age of twenty-five.

The Trustees were named and, this too, was a bit shocking. They were Judge John Wesson, Mrs. Iris Wesson, Dee Dee Wilson Fernandez, Sheriff Bartow Lewis, and Augustine Jackson, the local African American undertaker.

"Why in the world would they name him?" Dee Dee asked.

"*Because*," Destini told her. "He's really Mary Selena's great uncle. You see, Mr. Gus was his biological father. It's a long story, but most all the Jarrellsons knew about it. How do you think Augustine got that funeral home, and how do you think all his sons went to Meharry to medical school? They are Jarrellsons, honey," Destini explained.

"Gee, I thought I knew all the gossip around here," Dee Dee said, shaking her head.

There was one piece of news that no one in this small group of people was expecting. It came as a collective shock to all in the room. In the will, Mr. Carter read out loud that Stanley had left a sizeable chunk of Edison Energy stock to the senior Tate Esmerian's child, Sonny Boy. Of course, no one would ever know Sonny Boy had been Anna Mary's secret young lover, or so one would think at this point.

"What in the world?!" Judge Wesson gasped.

"Well, I suppose I can tell you all now, since Sonny Boy is dead, too," Mr. Carter began, and then he cleared his throat. "Tate Esmerian, or Sonny Boy, as he was known to most of us, was actually the son of Stanley Williams."

"What the hell?!" Dee Dee shrieked.

"Yes, he was Stanley's son," Mr. Carter said again. "The reason that Sonny Boy's father – who the boy thought was his father, that is – was so terrible to him, was because he wasn't really his biological son. The way I heard it was that Stanley had been smitten by the boy's mother during a visit to Philadelphia when he was a young man. He had gone there for a cousin's debut of some sort, and that's when he met her. Their relationship developed into much more than just a casual friendship, if you know what I mean. When she got pregnant, she knew it was Stanley's and not her husband's, Tate Esmerian Sr. She also knew Stanley was crazy about her and always had been since they first met, but he was a married man."

"So, she pulled one of the oldest tricks in the book," Dee Dee piped up.

"Yes, she did," Mr. Carter said. "But just like Anna Mary's own child had to pay a price for his association with Gus Jarrellson – and I can say that now that they are all dead and gone – Sonny Boy paid the price at the hand of his own father. Isn't it a strange and sad twist of fate that his own father killed him?"

"Has that been confirmed?" Carl Alvin asked.

"Yes, the sheriff told me personally that it was a double murder suicide at the hand of Stanley Williams," Mr. Carter said.

"My God!" Dee Dee gasped. "Can you imagine? Did Sonny Boy know that Stanley was his father?"

"I know the answer to that," Carl Alvin interjected. "First, though, may I ask permission to have my boyfriend, Chad, come in? He can shed some light on this."

"What did you say?" Dee Dee asked. "Did I hear you correctly, you old slut? Did you say boyfriend?"

Carl Alvin blushed. "I did, Dee Dee. I know it's hard to believe, but I am simply mad about him and I don't know why. I can't explain it to you or to anyone."

"No need," Destini interrupted. "Honey, love is either a misunderstandin' between two fools or it's blind… or both. There's one thing about love, Carl Alvin. Not a bit of explanation is needed. You been searching a long time, baby. I am so happy for you. Truly I am."

With that, Chad was summoned into the study and he sat down beside Carl Alvin.

"Mr. Clark," the attorney began.

"Please… call me Chad."

"Very well," Mr. Carter said. "Chad, you, of course, had associations with Dr. Watson Jarrellson Williams, the son of the deceased, Anna Mary and Stanley Williams. What exactly did you know about Sonny Boy Esmerian?" Mr. Carter asked, in a voice that had become a bit shaky all of a sudden.

"I know quite a bit about him, actually," Chad said. "I know he tried to kill his own brother by supplying dangerous, illegal drugs to him when he was up in

Pennsylvania. I know my distant cousin, who was cut off by his own father for being gay and now lives in a single-wide mobile home on a pittance compared to his sister, knew all about Stanley's affair with Sonny Boy's mother and the fact he got her pregnant. You see, my cousin was never one to keep secrets for any length of time. Anyway, he told me all this. He was good at two things. Tattling on others and not keeping his mouth shut."

"Who is or was this cousin?" Mr. Carter asked.

"I would rather not say," Chad told him. "You see, he's in terrible shape. He was beaten nearly to death by one of his muscle-bound boyfriends, one of many he had through the years, who took him for a great deal of money. He is so pitiful now. He lives in a government subsidized nursing home and his mind wanders a lot, so he wouldn't be a credible anything. He's much sweeter now, though, so you know he's not in his right mind. When he was in his right mind, he loved belittling people because they weren't as smart as he was, and, of course, he tried to buy friendship and love with what little money he had." Chad glanced over at Carl Alvin and said, "I have found that neither of those things are for sale."

"Very true," Mr. Carter said, and then he turned to the judge. "John, I guess we're done here, so let's get these folks buried as soon as possible and get this child back in school. I imagine that Destini will want to get moved into this house or wherever she wants to live. It doesn't matter where, but she needs to care for Mary

Selena since she is now her official guardian. Destini, honey, all of this ugly business with Stanley and Anna Mary and what they were trying to do to you... I want you to know I was paid to carry it out. I took no pleasure in it, and I tried my darnedest to talk them out of it."

Judge Wesson cut in, "That is the truth, Destini."

Destini straightened up in her seat and said, "Not a problem. I'm a tough woman."

"I'm sure you'll be quite busy with Mary Selena as she goes through the mourning process," the judge said to Destini.

"Ahhh, yes, grief... I know all about grief," Destini said. "It about killed me a few years ago losing my baby, Easter Bunnye, and my Mama Tee, but you know the Lord is never through until he's through. God has since given me a husband, a new baby girl, and now another one. Can you believe it? An old woman like me is now the mother of two children."

Carl Alvin interjected, "I can't think of anyone more loving or better to be a mother than you, Destini. You always mothered me. Both you and Mama Tee."

"Here, here!" Dee Dee added. "Where would I have been without you, Destini? Both Carl Alvin and me, as a matter of fact. Between you, Mama Tee and Uncle Hamp..." she trailed off, as tears trickled down her cheeks. She reached for Carl Alvin's hand and said, "God has been good to us, my dear cousin. I lost Mama, then Daddy, and then you lost your daddy..." she said, as she wiped her face. "You had Aunt Bessie, though, and we both had Uncle Hamp. Now look at us. Crazy as we are, we have both found love."

The judge cleared his throat and then he spoke.

"Before you all leave, Anna Mary was very specific about the funeral service," he said. "She wants a private graveside service for her and Stanley at the Jarrellson cemetery out near where the original plantation was located. She has named who is to attend, and she has asked for Dee Dee to speak. There is one specific request here, though. Dee Dee, she wants you to wear the entire Sapphire Suite and she has asked that the tiara be taken from the vault and that Mary Selena wear it. She wants everyone in pastel colors, she wants a cremation, and she wants the ashes to be placed in the mausoleum out there. One more thing before we go," he added, with a smirk on his face. "Sonny Boy Esmerian was her lover for many, many years. She tells it here in her own hand," he added, with a cunning grin, as he held up a stack of papers.

"My God!" Dee Dee shrieked. "Sleeping with her own stepson?! Well, I'll be! There was some of Uncle Gus in her for sure!"

"Lord Jesus, Dee Dee!" Destini gasped. "You is crazy!"

"Do you think she knew?" Dee Dee asked.

"With Anna Mary, there's no telling," Mr. Carter interjected.

"She has also mentioned a block of stock shares that Stanley wanted to go to his family," the judge went on. "She mentions specifically a million dollar bond given to her by her Uncle Gus, which is still in effect. She wants that to go to Sonny Boy Esmerian's oldest son, who is a medical doctor in Atlanta."

"You mean Trey Esmerian?" Carl Alvin asked.

"The very same," the judge said.

"Well, I'll be damned," Carl Alvin said. "I haven't thought about him in years. He was quite the handsome guy, and such a nice young man. His father had very little to do with him because…"

"He is gay," Mr. Carter said, finishing the sentence for him.

"Yes," Carl Alvin agreed. "He was quite awful to that boy."

"Well, that boy will be taken care of now, thanks to Anna Mary. Despite being misguided at times, Anna Mary suffered a terrible breakdown after her own son's death."

"So, she had a heart after all," Dee Dee said, with a surprised look on her face.

"Oh, she could act and bat her eyes, but at the core of it all, Anna Mary had a heart," the judge said. "She was just created by the Jarrellsons to be a Jarrellson and she played that role to the exclusion of being who she could have been. They controlled her. Maybe that's the reason for the bequest to young Trey Esmerian."

"Maybe so," Mr. Carter said. "I have been a part of this family's business for over fifty years, through three generations of the family, and I could never figure them out, except for one thing I knew for certain."

"What was that?" the judge asked.

"They took care of their own. They protected their own, right or wrong, and at all costs," Mr. Carter said. "Family loyalty ranked high with them. You have to give them that. They had an upper class attitude about child rearing and they really couldn't help that. Anna Mary was basically raised by Gussie Mae Jackson, and later sent to Ashley Hall in Charleston, and then to college up in Virginia. Her daddy died young. Her mother was a socialite, who cared more about her life at the country clubs in Jacksonville and their home in Cashiers, North Carolina. She seemed happiest when surrounded by a group of her lady friends, all dressed to the teeth, playing bridge or traveling to some exotic location. She wasn't maternal at all and, consequently, neither was Anna Mary."

"Well, I did the best I could for Watson, God rest his soul," Destini said.

"Yes, indeed," Mr. Carter agreed. "And now, Mrs. Abamu, it devolves upon you to do what you can for Mary Selena Williams, the child of the late Dr. Watson Jarrellson Williams. You are now that child's legal guardian. It's a tremendous responsibility. Do you think you are up to it? After all, you have a brand new family of your own right now."

"Mr. Carter, I will do my best by that chil'," Destini told him. "If unconditional love can count for anything, you may be sure she will be rich in that, as long as I have breath in my body. I am going to lean heavy on all of you here to help make this child's tragic past stay in the past. With prayer, maybe, just maybe, we can salvage this member of the Jarrellson family. Maybe she'll be a well adjusted and caring woman without all the stigma and false glory of being a Jarrellson."

"Very well, then," Mr. Carter said. "Very well."

Chapter 27

Bye-bye, Ruby, bye-bye

"Okay, now, Dee Dee... Carl Alvin... y'all come on," Destini said, barking out orders once the reading of the will was completed, and just seconds after Mr. Carter and the judge left the Jarrellson home. "We got to go back to New Orleans and get the rest of Mary Selena's things," she continued. "Matt, I want you to get our things moved over here. You and me, we got to stay here with Watson's baby girl and get her through these dark days ahead. Then, with the help of the trustees, we'll decide what to do about her future. I want her input, too. I think that was one of the major troubles in the past with the Jarrellsons. The family members had very little input about their own lives."

"You heard the woman!" Dee Dee said. "Chop-chop! Let's get a move on!" she added with a chuckle.

Later that evening around eight o'clock, Destini, Dee Dee, Mary Selena, and Lady Arabella arrived back in New Orleans, thanks again to Ricardo's private jet and pilot. Carl Alvin had begged out of accompanying them, saying that he had way too much business to attend to before he and Chad left for Barbados.

When they arrived at the New Orleans cottage, a maid in a white uniform opened the door.

"Good to see you, Ruby," Destini greeted her.

"Could you bring us some coffee and maybe some sandwiches or something? I believe we're all starving."

"I know I am," Mary Selena piped up.

"I shall bring it into the drawing room in a few minutes," Ruby said.

"Thank you very kindly, Ruby," Destini told her.

Into the drawing room everyone went. Mary Selena retreated to a love seat near the big bay window where she often sat to look out across the river and take in all the colorful lights of downtown New Orleans.

"You know, Destini," Mary Selena started. "Anna Mary and Stanley were all I remember, as far as family goes. I have no memories of either of my parents."

"Well, you were just a little baby," Destini told her. "You had your Aunt Arabella, though."

When Mary Selena turned towards Destini, she had tears streaming down her cheeks. Destini opened her arms and the girl rushed over to her.

"You cry, baby," Destini told her. "Cry it out. It's all right. You cry all you want, for as long as you want."

"What's going to happen to Ruby?" Mary Selena asked her through her sobs.

"What do you mean?" Destini asked.

"Ruby and Sam," she said. "They work here in this house and they support their grandson, who's in a special needs school. Could you phone Mr. Carter and tell him I want some money to go to them each year? Or, maybe they can come to Florida with us. Can you ask her? She's been so wonderful to me."

Just then, Ruby stepped into the room pushing a

wheeled cart with coffee and sandwiches. She had changed into a black uniform and she had a black turban wrapped around her head. In her pocket was a lace-edged handkerchief and it was evident from her bloodshot eyes that she had been crying.

"Oh, my baby, I am so sorry, honey," Ruby said to Mary Selena.

"Come sit by me, Ruby," Mary Selena told her.

Destini let Mary Selena go and after Ruby sat down beside her, Mary Selena continued.

"I am going home to Florida… to Seraph Springs," she told Ruby. "I really need to leave this house after what has happened to my grandparents. Would you and Sam like to come with me? We can find a school for your grandson there. If you want to stay here, that's okay, too. I will see to it that you are provided for and that your grandson's schooling is provided for, as well."

"Oh, Miss Mary Selena, thank you, but for the sake of our little Kenny, I think it would be best if we stay here in New Orleans," Ruby said. "It's not that I don't love you. I do. You know that."

"Of course, I do," Mary Selena assured her. "I will miss you, though. I promise I will come back here from time to time, either with Destini or Aunt Dee Dee, or even Uncle Carl Alvin, if that's okay."

"Oh, honey, that will be perfect," Ruby said. "You know we're going to miss you terribly."

"I know, Ruby," Mary Selena said. "I know," she added, and the two of them shared a long hug.

Chapter 28

The final nail

The funeral service for Anna Mary and Stanley was a simple affair. In total, there were probably about fifty people in attendance. One of them was sitting alone in the last pew inside the chapel and she had such a thick veil of black lace covering her head and face that it was hard to discern who she might be. It was almost as if she didn't want anyone to know she was there, as she kept totally to herself and spoke to no one. Destini, however, had no trouble picking her out when Mary Selena asked who she was.

"That, honey, is your grandmother's best friend, Sterling Randolph," Destini told her. "She works over at the courthouse. I remember the day your grandmother gave her that veil. It was a gift to her from Anna Mary when Sterling's mother died."

"Should I go say something to her?" Mary Selena asked.

"Oh, I wouldn't, baby," Destini told her. "I can tell just by looking at her that she would rather sit there all by herself and do her own mourning."

"Whatever you say, Destini," Mary Selena told her with a nod of the head. "I'm sure you know what's best."

As directed in their will, both Anna Mary and Stanley's bodies had been cremated. Their ashes now rested inside two beautifully carved, ancient-looking marble urns that Mary Selena had specially flown in from her mother's native country of India. The pastor from Seraph Springs Methodist Church presided over the services and he kept his sermon short, but respectful.

When he finished, he asked Dee Dee to come up to the podium to give the eulogy, since Mary Selena declined the honor, stating she would probably break down in tears before getting through with all she wanted to say. Dee Dee spoke a few words… very few, in fact, and she kept her plethora of conflicting emotions in check, for the most part.

In a surprise move, she then sat down at the piano and broke into an old Stephen Foster song, "Ah, May the Red Rose Live Alway".

Ah! May the red rose live alway,
To smile upon earth and sky!
Why should the beautiful ever weep?
Why should the beautiful die?

Lending a charm to ev'ry ray,
That falls on her cheeks of light.
Giving the zephyr kiss for kiss,
And nursing the dew drop bright.

Ah! May the red rose live alway,
To smile upon the earth and sky!
Why should the beautiful ever weep?
Why should the beautiful die?

When the service ended, the urns were placed in the back of a black limousine provided by Augustine Jackson's funeral home. Augustine himself then drove the ashes over to Anna Mary's requested burial site. Destini had convinced Mary Selena that Augustine Jackson's was the funeral home her grandparents would have chosen had they remembered to do so in their last will and testament. Unbeknown to all but a few, this was Destini's final nail in Anna Mary's high and mighty coffin, so to speak, and no one dared to call her out on it.

After the burial, many of the attendees congregated at Camp EZ. Wanda Faye, Nadine, and Miss Jewell, along with all the ladies from the House of Prayer, provided a funeral repast fit for royalty, even though everyone knew neither Anna Mary nor Stanley deserved it. It was all done for the sake of Mary Selena.

Ever the regal young lady, Mary Selena stood before the group like a royal princess. In her cultured Southern accent and with perfect enunciation, she finally got to say a few words.

"My dear grandparents would wish me to thank each of you for your kindness and generosity," she began. "I ask for your prayers as the burden and the glory of their legacy, along with that of my parents, is delegated upon me today. I am very fortunate to have Destini by my side, as well as many of you dear friends who are gathered here today. Words fail to express all that is in my heart. I simply say thank you from the bottom of my soul. I do thank you all so very much."

When she sat back down, Destini patted her on the arm and said, "You did real fine, baby."

Once everyone was seated and feasting on the delicious meal that had been prepared, Destini figured it was time to move on to more pleasant conversation.

"Would you like to talk about your schooling now?" she asked Mary Selena.

"As a matter of fact, I would," Mary Selena said, smiling for the first time today. "I have done some research and I wish to finish my education at Bolles Prep School in Jacksonville. I believe Dee Dee owns a condominium there. Since she and Ricardo are living here at the present time, maybe you and I could move to their condo… temporarily, of course. I could finish the school year there and then we could return to Seraph Springs. What do you think?"

After mulling it over for a moment, Destini said, "I think that's a marvelous idea, honey. Of course, we'll have to check with Dee Dee and Ricardo first."

"Well, Dee Dee already offered," Mary Selena said, smiling wide.

"Ahhh, of course she did," Destini said, smiling back at her.

"So, can we?" Mary Selena asked again.

"Well, would it be all right if I bring my husband and my other baby daughter with me?"

"Ohhh… Destini, you are so bad," Mary Selena said. "You know it is a given that I meant all of you."

"Yes, I know, honey," Destini said, laughing. "You know what? I have always wanted to try big city living for a while. You know... just to see how the other side lives. This will be the perfect opportunity. You can make your debut at the Bolles City Yacht Club over there if you want to. You are a legacy, you know, as far as the debutante coterie is concerned in Jacksonville."

"Actually, no, ma'am," Mary Selena said, quite abruptly and firmly. "I really don't wish to do that. In a few months I shall be sixteen. Perhaps, we could have a small celebration at the Jarrellson house," she added. "Aside from all our friends here in Seraph Springs, we could invite Aunt Arabella, Miss Sissy, Justin, and... umm... well, Justin has a very nice cousin. His name is Pierre. He used to help out at the house sometimes and he was always most kind to me. Do you think we could invite them?"

"Well, of course, we can," Destini said. "Anything you want, honey. If that's what you want, that's what we'll do," she assured her.

Chapter 29

Mysterious ways

The infamous Jarrellson and Jarrellson Cotton Factor used to be a bustling center for commerce in Seraph Springs in the early 1800's, for a small, rural town, that is. In its heyday, Jarrellson and Jarrellson Cotton Factor had been *the* place to go for small farmers and even larger cotton planters in the region, who all brought their product to Seraph Springs and sold it to the Jarrellsons.

The warehouse was built near the train depot for obvious reasons, and no expense had been spared in building it, along with a suite of offices. While other cotton factors stored their cotton in scantily-built wooden and tin sheds, the Jarrellsons went all out, using the most expensive materials they could find.

Once the Jarrellsons purchased the cotton from the local farmers and planters, offering them the lowest possible price, of course, they would often hold onto the product, sometimes for many, many months, until prices went up on both the foreign and domestic exchanges. When it came time to sell all the cotton they had accumulated in their warehouse, they sold it at a premium price with a considerably high profit margin. It was one of many ways the Jarrellson family had re-established their fortune following the War Between the States.

At one point, many, many years ago, the Jarrellsons decided to get more use out of the huge building and so they added on a third floor, which would be used as a nightclub of sorts on the weekends. They drew crowds and crowds of people every Friday and Saturday night, and consequently added more revenue to their expanding empire, as there was always a steep cover charge to get into the social events.

The exterior of the main building had been touched up a few times over the years, but after a while it was only minor cosmetics to make it presentable enough on the outside, in order to ward off any code enforcement violations. The building had been vacant for decades, though, just like numerous other buildings in Campbell County. In fact, one could barely make out what the faded old painted sign once said on the side of the red brick structure.

In recent months, though, the entire building was restored by the Jarrellson family, specifically under the direction of Anna Mary. The work was completed a few weeks ago, and a new sign with a new name was standing upright at the edge of the parking lot; Spencer Augustus Jarrellson Gallery of Art.

The warehouse itself covered a large area of land, so the restoration project was a big deal, not only for Anna Mary, but for the community, as well. Its grey slate roof and hardwood floors had all been either replaced or restored. The bulk of the funding for the project came from state historic preservation grants that Anna Mary had worked hard to procure. Of course, it was primarily for her own vanity that she took on the venture. That, and the legacy of her late uncle, Spencer Augustus Jarrellson, whom she adored to the end, and probably, albeit unwittingly rightfully so, if what Stanley told her on her deathbed was true about Gus being her father and not her uncle. Nonetheless, her objective was that the warehouse turned art gallery would primarily serve as a place where her Uncle Gus's world famous art work would be displayed.

In her original conception of restoring the Jarrellson & Jarrellson Cotton Factor, Anna Mary had visualized prominent art enthusiasts from all over the world would find their way to Seraph Springs. She just knew they would come to worship at the altar fires, as it were, of her late uncle's fame.

In addition, she told everyone involved in the project that the building could be used as a meeting place for county social events of a more secular nature; events where the hosts could opt for serving something stronger than Baptist fruit punch to their guests. Anna Mary had told Stanley that she couldn't necessarily think of the virgin punch with disdain, though. She said her fondest memories as a young girl had been when she stood attendance over cut glass or sterling silver punch bowls that were filled with what the locals called the standard Campbell County wedding punch. It was green in color, cold and frothy, with floating chunks of lime sherbet.

Tonight was the grand re-opening of the historic

building, which was fully restored from top to bottom and from one end to the other, with a brand new name. Inside would be the largest, most renowned art show ever to be held in the southeast for one of its own; a regional and now internationally known visual artist by the name of Spencer Augustus Jarrellson. Anna Mary would have been beaming at this premiere, had she still been alive.

The event had to be postponed for a couple weeks, due to the deaths of Anna Mary and Stanley, but it all worked out well, as it gave Carl Alvin and Chad time to enjoy their Barbados retreat and be back in time to attend the gala.

In all truthfulness, the entire evening had been carefully choreographed by Dee Dee and her aunt, Hattie Wilson Campbell. Each detail had been meticulously planned, including the lovely reception, the stunning buffet of cultural foods, the imported candles, and, most importantly, the silver from the Jarrellson safety deposit box, which had been emptied of much of its historic glory for the event.

"I wonder if we should have armed guards at all the exit doors," Dee Dee had suggested to Destini several days ago. "You know... in case people start shoving silverware in their pockets or purses."

"Hey, don't stop there," Destini told her. "I think you should have metal detectors, too."

"Say what?!" Dee Dee shrieked, but before she could go off on an expletive-laden tirade, Destini burst out laughing.

"You are so easy sometimes," Destini said, still laughing.

It was finally agreed upon that they would just have to trust their guests not to steal from them. After all, most of the guests were so wealthy that they would have no need to steal someone else's silverware.

Speaking of silver, the shiny, silver candelabras flickering on each of the dining tables looked as if they were ghosts whispering back and forth to one another, perhaps chatting among themselves about former soirees and parties that the Jarrellsons had hosted throughout the years. Needless to say, could the candles actually speak, it would have been certain they would have many tales to tell, some odder and more risqué than others.

Inside the main hall tonight, one could close their eyes and almost hear the string orchestra playing upstairs for scores of couples dressed in formal attire. They would waltz the night away in the third floor ballroom of what used to be referred to as the Jarrellson House on the Suwannee River. It wasn't actually on the Suwannee River, but it was close enough to be believable. As the candles continued to flicker, one could almost smell the sweet scent of beautiful red roses, see the sparkle of fine jewels, and catch an intermittent scent of gardenia mixed with bourbon.

Then, the fragrances traveled in time to the twenty-first century and the grand re-opening of what used to be the Jarrellson & Jarrellson Cotton Factor. Here now, in what used to be the cotton warehouse, there were beautifully dressed ladies and gentleman holding crystal flutes of champagne, as they talked among themselves. They ooh'ed and ahh'ed over Uncle Gus's art works, never knowing they were really looking upon a more organic piece than they could have ever imagined. These were pieces of art that in reality contained the bone and blood of human and emotional sacrifices; three innocent, young boys, who died at the hands of dear Uncle Gus and Miss Agatha Campbell.

As the dealers and representatives from Sotheby's of London and other renowned New York galleries stepped over to a bank of telephones to take international bids on the mural, *Black Runs the River*, Dee Dee introduced Mary Selena Williams. As if she was part of the ghostly effect tonight, Mary Selena seemed to float rather than walk to the dais. She exhibited the same grace and charm as her mother, the late Selena Jarrellson Dubois Williams. Without further ado, she was ready to speak eloquently, with dignity and clarity.

"Welcome to the Spencer Augustus Jarrellson Gallery of Art, named in honor and in memory of my late, great-great uncle, the world renowned visual artist and entrepreneur, Spencer Augustus Jarrellson," she began. "Tonight we have all been afforded the privilege of enjoying the works of one who saw so much of the world, but who never lost the love of his home here on the banks of the Suwannee River. I would be remiss if I did not share with you something about a person who loved me very much and who, to this day, lives on in my heart and in my memory as a very great lady. It was she who visualized this place as a gallery and art center, housed in a commercial building that was so important to the economy of this area when cotton was king. Now, we pray that just as cotton enriched this area with the funds to pay for so many of the improvements to the world during the late nineteenth and early twentieth century, that art born of the human emotion, including its toil, blood, sweat and tears, will add to the beauty of this land and this part of the world we hold dear."

There was soft applause for a few moments, and then Mary Selena continued.

"It is with great honor that I unveil a portrait of my paternal grandmother, the late Anna Mary Jarrellson Williams, taken from a portrait completed of her several years ago in Charleston, South Carolina."

With one swift, graceful movement, Mary Selena pulled a velvet cord to reveal a life sized oil portrait of Anna Mary Jarrellson Williams in all her glory.

Anna Mary was attired in a midnight blue formal gown that she had worn to Dee Dee and Ricardo's wedding a couple years ago. She was also wearing the famous Jarrellson Ceylon Sapphire Suite, which graced her ears, arms, hands, and neck.

"I can't help but remember the beautiful woman she was," Dee Dee said to Carl Alvin, who was sitting beside her at one of the dining tables. "With that alabaster white skin, those blazing blue eyes, her dark blondish-brown hair, and that look of power, privilege, and pride... well, it just can't be erased from her image."

"I like that diamond and pearl tiara myself," Carl Alvin said, although, it was clear he was being sarcastic. "Oh, yes, she looks every inch the queen she thought of herself... over this part of the world, anyway," he added.

Sitting at the table two seats away from Dee Dee, was Destini, who had her own thoughts about the lovely Anna Mary.

"Lord, what she wasted and missed with her own child," Destini said to Nadine, who was sitting next to her. "Oh, what she gave up for pride and trying to hide the truth about Uncle Gus. What she sacrificed for pride, and in the end, she died a death void of pride. It was a death full of tragedy and as twisted as the Jarrellson family tree with all its generations of inner-breeding."

"It's twisted, all right," Nadine agreed.

"All them Jarrellsons really showed out when Miss Anna Mary got married," Destini went on, recalling a story her Mama Tee had told her. "At the time, Mama Tee said she thought it was only because Stanley was a northerner and not considered their equal. She was partially right, I guess. It was the first time in three generations that a Jarrellson had married outside the family. They had always married cousins who owned banks or property, or both. They wanted wealth that could add to their own."

"That sounds creepy," Nadine said.

"Yes, it sure does," Destini agreed. "Is it any wonder that Anna Mary, Mr. Gus, and all that crowd was so mixed up and messed up? That whole bizarre theater of being a Jarrellson, mixed with all that inner-breedin' and all that same blood... until Mr. Stanley, that is. Even their baby, Watson, married his cousin, Selena Dubois Jarrellson."

"Talk about keeping it all in the family," Nadine said with a smirk.

"Yes, they sure did," Destini said. "Miss Anna Mary was a bit of a rebel, though. Oh, she bought into the whole Jarrellson magnolia and moonlight myth that was cushioned by money and all it implied, but she married someone she actually loved. Someone who was different. From a different world."

As the audience clapped, Mary Selena walked from the dais, resplendent in a pink, silk chiffon sari, with the Jarrellson tiara atop her head, and a pair of ornate pearl and emerald earrings. She looked every inch a picture of other-worldly beauty, yet with a down to earth temperament. She had a sweet and tolerant personality, and she took time with each individual she met.

Tonight, at her insistence, she had invited local public school students who had an interest in art, so that they could experience the evening. One of the art teachers, Mr. Andrews, was a tall, gangly man, who for two decades had guided his students as best he could in a place where the arts hadn't always been a priority. In fact, his job had been saved more than once by the late Anna Mary.

Anna Mary appeared only one time at a school board meeting. The fact she was asked to appear at all didn't bode well with her to begin with, and it indirectly caused the superintendent to lose his job by one of the largest electoral margins in the history of the county. She was quietly behind that effort, too. Most times, she only had to make a phone call to encourage the school board and the superintendent to utilize a fair portion of their tax revenue to perpetuate the arts for children.

Tonight, as Mary Selena watched the bright eyes of the art teacher, she realized he was as excited as his students. She felt true satisfaction that she had done the right thing.

As Mary Selena was returning to her table, Dee Dee stepped up to the dais, hugely pregnant now, but still looking radiant. Tonight, to honor Anna Mary, she wore the Jarrellson Ceylon Sapphire Suite. She asked the gentleman from the International Art Auction House to come forward, a Mr. Edwards from the United Kingdom.

"This is a historical moment in American art history," Mr. Edwards announced before the group of international dealers and all the other guests. "The mural entitled, *Black Runs the River,* will sell tonight and the funds will be utilized to help the families of many young people who are less fortunate," he added.

In the audience, Dee Dee and Carl Alvin looked at each other and smiled, as did Curtis, who was sitting across from Destini. At an adjacent table, Judge Wesson moved a bit uneasily in his seat. Meanwhile,

Sherriff Bartow Lewis, who was sitting across from him, took the hand of the woman sitting next to him, Miss Sissy Paquette, his longtime companion and friend from New Orleans.

Before the bidding began, the sheriff rose from his seat and motioned toward Mary Selena, who nodded at him. Then, he walked up to the microphone, while the room went deadly silent.

Bartow Lewis was never one to take the limelight on any occasion, so this was extremely unusual, especially at such a public event. He was dressed as the occasion befitted in formal attire, and he was actually smiling as he spoke, something he rarely did.

"My dear friends, I have a major announcement," he began. "In fact, I have two announcements I would like to make tonight. First, I would very much like to thank Mary Selena Jarrellson Williams and the always delightful Mrs. Dee Dee Wilson Fernandez for so much of the work that was done here tonight. Let's give these ladies a round of applause."

The audience stood to their feet with a rousing ovation for Dee Dee and Mary Selena, as Sheriff Lewis motioned for them to join him on the dais. He kissed them both on their cheeks and then continued.

"Dee Dee, I want you to stay here beside me," he said. "There's one more person I want to come forward now," he added. "She isn't on the program, but I am here to tell all of you that without this lady's great kindness, forbearance, Christianity and love, so much of what has happened in this room tonight would never have occurred. How do I know that? Because I have lived it. Some of you have and some of you haven't, but I certainly have," he added.

Tears were streaming down Dee Dee's cheeks, and as her eyes swept the room, she could see others getting emotional, too, including Phil, Carl Alvin, Wanda Faye, Nadine, and Miss Jewell, who had taken out her handkerchief to dab her eyes.

Meanwhile, Destini was in her seat shaking her head, as if to say "no" to the sheriff, but Miss Sissy came up behind her and guided her to the dais. The applause was explosive, as Destini hugged the sheriff's neck.

In typical Destini fashion, she shouted, "The High Sheriff, always my man!"

The sheriff laughed and so did everyone else.

"One more thing, folks, and this is going to shock the hell out of some of you," the sheriff said into the microphone, as he took Miss Sissy's arm. "This lady right here became my bride a week ago in New Orleans. She is now, by God, for all of you who know what a fool I've been not to have done it sooner, Mrs. Bartow Lewis."

The room exploded in applause and cheers for the happy couple, while Dee Dee, Destini, Nadine, Wanda Faye, and anyone else who was able, rushed forward to embrace the sheriff and Miss Sissy to offer congratulations.

"You sly old dog," Judge Wesson said, smiling, as he and his wife, Iris, came forward.

Some in the audience who were not from the area looked at each other a bit confused. Many others, however, knew just what Sheriff Bartow Lewis had achieved with his surprising announcement.

Although he was absolutely thrilled about his marriage to Miss Sissy, his objective tonight was to divert attention away from the unfortunate events surrounding the mural that was about to be sold. For sure, he succeeded in substantially lightening the mood, as well as the guilt of many who were present. He had made the evening feel much lighter and less burdensome. He had also squarely placed the ball back into play to display the care and compassion for its people that, to him, Campbell County characterized. It was much more than the dark, grisly mess on the wall and the terrible events surrounding the deaths of Stanley, Anna Mary, and Sonny Boy.

Dee Dee watched as the sheriff looked up at Anna Mary's portrait and winked. From behind her proud smile and the glint of sparkling jewels, it seemed to Dee Dee that Anna Mary winked back at him. She could almost hear her say, "You always knew just what to do when the world became too real, Bartow."

Once everyone settled down and returned to their seats, the bidding began on the mural. When it was over, the mural had brought an unprecedented amount of fifty-two million dollars.

"Finally, the deeds of the Jarrellson family are doing some good for folks," Judge Wesson said, and he said it loud enough that everyone at the two side-by-side tables heard him.

At the conclusion of the bidding, Mary Selena blew a kiss toward her grandmother's portrait. She thanked everyone for coming and encouraged those still present to continue enjoying the art exhibit and the refreshments. She then presented a check to Mr. Andrews for an undisclosed amount of money, but it was enough that when the shaking Mr. Andrews came to the microphone, he told the audience that Mary Selena had just paid for all twenty of his students to travel to the Louvre in Paris that summer. For one week they would enjoy Parisian art and explore the famous city. Mary Selena's gift incorporated all expenses, including airfare, hotel, meals, and extra spending money.

Destini sat back in her chair, closed her eyes, and quietly said, "God sure does work in mysterious ways."

The next day, Dee Dee, the judge, and Mr. Carter, the Jarrellson's attorney, took care of making sure the money received from the sale of the mural would be handled properly. The families of the three boys, who died at the hands of Uncle Gus and Aunt Aggie, all got an equal share of the proceeds.

That afternoon, everyone learned that Sterling Randolph had been involved in a head-on collision with a log truck on her way into work at the courthouse. She died at the scene. The sheriff said according to witnesses, the accident appeared suspicious, as if Sterling had deliberately crashed into the log truck.

Meanwhile, Mary Selena, Destini, and Matt were packing up a small moving van for their trip to Dee Dee's condominium in Jacksonville, as Mary Selena was due in school in a few days.

Chapter 30

A new dawn

Almost a year had passed since the deaths of Anna Mary and Stanley, and life went on as if they were now just a distant memory. Mary Selena was having the time of her life in Jacksonville where she excelled in everything she was involved with at the Bolles Prep School, including all her advanced studies. She was also extremely popular with her classmates, both male and female, which was an inborn trait she seemingly had no control over, no matter where she went to school. She had been selected Homecoming Queen for her senior year, and she was a star athlete on the school's swim team.

She would often host small events at her temporary home in Dee Dee's condominium for some of the students who boarded at the school; particularly international students.

Destini loved the slumber parties Mary Selena hosted, and she frequently invited Wanda Faye and Nadine over to share in the fun. They'd bring homemade fudge and a variety of Miss Jewell's homemade cakes with them. Even little Lily Dee seemed to enjoy these special events. Dee Dee would pop in whenever she was in town shopping for her soon-to-be-born twins, which was quite often, as she was assembling layettes for two babies.

It was during this time that Mary Selena, Destini, and the girls, along with Miss Sissy – now the proud Mrs. Bartow Lewis – had decided to host a baby shower for Dee Dee at the Jarrellson House in Seraph Springs. Invitations were already printed and the date was the second of June. It would be the Saturday following Mary Selena's combined graduation and sixteenth birthday party during Memorial Day weekend.

It seemed the academic programs she had excelled in at the Ursuline Academy in New Orleans had placed her at the top of the heap academically, and so she was privileged to graduate high school a year early. Because of the private tutors and the rigid instruction at the Ursuline Academy, Mary Selena had also become fluent in English, Spanish, and French.

Though the caste system had officially been banished in Mary Selena's mother's native India, in actuality, vestiges of it were still in effect. In essence, this three-thousand-year-old hierarchal societal system was developed to divide the Hindu people based on their talents and vocations.

Mary Selena was descended from a long line of the Brahmin caste, the highest of the Hindu caste system. Her ancestors had been educated, scholarly aristocrats of India, many of whom still had vast holdings there. Therefore, while Anna Mary was alive, she had seen to it that Mary Selena was tutored in Hindi and Urdu. She also learned how to read Sanskrit.

Part of her graduation present from her aunt, Lady Arabella, would be a summer spent in India, traveling the nation and visiting with relatives as a guest at her aunt's estate in Shimla, a mountain retreat of the British Raj during the time they ruled India. As the story went, for six months each year, the Raj would escape the heat of Calcutta and travel to the foothills of the Himalayas.

Here, in the cool mountain air, Mary Selena and her maternal great aunt, Lady Arabella Simpson-Keyes, would spend eight weeks in the company of Mary Selena's mother's family and she was truly excited about it.

Her family in India had phoned her, written her, and texted her, as they made plans for a grand reunion. In fact, they had such a large house, truly a palace of sorts, that they had offered the invitation to all of Mary Selena's extended family in Seraph Springs. At this point in time, with Lily Dee still being a young baby, and with Dee Dee about to give birth to twins, most of the family declined the invitation with the exception of Carl Alvin and Chad. They decided together that they would love to visit India, as it was one place they both had always wanted to explore.

This, of course, delighted Mary Selena. She was looking forward to a fun summer in the mountains. She longed to experience all the intriguing sights and sounds, and bask in the beauty of all the exotic flowers and trees. She was also anxious to become better acquainted with her extended family members. Having two friendly faces from home beside her would make it even more enjoyable.

On the evening of her graduation at the Bolles

School, there wasn't a dry eye among the many folks who came to share in the momentous occasion.

Mary Selena delivered the class valedictory address, and as always she spoke with dignity and grace. She talked about losing her parents at a very young age and also about the recent loss of her paternal grandparents. Then, she spoke about the wonderful people who were now a part of her life in Seraph Springs.

"Not long ago, I received a letter from my great-aunt, Padmini, who lives in India," Mary Selena told the crowd. "She wrote that my Hindu great-great grandmother had always been frightened of crossroads, as she believed demons dwelled there. My mother was Anglo-Indian and my father was as Southern as the day is long," she added, which drew soft laughter from the audience. "He was a great healer and a humanitarian, and I am told my mother was a very kind woman. About a year ago, I had the privilege of dedicating an art gallery in my small hometown of Seraph Springs. Many of you, I'm sure, have never heard of the town, but a lot of you figured out where it was when the event was written about in the Jacksonville Union Newspaper. My late great-great uncle, Spencer Augustus Jarrellson's famous mural, *Black Runs the River*, sold for an unprecedented fifty-two million dollars."

There was a collective gasp from the crowd, and when they quieted down, Mary Selena continued.

"I don't say that to brag nor to boast," she explained. "I can tell you, though, that I received not a dime from that sale. The majority of the money went toward helping some families whose plight in life has been extremely difficult. I used a portion of those funds to establish a foundation for children in Campbell County, which is one of the fifty poorest counties in the United States. I want them to always have access to the fine arts and also to be able to appreciate them."

Again, there was more applause.

"The Hindu goddess Saraswati is the goddess of music, the arts, and creativity," Mary Selena continued. "I believe the encouragement of creativity is one of the noblest ambitions we can have. There is a difference between creativity and replication. Creativity is creating something original. It is creating something that has never been conceived… something original. I believe in today's world, more than ever before, where so much information can be accessed at the touch of a button, where so much research may not be research at all, but rather an ability to utilize technology, that creativity should be valued more than ever before."

"Isn't she just the most beautiful child?" Destini asked Nadine, who was sitting beside her in the audience.

"She certainly is," Nadine agreed.

"Not too many days ago, I encountered someone I consider to be a creative artist," Mary Selena continued. "As creativity knows no bounds and is no respecter of persons, I found it to exist in a place one might consider rather unusual. A lady who works as a waitress at a small diner I often frequent here in Jacksonville was typing away on a small I-pad. I know her well and have encountered her many times. So, I asked if she was working on a letter or a term paper. You see, she began attending college at the age of sixty and has already raised two children. Now, she's rearing two grandchildren. She explained that she was working on a book and asked if I would like to read some of it. I must tell you, I was more than impressed with her writing, which was about this area of Jacksonville. She wrote about the ways she provided meaningful and educational outings for her children and grandchildren on her limited salary. She explained that on her trips to the zoo with her children, she would pack animal crackers for a snack in order to further discuss what they were seeing. She wrote about how she would take time to check out books from the public library about animals, so the children could see and discuss the countries where one might find such animals. That was when tears came to my eyes as I was reading, because she herself was the embodiment of a follower of Saraswati. More than that, she gave her children and grandchildren a gift worth more than all the riches in the world... unconditional love. With the little she had, she was abundantly generous with the gifts of her time and her love. To every one of you who are part of this graduation class, I know each of you have your own personal ambitions. No matter what they are, I encourage all of you to be generous with your time and your love, and always, always encourage and foster creativity. Our world, I believe, depends on it."

The huge stadium erupted in applause, which made Mary Selena blush, but she hid it well. When they quieted down, she added her final statements.

"Finally, I would like to say to my dear friends and family members gathered here tonight, I do love you with all my heart. Don't ever lose an opportunity to encourage someone, and let those you love know that you love them. Remember, love wasn't put in your heart just to stay. Love isn't love until you give it away. Thank you all and God bless you."

The audience of well-dressed family, friends and teachers stood to their feet and gave Mary Selena a deafening standing ovation that lasted for almost five minutes. Immediately following the graduation ceremony, Mary Selena joined up outside the stadium with everyone who had come to honor her.

"Would you like to go out and have dinner, honey?" Destini asked her. "The gang is all here. I'll take you wherever you want to go and you can invite whomever you like."

"Thank you, Destini, but really... and I don't want to put any of you out... but I would like to go home to Seraph Springs tonight," Mary Selena said. "I want to rock on the porch at Camp EZ with you and the girls, and Aunt Arabella until the wee hours of tomorrow, or for as long as we can hold out," she added.

"Well, now, did you hear that?" Destini asked, as she turned toward the others in the group.

"Honey, we heard it, and everything is being made

ready as we speak," Wanda Faye told her.

"How?" Destini asked, clearly shocked. "We're in Jacksonville, in case you haven't noticed."

"Yes, we are, but Mama and the Bible Drill group are in Seraph Springs," Wanda Faye explained. "By the time we get back to Camp EZ, our pajamas will be laid out, there will be trays of sandwiches, potato chips, potato salad, homemade fudge, and a couple of cakes. It will be enough slumber party food to last a week... if we were staying for a week, that is."

Mary Selena squealed with excitement and then she hugged everyone before they started for their vehicles in the parking lot.

Late that night, on the banks of the Suwannee River, the girls all joined in a circle. As was their custom, they cast flowers into the flowing river. In this case, they were magnolia blossoms. Prayers were then said, and Mary Selena was hugged and wished a happy and successful future. Then, it was lots of laughing and giggling, reminiscing, storytelling, and eating yummy food until the wee hours of the morning, just as Mary Selena had requested.

Chapter 31

Health, wealth, and goodness

The following day, Dee Dee, who was hugely pregnant and about to drop at any moment, was feverishly working with Daphne Gerald, her Aunt Hattie's longtime caterer. Daphne, it seems, had kept a notebook that detailed all the memorable parties she had catered over the years. One of those parties was the one given by the late Anna Mary and Stanley Jarrellson Williams in honor of their son, the late Dr. Watson Jarrellson Williams. She said it was one of the most lavish parties she had ever had the honor to cater at the historic Jarrellson mansion on the banks of the Suwannee River.

Today was spent retrieving massive sterling silver serving pieces, epergnes, and candelabras from the bank vault, and making sure the rare Porthault linens were starched and ironed. The entire menu and the set up exactly replicated the party that was thrown over a decade earlier.

The start of Memorial Day weekend dawned clear and temperate, and then scores of guests began to arrive at the historic Jarrellson mansion in Seraph Springs on Saturday evening.

From her bedroom window, Mary Selena watched as tables were covered in white linen. Then, she breathed in and imagined the sweet fragrance of pink and cream colored roses in big ornate arrangements.

The tables underneath various tents were groaning with all sorts of food, and a full liquor bar stretched the length of the solarium. She spotted ladies and gentleman, many of whom were familiar, plus classmates, close friends, and family members, who were all dressed in their finery. It was a sight to behold.

On her bedside table was a framed photo of her beautiful mother.

"Oh, how I wish you could have been here today," she wistfully said. "Well, I suppose I should get dressed," she added with a sigh, and so she rang the electric bell on the wall to summon Consuela.

Seconds later, Destini appeared in her doorway.

"Why aren't you downstairs with Matt and the other guests, Destini?" Mary Selena asked her.

"Because, baby girl, I need to be up here," Destini told her. "You see, I'm the one who helped your sweet mama get dressed the night she went down that staircase and saw your daddy for the first time many years ago. So, child, I am gonna be the one to help your daddy's little baby girl do the same."

"Awww, you're so sweet, Destini," Mary Selena said, and they hugged.

"Someone else is here, too," Destini said. "Someone who was there that night helping me."

Just then, into the room waltzed Miss Sissy, ready and eager to assist. For the next ten minutes, she worked on Mary Selena's luxuriant hair and swept it up into a perfect chignon. It was an exact replicate of the hairstyle worn by her mother. Then, she helped Mary

Selena with her makeup.

When it was time, Destini reached into a large box that was sitting atop the bed. Then, she unzipped a plastic bag that contained the white lace cocktail dress that Mary Selena would be wearing tonight. The sheath hugged her body, just as it had hugged her mother's body years ago. The Jarrellson pearls were then placed around Mary Selena's neck, and her maternal grandmother's diamond earrings were placed in her ears. They were teardrop shaped and a whopping four carats each.

An addition to the jewelry suite worn by her mother was a bracelet, a gift from her aunt, Lady Arabella. It was an ornate piece given to her by the child's natural maternal grandfather, who was the son of an immensely wealthy Indian maharajah. The bracelet consisted of emeralds, diamonds, and pearls. The stones were so large that Mary Selena was a bit reluctant to wear it, thinking it may be too gaudy, but she relented, since she knew how much it would mean to her aunt.

Before she descended the staircase that night, Mary Selena, in a gesture no one expected, reached into a velvet lined box, took out the Jarrellson tiara, and gently placed it on Destini's head.

"I want you to wear this tonight," Mary Selena told her. "You are the queen of my life, and since I am the rightful owner of it now, I want you to wear it for my party."

"Oh, baby, no, I couldn't," Destini said, shaking

her head, and trying to untangle it from her hair.

"Correction, Miss Destini, you are going to wear it. I insist," Mary Selena told her, as she grabbed Destini's hands. "Oh, and I have one more gift for you."

Mary Selena reached into a small box and took out a strand of south sea pearls that were absolute perfection. The necklace even had a diamond clasp. After she fastened it around Destini's neck, she rang the bell again. When Consuela appeared, Mary Selena politely asked her to have Wanda Faye, Nadine, and Dee Dee come up to her room. A few minutes later the girls stepped into the room and immediately they began fussing over Mary Selena's stunningly gorgeous appearance.

In yet another surprise move, Mary Selena brought out a box from Continental Planters Bank. Inside, were four cases containing strands of South Sea pearls identical to those she had given Destini. She ceremoniously placed them on each of the girls, as well as Miss Sissy.

"Now, we are all dolled up and ready for a party," Mary Selena said with a huge smile on her face.

"I have one more surprise for you, Mary Selena," Destini said. "Well, actually two, but you're gonna have to wait a little while on them."

"Ooohh, I love surprises," Mary Selena squealed.

The ladies all went downstairs, and at nine-thirty on the nose, a twenty-piece orchestra broke into the strains of Stephen Foster's "Old Folks at Home".

A young woman, quite other-worldly in beauty,

descended the stairs into the great room of the Jarrellson home in the same dress her late mother had worn. She radiated an essence of magnificent and stunning polish and class, as she floated down the staircase. Many in the room remembered that night from long, long ago, and a lot of eyes became misty as Mary Selena came down the staircase, looking much more mature than her sixteen years.

Mary Selena was scanning the room in search of familiar faces when she spotted two individuals in traditional Indian garb. The lady was strikingly beautiful in a deep pink sari and her jewelry was stunning. The gentleman with her was in traditional evening dress, but he also wore a white turban on his head, centered with one of the largest diamonds she had ever seen.

Meanwhile, Destini had made her way to the microphone, still feeling a bit uncomfortable wearing the Jarrellson tiara, but she did her best to wear it with style. Everyone in the room was chattering away and it was getting quite loud.

Destini raised her hand, and then Carl Alvin boomed in a loud voice, "Pray silence for Destini Wilson Abamu!"

Destini gave him a quizzical look, as if he had gone off the deep end, and then shook her head and smiled at the crowd.

"Ladies and gentlemen, thank you for joining us here tonight on this momentous occasion," Destini began. "Our beloved Mary Selena Jarrellson Williams has just turned sixteen years of age. She has also just graduated from high school, valedictorian of her class, by the way. Very soon she will leave with her aunt, Lady Arabella Simpson Keyes, on a trip to India where she will be welcomed by many members of her family. She may be only sixteen years of age, but her wisdom reaches far beyond those sixteen years. Ladies and gentleman, please welcome a beautiful young lady, inside and out. Let's give a round of applause for Mary Selena!"

The crowd exploded with applause. Before Mary Selena was asked to speak, Destini went back to the microphone.

"Tonight, I had to call upon a special friend to arrange a very special present for Mary Selena," Destini said. "It is now my honor and my pleasure to introduce a lady who can make it happen anywhere in the world."

Down the staircase in a beautiful light aqua formal gown came the internationally famous talk show host, and star of television and movies, America's most famous African American woman, Margot Smith.

"Ladies and gentleman, this is not my first trip to Campbell County, and I pray it will not be my last," Margot said, when she made it over to the microphone. "Tonight, we celebrate this beautiful young lady, who is on the cusp of starting a new phase in her life. Have you ever seen anyone so beautiful?" she rhetorically asked. "It is unfair for anyone to be this beautiful, and I can attest she is just as beautiful on the inside as on the outside. Mary Selena, darling, come here and hold my hand."

Mary Selena moved closer to Margot and it was clear she was more than a little in awe of the woman.

Margot continued, "Baby girl, Destini, and your family here in Campbell County wanted to do something very special for you, and I believe they have succeeded. Tonight I want you to meet your great uncle and aunt who have traveled here from India for this occasion. Mr. and Mrs. Singh, Charita and Gadin, would you come forward, please?"

The aristocratic Indian couple, whom Mary Selena had spotted earlier, moved with grace up to the microphone to greet their great niece. To say Mary Selena was taken aback would have been an understatement and it showed on her face. Seconds later, Lady Arabella came up to the microphone, while Mary Selena was speaking to her aunt and uncle in flawless Hindi, while tears trickled down her cheeks.

"No, no, my child," Lady Arabella told her. "This is not an evening for tears, but for joy, celebration, and dancing."

Lady Arabella then motioned to a young man standing beside the couple, who proceeded to unfasten a huge diamond and emerald necklace that was around his neck. It looked as if it belonged to the Queen of England and should have been stored in the tower of London. The bottom teardrop diamond had to be at least twenty carats, maybe larger.

After he placed it around Mary Selena's neck, her friend from New Orleans, Pierre Boudreaux, stepped forward, looking resplendent in his evening wear.

"May I have this dance?" he asked Mary Selena.

The orchestra broke into the classic, "Stardust", the same tune that was played years before for Mary Selena's parents. The young couple danced with perfection and grace to the applause of everyone in the room. Soon, other couples joined them on the dance floor.

Throughout the night, there was laughter, love and celebration emanating from the terrace and down the banks of the old Suwannee River, where the bright yellow moon shone down on the dark tannic water. Destini and Matt had retreated to a bench that overlooked the river, holding hands and sipping on champagne.

Destini looked up at the moon and said, "Baby, ain't she pretty?"

Matt hugged her and said, "*You* sure are."

Destini smiled, and then she kissed Matt's cheek, but the moon and the night knew she was actually speaking to Watson, her former charge. When the cicadas suddenly began to sing extra loud, it was proof to her that Watson had heard her.

"I'll be right back," Matt said. "I think we need a cup of coffee and a piece of Miss Jewell's coconut cake," he added, and he went inside.

Destini didn't hear Dee Dee and Ricardo walk up behind where she was sitting, as she whispered, "Baby, I've done the best I could."

Dee Dee wrapped her arms around Destini and kissed her on the cheek.

"No one could have done better," she told Destini. "Now, let me wear that damned tiara for a few minutes. Y'all don't call me Queenie for nothing."

Right behind Dee Dee came Carl Alvin, Chad, Wanda Faye, and Nadine, followed by Ricardo and Matt, who was carrying a small tray of coffee and cake. Destini proceeded to remove the tiara from her head and she placed it on Dee Dee's head.

"Long live Queenie!" Destini shouted and she laughed.

Everyone joined her in raucous laughter. Then, the girls curtsied, and Carl Alvin and Chad bowed down to her, as if she really was royalty.

"You can all go to hell," Dee Dee told them, but she followed it up with a cunning grin.

"We have already been there," Carl Alvin replied. "The gatekeeper said if we made a return trip, you had to come with us."

The sheriff and Miss Sissy had been watching the group from the terrace and enjoying their camaraderie. When everyone started walking down toward the river, they decided to join them. The sheriff was carrying another big tray of cake and coffee.

"We knew the party was down here," Miss Sissy said, when they caught up to the group.

"Honey, if we are all together, it's a party," Dee Dee said.

"Did Mary Selena's aunt and uncle bring someone with them other than that handsome Indian servant?" Miss Sissy asked.

"Who you callin' handsome?" the sheriff teased her.

"Oh, sweetie, you know you're the most handsome guy in this town," Miss Sissy assured him, and she followed it up with a big, juicy kiss on his lips.

"Honey, that is not a servant," Dee Dee told her. "That is their great-nephew and a cousin to Mary Selena. He studied at Harrow and is now enrolled at Oxford."

"Hmmm," Miss Sissy said. "I may be reading things wrong, but when it comes to the language of love, I rarely do. Mary Selena's cousin has got an eye for her. He's danced with her twice already and it's like they move in harmony with one another."

"I hope the chil' has a good time," Destini piped up. "God knows we all known enough sorrow… her more than most, but none of us leaves this world without tastin' somethin' bitter. If we didn't, we'd never appreciate a sweet thing… a good thing."

"So true," Ricardo said. "Well, let's eat up and celebrate this beautiful night and our lovely Mary Selena." He held up his coffee cup and so did all the others. "Here's to *our* Mary Selena. May God continue to bless her with health, wealth, and goodness."

"Here, here!" the rest of the group echoed.

"You have to admit, Ricardo, this Camp EZ Blend is some good stuff," Destini said, referring to the coffee.

"It certainly is," Ricardo agreed. "It has just enough Cuban coffee blended in to make it the best!"

Dee Dee, ever the one for some zany humor, had to insert some gaiety into the conversation.

"Can y'all believe that Doughnut Dawson?" she asked, rolling her eyes. "Excuse me, I meant to say Chef Cyril Darrow Dawson."

"Who is that?" Ricardo asked.

"I'll tell you all about him later, honey," Dee Dee said. "Let's just say it has something to do with bouncing boobs," she added, laughing. "Anyway, he phoned, he wrote, he sent flowers, and he even went over to Destini and Matt's home unannounced, cake in hand, no less! He told them how much it would mean to this area that he be present at tonight's event. He said he heard Margot Smith was going to be here, and that he used to work for her."

"Honey," Destini said, on the verge of laughter. "I have rarely seen Matt get upset, I mean truly upset about anything, but that afternoon, when Doughnut knocked on our door and woke up Lily Dee, well, I thought Matt was gonna lose it. When he started his big spiel about Margot… Lawd Jesus! I thought I was gonna lose it!" she added, laughing heartily now. "Oh, then he gave us one of his, and I quote, "famous hummingbird cakes". I have to admit it was pretty tasty and so we thanked him for it."

"You mean the guy can actually cook?" Ricardo asked.

"Well, the cake was good," Destini said. "Anyway, then he began recounting everyone he knew and that if he was invited to this party he would have to bring his husband, Pablo, along with some other woman," she added, batting her eyes like only Doughnut could.

"Talk about being pushy," Dee Dee interjected.

"Yeah, he said this woman owns an island in the Caribbean and she's so rich that she bought a bunch of businesses over in Turpricone," Destini continued. "I'll tell ya', my first thought was who the hell cares? Before I could stop myself, I was tellin' him what I really thought. I said, oh, she's the one threatenin' everybody and sayin' how she goin' tear everythin' down and everybody's a fool except her. I told him I hadn't met her yet, but I heard from your Aunt Hattie and Aunt Nanny that they figured she had never gone to Ashley Hall in Charleston for finishing school or went to any sort of charm school, 'cause she sure as hell wasn't charmin' the folks around here."

"These outsiders just don't understand the way things are in this part of the world," Dee Dee said.

"Well, I'd had enough, so I held up my hand, and told him thanks for the cake and that we appreciated it," Destini said. "Then, I told him I'd appreciate in the future if he phoned before droppin' in."

"Ohhh... you didn't!" Dee Dee exclaimed.

"Yes, ma'am, I sure did," Destini told her. "Then, I told him I'd invite *him* to the party, but not Pablo, and definitely not this lady friend of his, who I heard needed to have her roots done and also gain some charm."

"Good for you!" Dee Dee said.

"That wasn't the end of it, though," Destini went

on. "He asked if I thought Mary Selena would consider his partner doing an art show at the Spencer Augustus Jarrellson Gallery."

"Oh, wow," Dee Dee muttered.

"I told him I didn't know, but that there was a board of trustees that had the say-so over things like that," Destini said. "Then I told him who was on the board. You know... Judge Wesson and his niece, Celesta, who studied fine arts at the Rhode Island School of Design, my husband, Matt, Mrs. Neva Wesley, and my sister-in-law, Essie Wilson. I told him he'd have to submit a proposal and do a presentation, and if they happened to pass on him, he could instead come up with a non-refundable thousand-dollar fee as a security deposit. You know... since the gallery is internationally renowned and the name itself carries prestige with lots of money behind it, unlike his lady friend who was buying up all the buildings in Turpricone. I told him Pablo would probably have a great show if he did it that way. Well... 'ol Doughnut left the house that day with his invitation for one person and he wasn't very happy about it, but I noticed he was here tonight, anyway."

"Oh, yes, he was here," Dee Dee said. "He started handing out signed copies of his latest cookbook to some of the guests just minutes after he arrived... until Celesta got involved, that is."

"What did she do?" Ricardo asked.

"Well, she started shouting at him, asking him if they were all low fat recipes," Dee Dee explained. "She said he wouldn't want folks packing it on like he did for so many years. Then, she told him it looked like he had picked up a few more pounds since the last time she saw him in the grocery store a couple years ago. Then, she got really loud and told him to put the damned cookbooks in his car and that this wasn't his party. She said, "Go on, now, run! You can do that now since you're not a fat ass anymore.""

"Bless his heart," Destini said, laughing.

"Well, the big fat ass started crying and he told her she was a bully. Then, he left the party. All I can say is thank God for Celesta," Dee Dee said.

"The only one who has volleyed for more photos than him is that woman who moved here to Seraph Springs a few years ago with her husband," Nadine piped up. "Let's see… her name was Amelia Elbertson Parker. Her husband, Ted, was some bigwig at one time with one of the major tech companies."

"Yeah, she has a couple of advanced degrees," Wanda Faye said. "One is from an online college. Of course, there's nothing wrong with that, but one degree is from Rice University out in Texas. She served on the planning and zoning board for Seraph Springs and got elected to the town council. Then, she eventually served as mayor for a few years."

"She had lots of good ideas, but her ideas were rather shotgunnish," Nadine said.

"What do you mean by that?" Ricardo asked.

"Well, she talked about a lot of things, but she never really zeroed in on anything specific. There was no follow-through. Also, being a public servant, you'd expect her and her husband to open their home for Christmas or other social occasions, but they never did. It just seemed rather strange to me. She never liked it when folks disagreed with her, either. Kinda like, God rest his soul, dear Sonny Boy Esmerian. She has that same type of attitude that she's better than other people. Education doesn't make folks better. It just means they went to school a little longer."

"You damn sure got that right," Dee Dee said. "Lots of million-dollar educations put into ten-cent heads. I've run into her a few times. I wish someone would tell her that it doesn't matter that she wears tasteful shoes and clothes, and speaks well, but as a public figure, no one can get too close to her. Damn, she has some of the worst halitosis I have ever smelled in my life! Her breath would gag a damned buzzard! As you black folks say, Destini, stank-ass breath!"

Destini and the others laughed so hard they had tears streaming down their cheeks, even the sheriff.

"Girl, you crazy!" Destini said. "I tell you, though, she moved like an Olympic runner every time the local newspaper snapped a photo."

Again, everyone had a good laugh.

Just then, Mary Selena called out to the group down by the river, "Get up here!" she shouted. "Ricardo! You, Carl Alvin, Matt, Chad, and yes, you, too, Sheriff Lewis, I want dances with all of you before this night is over!"

So, up the hill the entire group trudged back

toward the Jarrellson house with Destini lagging behind for a moment, staring out across the river.

"Even Mama Tee wouldn't believe all of this," Destini said, shaking her head. "No, ma'am, she sure wouldn't.

Chapter 32

Love is an international language

The Himalayan Mountains, as well as the Ganges River are considered sacred by many Hindus. The beauty of the subcontinent of India with its colors, sights, and sounds brought much joy and wonder to Mary Selena. It seemed that the soul of India magically filled her senses as soon as the plane touched down on the blessed ground of her mother's homeland.

The unmistakable fragrance of frangipani surrounded her that first night, as she stood in the carefully tended gardens of her great aunt and uncle.

In some ways, the atmosphere of her family's home in India reminded her of the Deep South in the United States. Family of the first, second, and third generations all came to meet, eat, and greet, as well as dance, sing, and play music. Each family member graciously engulfed her with love, understanding, and compassion, just like back home in Seraph Springs.

Every one of them gave her a token or a gift of some sort, including a bracelet, medallions, and a small jeweled box. More than anything, though, they brought laughter to her, as well as stories of her mother's family that she had never heard before. Each time she walked through the gardens, gazed toward the majestic mountain peaks in the distance, or went on excursions of the area, she found herself oddly attracted to her handsome cousin, Gopal Sing. He was extremely attentive toward her, as well as compassionate, mature for his age, and very understanding.

One evening, the two of them went for a walk through the family garden. When they came upon an ornate bench, Mary Selena suggested they sit down for a bit. She completely surprised herself when she leaned over and kissed Gopal on the lips. Then, she boldly told him she loved him.

"Do you think me too forward to say that to you?" she asked Gopal, as her cheeks turned red. "Was it too immature?"

"No," he quickly responded. "I fell in love with you the moment I first saw you at your home in Seraph Springs. I believe I am in love with you, too. I want us to spend our lives together," he added, which made Mary Selena smile wide before planting another kiss on his lips.

The next day, the two of them departed with a chaperoned caravan on a pilgrimage to a holy place in the mountains. During that outing, Gopal and Mary Selena had the opportunity to talk for hours. The two of them finally decided they must tell their family about their plans.

"I have no one to tell here except my aunt, Lady Arabella, since Carl Alvin and Chad have already gone on to their next stop in the Caribbean. They said they enjoyed Barbados so much that they were going back for another extended visit," Mary Selena told Gopal. "I will have to tell Destini and Matthew over the phone. I want them to know what's going on. I will also call my cousin, Trey Esmerian. He's a doctor in Atlanta."

When the two of them returned to the palatial home of their relatives, they declared their love for each other to the delight of all who were present. The only one who had questions was Destini when Mary Selena called her a few minutes later. She had her on speaker phone so that Gopal could be included in the conversation.

"Baby, are you sure?" Destini asked her, after Mary Selena explained what was going on.

"I have never been more sure of anything," Mary Selena said. "Gopal is stable, and he is going to be a wonderful physician. He understands about me wanting to go to college, too. Destini, I just need someone in my life who is mine and mine alone. He provides all of that for me, and, most importantly, he is such a kind person."

"Lord, I wish Mama Tee was here," Destini said, but something flashed into her mind and it came to her clear as a bell. It was the words she spoke to Sheriff Bartow Lewis the day Easter Bunnye lay as a corpse at the county morgue "Mary Selena, unconditional love has no pride. We are blessed because we have the kind of love that Jesus had... the unconditional kind... the best kind."

"Yes, we are very blessed," Mary Selena agreed.

"Do you *know* your love for each other is unconditional?" Destini asked them.

They both simultaneously replied, "We do."

Destini felt something tug at her heart just then and she knew it was the spirit of Watson speaking to her. He was saying, "Destini, I love you, and our baby girl knows what she's doing. I entrusted her to you, but now it is time to let her go with the love of her life."

"Well, then, it sounds as if you two really know the meaning of love," Destini said. "You have my permission, Mary Selena. Go ahead and be happy," she added, as tears filled her eyes. "If you can hold off just a little bit, though, Matt and I would really like to come to the wedding."

"We would love that, too, and to have the blessing of our families means so much," Mary Selena said. "We will plan to marry a week from tomorrow, okay?"

"Okay," Destini said.

"We love you and we look forward to seeing you soon," Mary Selena told her, and they hung up.

The week went by in a flash, and before anyone knew it, Lady Arabella and Destini, who were standing in for the bride's parents, approached the altar to give away Mary Selena. During the complex Hindu ritualistic wedding ceremony, Mary Selena and Gopal were both beaming, especially when they uttered their vows before the priest.

"Today, our Mary Selena is Laxmi and her groom is Vishnu," the priest declared. "By joining their hands in marriage, we will repay our debt to our forefathers by continuing the next life cycle."

Gopal took Mary Selena's hand and the couple promised each other that while pursuing a life of

Dharma and Karma, they would remain ever faithful to each other.

Next, the sacred fire was lit at the center of the traditional wedding mandap, a covered structure with pillars, as it is considered to be the prime witness of wedding rituals. The young couple fed ghee, a clarified butter, into the fire as an offering, and they prayed to the gods for children, wealth, prosperity, and long and healthy lives. This part of the ceremony is known as the Vivaha Homa.

Next, Trey Esmerian, the first cousin of the bride, poured rice on Mary Selena's palms and the couple offered the rice to the sacred fire together. The ends of their ornate wedding garments were tied in a knot to perform the Agni Pardakshina, and they made seven circles around the Sacred Fire uttering the promise to each other to be eternal partners and complement each other in life's journey. At the end of the seventh circle Mary Selena moved to the left side of Gopal indicating she was now part of his life.

The final and most important part of the Hindu Ceremony, the Saptadpadi, or the Seven Sacred Vows now commenced. It was during this that Destini, Trey, and even Matt openly shed a few tears. Mary Selena took the seven symbolic steps while pushing a stone along the marble floor, as Gopal assisted her. The couple reiterated their aspirations for married life as each step signified a specific promise that the couple made to each other.

The first step was to respect and honor each other.

The second was to share each other's joy and sorrow. The third was to trust and be loyal to each other. The fourth was to cultivate appreciation for knowledge. The fifth was to appreciate purity of emotions, love, family duties, and spiritual growth. The sixth was to follow the principles of Dharma. The seventh and final step was to nurture an eternal bond of friendship and love.

Upon completion of the marriage rituals, the ceremony concluded and the couple received blessings from all the elders of the families. A huge reception followed with much celebration and merriment. During the reception, Destini offered a heartwarming speech.

"When I first heard my baby, Mary Selena, wanted to marry, I thought, she's too young," Destini began. "Now, I'm a spiritual person and I respect all peoples and their different religions, but I am a Christian. We believe if you pray, and pray hard enough and listen, the Lord will send you an answer. All you folks here have been so kind and nice, but I want you to know something. I pinned some of the first diapers on this child's father when he was born a number of years ago. I loved him with all my heart. I loved her mama, Miss Selena, too. As I prayed and asked God to give me guidance, I swear to all of you, my baby Watson's voice came to me. He said, "I entrusted you with the love of my child. She knows what she is doing. Let her go.""

As Destini looked out across the Indian faces staring back at her among a sea of rich and vibrant colors, she saw many of them nodding. Many others were wiping tears from their eyes.

"There's something else I'd like to say," Destini continued. "Love, like grief, has no pride, and if it's unconditional, then it will hold. I felt it here today. To all of you, I am going to tell you something. When our little girl and her new husband come back home, we're goin' have another wing-ding of a party, Southern style! All of you who can come, please… come on over," she added, smiling. "We have plenty of room, plenty of food, and I can guarantee all of you a good time."

Destini turned, and then she kissed and hugged Mary Selena and Gopal, and wished the newly married couple well. Matt and Trey followed suit seconds later.

"Is there anything you want to ask me, baby? Anything at all?" Destini asked Mary Selena.

At this, Mary Selena laughed. "No, ma'am, I don't, but I love you for asking."

As the young couple left for their honeymoon, the partying continued. Destini found that folks, no matter their culture, were a lot more alike than not, and that love really is an international language that everyone understands.

Chapter 33

The cycle of life

Preparations were in full swing at the historic Jarrellson mansion on the banks of the Suwannee River. Anyone who was anyone from the Jarrellson contacts list around the globe had been invited to a reception honoring Mary Selena and her new husband, the soon-to-be Dr. Gopal Sing, M.D.

On this day, by the time mid morning rolled around, it seemed as if steam was rising from the soil and enveloping one's entire being. In weather such as this, many older north Floridians would say, "If you get a breath of air, you'll steal it." Nevertheless, specially ordered air conditioned tents were being set up on the expansive sweep of lawn with its panoramic view of the ever-majestic Suwannee River.

Because of all the work being done at the Jarrellson home for the party, Dee Dee had wisely advised Mary Selena and Gopal, along with their coterie of family from India, to be guests at Camp EZ. Meanwhile, Dee Dee's in-laws and all the family members they brought with them were staying with Aunt Hattie.

Aunt Hattie had offered many times to build Ricardo and Dee Dee a large home of their own, which they always refused, but at the same time she kept imploring them to come and live with her. Her palatial home in Turpricone was huge, with two stories, plus a spacious attic. There was about six-thousand square feet of living space altogether, not including a private guest suite in the back of the house that was connected along a covered walkway to the main house.

Aunt Hattie was so tickled to host the Fernandez family that she was over the top, as they say in this town. She absolutely loved having company, and more than that, she enjoyed all the gossip and just having folks to talk with.

Ricardo's mother seemed to love it, as well. Dee Dee found it more than amusing how these two, oh-so-different ladies got along so well. One would be talking a mile a minute in heavily accented Spanglish, while animatedly waving her arms, and Aunt Hattie, with her mellifluous Southern accent, liquid of vowels and with no "r's" present in her pronunciation, would talk at the same time. They would just go on and on, and they really seemed to love each other's conversations and company. One day, Dee Dee, came in to find both of them holding hands and crying.

"What in the world is wrong?" she asked her aunt. "Did someone die or something?"

"No, no, honey. We were just sharing how happy we are with the thought of your babies on the way. Then, we both took trips down memory lane to our childhoods," Aunt Hattie explained.

"Trips?" Dee Dee quipped, attempting to lighten the ladies' mood. "Hell, the two of you must have taken a really long journey if you were talking about childhood."

Aunt Hattie playfully slapped Dee Dee on the arm,

and said, "Get away from here, you bad thing. Let us visit and have our drinks in peace. I don't how Ricardo puts up with you."

Later that day at the Jarrellson home, Dee Dee smiled as she recalled that conversation, while she waddled about working with the caterers. Nadine, Wanda Faye, Destini, Essie, and Miss Sissy were all working their fingers to the bone in the kitchen and elsewhere in the grand hall to make this event picture perfect for the evening's festivities.

Miss Sissy happened to glance out the window and then shouted to the girls, "Ladies, I'm going out to give my best sweetheart a kiss! I see him coming up the drive! I'll bet he's brought me that staple gun I told him I needed!"

"Don't ya'll be trying to slip off into the bushes!" Nadine shouted to her, as she walked out the door. "Ticks are bad this time of year!"

Everyone in the group laughed and Miss Sissy shouted back, "Hush your mouth, Nadine! I ain't scared of no ticks!"

After about ten minutes had passed, Wanda Faye peeked out the window toward the sheriff's car in the driveway and noticed Miss Sissy was leaning up against him and he had his arms around her.

"Something ain't right, sis," she said to Nadine, who had come up beside her. "She's crying, isn't she? And the sheriff ain't moved in quite a while. He's just standing there holding her. I think we ought to mosey on out there and see what's going on."

"Do you think we should?" Nadine asked.

"Yes, ma'am, I do," Wanda Faye told her. "I just have a feeling something's not quite right."

The two of them went outside and slowly ambled over toward the sheriff's vehicle. When he spotted them, he motioned them over.

"Listen, girls," he said. "Do either one of you have a cell phone on you?"

"I do," Nadine said, and she reached into her pocket.

"I want you to call Ricardo," the sheriff ordered her. "Tell him to get over here as fast as he can."

"What is it, Sheriff Lewis?" Nadine asked.

"It's Carl Alvin and Chad, honey," he said. "They are dead, both of them, along with the pilot they hired to fly them from Barbados to the airport just outside of Pittstown," he added, mincing no words. "They crashed somewhere in the Caribbean. The Coast Guard found the wreckage and positively identified the bodies from the information they procured at the site of the crash."

"My God! Oh, my God!" Wanda Faye shrieked.

Nadine took her sister by the hand, "Now, honey, we can't do this. Not right now. We have to keep our wits about us. The sheriff has to go tell Dee Dee, and then go tell her Aunt Hattie."

"I know, I know," Wanda Faye said, shaking uncontrollably. "Dee Dee's never been one to show emotion in public… not a lot, anyway, except with her Uncle Hamp's death. My God, that was awful enough, but now this with Carl Alvin? And Dee Dee in her condition? I don't envy you, Sheriff. My Lord, I just can't believe this."

By this time, Destini had joined the group with Essie not far behind her. When Nadine explained what had happened, Destini stepped over behind a large azalea shrub and silently wept for a few moments. When she collected herself, she went back to where the sheriff was standing with Miss Sissy.

"Sheriff, sir, I need to be the one to tell Dee Dee, if you don't mind," Destini told him. "You can stand behind me, but please, you have to let me tell her. I do thank you from my heart, but I need to be the one to break this news to her. She's been so good to me all through my scare with cancer and everythin' else I been through. Please, let me be the one."

The sheriff agreed, and then the entire group walked around to the rear of the property and over to the tent where Dee Dee was helping the caterer, Daphne Gerald, put the finishing touches on a floral arrangement.

"Well, by God, are y'all being put under arrest for something?" Dee Dee asked with a chuckle. "Sheriff, you've come out here to check that all the silver is accounted for?" she joked.

The sheriff didn't answer her and neither did anyone else. Destini took control of the situation and motioned for Consuela to come over.

"Consuela, baby, if you don't mind, run over to that cooler over there and bring us several bottles of cold water and put them on that table over there. If you will, too, honey, I need a clean dish towel or a little hand towel. Thank you, baby. I hate to be a pest, but please do this as quick as you can."

Consuela knew all too well of Destini's infinite kindness to her and to all the staff, unlike the manner of her former mistress, the late Anna Mary Jarrellson Williams. So, she brought the items over right away. Meanwhile, Destini fished around in her pocket for the small bottle of ammonia she had brought along, in case of a bug bite, although, now she might need it for smelling salts.

"Let's all sit down a minute," Destini said to the group, and they did. "You, too, Dee Dee. Come have a bottle of cool water and take a load off your feet. You look like you could use a break," she told her. "Ooohh, Lord have mercy," she quietly added, as she sat down.

"We have work to do," Dee Dee protested, but she was met with silence from everyone. "Okay, what's going on here?" she asked, looking suspiciously from one face to the next as she walked closer. "I know it's something and I'm not liking the looks on your faces. Come on, now. I was born at night, but it damn sure wasn't last night. Somebody better tell me what's going on," she demanded, and then she sat down beside Destini.

Destini reached over and took her hand. "Baby, there ain't no easy way to say this, so I'm just gonna spit it out. Our sweet Carl Alvin and Chad are gone. They was killed in a plane crash down in the Caribbean trying to make it here for this party. They're gone, honey. I'm so sorry."

Everyone at the table began to openly weep. Even the sheriff was dabbing at his eyes, as Miss Sissy held onto him.

"Destini, you're lying to me," Dee Dee calmly said, clearly in shock, and clearly not wanting to believe her. "Tell me you're lying to me," she said again. Then, she took Destini by the shoulders and shook her. "Tell me! Tell me you're lying!" she screamed, and then she broke down in tears.

"Oh, honey, I wish I could take away your pain," Destini said, crying, as she rocked Dee Dee in her ample arms. Then, under her breath, she prayed, "Help me, Lord Jesus."

About that time, Ricardo and his brother Justo arrived and started toward the group of mourners. Tears were streaming down Ricardo's face, and when Dee Dee saw him, she rushed over to him.

"Ricardo!" she screamed. "Make them tell me they're lying! It's all a lie! You tell them! You too, Justo! Tell them it's a lie! My Carl Alvin can't be gone! Not Carl Alvin! Not my Carl Alvin, and Chad..." she added, in a voice that reeked of pain and heartache. "They just found such happiness together," she went on. "Oh, Ricardo, please make them say they're lying!" she screamed again.

Miss Sissy covered her ears and leaned in closer to the sheriff. Nadine and Wanda Faye held on to each other, both of them weeping uncontrollably.

Meanwhile, Essie moved closer to Destini, as Dee Dee held onto Ricardo, still wailing in grief.

"Here, now, baby, here," Destini said, and she got up from her seat. "You sit down, Dee Dee, and Mr. Ricardo here is goin' take care of you."

Dee Dee screamed again, "Oh, Carl Alvin, I love you! I love you! I love you! I have always loved you, cousin! You were my heart when I couldn't find my way! Oh, my Carl Alvin!" she kept on, repeating his name over and over again.

Then, as if someone had just snuffed out the blazing sun, Dee Dee sat bolt upright in her chair. She turned to Ricardo with the oddest look on her face.

"We have to go to the hospital now, Ricardo," she said, much too calmly. "Actually, I don't even know if there's time, but we have to go now. I think my water just broke."

"What?!" he shouted.

Wanda Faye, now a seasoned registered nurse, shouted. "Yes, ma'am, we have to go!"

She asked Nadine to call Camp EZ to alert Mary Selena and Gopal, as well as Trey Esmerian, who was staying there as a guest.

Upon arrival at the hospital, young Dr. Celia Campbell met them in the emergency room. Trey arrived seconds later and asked if he could assist her.

"Of course, you can," Celia told him. "I would be delighted and honored. The rest of you need to wait out here. Wanda Faye, you can come in. I want you to scrub in and help us with this girl."

"Okay," Wanda Faye said, as an orderly wheeled Dee Dee into the delivery room.

"I just heard what happened to Carl Alvin and Chad," Celia said to Wanda Faye and Ricardo. "I don't know… Dee Dee's blood pressure is dangerously high right now and her pulse is racing. Thank you, by the way, for keeping abreast of that, Wanda Faye."

"Hey, I always carry my stethoscope and blood pressure cuff with me in my purse, as you never know when something like this is going to happen," Wanda Faye said.

"I don't want to alarm you, but this may be a difficult delivery," Celia went on. "I'm praying we can save the mother and the babies."

"What are you saying?!" Ricardo asked, clearly not expecting to hear those words.

"Mr. Fernandez, if Dee Dee was having these babies under normal conditions, she herself would be able to handle this, but that's not the case right now, so we must prepare for what I pray will be the best outcome. We cannot rule out what could be the worst, though. We will do all we can, I promise you. I would ask the rest of you to pray as hard as you can for this girl. If you have ever prayed fervently, you need to do it now."

"Oh, dear God," Destini said, shaking her head.

"One more thing," Celia said. "I insist on this, Ricardo. You call Dee Dee's aunt, your mother, your father, and anyone else, and tell them to stay home until we call them. Nadine, you do the same for your mama and her group. This hospital is not equipped to handle large amounts of people waiting on babies to be born. It's just too small. Besides, Dee Dee needs calm now. She doesn't need all the hoopla, especially in light of this terrible tragedy that just happened. Tell everyone to stay away until I say so. Don't get into the reason why just yet. Do you all understand?"

"We need to do as the doctor asked," the sheriff said, and everyone nodded.

Later, after phone calls were made to family and friends, the small group who had arrived with Dee Dee waited in the corridor of the hospital delivery room. The only other person to join them was Matt. Since he was a minister, he led the entire group in prayer. Then, Destini prayed, and then Essie, the girls, and then to everyone's surprise, even the sheriff and Miss Sissy said prayers. Again, the tears were flowing freely, as eyes were closed and lips silently uttered more prayers.

For a long while, time seemed suspended. Nothing could be heard but the slamming of doors and the sounds of various electronic beeps from the hospital apparatuses. Every once in a while, a lightly audible, "I beg you, give her the strength to bear it, Lord Jesus," came out of Destini's mouth.

About twenty minutes later, Dr. Trey Esmerian emerged from the delivery room with Dr. Campbell by his side. They were both smiling wide and giving a thumbs-up gesture. Destini, who had been pacing the floor, caught her chest and fell against the wall, shouting, "Glory, oh, Lord, thank you, thank you, dear

Jesus!"

Ricardo shot up out of his chair in the small waiting room when he heard Destini's cries of joy. A second later, Dr. Campbell walked directly over to him.

"Well, Mr. Fernandez," she began with a huge smile on her face. "I am pleased to report that you are the proud father of two bouncing baby boys."

"Two boys?!" Ricardo gasped. "Are you sure?!"

"Oh, yes," Trey interjected. "We are quite sure. "Aren't you happy, Ricardo?"

Justo rushed over and hugged his brother. "Two boys, Ricardo! Two fine Fernandez boys!"

"But it was supposed to be a boy and girl," Ricardo protested. "The tests said so down in Miami and over in Jacksonville."

"Well, Mr. Fernandez, all I can say is, sometimes even medical science is unsure and uncertain," Celia said. "I guess that's the reason they call what we do the "practice" of medicine." Everyone had a good laugh, and then Celia added, "Go in and meet your new sons, Ricardo, and give your wife a big fat kiss. She was a real trooper. As for the rest of you, wait until I say you can go in," she ordered them.

When Ricardo went into the room, Dee Dee was cradling the two newborns with her on the bed, one in each arm.

"Well Señor Fernandez, what do you think?" Dee Dee asked him. "Did I do all right by you?"

Ricardo kissed his wife full on the lips and then he kissed both of the boys on the forehead.

"You did more than all right, Dee Dee," he said. "You did perfect. They are perfect, just like my beautiful, perfect wife," he added.

"Is there a tape recorder in this room?" Dee Dee jokingly asked the nurse. "Damn, I would love to get that comment on tape," she added, laughing.

Ricardo, still with tears running down his cheeks, said, "Oh, it's so good to see you smile."

"I have something I must ask of you, Ricardo," Dee Dee said. "I know it's the custom for a boy to be named after his father, and I am willing to do that for one of these boys, but I want the other one named Chadwick Alvin Campbell Fernandez, in honor of Carl Alvin and Chad. This big boy, of course, will be named Luis Ricardo, Jr. in honor of you and Papa," she added, nodding toward what looked to be the bigger of the two babies.

Ricardo was beaming. "Whatever you want, sweetheart," he said. "I am so happy. Can you imagine the fun we are going to have with these two boys?"

"I can imagine a lot, now, kiss me again, you handsome thing, and then get Destini and Miss Sissy in here. I need to be fixed up to receive visitors. Oh, and tell Miss Sissy I want her to call the house and have Aunt Hattie bring that beautiful dark blue gown and peignoir set you bought for me last year in New Orleans... oh, and the slippers to match... oh, and to bring my long diamond earrings. You can tell them, too, that the party tonight is to go on as scheduled. Carl Alvin would have wanted it, and I don't want any moping about it. We loved him and we will mourn his passing, but Ricardo, he did find love, honey, and he died knowing what it was like to truly be in love. He died alongside someone he truly loved and cared for. For all that this hurts me, my God, I am more than blessed that Carl Alvin finally found love."

"I found it, too, darling," Ricardo told her, and then he kissed her again. "Before I go, I want to tell you something… something I never told you before. I fell in love with you the first time I saw you get out of that Range Rover with your poodle, Chanel, down at Camp EZ. You were so refined and polished, and part of a world so different from mine, but I was in love. I felt because of me going to the gym and working on my physique, I was a decent looking man. So, that morning you went into the bathroom… well, I did… yes, ma'am, I purposely put that towel around me and walked in on you, hoping you would like what you saw."

"Señor Fernandez, I do declare," she said. "Well, now you got three for one, my Cuban cutie. What do you think about that? Are you still happy you put the move on me with that draped towel?"

Ricardo kissed her again. "Yes, indeed. I was prepared to drop that towel, too, but I didn't have to, did I?" he coyly asked her.

"No, you didn't," Dee Dee said. "And you better never tell anyone about how that towel incident played out, either."

Ricardo was heartily laughing now.

"I won't tell," he said. "That is something sacred between a husband and wife. No one else needs to know. Well, maybe our little family when they get older," he added, still laughing. "Wow, family, Dee Dee. Our family... how wonderful that sounds."

☙☙☙☙☙☙☙☙☙☙

THE PARTY did go on that evening just as it was planned, with one addition. Before things got started, Destini made an announcement about the deaths of Carl Alvin and Chad.

"There will be no weeping and wailing tonight, though," Destini said. "Carl Alvin wouldn't have wanted that. He and Dee Dee had a favorite saying, "I am not here for a long time. I'm here for a good time.""

"Amen," Nadine said.

"Carl Alvin brought nothing but joy to so many," Destini continued. "He would do the craziest things to please others. He even dressed up like cupid one year on Valentine's Day. Remember that, Wanda Faye? Nadine, remember how crazy he used to dance with us? Finally, one day our baby, Carl Alvin, just like all my other babies, found something worth more than all of this," she added, with a sweeping gesture of her hand across the total grandeur of the Jarrellson estate. "He found love."

There was an entire chorus of "Amen's" from everyone in attendance.

"Now, let's hear it for this beautiful couple, Mary

Selena and Gopal!" Destini shouted with glee. "Let's raise our glasses to the happy couple!"

Sheriff Lewis shouted, "To the happy couple!"

Everyone echoed the sentiment and toasted the newlyweds.

Mary Selena looked as if she had just stepped out of a dream, dressed in an ivory-colored sari with peacock blue and green embellishments. Gopal was in a white dinner jacket and black trousers, and he looked quite the dapper fellow.

The rest of the evening couldn't have been more perfect. Folks reminisced, they pigged out on all sorts of food, and then they danced the night away. The visitors and family from India ooh'ed and ahh'ed over the magnificence of the Jarrellson home, while the folks from Campbell County were more than goo-goo-eyed over the jewels worn by the Indian visitors, from diamonds, rubies, and aquamarines, to emeralds and sapphires. To say this group knew how to sparkle at a cocktail reception was an understatement, and dance? Lord, they loved dancing.

About halfway through the night's festivities, Mary Selena and Gopal were asked to have a seat in front of a huge television screen in the main hall, while the rest of the crowd gathered around. Projected onto the screen was the one and only Dee Dee, in all her post-pregnancy glory, compliments of Trey Esmerian, technology whiz.

Dee Dee was sitting in a large recliner wearing a magnificent, yet conservative lace negligee, looking every inch a queen. Her face was glowing, her makeup and hair were exquisite, and she was smiling from ear to ear, thanks to Miss Sissy's magic touch.

"I am so sorry I couldn't be with you tonight, Mary Selena and Gopal," Dee Dee began. "I tried bribery and every other trick I could think of, but this is one time Ricardo said no to me. He's the best man in the world, by the way."

Ricardo waved to Dee Dee from where he stood behind Mary Selena and said, "I'm coming right over in just a few minutes, sweetheart."

"That's good," Dee Dee said. "Now, Destini, you better have me a damned care box of party treats as big as a number two wash tub. I'm not complaining, but you know all about this hospital food. Nadine, Wanda Faye, you heard me now. I want a *big* care box."

"We heard you, Queenie," Destini said, laughing.

"All right now! Strike up the band and let the good times roll!" Dee Dee cheered. "Dance until dawn… except you, Ricardo. You bring that food on over here."

"Yes, ma'am," he told her.

"Oh, Destini, Wanda Faye, Nadine, Miss Sissy, and now our precious Mary Selena, I am so overcome right now," Dee Dee said, as her expression softened.

"Oh, no," Nadine muttered to Wanda Faye. "I hope she doesn't start on Carl Alvin or we'll all be bawling here."

Just then, the nurse appeared on the screen with the two babies in her arms and she handed them to

Dee Dee.

"Look here, Destini, Wanda Faye, Nadine, all of y'all… look what I did all by myself… well, maybe not all by myself. I guess my Cuban prince had a lot to do with it, too," Dee Dee said, as her face lit up again. "These boys are already full of black beans, but hey, Aunt Hattie, Aunt Nanny… there's plenty of grits in them, too."

The two older women just shook their heads.

"All that money for that charm school," Nanny said, shaking her head. "Lord have mercy."

"We can't kill her now, though" Hattie said. "We have too much invested in her. Plus, now we have to help with these two boys."

"I heard that, ladies," Dee Dee said. "I love you, Nanny, even if you do make the second best lemon meringue pie in the county. You know mine is better."

"Hrmphh," Nanny muttered, and then she grabbed her sister, Hattie, by the hand. "Bye, Dee Dee, we're old ladies, you know, so we're going home now. We will see you tomorrow."

After Dee Dee signed off, Ricardo graciously escorted the two women to their car. As they were walking, Nanny, who rarely showed any emotion, began to cry.

"What in the world?" Hattie muttered. "My God, what's wrong?"

"Dee Dee, of course," Nanny said. "Why did she have to bring up that damned lemon pie? She knows mine is the best."

"Oh, now, come on," Hattie comforted her. "It was just her way of not breaking down about Carl Alvin, but now here you are. Lord Jesus," she added, shaking her head.

"We will get through this, I know, but it won't be easy," Nanny said. "Goodness, Carl Alvin could sure make you laugh, couldn't he? When you were at your lowest point, he could sure do that."

"Yes, he could," Hattie agreed. "There were times, though, my God, I wanted to wring his neck. Like the time he told me I needed an inexpensive pair of evening pumps and he came back with a five-hundred-dollar pair of Gucci's."

"Yeah, that was Carl Alvin, but you know, Hattie, I always worried about him not finding love. He finally found it, though. Yes, he did."

"That's what life is all about, honey," Hattie agreed. "It's about finding love, sustaining love, and loving love, even when it hurts you. You can't give up on love because love never fails. That's one thing I did learn in church. All those times you thought I was sleeping in the pew, but I wasn't."

When they finally made it over to their chauffeured limousine, Ricardo kissed the two ladies goodnight.

"I believe my two boys will be the most blessed in the entire world to have two wonderful great-great aunts with such wisdom," he said.

"Pshaw," Nanny gushed. "You go on and believe that, Ricardo, but know that we plan on ruining them all we can. We joke about Dee Dee, and you have to live with her, but we did our part there, too. She's all right."

"She's more than all right," Ricardo said, smiling wide. "She is the love of my life."

"Well, let's get some rest, now," Nanny said. "Tomorrow, they dedicate that monument down by the river in memory of Watson and Selena. I hope I can hold up. I'll be thinking of Carl Alvin and Chad the entire time."

Two others who had walked out at the same time as Ricardo, Hattie and Nanny, were Curtis and Neva. Ricardo smiled at them as they walked past, while Hattie cagily said, "Beautiful evening, and such beautiful company. Did you enjoy the party, Miss Neva?"

"Oh, very much," Neva said.

Neva looked truly magnificent in a tailored off-white evening suit with matching shoes and hat, as well as a perfectly made up face. Even the usually scruffy-looking Curtis had made an effort with shiny black shoes instead of worn brown loafers. He had also been to the barber shop, as his beard was trimmed and his usually unkempt hair was stylishly cut. Everyone bid each other goodnight and Ricardo went back to the house to get Dee Dee's food.

After Curtis and Neva drove off, Hattie and Nanny had some words to say after they piled into their limo.

"Curtis really is a handsome man behind all that fur on his face, but she has to be old enough to be his mother," Hattie said. "What in the world do you think he sees in her?"

"Honey, love is blind, and if they have found some companionship that suits them, well, it suits the hell out of me. I'm happy for them."

Hattie and Nanny could both be heard laughing as the limo pulled away.

Chapter 34

Black runs the river

An early morning fog shrouded the Suwannee River this morning. As it was beginning to lift, a small group of family and friends of the late Dr. and Mrs. Watson Jarrellson Williams gathered together on a high bluff overlooking the historic river that was immortalized by the legendary songwriter, Stephen Foster. A huge, dark marble monument in memory of Watson and his wife, Selena Jarrellson Dubois Williams, stood proudly amid the fecund landscape, sheltered by moss-festooned live oak trees and decades-old longleaf pines. It was rumored around town that over a quarter million dollars from the Jarrellson Trust had been expended on the obelisk-shaped marble structure, plus several thousand more dollars for the brick pavers, the marble fountains, and the wooden benches that surrounded the monument.

The designer of the memorial was a friend of Dr. Curtis Osborne. He made certain the entire project was appropriate for the environment, as well as the sanctity of the two who were being memorialized.

"This is indeed very impressive," Ricardo said to Dee Dee when they arrived for the ceremony. "It's not showy or pretentious."

"Yes, it's almost as impressive as this Ceylon sapphire ring," Dee Dee agreed, as she held up her hand.

Dee Dee had insisted she was feeling well enough to attend the memorial after just giving birth to her twins, who were still in the neo-natal care unit of the hospital for another day or two.

At the gate-enclosed entrance leading into the beautifully landscaped area, programs were given out by members of the staff of Augustine Jackson's Funeral Home. They had been engaged to erect the custom-made monument at Destini's request. Several dozen chairs had been set up in front of the memorial area, and after everyone had arrived, the program began with an opening speech by Destini.

"Good morning, everyone," she said, as she stood behind the podium. "I was so pleased and honored when sweet Mary Selena, the daughter of the deceased, asked me to donate this piece of land on which this memorial is situated. Her father, Watson, was the first baby I tended to as a fourteen-year-old girl. I loved Watson throughout his tragically shortened life and he never once forgot me. He never stopped loving me and I never stopped praying for him. He had so many talents. He was a brilliant doctor, a great cook… oh, that boy could cook," she added, smiling. "He had a marvelous sense of humor, and he wasn't a bad guitar player, either. Above all, he had a loving heart for others, especially those who were less fortunate than he was. He spent a great deal of his resources and efforts while he walked this earth trying to improve the life of others."

After a few hearty "Amen's" from the group,

Destini continued.

"For a long time, it was easy for Watson to give love and give it unconditionally, but I have to say, as hard as we all tried, he never learned how to receive love until he and Selena got engaged and then married. I watched my baby's eyes light up when he was with her. He had overcome so much in his life, and finally he found love. Today, I say to each one of you, love is a major element that boosts us through all the swift currents of life."

"Amen," Dee Dee softly said, as she grasped Ricardo's hand in hers.

"The Suwannee River is right in front of us here," Destini went on. "It is placid and smooth right now, but there are times it can be swift and angry. Life is the same way. During those swift and angry times we all need an anchor to hold onto that keeps us in place. That anchor is love, my friends. For many years my baby Watson was adrift, but he anchored himself with Selena's love and, hopefully, my love, too, which never wavered. If he could speak to any one of us today, I believe he would say, 'Don't be stingy with love. Give it freely and live each day to the fullest.'"

There was yet another collective "Amen" from the entire group, as well as a few tears from some.

"Thank you all and God bless you," Destini said, and she quietly retreated to her seat.

Up next was Phil.

"Even though we grew up in the same town, I didn't meet my friend, Watson, until a stormy time in his life," Phil began. "He was going through a rough patch, if you will. Having recently lost the love of his life in China, he was searching for a way out of that dark and dangerous web called depression. He eventually found what he had been looking for his entire life in the arms of his wife, Selena. She was, without a doubt, one of the most beautiful ladies I had ever met. Her physical beauty and grace were breathtaking, and she was even more beautiful on the inside with her kind and loving heart. She reached out to everyone and she gave our world a dazzling display of light that, sadly, went out too soon. Rest in peace, Watson and Selena," he said, ending his solemn tribute.

Mary Selena then went up to the podium. She was attired in a beautiful pale pink sari and walked with the grace and dignity of one who was sure of herself, but who was also in harmony with the world around her. She wore her grandmother's stunning pearls and pear drop earrings. It was undeniable that her beauty was ethereal, just like her mother.

"My dear beloved family and friends," Mary Selena began. "Most of you are aware that I never knew my parents. I was only an infant when they were killed in a fatal car accident outside London. I did, however, have the benefit of unconditional love shown to me by so many who are present here today, but especially from my paternal grandparents, the late Stanley and Anna Mary Jarrellson Williams. I also received much love from my maternal great-aunt, Lady Arabella Simpson Keyes, who is with us here today. I love you, Aunt

Arabella."

Lady Arabella was beautifully coiffed in a chic white and black Chanel suit with a broad black and white straw hat. At the mention of her name, she began to dab at her eyes with a lace handkerchief.

Mary Selena continued. "Just like my beloved father and mother, who loved the Suwannee River and spent as much time as possible near or on it, I, too, love it. This magnificent river is quite spiritual to me, as spiritual as the Ganges River is to my dear husband and his family. The Jarrellson legacy in Campbell County is an interesting one. We could all say that, I'm sure," she added, and many in the audience nodded. "One thing about the family, despite their flaws and shortcomings, is their resilience and determination to endure. Above us is an ancient live oak tree that shelters us. I am told it is close to one-hundred-and-fifty-years-old. Think of the changes this old tree has witnessed and the many storms it has survived. Its limbs go bare in the winter, but then they sprout forth new growth when spring comes. Think of the songs of the cicadas and whippoorwills during the summer, as they perch upon its branches. Just think of all the life this one tree has seen… and all the death, too."

Just then, Mary Selena's speech was abruptly interrupted by the arrival of a large black sedan that had motored up to the memorial site. From the sedan alighted a lady, short in stature, and dressed in a severely tailored black suit. She wore black hose, black patent leather pumps, and black elbow length gloves.

She also carried a small black handbag. On her head was a small pillbox with a flowing, heavy black veil. The veil was so thick that no one could see through it in order to identify who she might be. She walked through the gate and then sat down in an empty chair on the back row.

Mary Selena, ever the gracious host, as well as a curious young woman, asked, "To our dear friend who just arrived, we welcome you here, but may I ask who you are?"

All eyes were upon the woman as she lifted her veil. Destini, for one, immediately caught her breath and clutched at her heart. Aside from the distinct Amerasian features of the young woman, there stood a nearly exact likeness of Anna Mary.

The young lady, in precise English, stood up and said, "I see you are Mary Selena Jarrellson Williams. I am your half-sister, Jiang Ling."

Everyone gasped at this announcement, including Mary Selena. Then, Jiang Ling embarked on a long, well-rehearsed dissertation about herself.

"My mother was in love with your father when he was in China," she said to Mary Selena, as if it was just the two of them having a private conversation in the woods. "She hid her pregnancy and he never knew she was carrying me. When she was hit by a car in her native Peking, the doctors were able to save my life, only to give me over to my maternal grandparents, who wanted nothing to do with me. Through a network of relatives they had in San Francisco, they literally had me smuggled out of the country, first to Taiwan and then to San Francisco, where I spent my formative years living with an older cousin and his wife. I worked hard in their small restaurant, and I studied hard. No one in the family ever told me about my father, but I knew I had to be either Amerasian or Eurasian, judging by my facial features and skin tone. One day, when I was eleven-years-old, I found a letter in an unlocked box atop my cousin's dresser. It was written in Chinese and I recognized the signature as my maternal grandmother's. I took it to a local priest who I knew could read Chinese and he interpreted it for me."

"Oh, my goodness," Mary Selena said. "This is fascinating. Please go on."

"In summary, the letter explained my heritage and who my father was. I kept that translated letter close to my heart throughout my schooling. After high school, I received a full scholarship to Columbia University in New York City. It was there that I began researching the Jarrellson family, which eventually led me here to Florida," she explained. "I assure you I am not here for money or for any part of an estate. I am here simply to honor my father because he truly did love my mother. He didn't want to leave China, but he was forced to do so. By the way, I have all the documents to prove who I am."

Throughout this back and forth exchange, everyone in attendance had been completely silent. When Jiang Ling finished, Mary Selena stepped down from the podium and opened her arms.

"There is no need for further explanation or proof," Mary Selena told her. "I can look at you and know that what you are saying is true. It took courage for you to come here today. Please come and stand by me."

Jiang Ling did as Mary Selena asked and the two girls embraced before standing side by side, hands entwined.

"I would also like Trey Esmerian to come and stand by me," Mary Selena said, motioning toward him. Then, in a shocking declaration, she announced, "I know many of you knew Trey's father, Tate "Sonny Boy" Esmerian, as well as Sonny Boy's father, Tate Esmerian Senior… or at least who we all thought was his father. As it turns out, Sonny Boy was not Tate Senior's biological son. In actuality, Sonny Boy's father is my paternal grandfather, the late Stanley Williams."

Out in the wide open woodsy atmosphere up on this high bluff above the Suwannee River, you could have heard a pin drop, as all eyes were trained on Trey and the two girls, as they tried to digest everything they just heard.

"While we are talking about blood, I would also like for Mr. Augustine Jackson, and his sons, Deon and Oliver, to come stand with me," Mary Selena continued, as she was about to deliver another shocking statement. "A few people in Campbell County have known for years what I found out just a short time ago. The Jacksons are actually part of the Jarrellson family. I don't want any more exclusions in this family, and I definitely don't want anymore more secrets," she proclaimed. "My arms are open to all… to my newly found sister, to my uncle, to my great-uncle, and all my cousins. What my grandparents would have wanted here today is as much a part of your heritage as it is mine. So, please, join hands with me. Destini, I want you, Phil, Wanda Faye, Nadine, Essie, Duke, Curtis, and any others who want to, come join hands with my husband and me, as we all sing "Amazing Grace".

Once everyone was in a circle and holding hands, Mary Selena asked Destini if she would lead the group in the song and Destini nodded.

"Aunt Dee Dee, I am so thankful you are here," Mary Selena said. "You look beautiful, as always. Would you mind accompanying us on the keyboard?"

"I would love to," Dee Dee said.

"When we finish singing, I shall call upon Trey to close us in prayer," Mary Selena said. "Then, everyone is invited to the Jarrellson House where brunch will be served."

As the group sang, tears rolled down Destini's cheeks. When the song was over and the prayer had been said, Mary Selena asked her family members, including Destini and Dee Dee, to walk to the river's edge with her. Mary Selena took off her shoes and waded into the river ankle deep. The others removed their shoes and did the same.

Mary Selena looked down the river and reverently spoke to the tannic waters of the Suwannee.

"You have brought my family here, and just like them, you have remained the same, yet always changing. Today, I bring new members of my family into your waters. Let them always remember that you are a beautiful gift to this world we live in. You give life to this land. Let us also remember that in your righteous anger your waters run dark. In the words of my great-grandmother, who told your stories to my grandmother, who then told them to my father, who whispered them to Destini and to my grandmother, who both told me the exact same thing. "You are sweet and you are life-giving, but remember, black runs the river." I shall never forget those words, and I pledge to you today that for as long as I live, a portion of my earthly fortune will heal you and make you whole again. Indeed, black runs the river, but just as I find joy today that the sins of my ancestors are absolved with the joining of hands of all my relatives, I will work the rest of my life to make this black river, this magnificent Suwannee River, clean and whole again."

With that, everyone hugged everyone and there were smiles all around.

"The world has indeed come to the Suwannee River," Destini said to Dee Dee, as they walked back to the parking area.

"Yes, it sure has," Dee Dee agreed.

"If Anna Mary and Stanley never did anything else in their lives, at least they made this happen today," Destini said. "Despite the hatred, the abuse, and the misguided passions of the past, here we are with the people of Hindu Indian descent, Chinese descent, African Americans, Cubans, Sicilian and Armenian descent… and finally, the Jarrellson family has arrived in Campbell County."

As the group drove away from the monument that day, it seemed that Dr. Watson Jarrellson Williams and his wife, Mary Selena Jarrellson Dubois Williams, were smiling down on them. It was as if they were speaking the words of the old Hindu saying that were inscribed on the tombstone.

Here in this hallowed place,
Where Black Runs the River,
Lies the mortal remains of
Watson Jarrellson Williams, MD
September 5, 1985 - October 22, 2015
And his loving wife,
Selena Dubois Jarrellson Williams
May 22, 1988-October 22, 2015

☙☙☙☙☙☙☙☙☙☙

"It is better to live your own destiny imperfectly than to live an imitation of somebody else's life with perfection."
The Bhagavad Gita

About the Author

White Springs native Johnny Bullard was born in a place where two cities and two counties interconnect on the banks of the historic Suwannee River. His family roots run about seven generations deep into the sandy soil of north central Florida, a place he dearly loves and where his entire life has been spent as an educator, public servant, musical performer, and writer.

Born into a family of prolific storytellers, Bullard absorbed all the tales that were told aloud, as well as the ones whispered quietly inside screened porches and around the dining room table when family and close friends gathered together.

Bullard's grasp of the culture and life of this region is expressed by one who has not only lived it, but who loves it and is a part of it. He offers a humorous, poignant, and honest voice of a South that is still colorful, vibrant, rich, and real. Bullard is as much a part of the region as the historic Suwannee River, immortalized by Stephen C. Foster in the unforgettable tune, "Old Folks at Home".

An old turpentine distillery at the Eight Mile Still on the Woodpecker Route north of White Springs is where Bullard calls home. He boasts four college degrees from Valdosta State University in Georgia, including a B.A. in English. He also did post graduate work at Florida State University in Tallahassee, Florida, and was privileged to be selected to attend the prestigious Harvard Principal's Center at Harvard University in Cambridge, Massachusetts in 1993.

Bullard writes a weekly column, "Around the Banks of the Suwannee", which is published in the *Jasper News* and *Suwannee Democrat* newspapers. He has also written magazine articles for several well known publications including *Forum*, a quarterly publication of the Florida Humanities Council.

His weekly newspaper column always ends with his signature message to all his readers, friends, and relatives throughout the region. He writes, "From the Eight Mile Still on the Woodpecker Route north of White Springs, I wish you all a day filled with joy, peace, and above all, lots of love and laughter."

Johnny Bullard

Reviews

Nightshade

I was drawn to the descriptive beauty of Bullard's North Florida, contrasted by the lives of the characters and their story of struggle and triumph. *Laura R.*

The characters are believable and true to life. By story's end, you'll find yourself wanting to move to Seraph Springs to meet Wanda Faye, Nadine and Destini. *Lesleigh*

Truly Southern! A very good read, and written by a talented and eloquent writer. *Dianne Banks*

Old school Southern writing; a fantastic take set in the Deep South by a talented writer. *Charles B. Pennington*

The mystery, intrigue, redemption and "dirty deeds" are spot on; kept me wanting more. *Monica Chambers*

I loved this book! It was like reading about old friends. *Sharron Handley*

This book will keep you turning the pages as you anxiously await what will happen next! *Cathy F.*

Written by a true southern gentleman, Johnny just makes the characters come to life. *Amazon reader*

Secrets

Mr. Bullard brings to life the true meaning of friends and family, and sharing in ones lives. Johnny is an inspiring writer that can relate to people and their feelings. *Debra Mahaffey*

Secrets is a "can't-put-it-down" kind of book. It grabbed me from the first sentence and held on until the end, especially since I had already read *Nightshade*. Simply a must read for all those who enjoy sharing their secrets with best friends! *Shirley Smith*

Good story with familiar surroundings from growing up in the area. Lots of diversions, too. Another great job by Johnny Bullard. He is a great storyteller. *Amazon reader*

The first book I could not put down, so I'm waiting until I have a rainy day to read *Secrets*. Love the author! *Angela Townsend*

I enjoyed this book very much. I can relate to the small town setting and all of the drama that goes on daily. *Amazon reader*

This book cleared up the mysteries that left you hanging from the first book. I enjoyed both books very much. *Julie D.*

Destini

This book kept me interested from the beginning. There were times I laughed and times I shed tears, but in the end it all came together and one could be at peace with the ending. *Juli D.*

Written by one of my favorite Southern writers, Johnny Bullard makes everyone and everything so real that you want to be among them and share in their fun as well as the tears. *Shirley Smith*

No one expresses it better than Bullard. A hundred years from now, if you wanted to read and feel the real south, then Destini will take you there. *David B.*

This sequel fills in the blanks from the previous two books. Although a bit contrived at times, it moves quickly with a fascinating and intricate storyline. There are many surprising twists and turns with a storybook ending. Mr. Bullard has left enough loose ends for several more stories in this series. *Amazon reader*

This story traces Destini's life. Many of the same characters are present, but the story takes a different twist as it explores many of the environmental issues facing Florida, as well as continuing to explore the great events of life, birth, marriage, death, and all the humor, sadness, and tragedy, set in a landscape along the Suwannee River. *Amazon reader*

Made in the USA
Lexington, KY
25 November 2019